The Lost Son

To 1
of love

Eeanor

p.s. Eric is my son-in-law
you must meet him.
some Time.

Eric
Leclere

The Lost Son

(Xavier Lombard Et Le Fils Perdu)

Alibi

First published in Great Britain in 1999
by Alibi Books
PO Box 25334
London NW5 2ZP

ISBN: 0–9535562–0–4

Cover photographs © Margaret Leclere

Printed and bound in Great Britain
by Cox & Wyman Ltd., Reading, Berkshire

Pour Margaret...

Et merci à Richard et Shelagh
et au pays de Galles

Voici bien un millénaire
Que nous nous tolérons fraternellement
Toi, tu tolères que je respire,
Moi, je tolère tes fureurs.
Parfois, en des temps obscurs
D'étranges humeurs te prenaient :
Tes pattes pieuses et affectueuses,
Tu les baignais de mon sang.
Ces temps-ci, notre amitié croît,
Elle se consolide chaque jour
Car j'entre aussi en rage,
Et je deviens presque pareil à toi !

"An Edom", Heinrich Heine (1824)

ONE

It was one of those looks men give one another. An angry searching look. The eyes probe from under the ridge of the brows, the lips are closed, the cheeks tense and the jaw stiff. He had probably felt Lombard's eyes on him as he made his way head down across the expanse of grass from the bandstand to the café. He had probably reflected on the fact that he would have to walk right past Lombard's table. It couldn't be helped: Lombard sat right outside the café's steamy glass door. Perhaps he'd even considered turning around, giving up the idea of going to the café altogether, so as not to have to walk past Lombard's dark stare. There are men who will take such undignified precautions when they feel thwarted or vulnerable, to avoid the defeat of not returning the look, to avoid the humiliation of looking back but too humbly, or merely to avoid the confrontation that too proud or hostile a look might incite.

People stare for a reason. And when the stare belongs to a grim-faced stranger hardy enough to sit outdoors on a freezing winter morning in nothing more than a thin raincoat, black suit and white shirt, it can be intimidating.

But the man had walked on, determined, and the look he sent Lombard on passing his table showed that he had indeed felt his stare. Still, he wasn't intimidated. His eyes held no fear. He was a leader, a man used to giving orders, a man used to responsibility, as he had just proved, even though this time things had gone wrong.

Lombard stared at him purely out of curiosity, as one does on such occasions. The man had made a fool of himself, carried his wounded pride like a burden, and whether stupidity or clumsiness was to blame for his pain, Lombard neither knew nor cared. The fact was that an old man and his dog had conspired to make him lose his composure, effectively turning what a few moments earlier might have been seen as the symbols of his authority – his leather jacket, short ponytail, cell-phone and bunch of keys that hung from his waist along with a two-way radio tucked into a hip-holster – into a lot of silly-looking and seemingly useless paraphernalia. Yet, in the past hour or so, under his leadership, the bandstand and its surroundings had been commandeered. Two small trucks had been emptied of chairs, spotlights, cameras, generators, musical instruments and countless other props and pieces of equipment. It had been smooth, professional work. Eventually the quiet of the Heath had been shattered by the generator's drone, someone had switched on the spotlights set up high on scaffolding and the circular bandstand which, with its wrought iron railings and wooden roof, had looked a grey, uninviting structure – as English bandstands do on bleak winter days – was transformed into a gleaming movie set. Garlands of flowers, multicoloured balloons, steel chairs, brass musical instruments now glistened inside its railings. Yet more chairs, these of blue and white striped canvas, stood in neat rows on the grass around it. There were gaps here and there, for cameras, and a small trailer bearing a camera crane was already set up on tracks laid down to skirt the whole set. It was a strange sight. Whereas the rest of Hampstead Heath lay in dull morning mist, the bandstand area seemed bathed in bright sunshine. And it had been he who, leading his crew of about twenty, akin to a little general, bawling, conferring, consulting scripts and drawings, had overseen the creation of this summer island of light and colour.

Lombard had observed all of this from his table on the café terrace. He had drunk two espressos, smoked three Gitanes. Then the dog had turned up, little knowing its appearance would soon lead to the man abandoning his baffled crew and summery film set for the refuge of the café.

Lombard could see his anger; short, hurried puffs of breath from his nostrils clouded the cold air in front of his face. Little of his former confidence remained; the keys dangling from his belt swung with each of his steps, prompting him to clasp them tightly to silence their attention-drawing rattle. In this manner, head down, awkwardly clasping his now bothersome keys, he was a sorry sight as he neared Lombard's table. But Lombard had gone on staring. By then, he had perversely decided to keep his eyes on him, just to see if...

He'd been right. On passing his table the man had felt compelled to glance, to send one of those looks men give one another. Anger searching for approval or, if not that, at least some kind of sympathy. He was proud; humbled but proud. In the short moment their eyes met, Lombard saw he expected nothing less than approval.

'Jesus Christ! What's a guy supposed to do, huh!' he might have said had he chosen to speak. Doubtless he'd also have found room for a swear-word or two somewhere in there: 'What's a guy supposed to *fucking* do, huh!' He looked the swearing type, the type who interjects into every other sentence a 'fucking' or a 'bloody'. He was used to bossing people around, used to the privileges that the authority to do so brings, like the right to swear when addressing subordinates.

Lombard looked quietly away. He wished neither to reassure nor condemn him, to confront nor add to his embarrassment. He wasn't really interested in this man or what had just happened to him.

He heard the café door swing open behind him, felt the warmth escaping from inside hit the side of his nape, heard it swing shut again.

'Another day, another asshole,' proclaimed a voice, aloofly.

Lombard frowned. The French accent, the blasé tone of voice were Nathalie's. He looked over his shoulder. Nathalie stood by the door, in a long black overcoat, her hands in her pockets, gazing stoically towards the bandstand. The man must have walked right past her.

'How are you, Nathalie?' he said with a dry grin.

The dry grin was his way of telling her he was pleased to see her, because he only had twenty minutes left, because they'd have missed each other if she'd turned up after eleven, as she sometimes did. But Nathalie didn't know that yet. She just fixed her black eyes in his. It was a habit of hers. Sometimes she stared, created silence, a moment of suspension, as if to give herself the time to inspect the soul of her interlocutor before committing to a reply. Returning her stare Lombard saw she was stoned again. She saw he saw, raised one brow, pursed her lips, glanced at the two empty cups in front of him, turned to the door.

'Coffee?'

There was no need for him to answer this. She'd bring him another espresso. She always did. She always arrived after him and however many coffees he might already have had, he always had one more with her. Such was their ritual.

'Yes,' he said anyway as she stepped into the café. His eyes lingered on the door slowly swinging shut behind her. He nodded, gently, almost imperceptibly. He was upset. It was not yet eleven in the morning and she was stoned again. He turned away, reached for his pack of Gitanes and lit one with a frown, now oblivious to the bandstand where the film crew was back at work.

'*Merde,*' he muttered softly, pulling the lit cigarette from his mouth.

He'd already tried. He'd already wasted the time. Nathalie didn't need him to tell her what heroin did. Nathalie didn't need to be told anything by anyone. Was that not why they'd once thought they could make a go of it? Was that not what had brought them together in the first place and in the end caused her to break off their relationship? Neither of them needed to be told anything by anyone. They'd always understood that much about each other. Could they really have expected it to last more than the three months or so it had?

'It's not working. We're too alike, Xavier,' Nathalie had announced one day. She was already packing her bags. Lombard had not tried to dissuade her. She was right. Living together had been like living with an unforgiving mirror, each being a constant reminder to the other of what they were not, of what they had not, of what they'd lost. Even so, he still wondered if something good might not have come of it.

A gust of wind froze the air around him and went on to sway the garlands and balloons in the bandstand. Lombard was glad he'd got his raincoat back from the dry-cleaner. He owned a warmer one, a fur-lined buckskin coat which he'd bought at the Jones Brothers store on the Holloway Road just before it closed down. It had been one of those stores that still employed courteous middle-aged men in their men's department and, for some reason unknown to Lombard, the assistant who'd sold it to him had called it a 'car coat'. It was expensive, but he'd liked it, only to discover after wearing it a few times that he'd made a mistake, that he didn't really like it after all; perhaps this was because it had turned out not to be truly waterproof. He'd understood then why the store-assistant had described it as a 'car coat'. But, to bother manufacturing fur-lined buckskin coats without making the seams impermeable...? Be that as it may, even though it was raining that day, he'd still been wearing it the first time he and Nathalie had met in Perkins' butcher's shop.

At the beginning, Nathalie had put their meeting down to fate. Lombard already knew better, already distrusted such notions as fate. He preferred to think of their encounter as the accidental crossing of drifting lives. But Nathalie was still young, still desired things to make sense. So fate it was. It was as good a way as any to explain how two lonely French people both exiled in London had turned up at the same time at a small butcher's shop on the Essex Road to ask for a Mr. Perkins who had advertised a flat for rent. Had Perkins not thought so himself on seeing them together in his shop? The podgy middle-aged man in a blood-stained apron had certainly looked amazed, talked of a 'strange coincidence'. Two French people, there in his modest North London butcher's shop, a man and a woman, unknown to one another, yet both wanting to see his flat... Still, he'd overcome his early surprise quickly enough to allow himself to feel the situation warranted light-hearted comments about a second Norman conquest, about starting to trade in frogs-legs and horse meat from then on, at one point getting so carried away as to make barely veiled insinuations about his two callers hitting it off and moving in together. The circumstances had required that Lombard and Nathalie be on their best behaviour. They'd smiled politely at one another, exchanged a few platitudes, grinned at Perkins' tedious pleasantries, but between themselves they'd immediately known that each was performing only for the sake of their potential landlord.

The flat itself turned out to be above the shop, and by the time they'd followed jolly Perkins upstairs to tour its three rooms, each had guessed the other was not in London because of a job, a holiday sojourn or their love of England. The communication between them had happened silently, the understanding with barely a few glances. So much so that when Nathalie suddenly matter-of-factly declared the place too grubby, bade Lombard and Perkins a curt goodbye and stepped out the door, Lombard had been ready for it. Perkins on the other hand had not, was very disappointed, and not so much by her unkind comments about his property as by seeing her leave. Escorting them around, he'd been all eyes for her, had completely ignored Lombard. Who could blame him? Lombard remembered he'd almost felt sorry for the butcher, even bothered to send him a commiserating smile.

It was appropriate. Nathalie was the kind of woman men notice. In her early twenties, with shoulder-length dark hair, sultry black eyes, always dressed with a studied elegance that made her look mature beyond her years, she faced the world with the tranquil poise that comes to women who men favour. What healthy middle-aged butcher with a flat for rent would not smile expectantly at the prospect of becoming her landlord? And then there was her smell. Perkins could not have failed to notice it, although, working all day long amid the raw odours of bloody meat as he did it was conceivable his sense of smell had waned over the years. Lombard himself had noticed it. It wasn't perfume. Hers was a natural body odour, a warm smell which he would later observe could make men not yet aware of her presence turn or glance sideways to search for its origin; a smell which caused them to watch her with a pensive, sober, sometimes even guilty stare, and then to turn quickly away, as if fearful of being caught with their thoughts. Whether or not Perkins had discerned it, her blunt exit had left him foiled. He merely nodded on hearing that Lombard liked the flat, had to be prompted into giving his terms. He was a reasonable man though, had offered a six month lease against a moderate rent to be paid fortnightly in advance, and a deposit amounting to four weeks' rent. And no pets, unless confined to a cage or aquarium.

'And what is it you do for a living then?' he had eventually enquired.

'I'm a private investigator,' Lombard had replied.

'Oh…'

Perkins had raised his brows.

Lombard was used to this. It was unavoidable. People raised their brows or frowned as soon as he said it.

'I mean—you're French. Do you…' Perkins had gone on.

Lombard had given him his story, the one he always told with a polite grin:

'The company I work for wanted an agent here in London. I volunteered. Always wanted to come and see what life was like on this side of the channel.'

The butcher had nodded, thoughtful:

'I see…'

'Of course, the company pays my expenses. Did I mention I'd need receipts?'

'Receipts? Yes, of course.'

'Good.'

The butcher had gone on eyeing Lombard, unsure.

'Er, forgive me for asking, but you… You know, in your line of work… Will you be bringing a gun in here? Because…'

Lombard had laughed:

'No. No, nothing as exciting as a gun in my life, Mr. Perkins. I'm afraid right now my job consists mostly of spying on the staff of French companies with branches in London. I check that people off work sick for weeks on end are really ill. Investigate the lives of potential new employees or business partners. That sort of thing, you know? All very boring and gunless, I'm afraid.'

Perkins was still not satisfied, had looked Lombard up and down. Lombard was well-dressed and appeared trustworthy enough. He was in his mid-thirties, fit, quite a good-looking man, even in Perkins' mind not the type to volunteer to move abroad for a tedious job affording nothing better than the kind of flat he was offering above his butcher's shop.

'Ha… And you volunteered, eh?' he'd asked.

'That's right. I like football, you see,' Lombard had replied;

'This is England. Where the game's played as it should be. Couldn't resist. Besides, I like to travel.'

Earlier, still down in Perkins' shop, he'd spotted the Arsenal football club poster and memorabilia conspicuously displayed on the wall behind the counter.

He had done well to remember it. A Frenchman who liked English football! This was sweet music to Perkins' ears, had put Nathalie and any misgivings he might have had about a French private detective plying his trade in London out of his mind. He was grinning now, talkative again:

'All right! Got nothing against football myself... You're looking at an Arsenal man here... Never missed a home match in twenty five years... D'you know the Arsenal pitch is less than a mile from here?... Won the championship last year, you know.'

'Yes.'

'Been to see them play yet?'

'Not yet. But I intend to.'

'Good... Say...'

Perkins was looking him over again, but not in the same way as before; he was assessing his physique:

'Say, d'you play yourself?'

'Sorry?'

'Football. D'you play?'

Lombard was grinning, Perkins had lost him.

'I used to, in younger days.'

The butcher had nodded to himself. He obviously had something in mind:

'Any good?'

'I made *Paris St-Germain* junior team as a centre-forward. Why?'

Lombard was wondering what this was leading to. But Perkins was not yet ready to tell him.

'Well, this might be your lucky day, Mister Lombard,' was all he'd said; 'You and I must have a chat as soon as you're settled in, all right? Now, tell me, are you a vegetarian?'

Lombard was still grinning, on automatic now:

'No.'

Perkins was pleased about that:

'I didn't think so. Good. In that case I expect you to buy your meat in my shop, understood?' he had announced; 'I'm afraid it's an unspoken rule of living in my flat, ha-ha…'

Lombard had watched him, wondering if the man was serious, then said:

'Well, now you've spoken it, I guess I'll just think of it as a rule, eh?'

Perkins had liked that. Lombard had left him laughing.

He had claimed to be a company employee to reassure. Landlords liked company employees. He had claimed an interest in going to watch Arsenal play to please. He had no intention of doing so; he did not care for crowds, and besides, he was a Liverpool supporter, albeit an armchair one.

Nathalie had come back into his life a few minutes later as he unlocked his old Triumph 2000 a few doors away from Perkins' shop. Her smell had reached him before her voice. He was already looking at her when she asked:

'You have time for a cup of coffee?'

She'd spoken in English.

Je parle Français,' he'd replied with an amused grin.

She had looked straight into his eyes, for the first time giving him one of her silences, drawing him into one of her moments of suspension. He had not looked away; it wasn't that unpleasant…

'If I wished to speak French I'd have stayed in France.'

The tone was calm, casual almost, but the voice firm. Then, before he could reply:

'You took it?'

Lombard had not answered immediately, wondered why she was refusing to speak in their own tongue. Her accent was fairly pronounced, much more so than his.

'The dump. You took it?' she'd asked again. For someone who liked to keep people waiting, she was rather impatient.

Lombard had deliberately let a few seconds pass before asking:

'What's your accent like when you speak French, huh?'

This was meant to test her. He wanted to see how she'd react, whether it would infuriate her, ruffle those looks, that poise of hers.

It had not. She had stayed cold, just stared back with a small frown, her head slightly tilted to one side, and although they'd just met, and although almost a generation separated them, a lot had passed between their eyes during the next few seconds, things they would never talk about. Lombard had understood then why she'd accosted him, and she had known he would accept her invitation. But it wasn't time yet. Not just like that. Decency required that even he made it a little harder, didn't give in so easily.

He had broken the spell, finally answered her:

'The location's good, the rent cheap, the butcher a nice enough man. Unlike you, I've seen worse.'

She'd looked him up and down, with a malicious gleam in her eyes; if a game was what he wanted…

'Unlike me, you probably can't afford better.'

'Then unlike you I probably can't afford the time for coffee in the middle of a working day.'

She'd sneered, without enmity, an amused sneer, and after a moment's thought decided she'd rather not play after all:

'Playing hard to get, eh?'

'What can I do for you, Miss Dutoit?' That was how she had introduced herself to Perkins, as Miss Dutoit.

'Nathalie will do. What's your name again? I didn't quite catch it.'

Lombard doubted that:

'Lombard. Xavier Lombard.'

'Xavier, eh… C'est un beau nom.'

It was something in the way she said it. He was sure she'd finally conceded to speak French as a ploy, to placate him, make him feel he'd got to her, won that small battle, and so could lower his guard without feeling he'd lose face. Lombard had not liked it. It was cheap. Too cheap. For a moment he thought he'd misjudged her. He had turned away, opened his car door, saying calmly:

'So, you do speak French. It's not just a silly accent after all. Nice meeting you, Miss Dutoit.'

And he'd settled down at his wheel, conscious of her glare. But she was not frightened to fight for what she wanted. She'd grabbed his door before he could shut it:

'Right. If that's how you want it, I'll do all the work, okay? I'm lonely and dying to have a cup of coffee with a man. You look like you know better than to ask stupid questions and, unlike the other asshole with his flat, you haven't yet fantasised about fucking me. Will that do, huh? I know a place and I'll foot the bill. We'll talk about the weather.'

The words had come fast and, Lombard now realised, in an English tinged with a slight American accent.

'Okay.'

She had stepped around the car, settled on the passenger seat:

'Do you know Hampstead Heath…'

Nathalie was back, putting her cappuccino and his espresso down on the table, just as she had done on that first day when she'd introduced him to the Parliament Hill café on Hampstead Heath. She moved his two empty cups onto the next table, sat down, searched her handbag, lit a Marlboro and chucked her lighter in her bag which she put down on the empty chair beside her.

'How are you, Xavier?'

'Wide awake and clear-headed.'

He couldn't help it, he had to say something about it.

She smiled:

'Hope you're feeling good then.'

He looked hard at her profile. She was pensively watching the works around the bandstand. She had a good mouth for lipstick but today the red on her lips contrasted too sharply with her almost translucent complexion, reminded him of those teenage girls who make up before their time, when their skin is still too green to bear red fruits.

'Do you really?' he asked.

She kept her eyes with their dilated pupils on the bandstand. The light today was very similar to what it had been that first time they'd sat side by side on the café terrace. She had not been so pale then. It was she who had insisted on sitting under the roof of the outside terrace even though it had been raining. They'd drunk their coffees, smoked their cigarettes. The rain had eventually driven away the man on the tractor-mower who was cutting the lawn around the café when they turned up, and they'd gazed at the rain combing the autumn leaves from the nearby trees in the heady smell of freshly cut wet grass. Lombard had closed his eyes; he couldn't remember how long it had been since he had last smelt freshly cut grass. It had brought back a few deeply buried pleasant memories...

'Why don't you surprise us both by saying something unexpected for once, eh, Nathalie?'

She was not going to surprise him. She just glanced sideways at him, nodded towards the bandstand.

'It's pretty, huh? All that equipment, they must be shooting a movie.'

He could guess what she was thinking about. One of the things she'd told him that first time was that she was writing a film script...

'A love story,' she'd said; 'I'm halfway through.'

'Good,' he'd replied.

'Yes. It's very good.'

Had she really misunderstood him?

'Are you writing it in French?' he'd asked. He was still not reconciled to them speaking in English.

'No. In English. It's for Hollywood. For the Americans.'

For a moment he'd thought she was writing on commission.

'Ah. That explains the luxurious lifestyle...'

'No. My script will make me money when I sell it. Meanwhile I can afford luxury because men are prepared to pay for my company.'

This had not shocked him. She already knew why of course, had decided to tease him:

'Cops don't usually need to be tipped off about that.'

She didn't expect a reply and he had not volunteered one. As she'd promised, they had then talked about the weather. At some point she had disclosed she was from Nice, had been in London for the past six months. Lombard had reciprocated, revealing he left Paris a year earlier.

'I don't like London, it's ugly,' she had said; 'But I like the parks and the people here; the parks are peaceful and the people don't bother you.'

Lombard had agreed. He'd stayed in London because Londoners didn't ask questions. As for the parks, he hadn't yet discovered Hampstead Heath, but he knew Regent's Park where he'd had a couple of walks soon after his arrival in the city. Its peace and beauty had impressed him. Here in the land of the cold English people, of the football hooligans, the skinheads, squatters, hard rock and punk rockers, in the city of Jack the Ripper, Dickens' slums, Sherlock Holmes' villains and 'The Sweeney', one was not only free to walk on the grass but amidst elaborate and carefully-tended flower beds where not a bush, not a rose, not a stem was vandalised; yet, children played games on the nearby grass, students and unemployed adults killed time on the benches...

The man with the ponytail was back, walking past their table with a quick sideways glance at Nathalie. He had regained his composure, headed confidently towards his set to the sound of his rattling keys with his ponytail bobbing behind him. Nathalie watched him reach the bandstand where some of his crew gathered to welcome him back. A tap on the back here, a shake of the head there; 'Don't worry, he was an old bastard,' someone was probably saying.

'He's ripe. Why don't you show him that old script you wrote four years ago? Do you still have it?' said Lombard. It was cruel. He regretted it immediately.

Nathalie turned, gave him one of her silences.

'Sometimes I wonder which one of us is the ugliest, Xavier.'

He deserved that.

'You should have more self-esteem, Nathalie.'

'Should I? Just think how lonely you'd be if I did, huh?'

'It's funny you should say that.'

'Funny? Amuse me then.'

'You remember the time you first brought me here? When you left and let me know you'd be here the next Friday morning if I felt like it?'

'I'm still not laughing...'

'It's a long time ago.'

'Yes, Xavier.'

'So I don't know if I feel like it anymore. Not with you—'

He broke off, angry with himself. What was he doing?

'Don't turn your problems into mine, all right,' said Nathalie calmly.

Lombard looked away, stubbed his cigarette out in the ashtray, eyeing the nearby path where a group of six teenagers was heading their way. He knew them. Two girls and four boys. They were pupils of a red brick school that loomed up behind them. They would come to the café, sit a few tables away and, today, instead of showing off their adolescent genius to one another, instead of flirting, they would probably focus their attention on the bandstand, even perhaps decide to spend their entire lunch-hour there, hoping to see the actors who had still to turn up, hoping to witness the shooting of the scene that was being prepared, and then dream, like Nathalie once had. Once the news that a man with a bunch of keys was setting up a movie set had got around, the rest of their schoolmates would probably turn up. And doubtless all that youth would feel fortunate if the bandstand turned out to be the set for a pop video rather than a movie.

Lombard frowned. Predictably, the six teenagers were already eyeing the bandstand, their school bags slung nonchalantly over their shoulders. A few hands held burning cigarettes. The two girls were dressed with studied sloppiness, as the current teenage fashion clearly required. The boys all had long hair, affected a detached and world-weary air in their uniformly messed-up clothes. Lombard didn't usually mind them, except perhaps one of the girls who had a high-pitched voice and laugh. She was a tall, thin, pale figure with long wavy blond hair who wore too much lipstick and liked to sing and wave her arms to the music from a walkman which she always listened to with just one ear, the redundant headphone plug being left to dangle on her chest. That way she could take part in the others' conversation while listening to her tapes. There was something ominous about her; she carried a kind of doom which led Lombard to feel she would probably end up badly. This morning, because he was angry, the sight of her and her friends annoyed him. Nathalie, who had a way with voicing her opinions, had said it once:

'When teenagers think its cool to look like their parents did at their age, the world's in trouble. But then again, it might be stupid to draw conclusions from a bunch of stupid kids.'

The six had been sitting nearby at the time and she'd deliberately spoken loud enough for them to hear. That's how she was. Since then the boys had ceased their furtive glances at her, the girls taken to sending her scornful looks to which he'd seen her on one occasion respond with a haughty grin. He had casually wondered aloud what this situation would lead to if he and Nathalie decided to meet at the café every day instead of once a week.

'The little bitches wouldn't dare come here anymore,' Nathalie had pronounced with a perverse little laugh. It was one of the rare times he had heard her laugh.

He checked his watch. It was 11:05. He knew he would be back the following Friday. Heroin or not, he knew he couldn't let her make him be the one to bring to an end the ritual they'd established ever since meeting again at the café a few months after their separation.

'I have to go,' he said, standing up.

Nathalie looked up. Was that a hint of disappointment behind her eyes?

'Work,' he said.

'Ah…'

'Take care.'

'Xavier?'

'Yes.'

'What happened with the asshole?' she asked, signalling towards the bandstand with her eyes.

'He… You know the old man with his navy blue blazer and three-legged sheep-dog?'

'Uh-huh.'

'Well…' Lombard turned to the bandstand.

They both knew the old man and his dog. The two invariably turned up between ten and eleven from the direction of the Lido, one limping on his cane, the other hopping along on his three legs. They toured the bandstand and vanished again. Typically, today the dog had turned up first and, oblivious to the film crew, hopped along between everyone and everything to sit in the bandstand as usual to wait for its master who was even slower than itself. The old three-legged animal looked harmless enough. At first the crew had tried to shoo it away. But the dog refused to budge; after all this was his bandstand, his patch, he sat there every morning, had done so for many years, was not going to be seen off by a bunch of intruders. But the ponytail man had other ideas. There was work to be done, the dog was distracting his crew, and so he'd sent everyone back to work and taken charge of the tiresome animal himself.

Trying to grab its collar to drag it away had proved too dangerous, caused a show of teeth and a few growls. So, like a man who has faced such situations before, he'd fetched a blanket from one of the trucks, thrown it over the dog, grabbed it and carried it thus away from his set. However, on being released, three legs or not, the dog had set off on a dash back to the bandstand, with ponytail now running after it, stumbling over chairs and nearly falling twice before eventually he was close enough to kick the dog's hind-legs. The dog had yelped, turned and bitten his ankle, only to be kicked again until, wailing, it had cowered away towards its master who, unnoticed, had appeared at the scene. Furious at having been bitten, ponytail had set off in pursuit once more, cursing and kicking, not realising the dog was heading for the protection of its master who, waiting, his cane at the ready, had struck him across the head. In a flash, ponytail had struck back, slapped the old man, sent him tumbling to the ground beside his dog. Realising what he'd done, he had quickly tried to help the old man back to his feet but been beaten back by the dog who had run in front of his now helpless master to show his teeth again.

The old man had eventually struggled back to his feet, shouted a defiant 'I'd soon show you if I was younger', and limped away beside his faithful hopping pet with as much dignity as he could muster.

'It's too long a story,' said Lombard.

He walked through the six teenagers, ignoring the thin blonde with her walkman who, he felt, deliberately brushed against him. For some reason he was remembering how Nathalie had once led him to contemplate writing his story. She'd still been writing her script then.

'I don't know anything about movies. I wouldn't know how to start,' he had said.

'Then try a novel. Whatever. It's cathartic…'

Cathartic… He had tried, bought an old typewriter, only to realise he didn't have a clue how to start a novel either. Then, a short trip to the French bookshop near Regent's Street where he'd hoped to find inspiration had brought about the end of his literary pretension after he'd read the first line of an esteemed French novelist's work:

Life is a celebration in tears…

Writing was not for him.

TWO

Lombard was still pulling away from the kerb in front of La Sainte Union Catholic school for girls towards Highgate West Hill when the downpour had broken out.

For a few seconds scattered raindrops had thumped his Triumph, then the rain came hurtling down like a cascade, eclipsing what little there was of the December sky's ashen glow. He had switched on his windscreen wipers and headlights wondering how this sudden change of weather would affect those he'd left at the café. He guessed that the teenagers had moved into the warmth inside its steamy windows; that Nathalie remained at their table; that all eyes were on the ponytail man, who was now presumably running about bawling orders for his crew to shelter what they could of their equipment. Lombard was sure the man wouldn't pack up right away, that he'd wait, give the weather a chance to turn again. The recklessness of setting up an outdoor scene on the first dry day following two weeks of continuous rain suggested desperation. He or those he worked for were clearly anxious that the bandstand scene be shot without delay, or else he'd have waited for a more clement sky before venturing out to create at great cost a cheerful illusion of summer in early December. Was that why he was so keyed up, why he'd let a three-legged dog get the better of him? He was under pressure, and he would wait, and Nathalie and the teenagers would wait, she placidly, they conjecturing whether or not they'd get to see any filming now.

Lombard lit a cigarette, snapped his lighter shut, looked up through his swishing wipers. There was no more sky. The man was delaying packing up pointlessly; the teenagers would be disappointed and Nathalie might afford a grin at their expense.

Yes, she would, he thought, catching through the deluge ahead the fast approaching red glow of brake-lights.

He pulled hard down on his steering wheel, slammed on his brakes and skidded to a halt an inch from the stationary car in front of him.

'*Nom de*—'

He'd clenched his teeth on his untipped Gitane and his mouth was full of tobacco. He pulled the cigarette from his lips, wound down his window, spat the strands of tobacco from between his teeth with a frown. Two rows of cars blocked the way ahead, barely inching around the roundabout to The Bishops Avenue with its millionaires' mansions forty or so yards away. He sighed. He should have known better than to take Hampstead Lane across the top of the Heath on a rainy day. He should have taken the shortest route – Gospel Oak, South End Green and then up East Heath Road. Still, it had made sense. An excuse to make for Hampstead didn't arise every day; he thought he'd enjoy the drive along Hampstead Lane which, flanked on one side by the Heath's rolling landscape and on the other by opulent residences interspersed with green playing fields and woods, was more like a journey through rich countryside than the drive through bustling London that it really was.

He very nearly put his split cigarette back in his mouth, then flicked it out his window. It flew through the rain and hit the wet tarmac with a spray of sparks close to a woman in a peaked fur cap and gumboots who was locking a couple of dripping dogs into the back of an Estate car across the road. She peered at him through the rain with what could pass for a grin. He sent her a neutral smile and checked his watch without waiting for her reaction.

'*I will expect you at 11:30,*' Mrs. Spitz had pronounced in her strong German accent.

Lombard pictured the cars far ahead beyond the turn for The Bishops, creeping slowly through the narrow gap between The Spaniards Public House and the small concrete shed across the road from it. Together these two buildings were responsible for strangling Hampstead Lane; a fine standing reminder to Londoners that their city was once ringed with gatehouses, but also a modern day nuisance that led most drivers to reckon two cars could not get through the old gateway at the same time. Accordingly everyone stopped, a few cars from one direction went through, then a few from the other. This was a superfluous precaution, as could be seen on clear days when, on reaching The Spaniards, drivers just slowed down and manoeuvred through two abreast without thinking too much about it. But on rainy days, when vision was bad and traffic heavy, it led to long tail-backs, as if the rain and weight of traffic combined to narrow the gap even further in everybody's mind.

'I will expect you at 11:30.'

It was 11:20. Lombard was going to be late. By at least half an hour if he waited his turn to reach The Spaniards; by just about the same if he drove back down Highgate Road to take the South End Green way up to Whitestone Pond. He lit a new cigarette. He didn't like the idea of being late, even if, as was the case, he wasn't at all certain he was not wasting his time.

He wondered briefly if he wouldn't do better to turn around and go home. Mrs. Spitz could always call him again if she was so keen to see him. Earlier, he'd considered ignoring her call. He had not liked her bluntness, found her interruptions irritating. And she had called out of business hours.

'Mr. Lombard?'

'Speaking.'

'Good morning. My name is Mrs. Spitz. You are a private detective, am I right?'

'That's right. How can I—'

'We will speak when we meet. Have you got a pen and piece of paper within reach?'

Lombard had paused, told her to hang on in order to give himself the time to clear his throat and his thoughts. It was 8 o'clock in the morning, he was still lying in bed, had answered the call from his bedroom.

'Mrs. Spitz, I—'

'Right. The address is 89 Templeton Road, London NW3. Have you written this down?'

'No, Mrs. Spitz. Before we—'

'89 Templeton Road, London NW3. This is in Hampstead.

You know Hampstead, don't you?'

'I heard you the first time, Mrs. Spitz. If you would kindly let me speak, we might—'

'What is the matter, Mr. Lombard? Don't you want work?'

He had remained silent. She must have guessed what he thought, had reluctantly proffered an explanation.

'What I would like to discuss is important and I neither wish nor have the time to talk on the telephone right now. Do you understand, Mr. Lombard?'

'I do. But—'

'Good. 89 Templeton Road. I will expect you at 11:30.'

She'd put the receiver down. It could have been a crank call. Lombard was used to them by now. Some people found calling private detectives diverting, a cheap and easy way to get a thrill, to fantasise for a few minutes, to imagine a life they did not have. They'd put on whatever voice they thought appropriate, more often than not hinted at rather than told some crazy or distressing story, gave a bogus name and address and asked to be met, usually in a public place like a pub, car-park or supermarket. The better ones thought of enquiring about his fees. They of course had no intention of being at the rendezvous. Lombard had been caught on a few occasions, when he was new at this, just after his number had appeared in the Yellow Pages. By now he knew better, knew what questions to ask, if unsure declared that he didn't meet people outside his office until he'd seen their money. But Mrs. Spitz, if indeed that was her name, had said nothing and given him no opportunity to say or ask anything. He'd searched the phone book for a Spitz with a Hampstead address but found none. Still, in the end, he'd decided the journey might well be worthwhile. Because of Mrs. Spitz's voice. It was rasping, coarsened and worn by the years. Lombard did not know if she was German, as her accent suggested, but she was old, and, if her telephone manners were anything to go by, old and used to having her own way. And then because of the address – London NW3. He knew the area well from having once done some work there for a jealous French Restaurateur trading in Church Row. This was well-to-do Hampstead. Leafy avenues bordered with redbrick mansions, luxury cars parked in sweeping driveways. This was the London where quiet opulence resided.

A domineering personality and Templeton Road added up. The latter indicated money, the former what it takes to make it. And when supplemented with Mrs. Spitz's old age, the equation became even more feasible. On one hand it could stand for the time it takes to make serious money, on the other provide an explanation for her bluntness; in some wealth spawns bad manners – money brings confidence and confidence brings arrogance. But whether or not this applied to Mrs. Spitz, her age was relevant to Lombard for an entirely different reason; so far his experience had given him no reason to alter his belief that old ladies didn't find the idea of making crank calls to private detectives thrilling.

He decided to go on. Templeton Road was two minutes from Whitestone Pond. The oncoming lane was clear. He flicked his cigarette out the window, glanced towards the fur-capped woman who was now chatting heartily with a rough-looking youth in soaked trainers holding an Alsatian puppy on the end of a rope, smiled, pulled out and revved away past the crawling traffic.

He liked London. He liked its healthy desperation. He liked the way its people carelessly went on with their lives whether it rained or not. Except perhaps for the ponytail man...

If Lombard had been asked to rule out one property as the likely residence of an old lady amidst the mansions that lined Templeton Road, number 89 would have been it.

The house was a long, two-storey, brown-bricked, grey-tiled edifice, a bleak specimen of functional modern architecture. It stood back from the road, perched up on the slope of a mani-cured lawn. A gravel drive edged by a colonnade of potted poplars led to a red Ferrari and a blue Aston Martin parked by a flight of steps that rose to its front door. The overall impression was one of cold new money, an impression strengthened by the security camera trained on the hydraulic front gate which had started to open as soon as Lombard pulled up in front of it.

'Mister Lombard?'

The man had opened his door as he was still switching off the ignition and looked down at him from above his long nose with indifferent eyes, one hand tightly clasped around his umbrella, the other holding the car door open. Lombard had seen him hurrying down the front steps with his umbrella as he steered across the drive to park alongside the Aston Martin.

'That's right.'

The man looked him up and down, glanced at his passenger seat, conveyed his negative impression with a slight raising of the brows.

'Will you please come with me, sir,' he said.

Lombard turned to his passenger seat where a stack of sodden newspapers was soaking up the water dripping from his leaking sunroof. He kept them there for that purpose.

'That might depend on who you are and where you're going,' he said.

'I am Lawrence, sir. Mr. and Mrs. De Moraes' butler. They are expecting you.'

Lombard looked him over. The suit was impeccable, the smile tight, the hair slick, the middle-aged face pinched by the cold air jaundiced. He was a polished and well-trained domestic, straight out of the old-fashioned mould, the kind who could be expected to possess the skill of concealing emotions. Yet he had just betrayed disapproval of his car and...

'Did you say De Moraes?'

'Yes, sir.'

The raising of the brows must have been wilful. Lombard felt sure the man would not have batted an eyelid had he turned up in a Bentley or Ferrari, leaking or not; that he would then have done his job with a competence equal to the flawless suit in which he stood so rigidly.

'I believe I was called here to see a Mrs. Spitz.'

'That would be Mrs. De Moraes' mother, sir. Mr. and Mrs. Spitz are presently here with their daughter.'

Lombard let his eyes linger on the butler's polished shoes getting splashed against the gravel. Could it be that he resented being sent out in the rain to greet someone he regarded as a lower form of servant than himself?

'And what sort of car do you drive, eh, Lawrence?' asked Lombard, turning away without moving from his seat.

'When you are ready, sir,' he heard the butler say insistently after a brief silence.

'I asked you a question, Lawrence,' remarked Lombard calmly, now observing the Aston Martin through his passenger window. It was the DB5 model, all curve and power, a beautiful machine, probably even more expensive than the Ferrari beside it.

'I... I do not own a car, sir.' There was exasperation in the voice, barely veiled.

Lombard smiled:

'Don't you?'

'No. I don't, sir.'

'Well, good for you. That way you don't have to worry about leaky sunroofs, eh?' said Lombard, turning back to the man with a grin.

The butler understood, sent him one of his tight smiles:

'When you are ready, sir.'

Lombard peered at the house. An overbearing old woman, a soulless house hiding behind a security camera, a judgmental butler, fast cars, foreign names... He wondered what awaited him inside, already somehow felt he was not going to enjoy it.

'Thanks for the umbrella,' he said, finally climbing out.

'You're welcome, sir,' said the butler, closing the door after him.

'Would you very much mind wiping your feet, sir?' the butler enquired as he stood aside to let Lombard in the front door.

'Mister Lombard,' he announced soon after, standing in the double doorway at the end of the vast marble hallway inside the front door. The man had crossed its expanse at such a brisk pace that Lombard was still sauntering past the broad curving stair-case halfway across the hall, peering curiously at the abstract paintings and tubular sculptures that lined the walls.

'Thank you, Lawrence,' he said eventually, moving past the stony-faced butler.

He felt compelled to stop and survey the immense room he had entered as the door closed behind him. He didn't see or hear anyone right away, but realised why the butler had made a point of asking him to wipe his feet. Before him lay an immaculate white carpet. It stretched between smooth black marble walls. The furnishings and fittings were twists and angles and squares of chrome, steel, glass and black leather, all blending with modern artworks similar to those he'd seen in the hall. A sculpture made of gleaming tubes and blocks of metal hung from the dark ceiling which was scattered with scores of tiny star-like spotlights that radiated a colourless light. The only relief from this black and white abstract world was the garden and swimming pool which could be seen through the Venetian blinds over the broad French windows.

'You are late, Mister Lombard,' said a rasping voice with a German accent.

Four people scrutinised him from the depths of the room, shimmering in the light of the tall flames that rose in a monumental fireplace beyond them. Lombard knew which one had spoken. She sat stiffly at a glass table, her fingers drumming a large brown envelope in front of her. Buxom, with her grey hair pinned up in a bun, she wore a chequered suit over a white blouse with a neck-hugging frill collar. She was too far for Lombard to really see her eyes, but they were dark and he could feel their fierceness.

'I very much hope you are better at your job than at keeping time. Anyway, come and sit down,' she said, motioning to a chair of twisted metal opposite her.

Lombard didn't move. He'd more or less muscled his way through The Spaniards, angered many drivers in doing so, and was only five minutes late.

'Good morning, Mrs...?' He knew who she was, but sent her a wilful quizzical grin.

'Mrs. Spitz. We spoke on the telephone.'

'Right. Good morning, Mrs. Spitz.'

'Yes. Good morning,' she said with reluctance, distinctly displeased at being coerced into this protocol; 'My husband. My son-in-law, Carlos. My daughter, Deborah. Now will you please come and sit down,' she went on impatiently.

She'd spoken fast, waving perfunctorily towards the other three in turn. Lombard was still looking at the man she'd called her husband. He sat beside her in a casual shirt and cardigan; thin, white and bespectacled. He too had dark eyes, and they were distorted by his glasses, magnified, so much so that Lombard could see their uneasiness as they returned his gaze.

'Good morning, Mr. Lombard,' he said with a troubled smile, squeezing the coffee mug between his hands. He too had a German accent. Lombard turned to the one she'd called Carlos. He was nearest to the fireplace, dressed all in white in a black armchair with a glossy magazine on his lap. He acknowledged Lombard's glance with a flash of perfect white teeth. He couldn't be much more than thirty five, yet had the ageless look of dark and handsome South American men.

'Are you going to sit down or is it your intention to conduct this interview standing up, Mr. Lombard?' called the indignant voice of Mrs. Spitz.

'Come, come, give the man time to probe, Mummy. Don't you know private detectives like to appraise people?'

Mrs. Spitz scowled sideways at the woman she had introduced as her daughter, Deborah. She stood beside her mother, with her arms crossed and a cigarette burning between her jewelled fingers, looking Lombard over, a naked sneer across her lips. Her hostility was so blatant that Lombard had to remind himself his presence there had actually been solicited.

As if reading his thoughts, she took a drag from her cigarette, blew out the smoke and asked with a scornful grin:

'Aren't I right, Mister Lombard?'

He didn't reply. She was a striking woman, probably in her thirties, secure and commanding in the voluptuousness of her maturity, with brazen eyes, firm full lips and shoulder length jet black hair. A crimson wool skirt-suit hugged the full curves of her breasts and hips, and the skin above the low-cut buttoned-up jacket was bare but for a pearl necklace which set off her olive complexion just as it drew the eyes to her cleavage.

Lombard let his eyes linger on her for a moment, then looked up and sent her his most charming smile. The sneer was still there, immovable it seemed.

'I bet he's going to tell us which one amongst us does not replace the cap on his or her toothpaste tube,' she taunted him.

Why was it that he thought she would have said something cruder, obscene perhaps, if her parents had not been present?

He peered at Mrs. Spitz. She was waiting, stony faced and, judging by her crisp finger-drumming on the envelope in front of her, growing impatient.

'At night or in the morning, Mrs. De Moraes?' he said, heading for the chair of twisted metal across the table from Mrs. Spitz. He'd just decided not to walk out, to stay and find out what they wanted. He was curious, and besides, he'd left Nathalie and the Parliament Hill café for this, nearly crashed on the way, and it looked as if, supposing he was about to be offered a job which he could accept, he would get paid.

Deborah just pursed her red lips derisively and something stabbed Lombard's spine as he sat down. He twisted around to inspect the chair's tortuous metal back. Nothing appeared to be broken. He turned, pushed the chair back, settled on the edge of its seat and grinned into Mrs. Spitz's unfriendly eyes.

'Now, what can I do for you, Mrs. Spitz?'

'Are you sure you are settled, Mr. Lombard?' she asked.

It was not a question but a reprimand. He glanced at the cigarette in Deborah's hands, pulled his Gitanes out of his pocket.

'I think so. Thank you. May I...'

Mrs. Spitz glanced at his Gitanes, snarled her disapproval but waved a granting hand.

'Thank you,' he said.

'Before we start, may I ask if you are Jewish?'

Lombard kept his eyes on the cigarette he was lighting. The German accent, the dark eyes, Deborah's olive complexion... He should have realised Spitz was a Jewish name.

'Lombard. This is not a Jewish name, is it?' went on Mrs. Spitz.

'Don't you think so?' he asked, pocketing his lighter.

'I'm asking you.'

Like most people, she pronounced the 'D' at the end of his name.

'What about *Lombar*?' he said; 'That is the correct pronunciation. The *D* at the end is mute.'

She scowled:

'Really? Well, are you Jewish, Mr. Lombard?'

She'd left the 'D' out this time. Lombard grinned again. Was she always so ill-natured or was it just because she was talking to him?

'I wouldn't know, Mrs. Spitz. To be honest, I never pondered the question,' he said.

She sent him a hard critical look.

'I hope it is not too significant,' he ventured.

'What if it is?'

'Well, you must realise we could have sorted out the question of my faith and parentage this morning if you'd been more communicative. I wouldn't like to think I had kept you waiting for nothing.'

Her eyes widened ominously, then narrowed again. She went on eyeing him for a short moment, musing, then checked her watch, sent out a frustrated sigh of resignation and said:

'Whatever, you come recommended. We—'

'Recommended?' he cut in.

'Must I speak to you in French?'

'Didn't you say I came recommended?'

'Yes.'

'That's what I thought. May I know by whom?' asked Lombard, grinning.

'No. You may not. And besides, it is irrelevant,' she declared.

Lombard took a drag from his cigarette, nodded compliantly:

'Okay. Recommended…'

'Good. Now, as I trust you have already guessed, we are looking for someone to work for us. Someone whose discretion can be relied upon. Someone who once in our employ would give us the exclusivity of his services until the end of our association. We expect full commitment and loyalty, you understand? Under no circumstance must anything this person might learn about our family be disclosed to any third party. Do you think you could be that person, Mr. Lombard?'

Lombard peered at his cigarette to avoid letting the woman read his mind. Maybe he could still salvage the journey. Maybe it was worth hanging on for a little longer, just in case it was within these people to be a little more polite or tactful.

'Look, Mrs. Spitz…'

He paused, turned to Carlos who was leafing through his magazine as if nothing was happening. Lombard could now see it was a yachting publication. A phrase pushed its way to the forefront of his mind: 'Latin manhood in all its carnal glory…'

'Look, Mrs. Spitz,' he spoke again; 'I don't know to whom I'm indebted for the recommendation, but it would seem the person concerned didn't explain what I do properly. I'm not in the business of making oaths of allegiance or giving myself or anybody else character references. What I do is listen to what the people who care to call me have to say, and judge whether or not I can be of help. I hope you can appreciate that, Mrs. Spitz.'

She couldn't:

'What I can appreciate is insolence, Mr. Lombard!' she said, once again articulating the 'D' of his name.

'Please, Ethel,' muttered her husband.

One of his hands had let go of his coffee mug and now gently squeezed her forearm in a firm but placatory gesture. She turned to him, muttered a few quick words in what sounded like German. The old man sighed, replied in an appeasing voice and, as if Lombard was not there, the two of them began talking in what he now believed to be Yiddish. Lombard moved his eyes onto Mr. Spitz's hand still clasped on his wife's forearm. The skin was dry and furrowed, the fingers broad and slightly deformed by arthritis. This was not the hand of a pampered rich man but that of a hardworking artisan.

'Would you mind telling us what you're doing here anyway, Mr. Lombard?' the voice of Deborah suddenly demanded above her parents' mutterings.

The two old Spitzes fell silent as Lombard looked up.

'Would you mind explaining what a Frenchman is doing in London working as a private investigator?'

Deborah's eyes were fixed on him, probing, and it was difficult to say whether it was contempt or hatred that burnt behind them.

Lombard rose to his feet, leant across the table, stubbed out his cigarette in her ashtray:

'There was nothing left for me to investigate in France, Mrs. De Moraes. Don't disturb the butler. I remember the way out.'

'Sit down, please, Mr. Lombard. Sit down...'

It was Mr. Spitz's conciliatory voice. He looked uneasily up at Lombard through his spectacles, his magnified eyes set in a patchwork of deep wrinkles. Lombard realised how old he was, much older than his wife.

'Please forgive us. My wife did not mean to offend you. It's just that—'

'Why don't you let him go, Daddy,' cut in Deborah; 'This is a complete waste of time anyway. Wonder boy'll soon run out of cash and stagger back to the nest...'

'Deborah, please!' roared Mrs. Spitz.

Deborah glanced at her mother, shook her head and leant to stamp out her cigarette.

'We were hoping to ask you to look for our son, Mr. Lombard,' went on Mr. Spitz, once satisfied that silence had returned; 'He—he has disappeared...'

He paused, understood Lombard wanted to hear more before deciding whether to sit down again:

'He has been missing for nearly two weeks now. We are worried he might be in trouble...'

'Come on! If you must go ahead with this you might as well get to the point.'

It was Deborah again. She turned to Lombard:

'As for you, if you must hear about my dear brother's riveting persona, you might as well sit down again. Boredom is easier handled that way. And by the way, in case you're wondering, the *boy* Leon is 31 years old.'

She shook her head, lit a new cigarette and sent Carlos an angry look. Lombard turned just in time to see him shrug, then turned back to the Spitzes. Mr. Spitz was no longer looking at him but gazing morosely at his clasped hands against the glass table. Mrs. Spitz was frowning at Deborah, who had turned to face the fireplace and stood with her back to them all.

Lombard sat down again, remembering not to recline against the chair-back:

'I take it your son is called Leon?' he said helpfully to the Spitzes.

'Leonard,' said Mrs. Spitz, still frowning; 'What my daughter is on about, Mr. Lombard, is that Leonard is a bit of a bohemian. You might as well know that—'

'For bohemian, read ex-university dropout and ex-failed rock star recently turned Artist Photographer. Oh yes, and a most likely relapsing *ex*-heroin addict,' muttered Deborah without turning from the fireplace.

'We do not know this for certain, Deborah!' yelled Mrs. Spitz. This time she had not bothered to turn to see whether her daughter was facing her again.

'I said *likely*, Mummy,' said Deborah, taunting.

Mrs. Spitz clenched her fists, threw an irritated glance at Lombard:

'Leonard is a good boy, but unfortunately he likes bad company and is very susceptible… Two years ago we had to send him to a…'

She broke off, peered at the envelope lying in front of her, her reluctance to go on almost palpable:

'Two years ago we had to send him to a detoxification clinic in the USA,' she said finally. She sighed, was glad it was over, was much happier speaking her next sentence:

'It has had the desired effect… He has since been very happy living in the apartment we gave him, and until two weeks ago called and visited me and my husband regularly.'

'Money doesn't grow on trees,' cut in Deborah.

This time, like Mrs. Spitz, Lombard did not bother to look up. Mrs. Spitz carried on:

'Leonard has decided to devote himself to photography. It has been good for him. My husband and I have chosen to support him in this. But he does work, part-time.'

'He does?' asked Lombard.

'*Jah!* In a restaurant.'

'Why don't you ask in what capacity, Mr. Lombard?' intervened Deborah.

'He washes the dishes. Three evenings a week he washes the dishes,' declared Mrs. Spitz forthwith.

The words had lashed out of her mouth, and she was now, for the first time, looking awkwardly at her hands, almost exactly like her husband beside her. Lombard knew she knew what he was thinking in the ensuing silence. He felt Carlos' eyes on him, turned. Carlos immediately sent him a toothy smirk, an awkward glance that did not suit his handsome looks but which Lombard translated as meaning that this situation had nothing to do with him, that he was only the son-in-law and…

'What do you think may have happened to your son, Mrs. Spitz?' asked Lombard, turning away from Carlos.

'If I knew I would not be wasting your time, Mr. Lombard,' came the reply. Mrs. Spitz was not one to remain flustered for long.

'Has he ever gone missing in the past?'

Deborah answered first:

'Leon used to elope like this before his *treatment*.'

She was facing them again, her sneer back in place, and Mrs. Spitz glared sideways at her again:

'I am categorical Leonard has had no interest in drugs since he left the clinic.'

'But he's been missing for two weeks,' said Lombard.

Mrs. Spitz just looked at him. He smiled:

'You seem like wealthy people; have you considered the possibility of kidnapping…'

Deborah guffawed.

'Don't you think we would know by now?' said Mrs. Spitz.

'He could have had an accident, or decided to take a trip or—'

'We are not stupid, Mr. Lombard,' cut in Mrs. Spitz; 'We have made enquiries of the police and at all the London hospitals. And had he decided to take a trip, as you say, he would have let us and his employer know about it.'

Lombard smiled:

'Then why not ask the police to look for him, Mrs. Spitz?'

Deborah beamed at him, pleased, and she shone, briefly:

'At last, a pertinent question. Come on, Mummy—answer Mr. Lombard,' she said without taking her eyes off him.

It was Mr. Spitz who answered, his sad eyes on Lombard:

'Whether or not our son is taking drugs again is something we would rather not find out through the police, Mr. Lombard. I'm sure you can understand.'

'It might be difficult for someone like you to discern, but we are people of a certain standing, you see,' Deborah enjoyed saying.

Lombard was tiring of her contempt:

'Appearances can be deceptive, Mrs. De Moraes.'

She looked straight back at him, so consumed with animosity she froze for a moment. Her dark olive complexion probably saved her from blushing with anger:

'That depends what you're looking at,' she pronounced, eyeing him up and down.

He frowned, looked right through her, coldly. He was certain he saw her lips quiver, her pupils widen, the fingers clasping her cigarette tense. He wasn't altogether displeased by this.

'Don't worry, I noticed the public school accent,' he said with a grin of cruel satisfaction, and turned to Mrs. Spitz:

'My rates—' he began.

'We are aware of your rates, Mr. Lombard,' cut in the old woman, sliding the envelope she'd been fingering across the table.

'This contains Leonard's address, a key to his apartment and other information you might require. The £1,000 is on account. We will pay you double your rates plus expenses. In return, let me say it again, we expect discretion and undivided attention. I gather you are not very busy, so I trust this should not be too much of a problem. Is that to your satisfaction?'

Lombard grinned; not very busy…

The envelope was resting on the edge of the table in front of him and Mrs. Spitz awaiting his answer. She'd taken him by surprise. He wasn't ready yet. He'd only brought up the matter of his rates to find out whether it was worth his while continuing to put up with this unpleasant meeting. In his experience, while wealthy clients settled their bills, they could also be relied upon to haggle exactingly about his price, unlike the less fortunate who made no fuss, accepted it as a fait-accompli, as they did most other things in their lives, even if they couldn't always afford him, had to be harassed once it was time to pay up. But the well-off paid, whatever bad news he may have brought them. Their privacy was dear to them, they had a name, a front to protect, more to lose. It was essential that the private detective who now knew an embarrassing truth or two should not be unhappy, not be tempted to publicise what he knew out of spite at not being paid. Their money could be trusted to buy silence, they liked to think, sweeping aside professional ethics, integrity and goodness. If what one owned didn't help one feel better and more secure…

'Double your rates plus expenses…' And £1,000 on account. Mrs. Spitz was a woman who knew how to get what she wanted.

'I take it your son is single?' he asked her.

'That is right,' she said; 'And before you ask, no, he is not gay! He has had a few girls, nothing serious. Girls he photographs only,' she declared, waving her hand flippantly.

Lombard nodded:

'Forgive me for asking this, but I presume someone checked his flat to make sure he's not there.'

'Of course,' replied Mrs. Spitz.

'Good. Could you tell me who went there?'

'I did,' she said.

'And everything looks normal?'

'Yes.'

'Did you by any chance think of looking for your son's passport and—'

'It is there, Mr. Lombard. And I also checked with his bank. There have been no withdrawals from his account for over four weeks now.'

Lombard peered at her:

'Excuse me, but how did you do that, Mrs. Spitz?'

'What?'

'Check your son's bank account, Mrs. Spitz. Banks don't usually communicate information about their clients' accounts to a third party. It's supposed to be confidential information.'

'I said earlier that my husband and I have chosen to support Leonard with his photography. What this means is that since he returned from his American clinic I have been depositing fifteen hundred pounds a month for his use in a joint account we hold together. So as you see, I did not have to break any law or pull any tricks to find out if he used the account.'

'You hold a joint bank account with your son?'

She noted Lombard's surprise with a scowl:

'Yes, Mr. Lombard. Leonard was weak and confused on his

return from America. It looked like a good idea at the time for me to keep an eye on the way and speed with which he spent his money.'

'I see. Has he ever been in prison? A mental institution?'

'No.'

'When did you last see him?'

'Myself, over six weeks ago, when I last came to London. But he came here a few days before we realised he was missing…'

'To borrow money. I wasn't here. But he got to Carlos.'

The interruption was Deborah's again.

'That's right,' said Carlos.

He was smiling at Lombard:

'I gave him a couple of thousand pounds,' the man went on in his suave Brazilian accent; 'He said he needed it to get some photographs printed for an exhibition he had coming up. He promised to pay me back as soon as he'd sold some work but I told him not to worry.'

'I still don't understand how you could have been so stupid,' said Deborah. She'd spoken with the kind of contempt she had so far reserved for Lombard.

'I'm sorry, darling. How was I to know he does his own printing?' protested Carlos with a helpless shrug.

Deborah scoffed, turned to Lombard:

'Wouldn't want anyone to interfere with his *Art*, you understand.'

'Was it cash?' asked Lombard.

The question was addressed to Carlos, and Carlos was looking back at him baffled.

'The £2,000. You gave it to him in cash?'

Carlos understood now:

'Oh. Yes. We've always got money in… We always keep money in the house.'

'He seemed fine?'

'Er, yes. He was very happy about the money.'

Lombard turned to Mrs. Spitz:

'According to his bank statement, had your son spent all of his monthly allowance by the time he came here to borrow money, Mrs. Spitz.'

She did not know, could not remember, but:

'I should think so. It was nearing the end of the month. I credit the account on the first.'

'Why didn't he come to you to borrow the money, Mrs. Spitz?'

She looked back at him, not understanding.

'You are the one supporting him in his photography, aren't you?' he explained.

'Ha... No. Our understanding is that fifteen hundred pounds is all he gets from my husband and myself. That's it. Anything else he needs, he must fend for himself, you understand?'

'You mean borrow it from people even stupider than he is.'

Who could it be but Deborah. Lombard automatically peered at Carlos. He was frowning towards his wife, annoyed.

'What about friends?' asked Lombard.

'I telephoned the only friend of his we know about,' said Mrs. Spitz; 'He is the owner of the restaurant where Leonard works. He too has not seen or heard of him for the past fortnight. His name and address are in the envelope, as is everything else you might need, Mr. Lombard.'

She glanced impatiently at her watch. Lombard ignored the signal.

'Does your son drive a car, Mrs. Spitz?'

'No. He has no driving licence.'

'Why?'

'What do you mean why?'

'Is he frightened of driving? Is he physically unable to drive? Or has he just failed his driving test?'

'No. He never bothered with getting a licence, that's all.'

Lombard looked at the envelope again, then up at Deborah. He smiled:

'What do you think led your brother to think you would have lent him money if you'd been here when he came, Mrs. De Moraes?'

She understood at once why he was asking, delighted in her reply:

'Only the fact that he knew I would have given him the money, Mr. Lombard.'

Lombard didn't understand. She pre-empted his next question:

'Why am I upset with my husband for having lent it to him? I don't think anyone in their right mind should lend or give Leon anything, Mr. Lombard. They might as well throw it away. I, on the other hand, I do get something out of lending him money secure in the knowledge that he'll never be able to repay it. Isn't it terrible? Aren't you going to ask me what it is, Mr. Lombard?'

He could guess.

'If not for prints, what do you think your brother may have needed £2,000 for, Mrs. De Moraes?' he asked instead.

'Huh!' she retorted.

'Leonard is not back on drugs!' snapped Mrs. Spitz indignantly.

'If you say so, Mummy…'

'I say so.'

'Well, you better hope that our French detective here knows his job then.'

'What are you saying, Deborah?'

'What I'm saying is, if Leon is not back on drugs, has not been kidnapped, gone on holiday or been in an accident, something really mysterious must have happened to him. Who knows, he might have decided to run away and start a new life. After all, he never showed much sign of coping with the one he's had so far.'

Mrs. Spitz peered at her daughter sullenly:

'I do not understand you sometimes, Deborah. Leonard is your brother.'

Deborah shook her head, looked somewhat hurt as she said:

'Why don't you ask Daddy what he thinks happened to *the boy* Leon, huh, Mummy?'

Mrs. Spitz turned to her husband who resolutely kept his eyes on his hands. She opened her mouth as if to ask him something, then turned to Lombard, checking her watch again. It was the third time she had done so since Lombard had stepped into the room.

'I'm afraid I have other things to deal with now, Mr. Lombard. Am I to believe we are agreed? If not, you might as well leave now. I will of course assume that someone in your profession would not need to be reminded that everything he heard here was said in confidence.'

Lombard looked at the envelope, reached for it and stood up:

'I'll be in touch,' he said.

If Mrs. Spitz was pleased, she didn't show it.

'My husband and I are returning to our house in Scotland

tomorrow afternoon. So if we don't hear from you before, you will have to communicate with my daughter, understood?'

'Fine,' said Lombard; 'One more thing, Mrs. and Mr. Spitz, may I ask what is or was your occupation?

'We make and sell shoes and leather garments,' answered Mr. Spitz humbly.

His eyes were on Lombard again, still uneasy, but now, buried deep in the pupils, was strength, tired strength but strength, and through his furrowed face, Lombard finally noticed the proud jaw, the high cheekbones, the fine aquiline nose; Mr. Spitz must once have been a good looking man.

'And Mr. Lombard?'

Deborah was summoning.

'If and when you do find our lost boy, don't bring him here, all right?'

She meant it.

'I'll do my best not to. May I ask what is *your* occupation, Mrs. De Moraes?'

She looked back at him, hesitating, then:

'I have too much money to work, Mr. Lombard.'

He turned to Carlos.

'De Moraes. That's a Brazilian name, no?'

Carlos smiled his beautiful smile:

'That's right. Do you know Brazil?'

'No. Do you work, Mr. De Moraes?'

'Oh yes. I race motorcars and yachts, you know...'

Lombard peered into the fire behind him.

There was no smell in the room. He thought he could hear the hiss of the gas feeding the tall flames that licked the red hot logs in the grate. Hot blooded people in a cold house...

THREE

Whoever had recommended Lombard to Mrs. Spitz, they had certainly fully endorsed him, for if appearances could be trusted, had she so wished, the old woman had the means to hire one of London's top investigative agencies to search for her son. Yet she'd elected to call him, a small-time detective, a foreigner who, as she put it, was not that busy, and offered him twice his normal rates.

She was right about his business: his phone did not ring so very often, he had no need of a waiting room or secretary, but he managed reasonably enough, at any rate reasonably enough to afford not to get involved in assignments he did not approve of or wish for.

Had the information about the slowness of his trade come from the same source as the endorsement, or had Mrs. Spitz got it from another party? Lombard frowned. He would have taken the job at his normal rates. The thirty-one-year-old lost children of rich people are not that hard to find, especially, as seemed the case in this instance, friendless ones with a drug problem...

'Anyway, Froggy, got a funny one for us? Anything juicy, eh?'

The voice roused Lombard from his thoughts, dragged him back into the small group amidst whom he stood at the bar, and the din of conversation and ambient music of the smoke-filled pub reached his ears once again. He ran his eyes over the five faces around him, came to rest on the tall frame in a blue track-suit he knew as Mark the greengrocer, a bear of a man with bushy eyebrows that met above his nose. He was waiting for a reply with an expectant smile.

'No. Not this week,' said Lombard with a polite smile, and he brought his pint of beer to his lips and drank.

Mark didn't press him. He knew it would be futile. Like the other Essex Road shopkeepers Lombard joined every other

Friday at The Falcon for the ritual drink after their football match, Mark had learned over the years that when Lombard said no he meant no.

'What about you, Bombay?'

This was addressed to Larry, the thin Indian with a beer belly who ran the newsagent's across the road from Perkins' butcher's shop. Larry frowned, repeatedly blinked, as he usually did when thinking, then grinned and narrowed his glassy eyes into a squint. He was clearly already drunk, but judging from his mischievous look, had nonetheless managed to summon a joke from his intoxicated memory.

'All right, fellows!' he called; 'Has anyone heard the one about the gay man who goes to have a check-up?'

No one had.

'Yes, well,' said Larry; 'During his examination the doctor is shocked to find a bouquet of flowers lodged in the man's rectum. "Where the hell did these come from?" asks the doctor, removing a yellow rose. "I'm not sure," says the gay man; "Why don't you read the card?" '

Lombard smiled as the men around him burst into laughter.

'Bloody Bombay,' John Perkins proclaimed. He was smiling at Bill, the tall, hatchet-faced pet shop owner who had joined in the general laughter.

Lombard noticed the tactfully fleeting glances towards Bill. Bill was the team's goalkeeper, and everyone was pleased to see him enjoying himself again, pleased to see him laughing, pleased to contribute to his recovery.

'Anyway,' resumed Larry; 'The doctor's next patient turns out to be a lesbian contortionist, and on this occasion, his examination reveals a lollipop lodged inside her... you know, inside her bush. Better be cool, calm and collected about it this time, he tells himself. "So, your girlfriend has a sweet tooth, eh?" he remarks nonchalantly, pulling out the lollipop. "No," says the lesbian contortionist; "I have." '

'That ain't funny,' declared Andy in the renewed laughter.

Andy was sniggering, but looked as if he meant it. He was the local ironmonger, a stiff man who, with the exception of football nights when he proudly donned a smart Arsenal track suit, was never seen out of his blue overalls.

For a moment, Larry looked ruffled, but then squinted his impish squint again:

'Would you very much mind telling me why indeed, Andy, my friend?' he enquired.

'It just isn't,' retorted Andy.

'But why is that?' insisted Larry. He was enjoying this now, welcomed the opportunity to torment Andy who had carelessly committed to an opinion while putting down his joke. 'What's the difference between a gay man with a bouquet of flowers lodged in his rectum and a lesbian contortionist with a lollipop lodged in her bush?' he asked with a grin.

John Perkins intervened before Andy could reply:

'I know why he's so upset,' he said, breaking off to suppress his chortle; 'His old lady's having it off with a woman, ha-ha...'

Andy just peered at Perkins, then grinned. This was all light-hearted fun, drunk men relaxing after a hard week's work:

'Well, if she is having it off with a woman, it certainly ain't with your missis, Johnny Porky boy. She just ain't bloody good looking enough,' said Andy gleefully, and he turned back to Larry:

'And talking of having it off, some of us would be well advised to think about doing just that instead of dribbling over dirty magazines when the wife's not looking, huh?'

The source of Larry's jokes was no secret to anyone.

'Well, there are perks to running a newsagent, my friend,' said Larry; 'But don't worry, I am very careful not to dribble over the copies you buy, ha-ha...'

'Well, so long as you don't strangle your granny over them either it's okay with me,' snarled Andy.

'Strangle my granny?' queried Larry, not understanding.

'Yeah. Milk the cow, you know?'

Larry didn't know. He looked wide-eyed at Andy, confused, then frowned on seeing the other men's faces glowing with mirth at his expense. This was Andy's chance to have a little fun:

'What's wrong with you, Bombay? Don't they teach you proper bloody English in bloody India, huh? What about stroke the lizard? Bash the Bishop? Beat the dummy? Varnish the cane?'

Larry was blinking again, trying to ignore the stifled laughter that surrounded him.

'Maybe he was deaf during the relevant lesson,' said Mark; 'You know what they say about—'

'Oh!' interjected Larry; 'Do you mean wanking?' he asked in all seriousness but still unsure.

Mark and Perkins roared with laughter, Perkins so much that his face grew almost as red as his Arsenal jersey, which stretched and shook with each wobble and quiver of his podgy belly and shoulders. His earthy laughter was infectious, Larry and Andy joined in, and the crowded pub momentarily fell silent as all faces turned to observe them.

'Happy, are we?' called a voice.

'Don't choke on us, eh! The season's not over yet,' shouted another. These calls came from the table where the rest of the Essex Road Traders squad sat.

'Do you mean wanking! Ha-ha...' Mark threw at them between roars of laughter.

A few eyebrows rose, lips smirked, shoulders shrugged, and all faces turned away again, not understanding. No one but Lombard seemed to notice Bill's discomfort. He stood smiling into his glass, but his smile was tense and his posture rigid. Considering how gratified everyone had been to see him enjoying himself a few moments earlier, Larry and Andy's last exchange was unfortunate. It was bound to touch Bill, and it had. But in the circumstances, their thoughtlessness was understandable and excusable. After all this was the evening the Essex Road Traders had beaten the Upper Street Traders by nine goals to one. A unique feat, one which they obviously felt deserved to be toasted to oblivion, even if it had admittedly been achieved only as a result of a flu epidemic which had deprived the rival team of several key players, including their regular goalkeeper, a giant who had once played in the Arsenal reserves.

'Come on, it wasn't that funny,' said Andy, slapping Perkins on the back. Perkins was bent double, tears running down his cheeks; he gasped for air and hugged his chest trying to stop himself laughing.

'Jesus Christ almighty,' he muttered, at last managing to recover his breath and straighten up as the laughter subsided.

But Larry was not finished. With a great sense of timing he turned to Andy again and asked:

'So? Did you mean wanking then?'

A new roar, much louder than the previous one, filled the pub again. Lombard heard himself chuckle, gulped some beer, and gazed down at Perkins who now seemed in serious danger of choking. In his Arsenal jersey, with the little hair he had left still wet from the post-match shower, he looked even more middle-aged and podgy than in his butcher's bloodstained apron. Over three years had passed since he had introduced Lombard to his team-mates, three years during which he had simply grown pudgier and balder, turned into what he was now, a fleshy figure with a jovial face who scrupulously kept a forlorn lock of hair stretched across his bald head. Was it a desire to hold back the years or mere vanity that led Perkins to apply Brylcream daily to this lock of hair so that it would cling to his skull like a second skin? Did its manufactured existence really make him feel better when he looked in the mirror? Whatever it was that warranted its mothering inside Perkins' mind, at this very moment, it was out of Perkins' field of perception. He'd forgotten his lock of hair; it hung slack and forsaken at the side of his cherry-red face, floating helplessly in the air, lurching rhythmically against his shoulder with each of his spasms of laughter. One stray, carefully stuck together, lock of hair...

Perhaps Perkins was right, perhaps he did after all look better with it on than without, thought Lombard, gazing at his naked skull that glowed with sweat.

Good old Perkins. He'd waited three months before letting Lombard know why he'd been so curious about his aptitude at football on the day they'd met. Subject to a trial and his team-mates' agreement, he'd offered him a place in the Essex Road Traders' squad. This was a shopkeepers-get-together-for-a-little-exercise kind of affair. But it was to be taken seriously, Perkins had proclaimed, for every fortnight, running concurrently with the English Premier league season, rain or shine, the Essex Road Traders played the Upper Street Traders in a two-team championship. The rivalry between the two squads was intense, the games hard fought, not least because at the end of the season each player of the team with most wins was entitled to a case of Champagne from the losers, or, if preferred, £100 in cash.

'That's money,' Perkins had said; 'Each squad has a total of eighteen players for the season, and although we play eleven-a-side, all eighteen players qualify for the bubbly or hundred quid, whether they've been fielded or spent the whole season on the bench... That's money.'

Lombard had thought about it for a few weeks, agreed, and, after a trial in which he'd shown sufficient skill to convince Perkins' team-mates he was worth enlisting, had had to wait a further two months for the rules governing this local competition to be changed because the Upper Street Traders had objected to a private detective joining what was, by rule, essentially a shop-keepers' game. However, once again thanks to Perkins' vigorous campaigning, it had eventually been agreed that each squad could recruit up to three 'self-employed' players as long as they actually worked from premises on either of the streets. This amendment had been most welcome to Lombard's new team-mates for, although they were of course glad to put his talents to use, more significantly, it had helped redress in their favour a situation they'd come to see as unfair; Upper Street being a longer and busier shopping street than Essex Road, its team could recruit players from about twice if not three times as many shops. Be that as it may, only one other 'self-employed' had enrolled in the Essex Road Traders since Lombard's arrival, an accountant, and he had soon left, unable to commit every second Friday to the game; he didn't have a wife or assistant to look after the shop from five o'clock onwards.

Lombard smiled, remembering how let down Perkins had looked when he'd turned up for his first match on the plastic pitch in Market Road wearing a Liverpool jersey.

'We wear red and the other lot yellow,' Perkins had said.

'Anything red?' Lombard had asked.

'Yeah, as long as it's like an Arsenal jersey. Ha-ha...'

Still, all had been forgiven when Lombard had there and then taken his team to victory by scoring a hat-trick, a one-off stunt never since repeated as, having learned the hard way, the Upper Street Traders had from that day on seen to it that he was always tightly marked.

But he still managed to score the occasional goal, so ensuring he kept his place in the squad. This meant something to him. He enjoyed the games, they allowed him to keep in shape; but he also enjoyed the chance to be with men in pleasurable circumstances, enjoyed the rowdy post-match communal showers and trips to the warm beery atmosphere of The Falcon, the crude jokes and belly-laughs, the trivial chatter and rounds of drinks, even though he himself neither drank nor spoke very much.

But like Perkins, the others had accepted him. Perhaps it was that he was as good a player as any of them, or perhaps it was because when he was in the mood he was not averse to enlivening their evenings with some of the more amusing incidents he came across during the course of his work. He knew they found him a little strange. He never spoke of his past or private life, never expressed opinions about anything. They knew he was not one of them, probably still wondered and conjectured about him behind his back, had doubtless by now decided he was running away from whatever it was he was hiding. Yet, they never asked any questions. In some ways they were alike. In some ways, like Lombard himself, they were anonymous people; people with modest expectations who quietly looked after themselves, although in their case it was down to the fact that they belonged to London's nation of small shopkeepers, a nation seen and heard but never looked at or listened to.

Jo Papadopoulos, the elegant but greasy-haired Greek owner of the Taverna restaurant next door to Bill's pet shop, had left the table where the rest of the team still sat and joined Lombard's group to partake of their fun. Everyone called him 'Papadoo', except Lombard, who called him 'Jo'.

Jo was one of those men who liked to carry at all times a thick wad of folded £20 notes in his trouser pocket. In his case, the wad was bound by a gold pin. When the time came to buy his round, he would pull it from his pocket, hold it flat in his hand between thumb and fingers, open it with one flick of the thumb, slip out however many notes he needed with the thumb and forefinger of the other hand, put the notes on the bar, flick the wad shut again and leisurely slide it back in his pocket. This act was carefully performed, well-rehearsed and perfected, and, whatever might be taking place around Jo during its execution, Jo's eyes were always staring calmly at the wad of money in his hand, Jo's lips were always tightly closed in a proud sulk, Jo's expression was always one of serene fulfilment; and one realised that this ostentatious display was not mere affectation but something close to Jo's heart, that the performance was not executed for the onlookers' sake but for Jo himself; that Jo loved his money.

'… So the guy asks for the toilet and…'

Lombard had never taken to Jo's Greek accent, wad of money or slick suits. He stopped listening. It was an easy enough thing for him to do. Listening to English still took a conscious effort; unless he concentrated, the words entered his ears bereft of meaning – and at once, the four people he'd met a few hours earlier in the strange house in Templeton Road engaged his thoughts again.

He could still feel their tension, the open hostility and distrust with which they had welcomed him. That in itself was nothing remarkable. People rarely welcomed him. It was part of the job. The nature of his occupation meant he was required only where trouble had preceded him. His clients couldn't help but see him as the bearer of bad tidings, and resent him for it, identifying him with their trouble. It was nothing personal. He did not exist. Like Perkins, he was just someone who happened to have what they needed and wanted money for it. But whereas they could at least look forward to Perkins' joints and chops, they did not always look forward to the information they paid Lombard to gather. Nevertheless, clients generally took care not to be offensive; after all, his co-operation had to be secured, his integrity relied upon.

Mrs. Spitz had not even attempted to be civil. Had her husband not been with her, Lombard would probably have walked out. Yet Lombard was convinced she alone had made the decision to get in touch with him. Although her husband and Carlos had said little, both had seemed to share Deborah's belief that her brother would reappear when the cash ran out. Handsome Carlos had even made a show of his indifference to the fate of his brother-in-law. As for Mr. Spitz, it was apparently beyond him to conceal his shame at his son's behaviour. Only Mrs. Spitz, in spite of her cold exterior, had shown faith in her missing progeny, had bothered to stand up for him, rushing to proclaim, unprompted, his heterosexuality, committing herself to declaring, even if experience made it unlikely, that he was clean, purged, freed from his drug addiction.

She was a worried mother, worried enough to have already made enquiries at hospitals and police stations, worried enough to have brought a private detective into her hostile daughter's house to ask him to search for her son.

'Leonard is a good boy, but unfortunately he likes bad company and is very susceptible,' she had said in her stony German accent. These were not the words of an insensitive old woman who could domineer and terrify everyone around her into submission. Besides, her husband's gentle squeeze of her forearm, his interruptions and placatory tone, her daughter's forthright and provocative words, all indicated otherwise.

Then why had Mrs. Spitz been so rude? Was she putting a brave face on her son's disappearance? Was she, like the rest of her family, already resigned to the fact that in spite of all her efforts, her son was back to his old ways, and in her disillusionment already taking it out on the messenger? Had she had to fight her family about calling in a detective?

Lombard nodded his almost imperceptible nod, made a note to himself to try to find out who'd recommended him to Mrs. Spitz, and peered towards the clock above the bar. It was not yet eight o'clock. He had the option of spending the rest of the evening with the ongoing drinking party, of heading home to watch TV, or failing that, of making a start on the Leonard Spitz case…

He finished his beer, put his empty glass on the bar, picked up his kit-bag and, listening again, waited for Mark to conclude the story he was telling his captive audience.

' "So what's your problem?" I says,' said Mark, running his eager eyes from face to face; ' "I mean, if she's beautiful and great in bed, huh?!" "Well, she's kind of psychic," he says; "You know – precognitive." '

'Pre-what?' cut in Andy.

'Precognitive, you know, when you know things in advance,' Perkins clarified.

'What, like a fortune-teller?'

Mark glowered:

'Jesus Christ. Yes, like a fortune-teller, all right!' he growled, and resumed where he'd left off, smiling again:

'So she's precognitive, he says. "Well, if she's a good fuck," I says, "who cares, huh?" "That's just it," he says all gloomy; "Whenever we're at it, she keeps yelling *Anthony! Anthony!*" The guy's called Steve, right? "Sorry?" I says. And you know what the poor bloke says? He says: "She says she can't help it. She's got to yell the name of the next bloke she's gonna lay." Honest to God, ha-ha...'

Perkins opened his eyes wide, a concupiscent grin across his face:

'Jesus Christ! My second name's Anthony! John Anthony Perkins!'

Mark sneered:

'You don't say! Then let me tell you, the poor girl's in for a bad surprise; Steve's a lot better looking than you are, mate, ha-ha...'

The men were laughing.

'Goodnight everyone,' said Lombard, waving a hand around; 'Great game.'

No one was surprised to hear he was leaving so early, except Perkins, who turned to him with a worried frown:

'Oh... I must... There's something I wanted to talk to you about before you left,' he said.

Lombard looked down at Perkins' hand. The man's thumb gently rubbed his index finger in a circular motion. Lombard knew this to mean that Perkins was nervous, had something important or unpleasant to say.

'Can't it wait until tomorrow?' he asked.

Perkins glanced around him, looking suddenly ill-at-ease under his lock of hair which once again lay plastered across his skull. Whatever he wanted to say, he didn't want to say it in front of the others, but he apparently didn't feel that it could wait.

'Er...' he began.

'What is it, eh?' cut in Mark. All eyes were on Perkins now, roguish, waiting for him to speak and adding to his embarrassment.

'Er…' muttered Perkins again.

'Er? Er? Is this yet another way to refer to wanking?' joked Larry, peering around.

'Come on,' implored Perkins as the others laughed. He turned back to Lombard, his disquiet plain for all to see:

'I'm putting my rents up as from Monday. I already told Jane and—'

He broke off, let out a sigh, said the rest with his eyes down:

'I'm sorry, *Savieer*. I know this is not the time or place, but I didn't want you to hear it from Jane's mouth…'

'Talking of your little Jane's mouth I—' began Andy.

'Shut up!' cried Perkins.

Lombard knew Perkins well enough to know his discomfort was genuine. Perkins liked him, held him in high esteem, especially since the day he'd asked if it was all right for Nathalie to move in with him. This had done a lot to impress Perkins, and the fact that Nathalie had teased the butcher with relentless cruelty during her stay and then moved out again within three months had done nothing to lower his high opinion of Lombard; knowing Perkins, it may even have risen. Any man who could have an affair with a woman like Nathalie and then take her leaving in his stride, well…

'I'm truly sorry,' went on Perkins; 'It's that bloody new supermarket. It's costing me a lot of trade… Anyway, we'll talk about it, eh?'

Lombard grinned:

'Well, I just hope the increase won't mean I can no longer afford your meat, Mr. Perkins.'

'It's not that bad,' said Perkins. He smiled, relieved Lombard was not annoyed at having had this discussion in public.

'Yeah, sodding supermarket,' muttered Mark shaking his head.

Perkins' words had cast a shadow over the group. The 'sodding' supermarket had opened its doors at the Balls Pond end of Essex Road less than three months earlier, had already produced a great deal of grievance and talk of closure amongst the Essex Road Traders.

'Don't worry about it now,' said Lombard helpfully; 'Remember, nine–one… Have fun.'

'Are you going home?'

It was Bill. He looked at Lombard with his watery eyes, doubtless hoping for a lift as he didn't own a car.

Lombard hesitated. He was going home, wanted to change into a clean suit, Bill lived only two blocks down the road from him, but...

'If you are, could you drop me off?' asked Bill. He wanted to leave, had been waiting to do so for a while now. Given his state of mind, he would misinterpret a rejection, would be hurt, end up feeling even worse than he already did.

Lombard nodded:

'Of course.'

A few voices pleaded with the pet shop owner to stay for at least another drink, but there was not much heart in their appeals.

Lombard would have preferred that Bill had not asked to come with him. It was not a dislike of the pet-shop owner – his dour face and timid manner could hardly inspire anything as commanding as dislike – but merely selfishness that had caused him to hesitate before agreeing to give him a lift.

Leaving the noise of The Falcon for the quiet of Market Road, Lombard normally looked forward to the short walk to his car which he always parked near the gate to the football pitch three hundred yards away. It gave him particular pleasure in the winter, when the invigorating cold helped stir the mild numbness that invariably won him over in The Falcon's stale and overheated atmosphere, when all was darkness but for the glare of the spot-lights towering over the green pitches beyond their Victorian railings, when all was stillness but for the distant clashing players who cut the evening silence with their hardy screams; then, the road acquired a quality all its own, the crisp, vivid sounds and colours from the football pitches reminding him of childhood, of games hurriedly played in school playgrounds during breaks, of a safer, younger and simpler world. But tonight, as he'd expected, Bill undermined his pleasure by the mere fact of being there, because Bill was tense, had been since Larry and Andy's exchange earlier on.

Lombard raised his raincoat collar around his cold, wet neck. The day's rain had become an all pervading drizzle which hung in the chilly darkness and got into everything.

'It's cold,' he remarked, to break the silence.

'Isn't it?' replied Bill in an abnormally high-pitched voice.

Lombard glanced sideways. Bill walked with his shoulders hunched, gazing at the match being played across the road, one hand pushed deep into his overcoat pocket, the other holding onto his sports bag. He was well over six-foot tall, yet walked so hunched he barely stood taller than Lombard.

'Yeah,' said Lombard.

'Very cold,' confirmed Bill. He'd felt Lombard's eyes on him, had felt obliged to say something further, had said it with a strained smile and was now looking away again.

Did Bill now regret having asked to come with him? Lombard had once walked into his cluttered pet shop to purchase an aquarium and two goldfish, returned on occasion to buy fish food, had played many matches and spent many hours at The Falcon in his company, but this was a new situation, this was the first time the two of them were alone together in the street, with no clear purpose, with no convenient markers to guide their behaviour or conversation. They had nothing to talk about and the abyss that normally separated them could no longer be ignored, seemed to grow wider and deeper with each of their silent steps, too wide to straddle, too deep to fill, even with small-talk about the weather. Had Bill been feeling better he might have hidden behind words about tonight's match, goldfish even, but it seemed all he could manage was 'Isn't it?... Very cold...' And that only in a slightly high-pitched voice, the same voice he'd used a month earlier when he'd broken down in front of his team-mates, to talk about the girl, his girl.

'She was so beautiful... So beautiful...'

Lombard could still picture the naked men standing around him in the steamy shower room. Even Perkins, Larry and Mark had been reduced to listening in silence. No one had smirked or interrupted.

'So beautiful…'

No viciousness nor vulgarity had coloured Bill's words. Just pain, enough of it to make those who disapproved keep their criticisms to themselves, those who found him ridiculous refrain from taunting him, enough to move everyone to feel he was suffering enough as it was, that there was no need to judge or punish him. Besides, as Lombard had seen on the enthralled faces above the bare middle-aged bodies, all had understood, some had identified with his plight, some even been secretly envious; for in his pain Bill had spoken well of his beautiful girl, seduced them as she had seduced him:

'She was only about fourteen but… I'd never seen such… Never imagined… An angel…'

Bill had never been a young man. Bill had lived his entire life alone with his mother in the flat above his shop, and now Bill felt awkward trudging beside Lombard because Andy had amused himself exposing Larry's sketchy knowledge of English when it came to masturbation.

'Every night, for two years…'

Two years. Precisely since his mother had died. Everyone had of course kindly if wrongly assumed Bill's ensuing melancholy to be inspired by grief, believed his tormented eyes to be but a sign of distress at finding himself a lone thirty-nine year old bachelor with prematurely grey hair. Still, in a twisted way, his mother could be said to be responsible for his torment; had she not died when she did Bill may never have seen his girl.

'Whenever something broke in the house, Mother always called the proper people to get it fixed. But I… When water started dripping from my bedroom ceiling one evening soon after she'd gone, I decided to investigate myself, to see if I could sort it out on my own, save the money… Mother never trusted me to fix things, you see. Didn't believe in tinkering about. She believed a job done properly is a job done by experts…'

Lombard suddenly felt irritated; irritated by Bill's willingness to feel sorry for himself, irritated at the thought that he was going to spend the night in his lonely flat above the pet shop indulging in misery, and that he, Lombard, was going to help him do just that by dropping him there.

They were nearing the Triumph now, but there was still a ten minute drive to Bill's flat, too long a time to spend in silence with an anguished man, too long a time to pretend not to know, to behave as timidly as Bill.

'Talking about it was a brave thing,' said Lombard, keeping his eyes on the Triumph.

He felt Bill's eyes settle on him then look away again, heard his breathing stop then resume again, noticed the brief hesitation in his stride before it steadied again. But Bill did not reply.

You fool, thought Lombard. He wasn't feeling cruel. Not even angry. Just exasperated. He quickened his stride; the sooner he was rid of the lanky man now the better.

'We better hurry. I have things to do,' he said, without looking back at Bill who, taken unawares by his abrupt change of pace, was already three steps behind.

Bill muttered something that sounded like 'Sorry' and Lombard shook his head at the sound of the man's feet rushing to catch him up.

'The roof's leaking. The seat might be a bit damp,' said Lombard, pushing the sodden newspapers off the Triumph's passenger seat onto the floor.

'Oh...' said Bill.

Lombard frowned. The roof's leaking... Evidently, this was not Bill's night. But he spoke...

Maybe he'd found the quiet of the street where his words would have echoed in the surrounding darkness too unnerving, found more courage with his voice drowned beneath the purr of the Triumph engine; or maybe he just found sitting in silence with another person within the close confines of a car too trying, the silence acquiring a special significance, becoming full of damning implications, as if some unwritten law deemed it a sin for people to sit together in a vehicle without making conversation. Be that as it may, Bill spoke, as soon as Lombard pulled out into the road:

'There's nothing brave about breaking down in public.'

Lombard took a deep breath. He no longer wished to get involved with Bill's problem. He'd just lit a cigarette, was about to slot a tape into the cassette player to smother the silence, had started thinking about Leonard Spitz. Still, it was he who had instigated the conversation:

'That's not what I said,' he replied; 'I said talking about it was a brave thing.'

'What do you mean?'

'There was no need for you to tell us.'

'I didn't mean to.'

It was useless. Despite his irritation Lombard had chosen his words carefully, deliberately trying to be positive, hoping Bill would jack-up, get strength from being perceived as assertive. *'Talking about it was a brave thing…'* But Bill had chosen to reject the bait, finding self-pity too comfortable to undermine with attempts at self-respect. Lombard knew. While self-respect requires feeding, self-pity simply feeds itself; very convenient when weakness or cowardice hold sway.

'Why did you then?' asked Lombard.

'I don't understand,' replied Bill.

'Why did you talk about it if you didn't mean to?'

'It just happened. I had no choice,' said Bill.

'No choice?'

'No. It just happened,' said Bill again.

'Because they were going to throw you off the team?'

'Yes.'

'Didn't you see it coming then?' asked Lombard.

'What?'

'The team losing match after match because of your goal-keeping. It must have occurred to you that you'd eventually have to face up to it, no?'

Bill sneered ruefully:

'If it had I think I'd have tried to do a better job of stopping the ball getting into the net.'

Lombard could see his point.

'Still, you could have lied,' he said.

'Sorry?'

'You could have lied, pretended something else was troubling you. Something less…'

'Shameful?' said Bill, as Lombard searched for his words.

'Embarrassing,' Lombard corrected him.

Bill remained silent for a moment, then:

'What's the difference. Shameful, embarrassing, it means very much the same thing, doesn't it? Two different words to describe the same thing really.'

'Maybe,' conceded Lombard; 'Though I'd say you'd use one rather than the other if you weren't so determined to feel sorry for yourself.'

Bill fell silent, and Lombard decided to let him mull over his last words. He had not meant to be so blunt, but now that he had he was glad he'd said what he'd said; he'd found Bill's rueful sneer unsavoury, was curious to see what would happen now, what would result from Bill's brooding.

Bill was right of course. He had not been brave but had broken down in the shower room when the team threatened to get rid of him after a seven–two defeat. Mark the greengrocer had taken charge:

'Am I right in saying we've all had enough of Bill's miserable mug?' he'd called through the hiss of water spurting from the shower nozzles.

'I should bloody well think so,' someone had replied.

It was a cruel way to proceed, but the men's anger was forgivable. They'd just lost the fourth match in a row because of Bill's new-found incompetence in goal. He'd never been the convivial type, but until then, at least, he'd been a reliable goalkeeper.

'So we're agreed?' Mark had gone on.

There had been a few yeses, a few nods, not one word in Bill's defence.

'Right,' Mark had said, turning to Bill; 'You're out, Bill. Sorry but we've had enough.'

Bill had looked around him in dismay, completely unprepared for all this, turned to Mark:

'What's this all about… Why?'

'Why? Is that what you said? Why?'

'Yes. Why are you—'

'Are you having us on or what?'

'No. What's… What have I done?'

Mark was furious:

'It's not what you've fucking done but what you're not fucking doing, mate. And that is fucking do what you're fucking supposed to do in the fucking goal: Stop the fucking ball!'

Bill had gazed at him, tried to protest:

'I'm sorry. I—'

'No! *We're* fucking sorry! We should've got rid of you sooner instead of running our arses off game after game,' Mark had roared; 'Now shut the fuck up and don't make it worse than it is, all right!' And he'd turned away, started to wash, leaving Bill to search in vain for support amidst the uneasy faces around him. Everyone had avoided his eyes. In desperation he'd turned to Perkins:

'I've been the team's goalkeeper for eight years, John. You're the only one that's played longer than me. Tell them they can't just…'

Perkins had nodded, smiled sadly:

'I'm sorry, Bill… Maybe that's just it, eh? Maybe you've been playing too long. We're all getting older and…'

'Old… I'm… But I'm younger than you, John. I'm younger than…'

Mark had roared again:

'I don't care how old you are, if you've played since nursery school or if you're flipping going mad because of your mother, all right! You're out and that's it! And one more word out of you and I bloody punch you, understood!'

Bill was aghast:

'My mother…'

The mention of his mother had thrown him into a trance-like state. He'd gazed down at the water running around Mark's feet, his face devoid of expression. There was something ominous in his demeanour and high-pitched voice, which was perhaps why Mark had not carried out his threat or tried to make him shut up again.

'My mother?… It's not my mother… It's the girl. It's my girl who's gone. Not my mother…'

Mark had frowned, rolled his eyes, glanced around befuddled.

'What girl?' Perkins had asked helpfully.

'The girl... My girl...'

'Your girl?' As far as anyone knew Bill did not have a 'girl', had never had one, and certainly didn't have a daughter.

'Yes. She's... She's gone and I'm... I don't know if I miss her or dread her coming back... But we, I...'

He'd broken off, smiled to himself, and for a moment the only sound had been the gushing water, the expressions on the faces in the steam around Bill a mixture of concern and curiosity. Ten naked middle-aged men had stood hushed in a football ground's shower room waiting for another man to speak, and Bill had obliged them. What else could he have done now that he'd started crying:

'It's ironic you should have mentioned my mother, though... You see, when something broke or went wrong in the house, mother always called... But I... When water started dripping from my bedroom ceiling...'

Armed with a candle he'd climbed into his attic for the first time in years, had found two tiles missing from the roof.

'... They'd been gone for quite a time because the roofing felt underneath was rotten and the rain was coming in because it had finally given way. Anyway, I thought they might've slid down into the gutter, got stuck there, and so I put my head through the hole in the roof and...'

He'd taken a breath here, still dithering about whether to go on, but he'd said too much or not enough now, would probably not have been able to stop himself had he wished to:

'There are two dormer windows halfway up the roof of the house across my back garden. About thirty yards away. I'd noticed them before from my bedroom window, though looking up, because of the angle, I'd never seen what was behind them, just a little bit of white ceiling... But from the attic, standing with my head through the hole in the roof I just couldn't help... It was night and the lights were on and the curtains were open, you see...'

Bill had found himself looking down into a small bedroom and connecting bathroom, the private territory of an adolescent girl who, possibly feeling her windows to be safe from prying eyes, never bothered to pull her curtains, even when, as on that night when Bill had looked out of the hole in his roof, she was bathing – 'you know… just lying still in the clear water, her head flung back on the edge of the bath, her long black hair hanging to the floor where her clothes lay in a heap… She was only about fourteen but… I'd never seen… Never imagined… An angel…' And although it was raining and he was soaked through, Bill had stayed, turned into a voyeur, watched her wash, rinse, dry herself and brush her hair 'with long, slow sweeps in front of a full-length mirror', and had then stayed to watch her get into her nightie and 'snuggle up in bed with a ginger cat', and then stayed on, long after she'd switched off her bedside lamp, staring into the darkness.

'I couldn't move. I was numb. I was drenched. It was dark and cold. But I was numb with warmth. I was warm inside…'

He had not slept. He had not tried to fix his roof but put a basin under the hole to gather the rain. The next day he'd closed shop early, rushed to a department store, bought a pair of binoculars and rushed back to climb into his attic at nightfall, a climb he would repeat nightly for the next two years. Two years during which he'd watched his girl develop into a young woman and 'do things young women do when they think they're alone', as he'd decently put it. Two years during which her evenings had been his and his days hers, anxiously waiting as he was 'for the time I'd be with her again…' Two years during which his mind had been monopolised by nothing but his girl, now inciting pleasure with wild fantasies of reciprocated love, now inducing torment with 'dark rushes of guilt and shame'.

'… It was like a merry-go-round. I felt so bad, so guilty, the thought of her was the only thing that made me feel better… And then I would think of her and me again… And then of me, what I was doing and… I'd think about her again… A merry-go-round…'

In the end, Bill had lost his girl as suddenly as he'd found her. One evening her windows remained dark. At first he'd thought she was on holiday – 'it had happened before and it was summer then' – but September had come without her and, fearing the worst, he'd eventually plucked-up the courage to direct his binoculars at her windows in daylight, 'to see if her clothes and belongings were gone…'

They were, though something else was there, something he couldn't have seen at night with no light shining beyond her bedroom window. Two words, in red lipstick on the glass:

'I KNOW'

There could be no doubt about their meaning, nor who they were intended for; the letters had been drawn in mirror writing.

Bill had called someone in to fix his roof and got rid of the binoculars in a high street refuse bin the very same day, now missing his girl as much as dreading her possible return, fearing she might decide to expose him, that one day 'someone would walk into my shop and…' It was about this time that his goal-keeping had let him down. It was surprising it hadn't happened sooner. Still, after hearing him out, the men had taken pity on him. He was reinstated as goalkeeper. The decision had not been unanimous, but no one had had the heart to deprive him of friendship and recreation in a time of need.

'He needs us,' Perkins had said, simply. Bill had rewarded their compassion with a return to form, and until tonight, the appearance of recovery.

'Here we are,' said Lombard, pulling up in front of Bill's shop.

Bill had still not said a word, gazed grimly out through the windscreen.

'Here we are, Bill,' repeated Lombard impatiently.

'My mother used to say that people's wickedness is always deliberate,' said Bill without taking his eyes from the windscreen.

So, that's what ten minutes of brooding had spawned; a quote from his mother.

Lombard peered past Bill and out towards the man's pet shop which stood in the amber glow of a nearby street-lamp. Even at night, even through the rain, the small corner shop retained its picturesque character. One of the few in Essex Road not yet protected by a security grille or lit by a neon sign, with its glossy post-box-red front and display window crammed with colourful pet paraphernalia, it conveyed an impression of old-fashioned exuberance and abundance. So unlike its owner…

'Did she?' muttered Lombard.

'She said that people need to be wicked,' went on Bill; 'So that they can feel guilty. They do bad things so that they can feel guilty. Do you know why that is?'

Lombard raised his brows:

'I don't think I do.'

'People need guilt in order to accept the bad things in life,' said Bill; 'Guilt is a bit like a rubber ring.'

'A rubber ring?' said Lombard, intrigued.

'Yes. It helps people stay afloat. To cope and behave when bad things happen to them. Bad things hurt less when they can be accepted as punishments, as penance for crimes.'

Lombard peered at him. Was Bill truly trying to convince himself he'd watched his girl merely in order to fill himself with guilt so that he could endure the trials of life? Either the man was more resilient than Lombard had given him credit for, or he was even more of a coward. It was just too bad if he was going to while away the night wallowing in misery and self-pity. He would have anyway, with or without Lombard.

'Your mother said that, huh?' said Lombard.

'Something like that. Don't you think it's true?'

'Can I ask you a couple of questions, Bill?'

'What?'

'Your girl, did you watch her because of what your mother said or because she gave you a hard-on?'

Bill turned to him, lost for words.

Lombard grinned, more cruelly than he would have wished, but it didn't matter now, Bill had asked for it:

'Why are you feeling so sorry for yourself right now, Bill? Isn't it because you've been doing what lonely men do when they get a chance to leer at a girl doing what girls do when they think they're alone? I know you never admitted it, but still, it felt like everyone was laughing at you when Andy and Larry made their jokes, didn't it, Bill?'

Bill looked back at him calmly now. He wasn't hurt or angry. He wanted to talk. He opened his mouth. Lombard pre-empted him:

'I'm sorry. I haven't got the time for this. Just don't deceive yourself. It doesn't help,' he said, turning away to wind down his window; 'Whatever your mother told you,' he added, flicking his cigarette across the road.

'I understand what you—' began Bill, but he broke off, disturbed by three sharp knocks.

It was Jane. Her broad Irish face grinned at Lombard through Bill's window. Lombard smiled at her:

'Goodnight, Bill,' he said, keeping his eyes on Jane.

'Er… Yes. Goodnight. Thank you. I'm sorry,' mumbled Bill, opening his door; 'I—I… Thank you for talking to me.'

'Hi there,' said Jane as Bill stepped onto the kerb.

'Hello,' said Bill, hurrying past her to his door.

'Bye,' said Jane, looking back after him before crouching in the open passenger door with a beaming smile.

'Hi, *neighbour*. I didn't interrupt anything, did I?' she asked.

Lombard ran his eyes over her. Her blond hair was wet, drooped messily towards a bright ski-type jacket he had never seen her in before, one of those plump quilted nylon things. It made her look tubby.

'How are you, Jane?' he said, peering at her arms crossed over her belly above her bent legs. She seemed to be holding some object hidden under her jacket.

'Fish and chips,' she said, following his gaze; 'Keeping it warm. You're going home?'

Lombard glanced at Mrs. Spitz's envelope sticking out of the glove compartment. Bill had soured his mood, he no longer wished to stop at his flat, wanted to drive on.

'No,' he said.

'Ah…'

She looked disappointed.

'Get in. I'll drop you there on my way,' said Lombard. It was a five hundred yard drive.

She hopped onto the seat vacated by Bill and slammed the door shut:

'Thanks. How was the match? Did you lose?'

'No,' said Lombard, pulling out. The sweet greasy smell of the fish and chips filled the car. Lombard was hungry, wondered if the restaurant where Leonard Spitz worked was any good.

'Good. You saw Perkins then?' asked Jane.

'Uh-huh.'

'He told you about the rent?'

'Uh-huh.'

'Isn't it great? Can't sell your meat, squeeze the tenants!'

Lombard stayed silent. He didn't want to be dragged into a conversation about Perkins. Neither did Jane it seemed:

'You're going out?' she asked.

'I just said I wasn't going home.'

'Yes… It's a shame. I've got your accounts. I thought we could have a look at them tonight. Just need your signature really. Anyway, the good news is you won't have to pay much tax this year.'

'Good.'

'Yes. My boss reckons you'd do better setting up as a limited company, though. You know, for expenses and all that. Of course, you'd need a partner to register the company. But that's a formality. I mean, you could use me; I mean, just as a name, right?'

Lombard raised his brows. She just couldn't help it.

'Thank you for the offer, Jane. But as I think I've already told you, I'd rather we remained just the good neighbours we are,' he said, pulling up in front of Perkins' shop without switching off his engine.

'I'm only passing on what my boss said,' she protested.

'We'll have a look at the accounts tomorrow, all right,' said Lombard with a grin.

'Sure. Where are you off to then?' she asked, masking her frustration behind an innocent smile.

Lombard didn't know why, but when she smiled like that she reminded him of a purring cat. Perhaps it was the way her lips curled beneath the pug nose in the middle of her broad face. She was pretty though. Hers was an ordinary prettiness, a refreshing prettiness, one which was not compelling at first glance but bloomed as one got to know her, as if it fed from her ebullient personality.

'I have some work to do,' he said.

'Ah…'

She looked him quickly up and down, fixed her eyes in his, making no attempt to conceal her curiosity. If only… But she knew not to ask, that too he'd told her time enough. So, she smiled again, asking:

'Have you heard of a French film called *La Collectionoose*?'

Lombard frowned.

'*La* what?'

'*La Collectionoose*. It's about a young girl in the South of France who seduces a different man every night and then meets one who resists her. It's on TV later tonight and as I'll be in when you come back perhaps we could look at your accounts then and... The review says it's about the conflict between intellect and instinct. And witty. The director's supposed to be famous. *Rommel* or something. French. You must know him.'

Lombard peered into her eyes, amused.

'Should I?'

'I don't know. How many famous French film directors can there be?'

'That are called *Rommel* or something? I guess not that many.'

She shrugged, steered the conversation back to where she wanted it.

'Anyway, I take it you haven't seen this film then?' she asked enthusiastically. Her enthusiasm was genuine. Everything about Jane was genuine. She had not yet been hurt.

'What time do you think you'll be back? It doesn't start until midnight and—'

'Your fish and chips are getting cold, Jane,' said Lombard. He wanted to go, drive away, all of a sudden no longer felt like playing Jane's games.

'Don't worry about it. What time—'

Lombard interrupted her again: 'It's Friday night, Jane. What happened to your latest boyfriend?'

'Oh... We split up.'

'Well, I hope you're not too heartbroken and can go home and enjoy your fish and—'

'Oh no. I'm all right,' she cut in; 'He was a jerk, really. Another *boy*, you know? All I meet is boys. When I think of all the fuss about older men liking young girls. I mean, is it true?'

'I'm late, Jane,' he said, reaching for the pack of cigarettes in his pocket.

'No. Seriously. Is it true? I mean, what about you, *Savieer*?

– 63 –

Do you think older men like younger girls?'

He knew what she wanted to hear him say. Bill and his girl came back to his mind. He had better get rid of her. The only way he knew how.

'What do you think of our landlord, Jane?'

'What?' she asked with a frown; 'Perkins…?'

'I'm sure he'd enjoy a French film. He might even give you a rent rebate…'

She understood immediately. A flicker of anger darkened her eyes. She glared, hurt, a stung young animal:

'You…'

'You're welcome,' said Lombard, grinning.

She looked him over, eyes ablaze, tight-lipped, determined to let him know what she thought of him, then opened her door, stepped out, slammed the door shut and stormed away.

'You bastard!'

Lombard watched her open their front door beside the metal screen protecting Perkins' shop-front. He smiled. She knew he was watching her, her movements were jerky, she was struggling to get the key in the lock.

'Goodnight, neighbour,' he called through the window as she stepped inside the door. She slammed that one too, and he wound up his window with a sigh, lit a cigarette, reached for the envelope in the glove compartment and pulled out the one sheet of paper it contained. There were just two hand-written addresses on it, one with the heading 'Leonard's address', the other 'Leonard's workplace'. He ran his eyes from one to the other, unsure, finally fixed on the latter:

> The Four Seasons
> 12 Holmes Road
> London NW5
> Tel: 0171 267…
> (The proprietor is called Jeff Hyames)

FOUR

When, twenty minutes later, Lombard got to Holmes Road in Kentish Town, he changed his mind and drove on towards Leonard Spitz's place in Highgate. At nine thirty on a Friday evening, The Four Seasons was likely to be busy, it would be better to go there at a quieter time.

The apartment Mr. and Mrs. Spitz had given their son occupied the entire top floor of a luxurious block of flats at the summit of a steep residential street. Its door, of heavy wood and fitted with a spy hole, stood just outside the mirror-panelled lift in a white corridor above which a glass-domed roof arched into the blustery night sky. Lombard looked up at the rain cascading down the glass above his head, mesmerised for a moment by the waterfall-like sight and sound, then looked down again. To one side a metal door led to the roof; to the other a mountain bike reclined against a raised miniature garden of climbing plants.

He stepped forward, unlocked Leonard's door, pushed it open. A blast of warm air hit him, a faint, acrid chemical smell reminiscent of ammonia reached him, and, peering into the darkness, he delayed the moment, stood still, taking in the atmosphere, until his eyes had adjusted to the shadows and made out, beyond a far-off line of floor-to-ceiling windows, the lights of London stretching into the distance, until, just as he realised that a flashing amber glow came from within the room rather than beyond the windows, the corridor light behind him went out with a click and he found himself plunged into darkness. He stepped inside, felt around the door for the light switch.

A parqueted hallway gave into a vast drawing room tastefully if sparsely furnished in a mix of antique and modern styles. Shelves of books, compact discs, music and video cassettes lined one wall, all neatly organised. The windows, an uninterrupted screen along the whole length of the room, now mirrored the interior's every detail, along with the telephone answering machine which flashed its amber light from an oak dresser beside a television and video player. The parquet floor was unmarked. The couple of Persian rugs appeared new. Most surfaces were clear, the few visible objects, such as the television remote control box and a telescope mounted on a tripod, in their appointed places. The only noticeable mess, if it could be described as such, was to be seen through the glass-paned double door to the dining room where an acoustic guitar and a packet of sweets sat on a massive table skirted with a dozen matching chairs. Otherwise, even the magazines on the coffee table by the leather sofa were stacked in a neat pile. Otherwise, all was tidiness and order, to the point of impersonality, like a comfortable hotel suite, devoid of feeling.

Somehow, this was not what Lombard had expected of a man who, a few hours earlier, had been described to him as a confused, wayward and susceptible individual with a bohemian disposition. The prevailing impression was one of soberness, of diligence, of a tranquil if not rigid existence which even the large black and white photographs that hung around the walls in their glass frames failed to alter. Here a young girl in a see-through gown lay in a coffin as if dead. There a scantily clad girl sat twisted and contorted in a rubbish skip, what there was of her clothing torn and dirty. Elsewhere a naked girl spiked with arrows stood bleeding under the spray of a shower. Further on, yet another girl lay impaled on railings, her limbs hanging limply from the metal spears. And there were many more still, all girls, all in various degrees of undress, all in various distasteful situations, in gruesome condition. Yet, like the room around Lombard, the photographs were cold; too flawless, deliberate and melodramatic to inspire awe, disgust or, as the case may be, concern or desire. There was something puerile about the images, as if they were designed to impress or shock, as if, in spite of their lurid content, they were the product of innocence rather than experience. Nothing seemed felt, not even the girls' youthful sexuality, though many were attractive. Whether they had any artistic merit, Lombard couldn't say. Doubtless though, Leonard Spitz thought so. 'DOES DEATH FEAR DEATH', read the caption under yet another photograph. Lombard peered at it; this girl stood erect in a foggy landscape, naked, clutching a scythe, mouth and eyes open wide in a scream.

Lombard nodded his imperceptible nod, once again became aware of the acrid smell that hung in the air, of the stifling temperature, scanned the room in vain for a radiator, reached for his Gitanes and looked for an ashtray. There were none. He made for the kitchen to fetch a small plate and proceeded with it around the apartment.

Many years ago, when he was still young, still dreaming of making *Inspecteur*, Lombard would have welcomed the opportunity of searching Leonard Spitz's private territory. It would have satisfied his natural curiosity, his predatory instinct. Many years ago, he'd have experienced a sense of well-being, gratification even, dissecting the missing man's life, moving from room to room like a merciless hungry beast with a mission to feed, hunting for the one thing that would inevitably lead him to his prey. He'd have sniffed, swallowed, digested everything, not in order to survive but merely to capture. And for many years, on the many occasions that he had been called upon to track down missing people and criminals of one kind or another, he had done just that, albeit with a relative degree of success. But that was then. No longer. He no longer could, no longer felt the lust. People's affairs were no longer that stimulating or complicated. Besides, these days experience ruled, so Lombard proceeded around the rooms looking for no more than there was to see.

The kitchen was tidy, fully equipped and little used. There were a few ready-made pizzas in the freezer, a dirty bowl, mug and spoon in the sink, and a quick look in the pedal-bin revealed a milk carton, a few used tea-bags and an empty pizza box. From the kitchen a door led to a laundry room where an assortment of men's underwear, socks and dishcloths hung from a line rigged up above the washing machine. The dining room, but for the table and its chairs, was bare. The main bathroom, an expanse of pink marble with a central sunken bathtub below a glass dome similar to the one in the corridor, looked somewhat forsaken with its one towel, one bar of soap, one shampoo bottle, toothbrush, half-used toothpaste tube, pack of disposable razors and can of shaving foam all methodically arranged around the washbasin. The medicine cabinet held just a box of Q-tips and a bottle of aspirin. Of the four bedrooms, only the smallest was in use, the only one without a connecting bathroom. Most of Leonard's carefully folded clothes fitted into one chest of drawers. A leather bomber-jacket and worn winter coat hung in the wardrobe. The double bed was unmade, its duvet folded open to one side, two pillows heaped against the headboard on the uncovered side. A box of tissues, a book and a colour snapshot in a perspex stand sat on the bedside table. The snapshot showed a young couple in jeans standing holding hands by a mountain stream in a summery landscape. They appeared to be in their mid-twenties. Scrutinising the man, Lombard guessed he was looking at Leonard Spitz. Dark, thin, gaunt-faced, with long wavy hair straddling his narrow shoulders, he stood smiling with rather effeminate grace, looking remarkably like Deborah De Moraes, albeit a softer, bonier, more fragile version. The woman was short, had muscular arms and small pointed breasts which stabbed at her tight sleeveless T-shirt. Curly blond hair framed the toothy grin in her freckled face. They stood about two feet apart, smiling self-consciously, like couples sometimes prudishly do when posing in front of a camera.

Lombard inspected the back of the snapshot for a name or date, found none, glanced at the book – *Occult Bondage and Deliverance*, read its title – and moved on, at last discovering the source of the smell he'd noticed on first opening the front door. It was photographic developing chemical and came from what had once been yet another bedroom with connecting bathroom but now, with its blacked-out windows, hanging negatives, cameras, lenses and wealth of other photographic equipment, was a makeshift darkroom which, in contrast to the rest of the apartment, appeared very much in use. Ends of negatives, photographic paper and sweet wrappers littered the floor. A black rubbish bin, of the type more commonly seen in people's front yards, overflowed with more of the same. The built-in wardrobe, stripped of its doors which stood tucked away in a corner, was piled high with contact sheets and prints, as were the surfaces of every other piece of furniture in the room, whose walls, apart from a small area by the door where a wall-mounted telephone was surrounded with scrawled phone numbers, were plastered on all sides with layer upon layer of photographs. Some showed yet more girls in lurid poses, but most were of everyday London scenes. Unlike the girlie ones, these were un-scripted, impromptu moments furtively caught in streets, parks and market places, but somehow they too felt premeditated, as if the photographer had gone searching for them rather than merely come across them by accident. Here and there, Lombard spotted a familiar location. A boy in a sleeping bag sat in the doorway of a computer shop in Tottenham Court Road. The outline of London Zoo was just about discernible behind a park bench where an old couple sat eating sandwiches under an umbrella. A screaming woman dragged two crying children across a pedestrian crossing by the Angel tube station. There was even a shot of a crowded bus-stop in the rain that Lombard felt sure was in Essex Road. Curious, he scrutinized it for a moment, then let his eyes linger on a shot of a couple kissing in a tube train carriage.

He sighed, stepped into the en-suite bathroom which was almost entirely taken-up by a long worktable cluttered with enlargers and other printing apparatus, flicked his cigarette stub in the toilet bowl, emptied the ash from the plate he was still holding after it, pulled the chain, and returned to the drawing room.

Leonard's bills, bank and credit card statements, all meticulously filed in a desk, revealed that Mrs. Spitz's son was invariably in debit at the close of each month despite his £1,500 monthly allowance; that he owed nearly £5,000 to a credit card company, spent mostly in a couple of photographic shops; and that he made scarcely any phone calls from home. An inspection of his address book, which was virtually empty and turned up in a drawer with his passport and National Health card, suggested that he was indeed friendless, or else had a good memory, or owned another address book which, perhaps, he carried with him. Examining the passport photo, Lombard found himself looking at the man from the snapshot in the bedroom; he stared out at the world with dark haunted eyes, hair plastered to his skull, mouth shut tight in what may have been an attempt to display resolve but only succeeded in making him look sulky.

Leonard, Jozef Spitz... Born London, 16 May 19...

Leonard Jozef Spitz… Lombard turned towards the shelves. The spines of the books were of classic novels, of works relating to the holocaust, and to photography. The music collection primarily comprised 60s and 70s artists; the videos largely well-known old black and white thrillers. He leafed through the neat pile of magazines on the coffee table. These were fashionable art and culture periodicals, one claiming to be for *'The Modern Man'*, its glossy cover catching the eye with a shot of a young woman striding a crowded street in a skirt so short it revealed the crook of her legs.

Lombard rearranged the pile of magazines, checked his watch, turned to the telephone answering machine. Its amber light was still flashing. He lit a cigarette.

Leonard Spitz had been missing for two weeks and the only messages on his answer-phone were from his mother, who was upset that he was not getting back to her; from his employer, who was upset he was not turning up for work; and from a girl, who was worried not to have heard from him. Each had left several messages, each growing increasingly upset or, in the girl's case, increasingly worried.

'Leonard! It is Tuesday now. What is happening? I have been calling your work and they tell me…' uttered Mrs. Spitz.

'What the fuck are you playing at, you… If I don't see your arse here in the next…' cursed the employer, who introduced himself as 'Yeah. Jeff here, man.'

'Leon…? Are you there…? What is… I—I tried to reach you at work but Jeff said you'd left… I hope… I hope everything's all right…' said the girl.

Hers was the last message. Lombard had dialled 1-4-7-1 on Leonard's telephone to find out where she'd called from, but had instead got the number of the Hampstead house he'd visited earlier.

'Good evening. The De Moraes' residence…' the dry voice of the butler had answered.

After a moment's thought, Lombard had put the phone down without saying a word, re-dialed 1-4-7-1 and realised the call from the De Moraes' residence had been made in the early hours of that very morning. Mrs. Spitz, probably, checking that her son had not returned before getting in touch with Lombard.

The Four Seasons was located fifty yards or so down the road from Kentish Town police station, its steamy window tucked between two redbrick terraced houses. Medium-sized, displaying a menu that mixed ordinary with exotic dishes, like many restaurants in that corner of North London, it was one of those offbeat places that owed its existence to its proximity to fashionable Camden Lock market rather than to its chef's skill or owner's interest in gastronomy. The decor was decidedly informal, the atmosphere laid-back, with rock music playing too loudly for Lombard's liking over the wooden tables which at this late hour were mostly empty, and, oddly for a restaurant during opening hours, it smelt more of stale alcohol than of cuisine.

Standing inside the door undoing the buttons of his dripping raincoat while awaiting the attention of a young waitress who seemed to be looking after the dining-room all by herself and was busy clearing the plates and bottles from a rowdy table of four, Lombard observed a stocky man with a long ponytail and a young chef in a messy uniform standing behind the bar at the far end of the room. They were chatting, rocking to the music and taking drags from what was most likely a joint being passed between them.

'Hi, lonesome. Are we handsome tonight?' Lombard heard a man's voice call.

He turned to a nearby table. A couple of camp middle-aged men in baseball caps were staring engagingly at him. They sat side by side. Lombard had noticed them as he stepped through the door, ignored their eyes which had immediately fixed on him.

'Nice suit,' declared one, casting covetous eyes over Lombard.

Lombard followed his gaze, ran his eyes down over his black suit that showed between the open sides of his coat, grinned:

'Thank you,' he said, looking up; 'Nice hats. Why don't you take them off and try enjoying yourselves, eh?' And he turned back to the bar without awaiting their reaction, which reached him anyway in the form of a critical 'Oooo…'.

The men behind the bar were chuckling now, teasing the waitress as she passed them on her way back from the kitchen hatch. She showed them the finger without breaking her stride, left them sniggering behind her, and started across the room. Lombard had already decided against eating there. Now the staff's open show of carelessness also made him decide against disclosing who he was; he'd only meet with the kind of hostility those with the conceit to display their disregard for conventions feel they owe to those without it. What's more, he already suspected he was not going to get on with 'Yeah. Jeff here, man…'

'Evening. Table for one?' The waitress had stopped in front of him with a weary smile, absent-mindedly sweeping a bead of sweat from her hairline with the tip of her finger.

Watching her tired face, Lombard found the long black eyelashes and full scarlet lips that stood out against her white skin familiar, felt sure he'd seen her before. He sent her his most charming smile.

'No. Thank you,' he said, milking his French accent; 'Could you tell me if Leonard Spitz is here, please?'

She frowned, scrutinised him, lips pursed, as if she found it strange that anyone should ask for Leonard. Or was it because of his suit, or his accent?

'Leon? No. I'm afraid he left,' she said.

'He left? When? I just came from his place and there was no one there. A neighbour of his told me he worked here and—'

'No,' she cut in; 'I mean he left as in no longer works here. He hasn't been here for the last couple of weeks.'

Lombard had just realised who she was. It had come to him as he mentioned Leonard's place. She was one of the girls in the photographs. She was the naked one with the arrows.

'Oh—' he said; 'Really. This is… We'd arranged to meet tonight and I'm due back in Paris tomorrow… I…' He didn't finish his sentence, peered at her as if pondering something, waiting…

'I'm sorry,' she eventually volunteered; 'But Leon no longer works here.'

'Yes. I understand. You wouldn't happen to know where I could reach him by any chance?'

She didn't, shook her head with a shrug:

'Sorry.'

'Do you think someone else here might know? It's important,' insisted Lombard.

She dithered, opened her mouth to speak but Lombard beat her to it.

'I stopped off in London on my way back from Ireland just to see him, you see. We were meant to discuss an exhibition of his photographs at my Paris gallery next month. I know it means a lot to Leonard, and to tell you the truth, I don't know what to make of his forgetting our meeting like this. He knew I was coming especially to see him. And if I don't get to finalise everything with him before Monday I will have to call the exhibition off. Too many commitments. Too much pressure, you understand?'

The waitress examined him with a mixture of surprise and interest now, thought hard behind her eyelashes.

'You—' she began. She changed her mind, signalled for him to wait:

'Just a moment.'

She made for the bar, exchanged a few words with the stocky ponytail man, and went back to her duties with a quick look at Lombard. The ponytail man eyeballed Lombard, who returned the scrutiny with a dry grin, spoke to the young chef who stared back at Lombard in disbelief, then stepped out from behind the bar.

'Welcome to the club,' he said, eyeing Lombard with both hands in his pockets.

It was 'Yeah. Jeff here, man...' From afar, in the diffused lighting of the room, with his soft cheeks, he had appeared to be in his early thirties. Now he was close, Lombard could see the lines and furrows around his eyes and thin mouth. He was nearer forty, even forty-five perhaps, and peered at Lombard with glassy eyes.

'Excuse me?' said Lombard, grinning.

'I hear you're looking for Leon. That makes me, his old-lady, and now you looking for the little bastard. Leon's gone, man. Vanished. You interested in his photographs?'

'That's right,' said Lombard, looking straight into his eyes. He was either drunk or high. Probably high, on coke; his speech was too fast for a drunk...

'Forgive me for asking,' went on Lombard; 'But you are?'

'I'm Jeff. I own this place. So, is it on the level? You want to see him about his photographs?'

Lombard nodded, still grinning. Jeff looked back at him in wonder, cursing to himself between clenched teeth now...

'No shit! Well, I'm afraid I can't help you, mister,' he said finally, shaking his head; 'It's as I said, Leon's vanished.'

'Vanished?' said Lombard.

'Yeah. Vanished. As in disappeared. All of two weeks ago. Which is probably why he's become so popular.'

'I take it you don't know where he is, then?' asked Lombard.

For some reason best known to himself, Jeff seemed to find this question absurd. He sniggered:

'Huh! I've got some idea of where that might be, but let's just say it's kind of in a figurative sense, eh...'

Lombard peered at him, waiting.

'You could always try Suicide Bridge, know what I mean?' Jeff eventually elaborated.

'Suicide Bridge?'

'Yeah!' And, whistling between his teeth, Jeff made a diving motion with his outstretched hand pointing downward.

'Are you saying you believe Leon has killed himself?' asked Lombard.

'I'm saying the possibility might be worth considering,' came the reply.

'Really?'

Now it was Jeff's turn to peer at Lombard, which he did by narrowing his eyes and wagging his head slightly to and fro.

'You don't know Leon, do you?'

'I know his work better than I know him,' replied Lombard.

Jeff sniggered again:

'That figures... Let me put it this way then – the photographs and the man? One and the same, man, one and the same. At best fucking weird, at worst, fucked-up fucking weird. Maybe you should think yourself lucky. Some folks just ain't worth getting involved with. And Leon sure is one of 'em.'

Lombard looked him up and down. Jeff had put his hand back in his pocket, stood with his feet apart, held his head slightly tilted upwards, so that his nostrils showed above his thin lips which were set in a smirk that made him look resentful and self-satisfied at the same time.

'I see,' said Lombard; 'Let's just say, just in case you are wrong, that he is still alive. Do you know of any friend of his who might know where he could be reached?'

'Huh! Leonard's got no friends, man. Leonard's a loner. Too fucking self-absorbed. Too much of a rich fucking mummy's boy…'

'No friends?' asked Lombard.

'No friends,' declared Jeff.

'You seem to know him well, though.'

'Yeah, well…' sneered Jeff; 'I felt sorry for the little shit, didn't I? He walked his sorry arse in here a year back looking for a job and I gave him a job, didn't I? And how does the fucker thank me? Dumps me with the washing up on a bloody Friday night. You could say I know him well, all right…'

'What about his girlfriend?' asked Lombard.

'What about which girlfriend?' asked Jeff.

'She was with him the only time we met. Short, strong, with curly blond hair and freckles,' said Lombard, describing the girl from the snapshot.

Jeff frowned, Jeff thought, Jeff…

'Oh. That'd be Rhian.'

'Rhian?'

'Yeah. A Welsh chick he used to lay at weekends. She got wise and dumped him months ago…'

'You don't think he might be with her?'

'I doubt it… Though, now you mention it, she did call here a week or two back. Looking for him too, she was. So who knows, huh?'

So, the girl with the toothy grin in the snapshot and the girl with the worried voice on Leonard's answer-phone were one and the same…

'Would you know where she might be reached?'

Jeff sniggered:

'Yeah! Somewhere in Wales. That's where she's from.'

'In Wales?'

'That's right. That's all I can tell you. In Wales. I don't really know her. She used to turn up at weekends in a Transit van and flog old furniture at Camden. That's how come he only laid her at weekends, ha-ha…'

'Camden? Would that be Camden Lock market?'

'Where else?'

'She sells furniture there?'

'That's what I just said. Yeah.'

'Do you know where in the market?'

'I think she shared a stall around the old stables bit. But… What? You're planning on going to look for her or something?'

'Unless you can tell me some other way of getting in touch with her, I might just do that,' said Lombard.

Jeff peered at him in wonder:

'Shit!' he uttered at last; 'You really think his pictures are that good?'

Lombard grinned. This was the second ponytail man he'd encountered that day, and he felt as distant from this one and his restaurant as he had from the other and his bandstand.

He'd looked into this one's eyes long enough:

'Fucked-up fucking weird,' he said dryly, and he turned away; 'Thank you for your time.'

Why did he know Jeff frowned at his back as he opened the door? Why did he know the waitress eyed him from under her long lashes as he stepped out into the cold air? Why did he know the camp men in their baseball caps watched him as the door came shut behind him.

He fastened the buttons of his raincoat. He was glad to be back out in the rain, glad to be outside the noise and stale smell of the restaurant, even if, for just a fleeting moment, he let himself feel pity for Leonard Spitz; *'The proprietor of his workplace is the only friend of his we know about,'* Mrs. Spitz had said…

A burger bar occupied the corner where the restaurant's side street met the Kentish Town Road. He bought a coffee, asked for a hamburger without sauce or mayonnaise, which seemed to aggrieve the eyebrow-raising boy who served him, and settled back into the darkness of his Triumph which he'd left opposite the police station. About an hour later, as four policemen struggled to drag two reluctant drunks out of a police van which they seemed resolute not to leave, the waitress with the eyelashes stepped out of the door of The Four Seasons wrapped up in a dark coat and hurried away through the rain. Lombard climbed out of his car and caught up with her as she reached the shelter of the Kentish Town tube station. She looked surprised to see him.

'Oh… You're still here…'

'I am,' said Lombard, no longer bothering to overplay his French accent; 'And still looking for Leonard. I recognised you as one of his models. Am I right?'

She scowled, pursed her scarlet lips as she had done earlier in the restaurant, instinctively backed one step away from Lombard, glanced towards the station's ticket booth, greeted the sight of the man inside its window with relief and turned back with hostile eyes.

'What do you want?'

'It's all right,' Lombard tried to reassure her; 'I just want to ask a few questions. Are you sure you don't know where Leonard is?'

'Look, your business with Leon has nothing to do with me, all right? Now, if you don't mind, I have a train to catch.'

If sounding reassuring did not work…

'What exactly is your relationship with Leonard?' he asked.

'My relationship…' she said, glaring.

'Yes,' Lombard said; 'Forgive me, but you did pose nude for him, didn't you?'

She swallowed hard, still glaring, made as if to walk away but wasn't sure if it was the right thing to do. She chose confrontation instead. Lombard grinned.

'Are you some kind of pervert or something. Because—'

'You have a train to catch and I haven't got all night,' cut in Lombard; 'So it might be in both our interests if you could act your age. I'm working for Leonard's parents. They're worried about him and would very much like to know where he is. And

I'd like to know if you know where that might be.'

She just stared at him now, more perplexed than hostile.

'Do you?' asked Lombard, smiling again.

'What was all that gallery stuff and—' she asked.

'I lied. And don't ask why. So?'

'I… Whoever you are, I've got nothing to do with Leon. He's just a guy from work, all right?'

'Just a guy from work for whom you strip?'

She gaped:

'Hey! Excuse me but! What I do is no business of yours.'

'You're right there. But that could change. And I'm sure you wouldn't like it. I might end up having to find out who you are, if you take your clothes off for guys from work for thrills or whether you only do it when you get high. Tell me, do you all take dope with your boss in there?' He motioned in the direction of The Four Seasons.

'No. Not all of us, thank you,' she blurted out. There was indignation in her young voice, although she looked slightly intimidated now, even though she was trying hard not to show it.

'Not all of you?' returned Lombard. He'd spoken as loudly as she had, heard his words echo in the empty station hall around them; 'What about Leonard?'

'Leon…' She sent out an exasperated sigh, looked straight into his eyes; 'Look, I'm just a girl who's got to earn a living, okay? As for Leon, I only posed for him because for just a few pictures he offered me what it takes a month to earn as a fucking waitress. The only time I ever spent with him outside the restaurant was the hour or so it took him to take his pictures. I don't know the guy and never longed to do so, all right?'

'Hour or so?…'

'Yeah. Hour or so. And I never even saw any of the photos he took, so…'

'Who stuck the arrows on you?' asked Lombard; 'It must have been quite a job putting those things all over you?'

Lombard saw her guessing what he was getting at. She shook her head, grinned back at him:

'He did. But it's like I said. He's just a guy from work who paid to take a few pictures. And that's all.'

Lombard nodded, observed her with a critical eye:

'I don't know. Why should Leonard need to pay you? From what I've seen, there are enough girls willing to pose for him.'

'Huh! Most of them are waitresses. Leon's done most of the girls who've worked at the restaurant. And paid generously for it. The thing is, he's no pervert and doesn't sell his pictures to dirty magazines. He's weird but as safe as they come.'

'Leon's models are waitresses?'

'Yes.'

'That's a lot of waitresses for one small—'

'Well, the turnover of staff is rather high at The Four Seasons,' she cut in; 'Now, it was nice talking to you but I'm going to miss my train...'

'Just one more thing. Does Leonard take drugs?' asked Lombard.

'Huh! I haven't got the slightest idea.'

'You never saw him take drugs with Jeff?'

'Not that I can recall, no.'

'Did you ever see him stoned perhaps?'

'For all I know he was either high as a kite or sober as a judge every time I set eyes on him. I can't tell you. No doubt you'll see what I mean when you find him. Now, if—'

'Thank you,' said Lombard; 'I'll wait here a few minutes in case you've missed your train. I'll give you a lift home or pay your taxi fare if...'

She sent him a baffled look, flapped her eyelashes over her deep brown eyes, shook her head and turned towards the barrier to the escalator.

'Jesus Christ. Don't bother...'

Lombard watched her run down the escalator and out of view into the underground. For a moment, the sound of her racing footsteps reverberating in the tunnel below continued to reach him, then, all was silence. He turned towards the street, lit a Gitane and waited, wondering if he should pay Jeff another visit as he watched an ageless bearded tramp in a yellow waterproof stagger across the street in his direction. The man's alcohol smell reached the station shelter before the man himself.

'Evening, my good man. I wonder? Would you have any spare

change for a poor fellow down on…'

Lombard put some loose change in his swollen hand, accepted his blessing with a grin.

'… And what about a cigarette to warm the numb heart of a forsaken lover, my fortunate…'

Lombard sent him away with a frown and, satisfied that the girl had caught her train, made his way back past The Four Seasons to his Triumph. He had had enough of Leonard Spitz and his people for one day. Besides, Mrs. Spitz's morning call had got him out of bed earlier than he was used to and he was tired. He wanted to go home, to try to enjoy what was left of the day.

A little later, standing in the rain across the road from Perkins' butcher's shop, he just about made out the light of the television flickering behind Jane's curtains directly above his own flat's dark windows. Was she watching her French movie? He frowned, turned to the sky and let the rain lash his face and run down his neck, feeling the cold water work its way inside his shirt collar. It didn't matter. He'd have a hot shower and eat something before going to bed. He was still hungry. He peered at the kit-bag that hung at the end of his arm and started across the street. It still held his sodden football gear. He had better get his boots out tonight and stuff them with newspaper or the leather would be ruined.

FIVE

There were still clouds in the sky on Saturday morning, but the rain had died and through holes here and there the winter sun shone, for the first time in weeks illuminating London with its fresh and soothing light. It was a welcome arrival, a welcome change, like the end of a long night, and out on Essex Road's rain-washed pavements people strolled with lighter steps, at a tranquil pace, as they used to in the days when the weekend was still a time of rest.

Lombard, still in his pyjamas and warm from sleep, sat at his desk by the window sipping coffee. Across the street, Larry the newsagent, as was routine on Saturday mornings, cleaned his shop window with the help of his young son. At what hour did newsagents get up, Lombard wondered? A quarter of an hour earlier, he'd once again been dragged out of sleep by Mrs. Spitz.

'Mr. Lombard!' she had roared into the receiver; 'Did you go to my son's apartment yesterday evening?'

She was furious. And perhaps for good reason. After Lombard's call from Leonard's place the previous evening, after he'd put the phone down on Lawrence without speaking, Lawrence had checked their caller-identity-display and, dependable butler that he was, had alerted the sleeping Spitzes to the strange call from their son's apartment. The result had been that Mr. and Mrs. Spitz had got out of bed, tried in vain to reach their son and, in the belief that he had returned but was perhaps too troubled to speak on the phone, driven to Highgate where, finding no trace of Leonard, they had subsequently spent an anxious night wondering what was going on. The possibility that Lombard might have gone to Leonard's apartment so late on the evening of the very day he had been hired and was responsible for the call never occurred to them, and it was only in the morning, as she was about to leave for the airport on her way to Scotland, that Mrs. Spitz, at her daughter's suggestion, had finally thought of looking into the matter with Lombard, who explained what had happened and apologised.

'*Jah!* You should apologise indeed, Mr. Lombard! Tell me, everything else aside, *vat* kind of manners is it to telephone people and not talk to them, eh!' Her German accent was much more pronounced when she was angry. She put the phone down on him after reminding him to get in touch with her daughter as soon as he had any news about her son.

Lombard returned Larry's wave – looking up at the sky while chatting with one of his patrons, the Indian man had just caught sight of him in his window.

'Nine–one, my friend! Nine–one!' he heard Larry shout with a big grin and a thumbs-up.

Lombard grinned, went to the kitchen, stopping to feed his two goldfish on the way, and returned to his desk with a coffee and a slice of bread. Eating, with the telephone receiver tucked in the crook of his neck, he dialled the Hampstead number.

Mrs. Spitz's daughter answered.

'Good morning, Mrs. De Moraes. Mr. Lombard.'

A brief silence answered him, then:

'Mr. Lombard. Didn't you just speak with my mother?'

'That's right. I wonder if I may speak to her again. She put the phone down on me and I—'

'My mother has left, Mr. Lombard.'

'Then maybe you will be able to help me, Mrs. De Moraes. I just have a few questions. Do you know if your brother employs a cleaning lady?'

'Are you serious?' came the reply.

'Very. Your brother's apartment is remarkably clean for a bachelor suspected of being on drugs.'

He was convinced he heard her scoff.

'Are you a bachelor, Mr. Lombard?'

'I'm sorry?'

'Are you a bachelor? Do you live alone or have you got a nice wife to clean your mess behind you?'

Lombard frowned:

'I live alone, Mrs. De Moraes.'

'Right. So tell me, is your apartment or whatever it is you live in a tip, Mr. Lombard?'

Lombard scowled, ran his eyes over his front room which, with its desk and chairs, its filing cabinet and large aquarium in which his fish were eating, appeared bare and passably clean.

'My interest in the question pertains solely to your brother, Mrs. De Moraes,' he said.

'Well, in that case, I don't know, Mr. Lombard. My brother and I stopped living together a long time ago.'

'Do you know of a girlfriend of his called Rhian, perhaps?'

There was brief silence before she said:

'As I said, Mr. Lombard, my brother and I stopped living together a long time ago. Will that be all?'

'Not quite. Did Leonard ever smoke?'

'I'm sorry?'

'Did your brother ever smoke, Mrs. De Moraes? I didn't see any ashtray, cigarettes, or for that matter any alcohol or anything more harmful than aspirins in his apartment. I guess he doesn't smoke at the moment, but I was wondering if he ever did.'

'Forgive me for asking, but is whether or not my brother ever smoked really significant in the present circumstances? Shouldn't you instead be more concerned with trying to find him?'

'Did your brother smoke?' Lombard simply asked again.

'I don't think he ever did, no. Not if you are referring to tobacco anyway,' she retorted; 'Why is this so important, Mr. Lombard?'

'I'm just trying to establish who I am looking for, Mrs. De Moraes,' he said; 'One more thing. You wouldn't happen to know where the thermostat of his central heating system might be? It's quite stifling in his apartment. I might have to go back there and perhaps could turn it down a bit.'

She didn't answer.

'Mrs. De Moraes?'

'Yes. No. I've never had the pleasure of visiting Leon's, Mr. Lombard. And if I had, I very much doubt I'd have noticed the thermostat.'

'Right. Well, thank you, Mrs. De Moraes. That's all I wanted to know.'

'Have a nice day, Mr. Lombard.'

Lombard finished eating his bread, gulped down his coffee and lit a Gitane. The news that Leonard Spitz had never been a smoker didn't help. It wasn't important but, had the opposite been true, it would have strengthened his suspicion that Mrs. Spitz might after all be right about her son. Had Leonard shown the resolve to give up smoking in the past, it would be reasonable to presume he could show the same resolve towards another bad habit, reasonable to presume he had it in him to steer clear of drugs, in spite of what his family seemed to think, in spite of his history. And nothing Lombard had come across in the Highgate apartment or learnt at The Four Seasons suggested he was a relapsing heroin addict. On the contrary. The last morning Leonard had spent at home he'd got up, munched his cereals, diligently put his dirty bowl in the sink and empty milk carton in the bin. He'd also spent the night before alone, possibly eaten a Pizza, watched TV or one of his videos, or perhaps passed the hours playing guitar in the empty dining room while sucking sweets, or kept himself busy in his darkroom where he obviously spent a great deal of time. Perhaps, on his way out, when he last left his apartment, he had also stopped by the laundry room to hang out his washing to dry. Where was he going? He had not taken his bicycle. Had he got a camera with him? Was he intent on searching the streets to capture a shot or scene he had in mind? Or was he on his way to a camera shop? His photography used up most of his monthly allowance, with a fair portion of it – assuming the girl with the long eyelashes had told the truth – going on waitresses who felt safe enough with him to model for him. Yet, Leonard worked in a restaurant where the owner got high with his staff. Yet, his employer had found it apt to describe him as suicidal. Yet, his sister and father seemed convinced he had succumbed to his old addiction, although, to the best of their knowledge, he'd kept himself clean for the two years since his return from treatment in America.

But then again, Leonard hung lurid pictures on his walls. But then again – just before disappearing anyhow – Leonard had been going to sleep reading books with titles like *Occult Bondage and Deliverance*. But then again, Leonard led an austere and lonely existence in the barren apartment given to him by his parents, occupying the smallest of many bedrooms, keeping it all as tidy as only the most nervous or respectful guest would, as if he didn't really live there, didn't feel it to be home, didn't intend staying, but was just passing. But then again, Lombard had found no sign of drugs or drug-taking. Only aspirins. Leonard Spitz took aspirins. Not exactly the pain killer favoured by drug users. And although according to his mother and the waitress Leonard was 'safe', indifferent to desire, yet he kept a snapshot of a grinning girl on his bedside table, a grinning girl who'd called him repeatedly in the last two weeks, worried not to have heard from him. At least someone other than Mrs. Spitz seemed to think enough of him to be concerned by his unexplained absence.

'... I hope... I hope everything's all right...' she'd said on Leonard's answer-phone, in a nervous voice that suggested that maybe she had reason to believe everything was not all right. And according to 'Yeah. Jeff here, man...', she'd even called the restaurant.

Lombard searched the pocket of his damp raincoat hanging by the front door and found Leonard's address book. The page with the letter 'R' was blank.

He called The Four Seasons. The woman who answered in a young voice with a slight foreign accent said Jeff was not there, disclosed she was Jeff's wife, asked if she could be of help. Lombard told her of his visit the previous night, asked if she knew Rhian's surname. She didn't, nor did she know of Rhian.

'Did you know Leonard well?' he enquired.

'Not really. He worked here in the evenings and I'm only here in the daytime. My husband looks after the restaurant in the evening...'

After searching the streets around Camden Lock for a parking space, Lombard finally took his Triumph to the underground car-park of a local supermarket. By spending a minimum of £5 on shopping, he bought himself a couple of hours' parking 'free of charge'. That suited him fine. It was five years since he'd last come to Camden at the weekend, had hoped to avoid the crowds by getting there before noon, but owing to the break in the clouds perhaps – or was it because of the imminence of Christmas less than three weeks away – he found the streets already teeming with shoppers and the usual mix of wide-eyed tourists and relaxed Londoners in their weekend outfits who, he thought he'd remembered, usually delayed flooding the area until early afternoon.

This was one corner of London Lombard had never really taken to. An ordinary popular neighbourhood during the week, come Saturday and Sunday, its heart became a huge and hectic mercantile centre committed to trend and opportunity, a faceless humanity indiscriminately blending people from all walks of life, providing for all tastes, catering for all palates.

'The future…' Nathalie had once said, as they stopped for a coffee after walking silently between the stalls where one could find anything from old jeans and cheap leather jackets to new 'ethnic' furniture; from second-hand books and bootleg tapes to overpriced 'Victorian' kitchen taps; 'We're where the future is at. The new tower of Babel. A greedy and soulless street department store peddling dreams to suckers who confuse looking cool with freedom… Or is it originality with personality? But I suppose we all need our little pleasures…'

Earlier that day, they'd visited Highgate cemetery, strolled between the graves of its illustrious occupants, and only made the journey to Camden afterwards for lack of anything better to do. Looking cool back then had meant that young men wore black leather jackets, young women clumpy shoes, preferably of leather with laces.

Lombard had not replied. A few years earlier, Camden Lock market had still been confined to two open expanses of stalls a few hundred yards apart along the High Street; no more than an ordinary flea market where Londoners came searching for second-hand wares at bargain prices. As its name indicated, one such expanse was located by the old lock that still served the Regents Canal, with the other close to the tube station across the street from the local vegetable market. Now, entrepreneurs had moved in. Where once were grocers and butchers along the High Street, now leather shops advertised their gear with giant replicas of boots, aeroplanes and other gimmicks mounted onto the facades above their open fronts; where once were electricians and bakers, now brasseries, themed cafés and restaurants could barely handle the hordes of hungry week-enders; and the vegetable market, once the thriving hub of the local community, was but a shadow of its former self, a few ever-shrinking stalls tucked away in a side street, just another victim of the relentless growth of the more hip street market which extended its arms everywhere and further, devouring everything, like an uncontrollable, insatiable ogre.

The area known as The Stables, formerly the site of warehouses belonging to British Rail, was one of its latest captures. Its sprawl of caverns, tunnels and outbuildings teeming with people musing over old motorbikes, phosphorescent T-shirts, kitsch furniture and whatever other curiosities could be turned into money, echoed to the din of an anarchic medley of music which made it impossible to think. But perhaps, to think was not why people were there, thought Lombard, peering at a bunch of impeccably dressed young French boys who had congregated around a stall of police and army paraphernalia.

'Hey! Look, c'est cool ça,' drifted the voice of the tallest of them; he put on a police helmet, waddled comically on the spot in a manner he clearly reckoned mimicked a strolling English bobby.

Lombard spent all of three quarters of an hour in this setting. He failed to find Rhian but, questioning one 'antiques' stall-holder after another, he eventually learnt, from a tall greying hippie-type brunette in a fur-trimmed suede jacket, short skirt and fishnet tights who went on swaying to a popular American ballad as they spoke, that Rhian did indeed sell furniture there but had not been seen for a few months.

'Yeah... I wonder what happened to her. She was nice... She was from North Wales. Some place in Snowdonia...'

'I'm told she shared a stall with somebody else...'

'Yeah. A bloke called Bob. But he doesn't come here no more neither. Someone heard he had a car crash and...'

'You wouldn't know anyone who knows where...'

'Sorry...'

'What about her boyfriend? Leon. Did you know him?'

'Sure. He often hung around here with her. Taking photographs and stuff... We never talked much though. I think he was shy. Anyway, you're from France?...'

Lombard left Camden Lock just as it started raining again and returned to Leonard's flat in Highgate. He was in a bad mood. It had nothing to do with his failure to find Rhian, but, walking away from The Stables, he had stopped to light a cigarette next to a young man in a thin jacket hopping up and down to stay warm behind a display of cigarette lighters on a cardboard box with a sign reading '10 LIGHTERS FOR £1', and, presented with the opportunity, he had ventured to ask something he'd always wondered about:

'Is there really a living in this?'

There was no malice in his question. The man however had thought otherwise and, vexed, had turned away muttering, loud enough for him to hear:

'What would you know about living, you old shit…'

Old… He had never been called old before. He had never taken to Camden, and this visit had not changed things.

During their night-time visit, the Spitzes had switched off Leonard's answer-phone. However, they had not erased the tape and Lombard managed to replay the messages. Rhian had left four messages, ending the first two with 'I'll call again…' She was worried, kept calling, but instead of asking to be contacted as both Mrs. Spitz and Jeff had in their initial messages, she only proposed to call again. Did this mean she could not be reached by phone? Lombard took another look at Leonard's phone bills but they were not itemised. He was considering calling The Four Seasons again when he remembered the phone numbers scrawled on the wall around the telephone in the darkroom. Would Rhian, who could not be reached on the phone, use friends' or public pay-phones? Would Leonard, to save her money, or because she'd run out of change, call her back, quickly scrawling her number on the wall as one did when…? On occasion she must have caught him in while he was busy in his darkroom.

There were about two dozen numbers on the darkroom wall, most of seven digits, a few six digits long, and a couple preceded with the area code 01766… Lombard picked up the phone, tried one of the coded numbers, got no answer, then tried the other. After a few rings, a little girl's voice answered:

'Hello?'

'Hello. Who is this?' asked Lombard.

A giggle quickly followed by the sound of whispers and laughter reached him.

'Hello? Can I speak to your mother?' he called.

'You have reached the wrong number,' replied a new young voice with suppressed giggles; 'This is the speaking sheep. At the third baa it will be time to have a pee—baa, baa, baa!'

Lombard pulled the receiver away from his ear as a high-pitched roar of laughter reached him.

'Listen, you—' he started.

'This is the speaking sheep,' cut in yet another girl, speaking very fast; 'At the third baa it will be time for a poo—baa, baa, baa!'

And she hung up amidst yet more laughter.

Lombard glared at the handset, called the operator.

'I'm trying to reach a friend but I can't get through. The number is 01766 770...' It was the number he had just called.

'Let me check it for you, sir...'

Lombard pulled a pen from his inside jacket pocket and, not finding anything to write on, reached for one of the contact sheets from a small pile on a nearby table.

'There's nothing wrong with the line, sir,' declared the operator; 'Are you sure you have the right number? The number you gave me is of a public phone in Penr—'

Lombard didn't understand what she said.

'Pen–what?' he asked, writing down 'Pen' on the back of the contact sheet.

'Penrhyndeudraeth.'

'How do you spell that?'

'P–E–N–R–H–Y–N...'

'Oh. My mistake,' he said; 'I gave you the wrong number. The one I want is...' He gave the first number he'd called, the one which had remained unanswered.

The operator informed him that it too was a public phone box.

'In the same place?'

'No. In Garreg...'

Lombard returned to Leonard's bedroom, made for the bedside table, withdrew the snapshot from its perspex stand and pocketed it. Replacing the empty stand, he noticed that the bed was made, and became aware that the apartment was no longer overheated. In the kitchen, he found the bowl, mug and spoon that had been in the sink, together with the plate he'd used as an ashtray, washed and put away on the drainer. The bin had also been emptied and, in the dining room, the table cleared of sweet wrappers and the guitar moved to a corner where it stood against the wall. Not finding her son home, had Mrs. Spitz gone around his apartment tidying up the little mess Leonard had left behind him? Had she done so to calm her frayed nerves, in a maternal response to disappointment? And what was Mr. Spitz doing while she kept herself busy washing-up and turning down the central heating? Had he sat in the dining room? One of the chairs stood slightly askew from the table. Perhaps he'd sat where Leonard had sat a few weeks earlier playing his guitar and sucking sweets, silent, waiting for his wife, peering sadly at his dry and furrowed hands as he'd done in his daughter's drawing room… What had they said to each other?

Lombard switched the answer-phone back on and left, realising, as he waited for the lift, that the mountain bike had gone from the corridor. He went back in and found it in the laundry room.

Garreg and Penrhyndeudraeth stood a few miles apart on the western border of the Snowdonia National Park in North Wales, roughly 250 miles from London. Judging from the road map, the two localities were small villages in mountainous coastal country. On clear roads, Lombard estimated the drive would take four to five hours, which meant it would probably be dusk by the time he got there. He'd never been to Wales, but all the same, he made straight for the motorway from Leonard's place in Highgate.

Sitting in his Triumph under the grey sky, gazing at the Welsh names scrawled on the back of the contact sheet – its front showed a series of park scenes, most focusing on a tramp laden with plastic bags trudging along a fence by a busy road, in the last few shots swearing angrily at the camera on realising he is being photographed – Lombard had decided he might as well get on with the task of finding Rhian, decided that, were he to fail, or the journey prove a waste of time – for it was evident Leonard was not with her – he'd call Mrs. De Moraes the following morning to inform her he no longer wished to keep the job. He did not care much for the places Leonard Spitz took him to, from the soulless house in Templeton Road to The Four Seasons restaurant and Camden Lock market. He did not care much for the people Leonard caused him to meet, from Lawrence the judgmental butler, to 'Yeah. Jeff here, man' and ill-mannered men who sold cheap lighters. Besides, for two mornings in succession now, he'd been roused early from sleep by Mrs. Spitz.

It was still light when he pulled up at the kerb opposite the grey chapel which, together with a couple of public houses, a police station and a few stores, made up Penrhyndeudraeth's central square. Contrary to what his road map had led him to expect, Lombard found himself in a colourless medium-sized town of pebble-dashed terraced houses that unrolled on a misty hillside. He made for the two phones boxes in front of the chapel, compared their numbers with those on his list from Leonard's darkroom, found that neither matched, and drove on towards Garreg which he found a few minutes later at the end of a long straight road that cut through flat marsh lands. An odd collection of bleak new housing and quaint old cottages, the village hugged the bend where the road turned at a sharp angle into a rolling green valley crowned to one side by a pointed mountain that peaked into the dusk sky a few miles away. The village lay still and silent, weaving with the road between rock and wet fields, its one phone box in a muddy parking bay opposite the pub, the last house in a small row of whitewashed cottages.

This one's number was on his list, and, finding the pub door closed, he made for the lights of the local shop.

'… She sold me a couple of chairs in London and I've come to collect the matching pair,' he explained in his best French accent; 'Unfortunately, I seem to have mislaid her address on my way here and she's not on the phone. Her name is Rhian. She's small, strong, with blond hair and freckles. I think she drives a Transit van…'

'Oh yes. I know,' said the plump girl standing behind the till, smiling back at Lombard with glowing blue eyes. She was tending the shop alone, had been reading a teenage music magazine when Lombard stepped inside, seemed only too pleased to come to the aid of a dark stranger.

'You're looking for Rhian Pentraeth. She goes to London sometimes...'

Rhian lived two miles away, in a cottage in the valley below the pointed mountain. It was difficult to find and the girl drew him a map on a paper bag, warning him he would have to walk as it was in the wilderness, remote from the road.

'Thank you. You're very kind,' said Lombard before leaving.

She sent him a shy smile, quickly looked down at her hands: 'It's all right...'

He was grateful for her map. Without it, it was doubtful he would ever have reached the bottom of the small field dotted with grazing sheep that sloped gently upwards to Rhian's stone cottage and its smoking chimney. With it, it had taken him a good half-hour to do so, would have taken even longer had he not given up trying to keep his shoes and the bottoms of his trousers from being splattered with mud.

First, he'd had to leave the main road past a small bridge, drive over a cattle-grid and steer along a bumpy track meandering between a flooding river and a steep rock-face. Then, reaching a small clearing where a battered Transit van sat, he had left his Triumph as instructed and continued on foot through a metal gate and on along the river into a wood, eventually coming to a narrow strip of ground that stood barely above the surging waters of the river on one side and an overflowing ditch on the other. This all but submerged ribbon of ground was what the girl had described on her map as the footpath to the cottage, but, dividing the roaring waters as it did to wind its way upriver under the canopy of trees, it appeared to lead nowhere but further into the wilds. Lombard had lit a cigarette before committing himself to it, glad he'd made it there before night, for there was no way he would have ventured ahead in the dark, and on reaching the field leading to the stone cottage many long minutes later, he had welcomed the sight of people – the light was fading fast; he realised he would need either a torch or a guide to make the journey back safely.

Three people stood upfield by the cottage, in waterproofs and gumboots. Two were small children. They were playing football, kicking a bright yellow ball across the wet grass between them. The other was a woman. She was splitting logs with an axe. The poor light and distance prevented Lombard seeing them clearly, but the woman's fair curly hair and short height indicated she might be Rhian. He stopped to observe her, flicked his cigarette towards the river, watched it bounce against a boulder before being carried away by the current, and, still unnoticed, tucked his hands into his coat pockets and set out up the field, in so doing disturbing the grazing sheep who flocked together and launched themselves, to the sound of their dashing hoofs, towards a gap in a stone wall halfway up the field.

The first to see him was one of the children, an Asian-looking boy who appeared about ten years old. Gawking towards Lombard, he froze where he stood. The other child, a blond girl of about the same age, followed his gaze and cried out to the woman who, when her turn came to catch sight of Lombard, also froze, her axe suspended in mid-air above her head. It was Rhian all right. She looked much the same as in the snapshot from Leonard's bedroom, except the toothy grin was missing. As Lombard met her eyes, he immediately realised something was wrong; through the twilight and distance between them he guessed rather than really saw her apprehension. He stopped, opened his mouth to speak but, before he could say a word, Rhian had turned away and, yelling to the children, hurried towards the cottage with her axe and disappeared inside. At the same time, the blond child, who had darted for the boy and grabbed his hand to drag him running behind her, vanished into the woods beyond the cottage.

Alone in the empty field which only moments earlier had struck him as an image of rural peace with its sheep, playing children and wood-chopping girl, Lombard stood still, frowning towards the cottage. Why should his appearance be so alarming to people who couldn't possibly know who he was? He raised his brows, lit a Gitane, and started upfield again, only to stop again as Rhian reappeared outside the cottage. She was heading his way holding a double-barrelled shotgun across her midriff.

'This is private property,' she shouted, stopping ten yards short of him; 'The public footpath is back to the left of the bridge by the road.'

Lombard peered at the shotgun; she held it firmly in both hands, the barrel pointed towards the ground, her index finger resting on the trigger guard. He looked up into her eyes:

'How are you, Rhian?' he asked.

She didn't answer but stared, a worried frown forming above her dark eyes. Something was definitely wrong. Lombard instinctively peered at the shotgun again, saw her finger move onto the trigger, watched the barrel rise up in his direction.

'I—'

'On—on the ground! Lie down on the ground!' cut in Rhian.

'You...' started Lombard.

She pulled the trigger. He heard the sound of the detonation echo against the surrounding rocks as he ducked, felt the small-shot charge fly above his head, heard its hiss through the damp air.

'Get down on the ground, I said!'

Lombard straightened up, scowling...

'On the ground, I said!' Rhian shouted again, looking straight back at him; 'I've got one more cartridge in this thing and I won't fire too high next time, you hear me! On the ground! Now!'

Lombard considered making for her, would have, had she not looked so frightened... He wondered if the blast had been heard from one of the other cottages he'd seen in the valley from the road. It was likely. But this was farming country...

'Whatever little secret I've stumbled upon here, it's no concern of mine, okay?' he said, slowly raising his hands.

'Shut up and lie on the ground!' she repeated.

Lombard sighed, glared at the sodden grass, reluctantly started to kneel.

'If you don't mind, I'd rather just kneel. It's wet and I got dirty enough as it is making my way here,' he said calmly.

His apparent calm, the mundanity of his remark, had the desired effect. She peered at him, dithering, obviously not knowing whether to insist.

'I'm looking for your friend Leonard Spitz,' he went on with a forced grin, all the time keeping his eyes fixed in hers. He had said this hoping to reassure her, but instead she was now staring at him with as much dread as hatred.

'Are you now?' she said after a moment; 'Your wallet! Where's your wallet?'

'What?'

'Where's your wallet?' she screamed.

Lombard hesitated, peered at her finger on the gun trigger, nodded his imperceptible nod, started to lower his hands to reach for his wallet:

'If this is—'

'Up! Keep your hands up!' she ordered; 'Where is your wallet?'

'In my jacket. Left inside pocket,' he said between clenched teeth, hands up again.

'Reach for it with one hand and throw it to me. And don't try anything. Come on!'

Lombard swallowed without parting his lips and did as he was told. He tossed his wallet across the grass, watched it land by her gumboots, watched her pick it up and, struggling to keep the gun pointed at him, start to search through it. She pulled out his French driving licence, scrutinised it, checked his bank and credit cards, found his business card. She stared at it for a long time, perplexed.

'You're a private investigator?'

'That's right,' said Lombard.

'You're not Austrian?'

He just peered at her.

'You're not Austrian?' she insisted.

'Should I be?' he queried.

She looked him over, unsure, held up his driving licence:

'What's this?'

'My driving licence,' he said; 'It's a French driving licence,' he added, realising she must be unable to speak or read French since she had to ask the question.

'You're French?'

'Uh-huh.'

She peered hard at him, frowned at his driving license again, and Lombard was pleased to see uneasiness creep into her eyes. She seemed less frightened, seemed to be pondering now what to ask or do next. Had she thought he was Austrian because of his foreign accent? If she had, she now realised her error. He saw her finger move away from the shotgun trigger and back onto the guard. She was obviously familiar with guns, knew how to handle them safely, even under stress.

'Can I get up now?' he asked.

'No!' she said, tossing his wallet back; 'What do you want here? How do you know me?'

'As you know from speaking to Jeff on the phone, Leonard has disappeared, Rhian. His family have hired me to find him.'

He knew what would come before he finished his sentence. It took a few seconds and Rhian came up with it:

'You're French. Why would they hire a French detective?'

'Because this one plies his trade in England and, it appears, enjoys a good reputation.'

She didn't know what to make of this, nervously shifted her weight from one leg to the other.

'Whether or not you believe me is your problem, Rhian,' he added, pre-empting her; 'But I sure would appreciate it if you stopped making it mine, eh?'

'Really…? How do you know me? How did you get here?' she asked.

He sighed.

'How did you find me?' she persisted; 'Jeff, Leon's family, none of them know where I live.'

'Well, I obviously do,' he replied; 'But that's not the point. As I said, I'm looking for Leonard. I came here hoping you might know where he is.'

'I don't,' she blurted out; '… He's not here. Leon's not here. You've made a mistake if you thought he was.'

'I know he is not here, Rhian.'

She looked thrown:

'You know. Then…?'

'I thought you might point me in his direction.'

'You thought wrong. I—I haven't seen Leon for months.'

Lombard stayed silent. She was a bad liar; uttering her last words she had found it impossible not to hesitate or avert her eyes from his for a fleeting moment. And now she stared back with too much determination.

'Haven't you?' he asked.

'No.'

'Then why the worried messages on his answer-phone, Rhian? You must at least have spoken to him on the phone recently. I'd swear you think he must be in trouble.'

'You—you're wrong. I just called to ask if I could stay with him the next time I'm in London. That's all.'

'That's all?'

'Yes.'

'So you're planning to go to London, are you?'

'... Yes.'

'I thought you'd given up selling furniture at Camden, Rhian. According to what I heard, no one has seen you there for at least six months.'

She looked surprised he knew so much about her:

'I don't just go to London to sell furniture,' she declared.

'I'm sure. So you cannot help me, right?'

'No. I haven't seen Leon for months. I called him to ask if I could stay at his place next time I'm in London,' she repeated.

Lombard grinned and picked his wallet up from the grass. She was frightened of an Austrian she had never met, enough so to send her children away into the woods and threaten a stranger with a shotgun. Yet, she'd seemed anything but reassured on learning that Lombard was only there because of Leonard. Rather, at first, the news had had an adverse effect, incited hatred, as if there existed a connection between the feared Austrian and Leonard. Or could she perhaps have thought that the Austrian had traced her through Leonard, had only mentioned his name to...

Her conduct so far suggested further questioning would be pointless. But she was no killer, and now she knew Lombard knew where she could be found, now she knew he knew of her fear of an Austrian, could she afford to let him go...?

'Well, since you have a gun, I'll take your word for it, Rhian,' Lombard said, pocketing his wallet after rearranging the papers inside; 'Now I'm going to stand up and quietly return to my car, all right?'

She stayed silent. Lombard rose to his feet and inspected his trousers. They were wet and muddy from the knees down. He heard himself curse before starting to sweep the dirt from them:

'By the way. Do you think Leonard might have killed himself, Rhian? That's what Jeff seems to think. That he committed suicide.'

He looked up. Rhian stared back, too perturbed to speak. He smiled, his charming smile:

'Never mind. You were my best hope of locating him, so I guess I'm now out of a job. I expect his family will relay my findings to the police who may or may not decide to pay you a visit. I trust you have a shotgun licence,' he said, grinning at her before looking away to survey the landscape around them; 'A nice place you have here. It must be very beautiful in the summer. My apologies for sounding Austrian and frightening your children away. Goodbye, Rhian.'

He turned and started down the darkening field, pulling his Gitanes from his pocket.

He'd already had a few drags of his cigarette and given up on Rhian to worry instead about the trek back through the raging waters when he heard her shout:

'Wait!'

He stopped, turned. Rhian was slowly walking down the field. As before, she stopped about ten yards away, and through the twilight, he saw that she was crying.

'I hope you're not a bastard, Frenchman.'

Lombard took down the smoke from his cigarette, smiled:

'My name is Lombard, Rhian.'

'Well, I hope you're not a bastard, Mr. Lombard.' And she turned on her heels, sent out a strident syncopated whistle, like sheep farmers do to command their dogs, and started upfield:

'Come.'

As they neared the cottage, the silhouettes of the two children reappeared from the wood. They still held hands. Rhian cried out a few sentences in a language Lombard didn't understand and, just like before, the blond little girl ran pulling the boy behind her, this time into the cottage. Had they been hiding in the woods, waiting for Rhian's whistled signal to reappear?

'What language was that?' asked Lombard, striding a few feet behind Rhian.

'Welsh,' she said after a moment; 'Didn't you know you were in Wales, Mr. Lombard?… Watch your head.'

She was sobbing now.

He stepped after her through the small front door and into a cluttered kitchen with a grey flagstone floor and whitewashed stone walls. Rhian put the shotgun down on a table buried under a mass of crayons, felt pens and children's drawings, got out of her gumboots and waterproof, picked up the shotgun, unloaded its remaining cartridge and put it away in a cupboard under lock and key.

'You better go in the sitting room and sit by the fire to dry your trousers,' she said, grabbing a kettle on her way to the sink, avoiding Lombard's eyes and suppressing sobs.

Lombard surveyed the room. A bare light-bulb hung above the table. A potter's wheel and what he took to be buckets of clay occupied the space around a burning stove. The cooker and fridge were rusty, the rest of the furniture bruised by time and use. Nevertheless, unassuming and chaotic as it was, perhaps because it appeared fully in tune with the wilderness outside, like a stone refuge of essentials for survival, the room possessed a cosy and welcoming character. Clusters of wild heather and crude clay figurines fought for space on the windowsill with collections of trinkets and old-fashioned glass bottles.

'Do you want milk and sugar in your tea?'

Lombard didn't drink tea.

'I'm afraid I haven't got any coffee to offer you,' she added, as if reading his thoughts.

'Two sugars, no milk,' he said; 'Where is the sitting room?'

'Through the passage,' she replied, motioning towards a dark, narrow gap in the stone wall across the room; 'I'll be with you in a minute.'

'Is it all right if I smoke?'

It was. Lombard peered at her back. She stood in front of the stove waiting for the kettle to boil. The man's woollen jumper she wore sagged rather than hung from her strong shoulders to the middle of her thighs, giving her a shapeless figure. Whatever she'd called him back for, she was not yet ready to tell him, and since he didn't relish driving all the way back to London with wet trousers clinging to his knees, he stepped around the table and made for what she'd called the passage, stopping as he emerged on the other side.

If not for the dim light-bulb hanging from its wire, a TV set balanced on a barrel, various children's toys and a cassette player crowding the deep sill of the room's small-paned window, he might have thought he'd stepped through time, entered a ghostly world belonging to the past, like a quaint scene from a picture book or movie, complete with fat tabby cat who, perched on the edge of a double bed covered in ragged blankets and cushions, stared with glazed eyes into the flames of a log fire that burned in an open fireplace set back beneath a massive oak beam. Here too the walls were made of craggy stones and the floor of flag-stones. A couple of beat-up leather studded armchairs stood by the fireplace, one draped with layers of fabric, the other so worn its shiny leather reflected the dancing light of the fire. A wall was stacked with drying logs covered in moss. The ceiling, ridged with beams, hung so low Lombard could barely stand upright, and a few threadbare rugs led the way to an opening in the fire-place wall where a stairway, also of stone, curved to the floor above. From there, came the soft whisper of childish voices.

Lombard listened to them for a moment, observed a black and white portrait of Rhian that hung above the bed, reckoned it was Leonard's work even though this was more pleasant and sensual than anything of his he'd seen so far, made for the fireplace and settled into one of the leather armchairs under the oak beam. As the tabby cat sent him a wary glance, the sound of muffled sobs reached him from the kitchen, then that of footsteps hurrying against the hard floor and a door opening and closing. Rhian had left the kitchen.

He took a deep breath, reached for his Gitanes and peered into the fire. The flames licked the darkness in a seductive dance. The glowing logs crackled, spat and hissed. Already, the comforting heat was causing the wet fabric around his knees to steam. And, before he knew it, the earnest kid yearning for adventure who used to sit like this around the camp fires of his boy scout days rose to the fore of his mind; before he knew it, he fell under the spell and, like the tabby cat on the edge of the bed, found himself staring with glazed eyes into the flames, forgot Leonard Spitz and Rhian, stopped hearing the whispers from upstairs, forgot to light his cigarette…

He didn't know how long had passed when Rhian appeared with the tea. She shooed the cat away and settled in its place on the bed with a quick glance at the ceiling from where he once again heard whispers. It was just a girl's voice now. From her monotonous drone it sounded as if she was reading.

'Do you make a good living as a private detective?' asked Rhian.

She was no longer crying, had pulled her hair back into a bun and changed into a small buttoned up cream cardigan that fitted so tight against her bare freckled skin that, like in the snapshot, the points of her breasts stabbed at the fabric as she sat with her hands clasping the mug of tea on her lap.

'I survive,' Lombard said. Her deep blue eyes stared into the fire and, like the shiny armchair leather, reflected the flames in front of her.

'What's your speciality? Marital problems? Insurance fraud?'

Lombard sipped some tea. She'd spoken in a mild, even tone, but contempt had somehow crept through the question. Whether or not it was deliberate…

'I do what I can,' he said patiently.

'Well, this might be your lucky day then,' she declared.

Lombard remained silent. She sent him a quick glance, he sent her a warm smile, and she looked away again.

'Do you live here alone?' he asked.

'Yes. I mean, no,' she corrected herself; 'With my daughter…'

'The blond little girl?…'

She nodded, glanced up at the ceiling again, turned to Lombard as if to say something, changed her mind and looked back into the fire with a sigh.

Lombard lit his cigarette. She was fighting inside, had a heavy heart. There was no point in hurrying her.

'What's the worst thing you've ever been told?' she eventually asked.

Lombard thought for a moment, then:

'Someone once suggested I should become a Buddhist,' he said perversely, remembering a particularly unpleasant individual; 'Leonard's?' he went on to ask helpfully.

She followed his gaze towards the black and white portrait on the wall above the bed, nodded:

'Yes. My London drama school days. It's the picture I used in *Spotlight*.'

'What's that?'

'It's a catalogue of photos of aspiring and unemployed actresses. You advertise your stuff in the hope of being spotted by casting directors. The film world's equivalent to a cattle market, on glossy paper...'

Lombard raised his brows, thought of Nathalie. Like her, Rhian had wanted to break into the movie world and obviously failed. He peered at the portrait again. Now she mentioned it, it was true that she appeared younger in it, though only just. Perhaps he had failed to notice this because it showed her wearing make-up, which made her look mature beyond her years. She wasn't wearing any now.

'You've known Leonard a long time?' he asked.

'Yes. Well, five years. We met in a pub. He was the hopeful guitarist of the live band and I was the hopeful country girl looking for excitement in the big city. Later that night we got high together and became friends.'

'Friends?'

'Friends,' she maintained; 'I was still married to the father of my daughter then. It was only when Leon came back from America two years ago that we... Well, we didn't quite make it as lovers but we remained good friends... Whatever you may have heard, Leon is a good man. Too good a man perhaps...'

'His family seem to think he is back on drugs,' he said.

Her lips twitched in a half-scornful, half-sad grin:

'Do they now?'

'Aren't they right?'

'Huh. Leon did drugs. A lot of drugs. Went through his self-destruct phase, you know? Things to come to term with. Demons to fight. Some people's minds are gloriously uncomplicated. Not Leon's. He did beat the drug, though. He did.'

'His mother will be pleased to hear that,' said Lombard.

'Will she?'

It was not a question, merely a bitter remark.

'But he didn't beat the demons…' she went on; 'Tell me, what do you know about Leon's parents, Mr. Lombard?'

'Aside from the fact they're wealthy, not much. We only met briefly yesterday morning.'

She sent him a puzzled glance, wondering how…

'You're not on the phone. Leonard calls you back when you ring him from phone boxes,' he explained; 'Scribbles the numbers on his wall. I might not have found you so soon if you lived in a big city.'

'What about my name? I asked him to—'

'I was lucky. I gave Jeff a description of the girl in the snapshot Leonard keeps on his bedside table.'

She turned away, looking worried and frightened again.

'That's right. It wasn't very hard to find you. So, even though you still haven't told me why you're afraid of an Austrian and I somehow guess it has something to do with your friend Leon, I wouldn't make a habit of greeting strangers with a shotgun if I were you. If your Austrian was looking for you, I reckon he'd have found you before I did. And if you're that scared of him, and your fears are justified, I very much doubt he'd broadcast his arrival by calmly walking up your field while you're busy chopping logs. But then again, perhaps I don't know what I'm talking about.'

Rhian peered straight into his eyes, but he could see, she wasn't looking at him. She sighed nervously and turned to the ceiling, calling:

'Carys! Tell Shiva not to be scared. The man is just coming up to have a look and he won't come inside or touch him, okay?'

'Okay, Mam,' Lombard heard the girl reply.

'Good,' Rhian said before turning back to Lombard; 'Go upstairs and have a good look at the boy with my daughter, Mr. Lombard. Stay on the stairs and don't go into the room, all right. He's terrified of men.'

Lombard frowned. She looked back at him, unflinching. Hurried whispers and the sound of footsteps across floorboards resounded now above their heads.

'Go and have a look at the boy, Mr. Lombard.'

'If it's the boy I saw earlier with—'

'Have a look at the boy, please, Mr. Lombard. Upstairs.'

Tears were welling up in her eyes again.

Lombard flicked his cigarette into the fire, put his tea down and climbed the curved stone stairwell. It opened into a door-less bedroom beneath a skylight and the roof's sloping beams. Before he reached the top, in the light of yet another bare light-bulb, he caught sight of the two children standing on a mattress on the floor deep inside the room. They still had their gumboots on. The girl stood in front of the boy, her arms hugging him behind her as if to shield him, looking back at Lombard with sullen eyes. The boy, taller than her, also looked at him, but there was no expression in the big dark eyes in his dusky brown face.

Below, Rhian must have heard his feet stop on the stone steps.

'Meet my daughter Carys and her friend Shiva, Mr. Lombard,' he heard her yell; 'Shiva doesn't speak English so we're not quite sure where he comes from or what his name is. But we have to call him something, so Shiva it is. He cost £15,000. Leon bought him. From an Austrian who sells little children to perverts. Aren't you glad you came, Mr. Lombard?'

Lombard scowled into the reproachful eyes of the blond girl.

'What are you going to do now? Call the police so they can take him away and dump him with the social services? No doubt that will enhance your good reputation, eh? Private detective finds Asian boy for sale in Welsh cottage! Aren't you glad you came, Mr. Lombard?'

Rhian spoke in a high-pitched voice now, in fast succinct bursts. The little girl in front of Lombard had begun to look frightened. He sent her a reassuring smile, glanced at the boy and returned downstairs to find Rhian on her feet, crying in front of the fireplace with her arms across her chest. There was no need to wait or to question her anymore. The words poured out of her mouth as fast as her sobs allowed, and Lombard just let her speak.

Four weeks earlier, Leonard had turned up unannounced at the cottage with the boy, she said. He was both frantic and exhilarated, kept repeating 'I saved him! I saved him!'. He told her he bought him in London from an Austrian for £15,000, wanted her to look after him, had given her £3,000 in cash for his keep, and had left apparently intent on buying another child after insisting there were plenty more where this one had come from. At first, Rhian had not believed him, suspected he'd flipped or was on some bad drug trip and had either kidnapped the child or got hold of him in some other fantastic way. But the boy was obviously very distressed, and Leonard had come prepared, had showed her a video of a movie he claimed also came from the Austrian. He'd told her it was a snuff movie involving children. She'd only been able to bring herself to watch the first few minutes, but that had been enough to convince her Leonard was not lying, and she had then tried to persuade him to take the boy and the video to the police and tell them what he was telling her. Leonard had refused, declared he had 'good reasons' not to, that he couldn't divulge them even to her and that, in any case, he reckoned the police would not believe him. He had a much better idea. A much better plan. He would buy and rescue other children, and only if he failed in this enterprise would he consider informing the police. All the same, Rhian had gone on pleading with him, arguing that even if she could and would look after the one boy, she couldn't possibly look after another, let alone two or three, and had pointed out the danger Leonard was putting them both in by trying to deceive people who thought nothing of selling children. 'Don't worry. There's no way anyone can find out what I'm doing,' Leonard had assured her; 'I just did it and it worked. As long as his kids are paid for, the Austrian couldn't care less what happens to them.' As for the next child, he'd find a way to get it looked after without her help. And when Rhian had asked how he could afford thousands of pounds to buy children, he had been evasive, refused to say anything other than that he'd been lucky and money was no object. After his departure, Rhian had considered going to the police herself or taking the boy to the local social services, if for no other reason than that the boy refused to eat and just sat placidly in the bedroom upstairs and she was worried he might get ill or starve. But he'd quickly enough taken to her daughter, had begun to come out of his shell, withdrawing back into himself only when strangers, especially men, visited the cottage. She didn't know how long she'd have been able to look after him without it being found out, but had hoped it would be at least until he might have 'learnt enough good things about life to have one for himself'. As for Leonard, she hadn't heard from him since he'd left the boy and worried he'd got into trouble with the Austrian, was maybe even dead. For all she knew, he'd been made to tell where he'd hidden the child. That was why, when Lombard had turned up with his suit and his foreign accent, she'd feared he was the Austrian who'd come for the boy and also, perhaps, to get rid of the people looking after him.

'I didn't think of asking Leon how he met the Austrian in the first place. Now I just hope nothing terrible has happened to him,' she said eventually, turning to Lombard and drying her tears with the sleeve of her cardigan; 'Perhaps it's a good thing you found me. Perhaps the police should be told about all this. Anyway, what are you going to do now, eh?'

Lombard was gazing at the tabby cat who had returned to his spot on the bed in front of the fire. He had no reason to doubt Rhian's story. But watching and listening to her speaking through her tears, he had felt it coming, growing, gradually, and now the old familiar warmth in the back of his neck had almost reached its full intensity. He knew. He'd lived with it long enough.

'In your line of work you know about these things, don't you?' he heard Rhian say. She had misinterpreted his silence, thought he was shocked or didn't believe her.

'In my line of work I know people do anything for sexual gratification and money, Rhian,' he heard himself say.

She frowned, looked almost frightened of him again. He found her beautiful.

'Where is the video tape, Rhian?'

She didn't understand.

'The one you couldn't watch?'

'Oh... Leon took it away with him.'

Lombard peered at the television set on the barrel.

'Have you got a video player?'

'Upstairs. My... Carys has one. I don't watch much television. We watched it upstairs. Why? Do you think I could have inven—'

'I didn't say that, Rhian.'

'Good. Because I saw the sick thing…'

She described how the video tape had been disguised as a Disney film, from the cover on the box to the sticker on the tape.

'… *Sleeping Beauty*. It looked just like the real thing. I'd heard of snuff movies, but, Jesus—'

The whole of Lombard's nape was warm now. He felt his shoulders tense up. He told her he believed her, asked if she had any idea why Leonard had all of a sudden taken the fate of maltreated children so much to heart. He might as well have insulted her. She gazed at him speechless.

'From what I know he's mostly interested in photography,' he added as an explanation.

She understood, relaxed:

'I guess he finally found himself a crusade…'

'A crusade?'

'His demons. As I was telling you earlier, he beat the drug but not the demons.'

Lombard just looked at her. His temples had become numb and heavy. He felt the blood beat against the bones beneath the skin, felt the void in his chest. That was it. His neck was as hot as it would get. He knew, he could hear his heartbeat. Some called it fear, and soon – this he also knew – he would no longer know or feel it. He'd just be himself, be one with it. The mind is as adaptable as it is predictable.

'Probably a fifth off all the shoes sold in Europe are made by or retailed through Leon's parent's leather empire. All started in the late forties from a small cobbler's shop in the East End of London with war reparation money for holocaust victims,' Rhian was explaining.

'I'm afraid I don't understand,' he said.

'They're German Jews. Came here before the war. They both lost all their families in extermination camps, but were actually never inside one themselves. Their parents had sent them here just before the war. The idea that his family wealth was started with money he believes should have gone to camp survivors has been haunting Leon. It's not guilt, more of a curse… And then there's also a story about them being involved with some group of Nazi-hunters. Though I wouldn't be surprised if that was just one of Leon's dark delusions. Still, he reckons they settled on hunting ex-Nazies to purge themselves of a bad conscience for having misappropriated what was rightfully camp survivors' money. As a kind of catharsis, if you like...'

Catharsis... That word again, but...

'Do you know Leonard's parents' names?' he asked her.

'Er... Albert. Albert and Ethel Spitz. Why are you—'

They turned together as they heard the kitchen door open and a man's shout:

'Rhian!'

She froze. Someone ran across the kitchen's stone floor and a burly man erupted out of the passage and came to a stop, scowling at Lombard. He was young, dark, roughly dressed, drenched from the waist down, with a crowbar held in his thick hands.

'Shit!' uttered Rhian, before yelling angrily at the man in Welsh. He yelled back, keeping his eyes fixed ominously on Lombard as the kitchen behind him echoed to the sound of yet more people running in – from the sound of it, all men.

'Shit!' Rhian swore again before making for the one in the room and shoving him back into the passage; 'And don't you move!' she commanded Lombard, stepping out of view.

There was great commotion in the kitchen now, with several men fighting to be heard above Rhian's angry and uninterrupted voice. Lombard heard the sound of running footsteps on the floor above and turned to see Rhian's daughter appear at the bottom of the stone stairwell where she stopped to gaze towards the kitchen.

'It's all right,' said Lombard; 'I think your mother is in control of the situation,'

The girl sent him a fierce glance:

'They are my uncles. And if you do anything bad they'll beat you up,' she said.

Lombard scowled at her, but already she was looking away again, listening intently to what was going on in the other room.

'They found your car and let the air out of your tyres so that you can't take Shiva away,' she added with a satisfied little smile.

She was not lying. When Lombard stepped into the kitchen, Rhian introduced him to six of her brothers. Each of them held a weapon of some kind, from crowbars to cricket bats, and eyed him menacingly. All six were small and dark and, like the one he'd already seen, wet from the waist down. Be that as it may, Rhian had succeeded in calming them down and sent them out of the door before explaining to Lombard the reason for their unfriendly visit. As it turned out, another member of Rhian's family, her sister, had stopped at the village shop soon after Lombard and heard of his visit from the helpful girl who worked there. This sister knew about the boy because Rhian, needing a sitter sometimes, had had to tell someone she could trust, and, like Rhian before her, she too had instantly assumed the prying stranger to be the Austrian. Fearing for Rhian, she'd driven to the family house a mile or so across the valley knowing that most of their nine unemployed brothers would be there. She'd found six of the nine, told them the whole story and sent them to the rescue. As the journey was shorter by foot than by road, the six had dashed cross-country and waded the river to get to the cottage, letting down his tyres on their way. Rhian had just sent them to pump his tyres up again. But she was upset that thanks to her well-meaning sister, her whole family now knew about the boy.

'But,' she said after a moment's thought, 'I suppose it doesn't matter now. You're going to call the police, aren't you?'

Lombard had just reached for his wallet and now gave her his card:

'My number if anything happens. I'll get back to you within 48 hours. Is there anywhere I could leave a message if I need to contact you?'

'You're...'

'No. I can't think of any good reason to take the boy away or go to the police — for now anyway...'

She was so pleased she started crying again.

'What are you going to do?...'

'Try to find out if the story Leonard sold you is true.'

She gave him her sister's phone number and led the way with a torch back through the dark waters leading to the clearing where he'd left his Triumph. There, in the darkness, they found his tyres were up again and her brothers lurking like a pack of wolves, still hanging onto their weapons, except for one who was now holding a foot-pump.

'What do you do for a living, Rhian?' he asked, settling down behind the wheel.

'I'm on the dole.'

He nodded.

'I've got the snapshot and I'll erase your messages from Leonard's answer-phone. You'll be all right?'

'Don't worry, Mr. Lombard. This is my valley,' she said, shivering. She'd come out wearing only her cardigan.

Lombard had glanced at her breasts, run his eyes over her brothers and grinned:

'No sick people in the country, eh?'

As he drove over the cattle-grid at the end of the track and onto the road, he caught sight of Rhian's sister in his headlights. She was running along the kerb in a heavy winter coat. He knew who she was because of her freckles and curly blond hair; Rhian had forgotten to mention that her sister was her twin. A few hundred yards further on he passed a small car stuck nose down in a ditch along a sharp bend in the road. Its headlights were still on and its door was open.

SIX

Perhaps Leonard's reluctance to get in touch with the police was understandable. There could be several explanations for it; for one thing he'd have had to compromise himself and face the unpleasant consequences.

At midnight, Lombard was back in Highgate. Presuming he had not disposed of the video tape, Leonard Spitz, being a methodical type, was likely to have concealed it either where it could not be discovered, or in the most obvious place, where it would appear reliably inconspicuous.

Lombard found it on the video shelf. It matched Rhian's description, looked just like Disney's *Sleeping Beauty*, with colourful illustrations on both the box jacket and the cassette label, and any doubts he may still have had about Leonard having got himself involved with a professional child trafficker rather than a back-room paedophile evaporated the moment the film started playing on the television screen. Already, too many details tallied: the price of the boy, which, insofar as Lombard knew, was about right; the race of the boy, and the fact he did not speak English, which suggested he'd been brought into the country only recently; the nationality of his seller, for more often than not such men operated outside their own countries; and Rhian's description of the video packaging. All this had sounded too authentic for Lombard to mistrust the story Rhian claimed Leonard had supplied about the boy's provenance, however sketchy and improbable it still appeared. For, even setting aside the question of Mrs. Spitz's son's sudden access to an unlimited source of money, it was difficult to imagine someone of his calibre could have fooled a child trafficker into doing business with him. People who peddle children for a living operate in secret rings, belong to the invisible world. Besides money, it takes connections, references and know-how to get to them, let alone to win the right to enjoy their services. Either Leonard had come across the dumbest, most careless child trafficker there was, or he'd been more than economical with the truth. Nevertheless, there could be no doubt he'd got mixed up with bad things and bad people.

The thing running in Leonard's video player bore no relation to the badly shot, run-of-the-mill porn films Lombard had come across before. This one was shot on film, faultlessly produced and edited, and had doubtless been scripted. This one was the expensive work of professionals and, bar its storyline, looked as good and as slick as movies came.

On the television screen, a little girl slept, her blond hair splayed out on the pillow beneath her head.

'Renatta assures me she's got something special in store for us this weekend,' said a man's voice in stiff dubbed English.

'Well, after last time there can only be one thing: the perfect love machine, ha-ha...' replied another.

Through a dissolve, the men appeared on the screen. They sat against a decor of painted palm trees in an exotic restaurant, eating, big, blond and tanned, their laughter cutting through the soft background music.

Lombard swallowed, lit a Gitane, turned the volume off and settled in the leather sofa. He wished he'd never gone to Wales. He wished he'd phoned Mrs. Spitz's daughter on leaving Camden Lock to tell her he didn't want the job. Now... He surveyed the orderly room around him. Leonard Spitz had chanced upon kiddie porn and child trading, had been horrified enough to embark on a mission of rescue, and yet, on the last morning he spent home, he'd got up, munched his cereals, diligently put his dirty bowl in the sink and...

At two in the morning, he found Nathalie at the all-night brasserie in Brewer Street that he knew she haunted between engagements or when she couldn't sleep.

Bad as he felt, he still couldn't help but pause inside the door to observe her before proceeding with what he had come there to do. Amidst the mixed clientèle of lonely men and weary groups who talked quietly around the tables, she was the only woman alone. She sat at a corner table over an espresso and a pack of

Marlboro, reading *Le Monde*, dressed in a becoming green silk shirt trimmed with a white lace collar and a black ensemble with matching stiletto-heeled shoes. In the diffused, smoke-filled light, she was radiant and intimidating, her pallor equal to the night; it struck one as a splendid performance, and, if none of the men were bothering her, it was probably only because this late hour belonged to regulars and night-wise creatures who either knew her or simply knew better.

She looked up as Lombard settled onto the chair across her table, eyeballed him in a sullen show of surprise and displeasure. This was the first time since their 'break-up' that they had met anywhere but the Parliament Hill café. Showing up here, Lombard was breaking the rules.

'*Comment vas-tu, Nathalie?*'

He'd thought long and hard before doing this, in the end had decided he had to...

She just went on observing him, ran her eyes over his face, dwelt on his tense shoulders. She saw, understood...

'You look like shit, Xavier.'

He didn't reply, just looked into her stoned black eyes, and she into his, serenely confrontational... Was she going to suggest she had a remedy for troubled minds? Or would she dispense with sarcasm?

Whatever she was, she wasn't cruel. Not to him anyhow. She glanced at her watch:

'*Qu'est-ce que tu veux?*'

In normal circumstances, Lombard would have pondered over her use of French. It was a rare event, invariably held some significance.

'*Un Autrichien. Négociant en pré-pubescents,*' he said.

She gave him one of her silences, raised her brows, turned back to her paper, which was more or less what he'd expected.

'*Les histoires d'enfants ne m'intéressent pas, Xavier.*'

He grinned, angry, said it:

'*J'ai besoin de ton aide, Nathalie.*'

She barely frowned:

'I'm expecting company, Xavier,' she announced, reverting to English.

'Un putain d'Autrichien, Nathalie!' he spat out between clenched teeth; 'He operates in London. Deals in kids and snuff videos. You must know him or know of him, eh? Aren't shitbags and sickos right up your street?'

He'd never spoken like this to her before. Still, she was not going to lose her composure for so little. She just stared back, as unruffled as always, tilting her head slightly to one side as she sometimes did, expecting her eyes to do their work, set the spell, and then for their eyes to speak. What was supposed to happen? Lombard would leave and they'd both wonder whether or not the other would turn up at the café the following Friday?

But nothing passed between their eyes. Lombard scowled, impenetrable, and more than any word he could have said, it touched something in her. He lost her. She gave him a look he'd only ever seen her give to other men before and turned back to her paper:

'I'm expecting company.'

Lombard had just seen himself in her eyes and did not like what he saw. The warmth in his nape let itself be felt, his temples…

'I…'

In quick, short sentences, he told his story:

'… poor little rich boy who thought he'd save a few kids… Went missing on his second shopping expedition… Could be dead… Can't go back to his loving family with this without evidence the Austrian exists… Possibly have a chat with him… I need a name or an address…'

She was sneering. This was the longest speech he had ever given her, the only time he'd ever spoken to her about his work, but he'd got her back. She was sneering:

'So?'

'So? You're not going to make me repeat myself, are you?'

'I don't know any Austrian, Xavier,' she offered after a long silence.

'But maybe you know someone who does. An Austrian peddling kids in London. How many can there be? These people supply to order. He has to be known, reachable.'

'Then why don't you reach him?' came the reply.

'I'm sure I could, Nathalie. But it would take me too long.

Besides, I don't have your credentials.'

She looked back at him, reproachfully almost, took a drag from her cigarette and turned back to her paper:

'Les histoires d'enfants ne m'intéressent pas, Xavier.'

He had thought about it on his way there, had hoped not to have to stoop to it, but...

'What's an hour of your time worth these days, Nathalie?'

She looked up again, softly blew out the smoke from her cigarette.

'Combien, Nathalie!' he insisted.

'Five hundred.'

'Viens,' he said, rising to his feet.

She peered into his eyes, surprised, amused and pensive at the same time. He was really breaking all the rules tonight.

'This is... Are you sure your interest in this Austrian is purely professional, Xavier?' she teased him.

He looked hard at her:

'I guess as professional as your interest in money, Nathalie. Come on. Let's go.'

She looked beyond him, grinned. He looked back. Across the room, two middle-aged men had just stepped through the door. They wore expensive coats, looked like money, already one was beaming past Lombard towards Nathalie.

'I'm afraid you'll have to wait,' she said.

'When?' he asked, turning back to her.

'Not before early afternoon...'

He nodded:

'You know where to find me.'

And he turned and nearly bumped into the two men on his way out. He scowled at them and hurried away.

'Michelle! Long time no see, ha-ha...' he heard one of them say behind him with an American accent.

'Gerald. I was so thrilled to get your call...'

He glanced back just once before stepping outside. Nathalie was all smiles, folding away her newspaper.

A splendid performance...

The chilly night air calmed him. Had he been able to leave his Triumph parked overnight in the West End without the risk of having it clamped or towed away, he'd have walked back to Islington, hoping the half hour trek would tire him out. He was not ready for home yet, knew sleep wouldn't come easy. There was still one thing he could do though, one thing he'd put off doing on his way back from Wales. At this time of night, he'd wake Moreau up, but at least he'd find him home, and since he still only ever contacted him from pay-phones, he wandered through the streets towards Leicester Square. In the days when he was still new in London, the square's phone boxes were among the few in town from which one could make direct international calls, and many a time, not quite used to his new life, still giving in to anguish, he'd made his way there on foot – he hadn't yet bought a car – to hang around the crowds of tourists, cinema-goers, buskers and down-and-outs and wait in stony suspense for his fear to make its mind up. It had gone on for weeks, and then months, but he'd never made the critical call; merely, whenever needing a favour, or at times, needing to talk, he'd step into one or other of the phone boxes and call Moreau. London's phone boxes were still red and cast-iron then, and Moreau still just an *Inspecteur*. Now, bar the layers of obscene cards advertising sexual services that perpetually inhabited them, the former were all grey and glass, Moreau had made it to *Commissaire*, and Lombard still rung him from time to time. He always had mixed feelings about getting in touch with his old friend though. He found it painful, the mere thought of him reawakened memories, and then, Lombard owed him the kind of debt that is just too heavy to make good. Also, there was the long ringing tone of the French telephone exchange...

It rang for a long time before a hoarse voice dense with sleep answered:

'*Allô?*'

'*Salut Moreau. Laurent...*'

'*Laurent! Merde! Qu'est-ce qu'il y a? T'as des Problèmes?*'

Good old Moreau. Lombard calls him in the middle of the night and instead of being angry he is instantly concerned for his well-being.

'*Non. Je suis désolé de t'appeler à cette heure mais...*'

Lombard asked him if he could check the French police computer for information about Albert and Ethel Spitz.

'C'est qui? Des clients?'

'Ouais… Il se peut qu'ils soient impliqués dans des histoires de Nazis…'

Moreau understood, Moreau didn't ask any questions, Moreau promised he'd look into it and turn to his *confrères Britanniques* if he failed to come up with anything at his end.

'Alors, dis-moi? Tout va bien là-bas?'

'Ça va. Il fait froid et il pleut mais—'

'Non mais dis donc, Laurent! T'es devenu un véritable Anglais où quoi?'

'Pardon?'

'Tu te mets à causer du temps dès qu'on te demande…'

They exchanged a few more banalities, Lombard said he'd call the following evening and lit a cigarette, gazing at a girl sleeping under a blanket in the brightly lit shelter of a cinema entrance. He only guessed she was a girl because there was nail polish on the hand that lay over the dog asleep beside her. A couple of bobbies walked past…

He'd meant to ask Rhian why Leonard had so few belongings, why he behaved like a guest in the apartment his parents had given him. He would, next time he saw her.

'Savieer!'

Moreau had grabbed his arm and was pointing towards the bright white convertible cruising the stretch of road in the no man's land between the Spanish and French border posts. A dark woman in a red head scarf and sunglasses was at the wheel.

'Savieer!'

Wasn't Moreau gleeful? It was one of his own informers who'd come up with the good news, it was he who'd got the tip-off. The Paris bureau had immediately dispatched every available cop who knew what she looked like to the Spanish border and, jointly with the local boys, they covered every road into the country, had been enduring the summer heat for nearly eight hours now. A moment ago Moreau had still been as pissed-off as he was thirsty. The two of them had been assigned to a secluded road, off the beaten track, and Moreau was convinced she'd try to get in via one of the busy main routes, taking cover amidst the herds of summer holiday travellers jamming the roads elsewhere, and some other son of a bitch was going to either miss her or reap the rewards. But there she was. And if the information was right, with her in the fancy convertible were two kilos of cocaine. And with the cocaine… This was José's woman, the wife of the fucker who two years earlier had broken free from an ambush, killing two Paris colleagues. Now his wife carried for him. Now they were going to get her and… It was Moreau and him who were going to do it…

She reached the French border control, smiled, and the young customs officer waved her through. She was on French territory.

'*Allons-y!*' bawled Moreau into the two-way radio.

Tyres screech. A car blocks her way back. A car blocks her way forward. She slams on her brakes and they're already on her, guns in hand, aiming right at her pretty face. Who got there first? Moreau or… They can't see her expression behind her sunglasses but… Is she wearing a green silk shirt with a white lace collar? And who saw the baby sleeping in the cradle strapped to the back seat first? They both frowned together. Have they got the wrong woman? No. It's her all right. She just took her sunglasses off, eyes them with those turquoise green eyes of hers. Perhaps she's not carrying. Perhaps she thought a woman with a baby would look innocent. Perhaps… But she's scared all right. She is facing their guns and doesn't even look surprised. She just stares, tight-lipped, more worried than scared really. But she's got to put her hands up, she's got to be got out of the car, be searched, and then her bags will be searched, and then the convertible. Everything's got to be searched. Two kilos of cocaine! Hello José! We haven't forgotten you. The coke better be there or…

'*Merde! Qu'est-ce qu'on va foutre du marmot, Savieer?*'

But why does Moreau keep calling him *Savieer*? He was not called Xavier then, he… Why is Moreau still holding onto his arm? He wasn't even touching him at this point. He was standing across the convertible, holding his gun and saying…

'*Savieer! Savieer!*'

Lombard opened his eyes, felt the hard wood of his desk against his cheek and the stiffness in his neck. He focused on a blurry pile of banknotes right in front of his eyes, then on the empty bottle of Cognac...

'*Savieer!*'

Behind him, Moreau was still shaking his arm, but his voice... He lifted his head, felt the fingers clasping his arm release their hold as he started to turn around.

In the dull light from the window, Jane was stepping back from him, frowning disapproval:

'Are you all right?'

It proved necessary for him to tug his raincoat sleeve to check his watch. It was 12:30. He glanced at Jane again. She wore her smart black coat and handbag. She must have just returned from mass. It was Sunday and he'd fallen asleep at his desk.

'Yes. Thank you, Jane.'

'Your door was open,' she said; 'This... This woman was downstairs ringing your bell...'

Lombard turned. Nathalie stood just inside the open door, a laconic smile on her lips. She was still in her black ensemble and high heels and gazed deliberately at Jane, studying her in a way, he knew, designed to make his neighbour feel uncomfortable.

'Thank you, Jane,' said Lombard. He was telling her to go.

'Yeah, well... Your accounts,' Jane said, gesturing towards a red folder on his desk; 'They just need your signature. I've got to go.'

Lombard nodded and Jane edged her way to the door and past Nathalie, who gave her one of her smirks.

'Bye. And thanks... Jane.'

Lombard scowled. Although Jane had her back to him – he could see it in her body language – she felt intimidated, was probably returning Nathalie's cold glance with threatened eyes.

'Goodbye...' said Jane.

Nathalie raised her brows and gently closed the door behind her, her eyes surveying the room and eventually settling on the goldfish in their aquarium:

'I see you still got your fish but lost your sitting room.'

'I couldn't really afford a proper office,' Lombard said, reaching for his cigarettes.

'*Eh bien...* Are you sure you need me?'

'What?' he replied too quickly, realising too late that he was swallowing her bait.

'*La petite m'a l'air assez bien foutue, non?*'

He peered at her, shook his head, lit his Gitane, picked up the wad of banknotes from his desk and made for her.

'Your money,' he said grabbing her hand and pushing the notes into it. He closed her fingers around the wad, grinned and turned to the kitchen.

'In here. *Café?*'

Coming back home during the night, he'd remembered he didn't have a video player. He could have taken Nathalie to the Highgate apartment, but it wouldn't have been right, and so he'd made a detour to borrow Leonard's video player which was now connected to his television above the fridge in the kitchen. Nathalie, settled on the chair which had been hers when they used to have dinner together across the Formica table, watched the screen, well aware, Lombard knew, that he was watching her.

He had to hand it to her. She was tough. She held out for twenty seven minutes before her eyebrows twitched and a spasm in her cheek caused her to tighten her jaw. It happened very quickly and she swiftly enough regained her composure, but she knew he wouldn't have missed it, stubbed out her half-smoked cigarette just to prevent herself from glancing towards him. Somehow, he was surprised at her. She ought to have known better. She was never going to win this one. The odds were always against her. She ought to have guessed as much when Lombard placed her in the windowless kitchen alone with the television set and positioned himself at his desk in the office, so that he could observe her through the open door between them without also having to see the television screen. He couldn't have made it more awkward for her.

It was good she had not turned towards him. She'd have caught his cruel grin and walked out perhaps. Because, however short-lived, Lombard greeted the crack in her placid mask with quiet satisfaction. Still, this was not meant as an endurance test, and he announced that he was going to have a shower. Now he'd seen what he wanted to see, he needed to freshen-up, and she perhaps needed to be allowed to look away from the screen without losing face. It was not that Lombard did not wish, or did not dare, to embarrass her further; neither could embarrass the other, they were both past that and, if anything, Nathalie could only be embarrassed by Nathalie, as she had just shown; it was just that he felt, now that she'd cracked, it would be counterproductive to let her use his presence as a helpful glue to seal her feelings. Alone, she'd open up, let it all in, and perhaps, just perhaps…

'Sometimes I wonder which one of us is the ugliest, Xavier…'

'I still don't know any Austrian, Xavier' she said, putting her coat on; 'Call me a taxi, will you?'

Lombard was in his dressing gown, had stepped into the kitchen as the film ended.

'Is that it? Is that all you've got to say?' he asked.

'Say? What do you want me to say, Xavier?'

'Why don't you tell me what you think of what you've just seen, huh? You should at least have to say something for £500.'

She peered at him, then at her watch.

'Your hour is over. But—' She broke off, smiled to herself; 'What you have there is collector's stuff, Xavier. It's not available on the free market and usually never surfaces outside their restricted world. Only the most select clientèle would ever be entrusted with something like that. It probably sells at around £5,000, but generally, this kind of material is kept aside for prearranged screenings costing anything up to five hundred per head. But it could be more. I don't know. I've never seen anything of this quality and, at the risk of disappointing you, I have to confess it's not really my sort of thing. It probably comes from Germany, Holland, Belgium or one of the Scandinavian countries. But since three quarters of all decent kiddie porn is produced in one or other of those places, this in itself is of no significance. I would guess it's German or Dutch though. They're the big boys. Hard porn, snuff movies, kiddie stuff—you name it, they make the best of it. I could also tell you your tape would be referred to in the trade as a *Lolita*, but I'm sure you know that and I've got to catch up on some sleep. So I hope that will do.'

He scowled:

'I was not asking for a lecture, Nathalie. Only what you thought about it.'

She looked coldly at him, then grinned:

'Would you like me to use the word sick perhaps, Xavier?'

He didn't reply, just returned her cold stare.

'Last night the two gentlemen you briefly met requested to be taken to a flat in Clapham just so they could watch me relieve my—'

'I don't want to know about your work, Nathalie,' he cut in. He meant it.

'Afterwards we drove back to their hotel and drank until dawn chatting about their problems. Then they paid me and I guess went to bed to rest before their business lunch.'

'I don't want to know about your work, Nathalie,' he repeated.

'You brought your work to me, Xavier. That's why you paid me to watch your film, remember? I just wouldn't want you to think you've got a monopoly on filth. You might start to feel righteous and turn judgmental.'

She was right. He was out of order. And she'd just done him a courtesy by bothering to point it out. It would have been more like her to just give him one of her silences.

'It's Sunday,' he merely said.

She sent him a puzzled look.

'Business lunch,' he observed, turning away to make for his cigarettes on the desk; 'Thank you for your time, Nathalie. If the Austrian exists, I'll find the son of a bitch myself.'

He inhaled the smoke deeply, staring out the window, and caught sight of Bill. He was walking a black and white puppy along the gutter. He seemed taller than usual. Was that a proud smile across his face? Bill the pet shop owner had acquired a puppy and no longer walked between hunched shoulders. The pet shop owner had acquired a pet and found happiness.

He blew out the smoke from his lungs and took a deep breath. Nathalie's warm smell filled his head, took him over, and for a moment he gorged on it. It was such a long time since... It had been what he'd missed the most when she left. Stepping through his front door a couple of days afterwards, he'd realised how hollow his flat felt without it. That had somewhat contributed towards his giving up the office he rented a few blocks away at the cost of his sitting room.

'But you want me to call a taxi, you—' he started, turning to face Nathalie who had gone silent behind him.

He broke off. Nathalie stood in the kitchen doorway staring ahead of her with a coy smile across her lips. Or was it a rueful smile? Or was it smugness perhaps that curved her lips? Or irony? Or happiness, hope or even gratitude? She was smiling though and, from the glow in her sultry black eyes, adrift in her own world and happy to be so. Had there been a little more colour in her cheeks, had she not been so elegantly dressed, she could have passed for one of those fresh but brittle young women who are used in advertisements because they arouse man's protective instinct.

'I would have thought…' She trailed off and, after what felt like an eternity, looked up, met Lombard's frown and twisted her smile back into a familiar grin.

'Can I use your bathroom?'

Lombard automatically glanced at her handbag… He nodded, tight-lipped.

When she reappeared he swore there was a spring in her step, even though her enlarged pupils betrayed what she'd just used his bathroom for. Light, cheerful almost, she announced she'd do what she could to try to locate his Austrian and asked if he had any more cash. She wanted five hundred pounds in an envelope and the same again for herself. It was Sunday, the banks were closed, the only cash Lombard had in the flat was the five hundred pounds left in Mrs. Spitz's envelope. She took them, said he owed her the balance, and left.

Lombard was puzzled and unhappy.

'Can't you just give me a name?'

'I don't know any Austrian, Xavier.'

'I don't want you to compromise yourself, Nathalie. It—'

'Aren't shitbags and sickos right up my street?'

'I didn't mean it like—'

'Take it easy, Xavier. If your Austrian exists, I'll point you his way. That's all I'll do.'

'Why suddenly—'

'Stay home. I'll call you later. And by the way, there's no refund if I fail to deliver.'

'In that case you better give me a receipt.'

'Huh… When I get the rest of the money…'

She was as good as her word. She rang at 20:30, much sooner than he'd expected. There was loud music playing and the sound of laughter behind her, as if she was in a pub or night-club.

'Can you afford a few hundred more?'

'What for?'

'You've got yourself a room at the Métropole on Piccadilly. Just go to reception and ask for room 142. No one will ask any questions. If you haven't got the cash ready just charge it to my account. Your name is Mr. Marchand and mine is Miss Dutoit.'

'When and why?'

'Now and because it will look better. You're here on a short business trip. You're a trustworthy sicko of mine who's heard only good things about the Austrian's products and doesn't want anything else. My contact claims not to know the Austrian but he encouraged me to leave him your money. I told him you were in a hurry. If I'm right, you should get a call tonight. If you do, I can't tell you what course will follow. If you don't, too bad. That's all I can do.'

'Is your contact a friend or…'

'I have no friends, Xavier.'

She hung up.

Lombard still didn't understand what had brought about her sudden change of heart. The answer was in the strange smile that had lit up her face, but, visualising it time and time again, he still couldn't give it meaning, only that, for a moment, she'd perhaps looked like the young woman she might have become if…

He swallowed without parting his lips and peered at his goldfish. They hung still in their water. Did fish actually sleep? He'd forgotten to feed them.

A little over an hour later, at ten o'clock, he walked into the Métropole's glistening lobby, presented himself at the reception desk as Mr. Marchand, asked for the key to room 142 and instructed the balding uniformed receptionist to charge his bill to Miss Dutoit's account. The man, despite an initial effort to the contrary, could not restrain himself from giving him a knowing look and wishing him a most pleasant evening after remarking, in bad, insinuating French:

'Je vois Monsieur a ne pas de bagages. Je comprends…'

The room was on the first floor, had a double bed and a window overlooking the traffic on Piccadilly. Lombard found it overheated, opened the window, took his jacket and shoes off and lay on the bed with the telephone on his chest. He ordered a ham sandwich and a coffee and called Paris.

'Moreau? C'est moi. Alors?'
'Salut, Laurent. Ouais. Bon ben dis donc…'
Moreau wanted to know what business Lombard had with the Spitzes.
'Ils ont perdu leur fils. Pourquoi?'
It had not been easy, but Moreau had managed to get hold of information about the Spitzes through Interpol. It turned out there was quite a dossier on them going right back to the early fifties. It appeared that in their younger days Mr. and Mrs. Spitz had been actively involved with a German-based covert group of Nazi hunters who called themselves *Never Forget*. Over the years, the group was suspected of having carried out over two dozen execution-type killings. All of their victims were affluent German and Swiss citizens, and all had been found dead in secluded spots with a single bullet hole through the head. Although the group seemed to have slowed its operation down in the last fifteen years, they were believed to be still operative and responsible for the killing of an eighty-two-year-old Swiss banker who had been found in a wood by lake Geneva with the trademark single hit through the head two years earlier. Whether the Spitzes had ever been directly engaged in any of the killings was not known, but there was positive evidence they were implicated with the group and were currently its main paymasters.
'How come they're not being bothered?' asked Lombard.
'That's just it, Laurent. I'd watch my step if I were you. Your guys are loaded and well-connected. I mean big money and big friends;

former Israeli prime minister, etc... The lady's also president of an
international Zionist fund-raising organisation. I don't know how
you got to work for them but... Anyway, you get the picture.'
   'Mossad?'
   'It's a good guess...'

Intrigued, Lombard had barely put the receiver down when
the phone rang.
   'Hello?'
   'I spoke with your friend earlier,' said a man with a London
accent at the other end before falling silent.
   'Yes?' replied Lombard.
   'Are you the person?'
   'Yes.'
   'Right, Mr. Marchand. You got something to write with?'
   'Just a moment.'
Lombard sat up on the edge of the bed, pulled a pen from his
jacket and grabbed a brochure from the bedside table.
   'Go ahead.'
   'You want Mr. Friedman — 0171 435... Say you're calling
about the puppies.'
   'The puppies...?' said Lombard, noting down the number.
   'Yeah. The puppies. And say you saw the ad at George's, all
right?'
The man hung up.

   'The puppies...' Lombard heard himself say, still hanging
onto the receiver.
   'Merde! What the hell are we gonna do with the kid, Laurent?'
asked Moreau.
   What had he replied? Wasn't it something witty referring to
Moreau's boasts about the reputation he enjoyed amongst women
for his smooth and soothing fingering technique? *'I don't know.
Hey! You better look after it since...'* They were young. They were
happy. They'd just got José's woman and they and everybody else
were laughing. Everybody but José's woman that is...

   Lombard rose to his feet and slammed down the receiver. So
the Austrian existed. Everything Leonard had told Rhian was

true. Less than three days ago he had undertaken to track down a wealthy old couple's mixed-up son and now the trail had led to... Even the old Spitzes weren't quite what they'd seemed.

He made for the bathroom, took off his shirt and let the cold water from the shower nozzle run over his neck and shoulders, until he no longer felt the cold, until his head was clear. He put his shirt back on, combed his hair, returned to the bedroom, lit a cigarette and called the number he'd just been given.

A woman answered:
'Hello?'
'Can I speak to Mr. Friedman?'
'Just a moment.'
He heard a few clicks, as if the line was being redirected through a switchboard, then the ringing tone again.
'Yes,' responded a man. The voice was old.
'Mr. Friedman?'
'That's right.'
Now Lombard noticed the German accent. It wasn't as pronounced as Mrs. Spitz's but nevertheless quite evident.
'I'm calling about the puppies,' he said.
There was no reply.
'I'm calling—'
'Have we done business before?' asked Mr. Friedman.
'I saw the ad at George's,' replied Lombard; 'I'm passing through town, I'm in a hurry and was told you could help me.'
'Were you?'
'Uh-huh.'
A long silence answered him. Lombard could hear the man across the line breathing. Then:
'May I have your name and phone number, please?'
'Why?'
'This is a bad line. I'll call you back...'
'When?'
'Soon.'

Lombard gave him the information he needed. Friedman, if that was his name, would now doubtless check with whoever the code phrase 'Ad at George's' referred to whether Mr. Marchand's call was in the clear. It could take ten minutes, several hours or forever, depending on how keen Friedman was to do business and how easily 'Ad at George's' could be reached. Lombard found himself hoping the man had a cell-phone, found himself hoping Nathalie's contact was high up enough in the criminal hierarchy to warrant being trusted. If not, he'd probably never hear from Friedman again. But now at least he had a phone number which led to a woman who obviously knew where Mr. Friedman could be contacted.

Nathalie had clearly knocked at the right door. The phone rang an hour later as Lombard stood gazing at the smooth running traffic in the wet night below his open window. He flicked his cigarette and, as it bounced against the roof of a black taxicab, he picked up the phone.

'Yes?'

'What sort of puppies are you looking for?'

It was Friedman.

'What sort have you got?'

'Pups. Bitches. From three to twelve months. Trained and untrained ones. White and brown ones. You understand?'

Lombard had thought he was ready for this. Yet, he had to swallow hard before replying:

'Yeah.'

'We also provide a 24-hour after-sale service. In the event of the puppy falling sick or any other accident, we would unburden you, you understand?'

He heard himself clear his throat.

'Yes… Good, good…'

'So what are you looking for?'

'What about an untrained pup, white…' he said.

'How much of a hurry are you in?'

Lombard quickly thought:

'Tomorrow?'

'I'm afraid the only pups currently available at such short notice are brown and trained. But they are all very cheerful and have been thoroughly checked for diseases.'

'Have they?' let out Lombard.

'Yes. I assure you they have,' Friedman said, misunderstanding.

'I see. How much?'

'Fifteen for straight delivery. Twenty with the provision of a safe place. Visitors tend to find the second option more convenient.'

'Right... Fine. I'll go for the safe place.'

'Good. Can you have the money ready by 11am. As I'm sure you know, we only deal with cash.'

'Of course. I'll have the money.'

'Good. We'll call you.'

The time had come to get back to Leonard's family. He checked his watch. It was 23:50. He needed to go home to fetch *Sleeping Beauty* but still, he'd make it to Hampstead before one. He very much doubted Mr. and Mrs. De Moraes were the early-to-bed type. He perhaps, but not she.

Lawrence was not pleased to see him. And for good reason. The house had been plunged in darkness when Lombard rang the bell. When the butler finally turned up, puffy-eyed in a striped dressing gown, it was clear he'd just got out of bed. Regardless, Lombard met his frosty attempt to deter him from entering by shouldering past him and making straight for the drawing room.

'Just go and tell your masters I'm here, Lawrence...'

The butler didn't really have any choice, and when Mrs. De Moraes walked into the drawing room several minutes later, Lombard was peering at a photograph of her husband standing smiling triumphantly on a podium wearing driver's overalls, a garland of flowers around his neck, Magnum of Champagne in his hand.

By the look of her, she too had been asleep. She sent Lombard one of her hostile glances without stopping, settled down on the sofa and quickly arranged the tails of her clinging dressing gown around her bare legs.

'Thank you, Lawrence,' she croaked, reaching for a cigarette case from the low marble table in front of her.

Lawrence, who had stood silent in the doorway warily eyeing Lombard for the last few minutes, stepped out and closed the door. Now they were alone, Lombard observed her as she lit her cigarette. Her eyes were swollen with sleep but still bore her make-up. Mascara and eyeliner formed dark clouds around her eyes, the lipstick on her fleshy lips was smeared, as if she'd fallen asleep drunk, or been crying. Still, even like this, she remained a striking sight.

'I won't comment on the time but you'll understand if I don't invite you to sit down,' she growled, snapping her lighter shut; 'Now, what are you waiting for, Mr. Lombard?'

She ran her dark eyes over him and focused on the briefcase he was holding.

'I'm sorry to trouble you at such—'

'Spare me the apology and get to the point, will you?'

'Where is your husband?'

He had hoped to see both of them. He was a bad messenger, knew what he was about to say would not go down well. In such instances, two listeners were always better than one. Indeed, the more the merrier. People who are close have a calming effect on one another. Or at least one always tries to calm the other.

'My husband's away playing with his motorcars, Mr. Lombard. Now, I'm still waiting.'

Lombard nodded his nod.

'I'm afraid I have bad news, Mrs. De Moraes. I have reason to believe your brother is in serious trouble.'

She sneered:

'For your information, Mr. Lombard, trouble is possibly the one thing Leon is capable of getting into all by himself. Though I don't doubt he will ultimately fail even at that.'

He grinned. He couldn't help it. Her open antagonism got to him. Perhaps, if she weren't so good looking he could…

'I don't know,' he retaliated; 'He seems to delight in so much sisterly love, he might become determined.'

'Oh!' she snarled; '*Touché*, Mr. Lombard. But tell me, what would a French private detective languishing in London know about sisterly love?'

'I guess possibly as much as you seem to, Mrs. De Moraes.'

He returned her icy glare.

'Don't speak of things you don't understand,' she spat; 'You might get confused and we need you clear-headed, at least until you've done what we're paying you for.'

'Now you are confusing me, Mrs. De Moraes,' he replied.

'Can it be that easy?' she asked, taunting.

'Can it be that you really want your brother to be found?'

'Anything is possible.'

'Yes, like hiring me.'

She raised her brows.

'Now it's my turn to be confused, Mr. Lombard.'

'Why me? Why did you hire me, Mrs. De Moraes?'

'Don't ask me. It wasn't my decision.'

'I don't doubt it. But why did your parents want me?'

'Huh! Please, you needn't go around imagining anyone in this family wants you, Mr. Lombard.'

He grinned:

'Don't worry. You're not my type.'

'I understand,' she replied, dismissive.

'Why did your parents—'

'Maybe they're getting too old to make decisions,' she cut in.

'What do you think?'

'It's a bit late for riddles, Mr. Lombard. What are you getting at?'

'Why should such well-connected people as yourselves hire a small-time French detective to track down their missing son, Mrs. De Moraes?'

She almost laughed:

'Ha-ha! Who do you think we are, Mr. Lombard?'

'Couldn't Nazi hunters do the job? Or should I say Nazi killers, Mrs. De Moraes?'

It took her aback. She looked at him, incredulous, then took a drag from her cigarette, sizing him up. She was too intelligent to waste time trying to deny what he obviously knew.

'So, you do do other things than bother your clients at unsociable hours.'

'Why did your parents hire me, Mrs. De Moraes?' he asked again.

'As I recall you were told, Mr. Lombard, we'd all prefer that Leon's antics remain our little family secret.'

'And that of a stranger?'

'Let's just say some strangers matter less than others, Mr. Lombard,' she said with a provocative grin; 'Especially those whose silence is for sale,' she went on; 'Besides, why call the experts to go after a predictable mind like my brother's... Or is the job too formidable for you, Mr. Lombard?'

Lombard returned her grin, looked right through her, coldly. Hadn't this happened the morning they'd met two days earlier? But this time, her lips didn't quiver like they had then. This time, she froze, her eyes filled with dread. It was not just contempt he was returning. She was perceptive enough to see it.

'Why don't you judge for yourself?' he said, opening his briefcase; 'I found this at your brother's.'

He threw *Sleeping Beauty* onto the table in front of her.

She glanced at the colourful illustration on the cover, frowned: 'Sleeping Beauty! How inter—'

'It's a snuff movie,' he cut in.

She frowned, unsure. She obviously didn't need a definition. 'What?'

'Prime paedophile material. The best there is. I'm told it's collector's stuff and retails at around £5,000.'

She turned from him to the videotape, rigid.

It wasn't the way he'd planned to deal with this, but...

'You seem surprised. Could it be you don't think that badly of your brother after all, Mrs. De Moraes? Has he never been into this kind of thing before?' he asked, callously.

She opened her mouth to speak but he went on, relentless:

'Do you think it possible that Leonard tired of taking photographs of young girls and decided to graduate to better things?'

She could just manage a frown.

'And there's more. Leonard also purchased himself a little boy. For all of £15,000.'

'What?'

'You needn't worry, though. It seems his motives were pure. From what I can make out he bought his boy to rescue him from further abuse. Your brother got himself mixed up with child procurers, Mrs. De Moraes, embarked on a rescue mission, and right now my guess is he's either being held captive, running for his life or dead.'

'What—what are you talking about?' she interjected.

'I have reason to believe Leonard vanished while attempting to buy a second boy, Mrs. De Moraes. Having succeeded in saving one little life he unwisely set out to repeat the exercise. It's a bad idea. You don't mess around with child procurers.'

Either she didn't understand what he was saying or she was just too horrified. Either way, she stared, all the usual brazenness gone from her eyes as if for good.

Lombard adopted a more placatory tone of voice.

'Your brother got mixed up with a child procurer and tried to make the world a better place, Mrs. De Moraes.'

She was thinking now.

'What are you saying? How do you know all this? How... How do you know this... this even belongs to Leon?' she asked, staring at the tape again.

'I know I found it in his flat, Mrs. De Moraes. I know he showed it to someone else. I know he bought a boy because I met the child. And this evening, posing as a potential customer, I also made telephone contact with the man he claimed sold him the child before he disappeared. Which leads me to the purpose of this late visit. I need £20,000, in cash, by eleven this morning.'

'This is not possible,' she muttered between her teeth, still looking at the tape.

'I understand your misgivings, Mrs. De Moraes. For one thing, I can't explain how Leonard suddenly got access to the sums of money involved. For another, I can't quite figure out how someone like him could possibly have infiltrated the world of child procurers. But I intend to try to find out these things as soon as I meet with the man who sold him the boy. I need the money to smooth my way, you understand? Now, do you have that sort of cash here or do we need to meet in the morning after bank opening time?'

She still wasn't looking at him, was still staring at the videotape.

'Not Leon,' he heard her mutter between her lips; 'Not Leon...'

He frowned, spoke again as she remained silent. Somehow, he had not made her out to be so emotional.

'If anyone knows what happened to your brother it will be that man, Mrs. De Moraes. That's why I need the money. I will of course do my best to hang onto it.'

At last, she was turning to him. Her bewildered expression had just turned into one of indignation:

'Where is it?' she asked.

'I'm sorry?'

'Where is it?' she screamed; 'He! The boy you say my brother bought. Where is he?'

'I can't tell you that yet. But I can assure you he's safe and being well looked after.'

'You can't… What do you mean you can't tell me that yet, Mr. Lombard?' she demanded.

He sighed:

'Right now the boy's whereabouts are of no significance, Mrs. De Moraes. He's better off staying put. He's being well looked after. What matters at the moment is Leonard.'

'Oh no. You'll have to do better than that, Mr. Lombard,' she uttered ominously.

Her eyes were ablaze again. He could feel his anger…

'Look, Mrs. De Moraes, whether you like it or not, your brother's not back to his old weekend tricks! Impressionable as he is, I believe he grew bored of his girlie pictures, tried moving onto bigger things, came upon more than he'd bargained for and somehow fancied he could take on the big bad world. You see, Mrs. De Moraes, most of us accept that greed, sex and fear are the only constants of humanity. Perhaps your brother can't. Never could. I wonder? Could that be why you hate him so much? Because you two are so unlike one another?'

He regretted having provoked her. It was a mistake. It took a good few seconds before she said:

'How dare you!'

'Why don't you watch the tape, Mrs. De Moraes,' he replied, trying to calm her; 'Perhaps we should resume this conversation afterwards, eh?'

'You're not even sure this tape really belongs to my brother, are you, Mr. Lombard?'

'The question now is whether or not your brother still owns anything at all, Mrs. De Moraes.'

'No. The question now is how long it's going to take you to get out of my house, Mr. Lombard.'

Lombard just peered at her.

'Get out of my house. You're fired, Mr. Lombard.'

'What's the problem, Mrs. De Moraes?' he asked, sounding as calm as he could; 'Do you think I would jeopardise a flourishing career by coming here with such a story to con you out of £20,000 perhaps? Why don't you watch the—'

'No! You're fired!' she cut in, suddenly getting to her feet and reaching for the tape; 'Get out of my house. And take your sick tape with you—'

Lombard just about managed to duck in time to avoid being hit by the tape which crashed into the wall behind him. He turned, stared at it where it lay on the immaculate white carpet. Mrs. De Moraes was summoning the butler:

'Lawrence!'

Lombard turned to face her again, straightened up. Her cold, disdainful look was back, aimed straight at him. Why should she be so offended? She'd displayed such contempt for her brother Lombard had wondered if she would not delight in hearing the gravity of his situation.

'Perhaps I should come back after you've—' he started.

'You're fired, Mr. Lombard,' she repeated.

'I'm afraid I can't let you fire me, Mrs. De Moraes. I was hired by your parents and—'

'The family hired you and I just fired you, Mr. Lombard.'

Lawrence appeared in the doorway.

'Madam?'

'See Mr. Lombard to the door, Lawrence. He is leaving,' she said, keeping her eyes fixed on Lombard; 'And he needn't worry; he can send us the bill if he is still owed anything,' she added.

He'd lost this one. He wasn't going to get anywhere with her now. He grinned, searched his pockets, pulled out a Métropole matchbook and threw it on the table.

'I'll be in room 142 until eleven. Keep the tape.'

'*Merde!*' he cursed, stepping out into the dark rain.

He felt angry and grim. And he had only himself to blame. He'd gone about this in the worst possible way. He should have remained calm. He should have known better than to let her get to him. He didn't know why, but Deborah De Moraes just stole his self-control, made him irritable. She just affected him that way. Perhaps it was all that voluptuous petulance.

SEVEN

Even with the window open the hotel bedroom was too hot. Outside it was a mild, still night which even the rain failed to stir. Still, the permanent drone of the surrounding West End traffic provide a welcome intrusion. Had Lombard been home, in his bedroom, lying on his bed, he would have heard only silence.

He couldn't sleep. He couldn't shut his eyes. As soon as he did so, the sunny little tableau of the convertible, Moreau, José's wife and the baby took over his mind, projected itself against his eyelids with frightening clarity. So he opened his eyes again, but as he was drowsy with tiredness, the scene remained etched on his mind for several minutes, only eventually fading in the entanglement of his jaded thoughts. But then, his eyes would close again and again he would quickly snap them open, because, given the choice, he preferred thinking about it to seeing it; words followed a thread, could only describe, but could also challenge things, while the images just hit him, senseless and merciless. Even though, even now, words were barely up to the task, still fell short of giving it sense. They offered a progression, but no clear explanation. But at least, they raised questions, provided some distraction, while the images...

What had been in Moreau's mind when he stepped towards the baby sleeping in the cradle on the back seat of the convertible? A dark beard had given a shape to his round face in those days. With his stocky body and thick fingers clasping his gun he had just moved forward, peering at the child. All he said afterwards was that he wanted to have a closer look at it. He couldn't explain why. It had been instinct. Lombard had light-heartedly suggested he should look after the child and Moreau had felt compelled to see what the child looked like. Just like that. What had Lombard thought? Did he believe Moreau was then and there going to get hold of the baby, free him from the straps of his cradle? It wasn't right. José's wife was still at the wheel. It wasn't the proper thing to do. Moreover, perhaps it wouldn't prove necessary to separate mother and child. Not right away anyhow, not without discussing it first. They weren't even sure she was carrying the cocaine yet.

'*Merde! Qu'est-ce qu'on va foutre du marmot, Laurent?*'

'*Je n'sais pas moi. Ben t'as qu'à t'en occuper comme t'es tellement adepte avec…*'

They were young. They'd got José's woman and they were laughing. Everyone but the woman, that is. But no one paid her any attention. Lombard, like everybody else, watched Moreau, wondered what he was up to, would have asked him as much had he not caught sight of her movement from the corner of his eye. He remembered. What had actually caused him instant worry was the speed at which the woman had moved. He didn't know what she was up to but, whatever it was, she was moving fast, and it couldn't be good, not under the circumstances. In the moment it took him to move his eyes from Moreau leaning inside the back of the car to the woman in the front seat, she had turned around, had her back to him and was raising a small silver handgun over the back of her seat.

'*Alors. C'est du mouflet ou de la mouflette?*' Lombard heard Moreau ask as this was happening, though neither Moreau nor anyone else ever could remember this.

But the woman held a gun all right. Lombard could still see it gleaming in the sunshine as she aimed it over her seat, towards Moreau. Without thinking, faster than he thought it possible, he'd aimed and fired. He heard only one blast, the one from his gun, saw the woman jerk under the impact, twist into a 180 degree turn, jolt back across the front seats and slam into the passenger door. Lombard had hit her between the shoulder blades, and now she lay facing him, the place where her chest had been all gurgling blood and ripped flesh. The exit hole, he had thought automatically, the exit hole is always messy. She wasn't dead yet though. She stared at him, with strangely indifferent eyes, and he had just looked back at her, rooted to the ground, holding his breath, seeing nothing and no one but her, until, with a last twitch, as if on a spring, her head slumped to her chest. Only then had he thought of Moreau, had he looked to see if his friend was all right. Moreau wasn't. He stood rigid, still leaning slightly into the back of the car, mouth shut, his face and shirt covered with shreds of flesh. Lombard had thought Moreau was hit, that the woman had got him and he was dead on his feet perhaps, about to drop. But Moreau was alive. How long had it taken for Lombard to realise his friend's lips were moving, rapidly, as if delivering a crazed and mute incantation? How long had it taken him to realise Moreau wasn't dead or dying but gazing at something inside the car? Then, it had all happened quickly. He'd seen the bloody cradle, failed to find the baby's face, mentally processed how his shot had gone through the woman's body and hit the child in the head, felt his legs give way and collapsed onto the hot tarmac, sick. Five years he'd been a cop, but he'd never shot at anyone until then, let alone killed anyone, and when Moreau had regained his voice and told what he'd seen, Lombard wouldn't have it, assumed Moreau was trying to comfort or cover for a friend and colleague.

'Mais putain, Laurent! I'm telling you! She went straight for the kid. She never went for me...'

Lombard was convinced that if that was so, if she had indeed shot the child, it was only because he'd got her before she could aim and had pulled the trigger on being hit.

'No! She fired before you...'

'How can you be so damn sure...'

'I was standing right there. I...'

Their hearts were pumping, their blood rushing. They had begun to fight, been forcibly pulled apart by the others. But Moreau was right. The woman's gun was still warm when they thought of examining it. She had fired it. And later, ballistics confirmed the child had been shot with her gun. And later still, forensics revealed she was on speed, had not eaten for at least 48 hours, and that the child had already been dead for a few hours at the time it was shot. The two kilos of cocaine they were after were found in its abdomen, in two one-kilo bags, and some of its organs had been removed – possibly to make room for the drug – though none of the vital ones; indeed, it was established that the surgery had been the work of an expert, that the child had survived the operation, died only later as the result of an internal haemorrhage. The post-mortem examination of its body had only been carried out because of its scarred and distended stomach. The scar was still raw, the stitches still in place.

People were shocked. Explanations had been sought, hypotheses put forward, especially after it was also determined that the woman and child were not related. In the end, for lack of any other answers, everyone had settled for the theory that the child had been either bought or kidnapped so as to serve several useful purposes, from supplying a secure cover – who would suspect a woman with child of smuggling drugs – and providing the most unthinkable and therefore safest hiding place, to generating income as a living organ donor, which would probably have brought in as much money as the drug it was carrying. There had been a lot of talk about the business of organ trafficking, of living organ donors, about how lucrative and, if not widespread, how recognised it was. This was all new to Lombard. At first, he'd rejected the mere idea of it, but then he had been shown a few dossiers, been brought together with a few people in the know, and like everyone else, had eventually come to accept the agreed theory, although in his case it was more a question of resignation than conviction. He needed something to give the events some sense and, however hard he'd tried, it had proved beyond him to come up with any other explanation for what had been done to the child, or for José's woman's actions.

The way the theory went, as the bloodstained passport they found in the convertible described her as the child's mother, she would not have panicked if the child had still been alive when they'd stopped her, would have let them search her and the car, confident the drug couldn't be found and she was safe. In the event of the baby's scar being noticed, she'd probably have had a ready and convincing explanation. And in the event of finding herself threatened with detention for a thorough examination, so that her car could be taken apart and it could be determined that she had not swallowed the drug to get it through customs, she'd have raised hell, invoking her child's welfare and, if all else failed, demanded she be allowed to have someone come and take the child away. And it would probably have worked, the drugs would not have been found and she would have walked away. But since the child was dead, it couldn't work. Perhaps, for a time anyhow, people might have thought it was sleeping, as Lombard and

Moreau had done, but eventually someone would have realised something was wrong. Babies cry, or certainly don't sleep for hours on end. So what had happened in her head when she found herself surrounded with armed police? Had she guessed they'd been tipped-off and in her drug-induced panic decided that shooting the child was her best option? That once it had died so violently no one would think of opening its body? Would she have claimed it was an accident, that she was going for Moreau, had missed, pulled the trigger at the wrong moment? Did she think she could have got away with it, would have received a more lenient sentence for unintentionally killing her child while attempting to shoot a police officer than she'd get for the ghastly crime she was really perpetrating? She certainly wouldn't have looked as bad, might even have secured some sympathy. Starving and intoxicated, sitting in front of a dead baby stuffed with cocaine, she just might have thought something like that when finding herself confronted by police; unless of course, like Moreau before her, when he was approaching the baby, she had not thought at all, simply followed instinct, in a moment of madness sought to destroy the evidence of her wrongdoing, like children do when caught red-handed.

Whatever the truth, it was never established, and Lombard was never able to think of those events in a way that satisfied him. At best, he'd come up with a long list of questions; like why didn't she cancel her trip and turn back when she realised the child was dead? Was she trying to salvage the situation? To cut her losses? Did she believe that by going ahead she could still sell the child, get a good price before its organs became useless? The fact was, for all anyone knew, she didn't even know the child was dead; for all anyone knew, it had died quietly in the cradle behind her as she drove and she was still unaware of it. But crazed on speed or not, no one believed she'd shot it by accident while attempting to kill Moreau. Surrounded with armed men as she was, it would have been suicidal for her to go for Moreau. And if she had resolved to end it all in a blaze of glory, as people sometimes do, she'd have gone for Lombard, who stood to the side in front of her; she wouldn't have needed to turn to face the back of the car to fire at him, might even have had time to shoot someone else as well before anyone could react. Be that as it may, that was how it had begun.

'*La revanche est un plat qui se mange froid*', read the note Lombard had received a few days later.

It was simply signed 'José'. Lombard hadn't known it yet, but, although he had no qualms about letting her do his dirty work or putting her life at risk, José loved his woman deeply. And José, secure somewhere in Spain, was convinced that the facts as reported by the press of the day were a lie, that his woman had been set-up, cold-bloodedly executed by the colleagues of the cops he'd killed a couple of years earlier. Lombard had hardly paid the note any attention. At that time, he was still recovering from his first 'kill', and still receiving praise from his colleagues for his swift reaction. For, whatever people thought, no one was really sure what José's woman might have done had he not fired so quickly after seeing her silver gun gleaming in the sunshine. And of course, of them all, Moreau was the most grateful. After all, had Lombard not reacted when he did, Moreau might have been her next target once she'd dispatched the child.

By seven o'clock, Deborah De Moraes had still not called, Lombard had run out of cigarettes and his grim thoughts finally forced him to sit up. For the past hour he'd tried to bring Leonard, Mr. and Mrs. Spitz, Mrs. De Moraes and Friedman to the fore of his mind, but they just wouldn't stay there, became blurred and turned, like composite characters, into Moreau, José's woman and the others. The traffic outside his window was increasing now, would soon bring the morning rush-hour, and, more than cigarettes perhaps, he needed to do something to unchain his mind. He stepped out into the corridor after instructing the hotel switchboard to transfer any calls to the restaurant. He missed the sight and sound of people, had to connect with the outside world again.

It was the right thing to do. He found the ground floor restaurant a quarter full despite the early hour, smelling of fresh coffee and purring to the sound of hushed conversation. For a moment, he even perceived the soft clatter of the cutlery and crockery in the hands of the breakfasting clientèle, and by the time the blond waitress in her frilled apron who had welcomed him with a smile invited him to sit down at a small corner table, his mind was free, his night come to an end. The waitress even managed to get a grin out of him.

'I suppose you don't sell Gitanes in this place,' he said.

'Er... I don't think so but we could always get some for you if you wish, sir.'

'You could, eh?' he grunted.

'I'm sure it could be arranged,' she returned, her lips set in a conspiratorial smile, eyes aglow.

Lombard found himself peering at her. She was in her late teens, had soft sensual cheeks and a wide engaging mouth. She'd obviously found his grunt amusing, could see he'd had a bad night and either jumped to the wrong conclusion as to the cause of it or her winsome smile was just her way of dealing with prickly early morning customers.

He grinned, involuntarily, won over by her charm:

'Well, then I'll have a couple of packs. Untipped, please...'

She duly delivered them a little later, still smiling. Eating his breakfast, Lombard barely glanced at her. The interlude was over, his day had begun and Leonard Spitz once again occupied his thoughts. Now that he had confirmation the Austrian existed, he found it even harder than before to accept that Mrs. Spitz's son could have succeeded in conning his way into being handed the boy he'd seen at the Welsh cottage. As was to be expected, Friedman had behaved cautiously, insisted on checking Lombard's credentials before proceeding with business. Where had Leonard's credentials come from? Did he know a Nathalie? Presuming he did, could he then have handled the puppy conversation? It was unlikely, but it couldn't be ruled out. After all, Lombard had never met Leonard. Perhaps, like many people facing tests and trials, the poor confused little rich boy had discovered a resolve no one knew he possessed, a backbone that neither his reputation nor appearance suggested. In any case, if that was so, Friedman would be able to clear up the matter. And Lombard was intent on meeting Friedman, with or without Deborah De Moraes' money. One of the perks of his job was that as a rule people paid in cash and didn't ask for receipts. The fear of ridicule, embarrassment or scandal kept them from declaring his employ to their accountants or the Inland Revenue and, accordingly, over the years he'd been able to put some cash away for contingencies in a High Street bank's safety deposit box. He'd never bothered to count the total but reckoned it amounted to more than £20,000. At any rate he didn't intend to part with it and, if need be, he could always ask Mr. and Mrs. Spitz to reimburse him. After all, he was tracking Friedman on account of their son, and could conceivably still save his life. If Friedman was indeed responsible for Leonard's disappearance, it could be that he had not killed him yet, but was keeping him alive to make him divulge where he'd hidden the boy.

Because Friedman should be worried about the boy. Feasibly, with proper handling, the latter might be made to reveal where he'd been kept, might be made to talk about what he knew, what he'd seen, and could cause a lot of trouble. One thing was certain: whether or not Leonard was in Friedman's hands, Friedman didn't know about Rhian. Had he done so, Lombard would not have found her, her daughter and the boy alive and well. So either Leonard was dead, or he was defying Friedman's methods of questioning, however unpleasant and compelling they might be. Because Leonard just might be up to keeping his secret, however much pain and fear he was made to endure. After all, hadn't Rhian said he'd found himself a crusade?

Lombard hoped she was right. People on self-appointed crusades might reasonably be the only ones who could be relied upon to suffer torments and tortures without breaking down. If Leonard was determined not to reveal the boy's location, he just might not talk. And not talking just might be the only thing he could still do to remain alive, or at least to postpone his death. Perhaps, by now, Leonard had even figured that much out for himself.

'Would you like some more coffee?'

The waitress was back, no longer smiling but peering at him with raised eyebrows, as if concerned by his dark and stony stare.

'Yes. Thank you,' said Lombard, moving his eyes onto the coffee pot in her hand.

Lighting a cigarette, he observed the dark liquid flowing into his cup.

'Thank you for the cigarettes,' he said.

She smiled again.

'My pleasure,' she replied; 'Is everything to your satisfaction?'

He nodded. She beamed and turned to a nearby table where a smartly dressed old couple sat poring over tourist brochures.

'Would you like some more coffee?'

They would, and asked her if Monday was a good day to go and see the changing of the guard on Whitehall. She didn't know, but offered to find out for them.

'Oh, really,' exclaimed the woman; 'That would be very kind of you.'

They were Americans, all white teeth, tanned skin, silver hair and aplomb. When the waitress had left them the man voiced doubts as to whether the changing of the guard was still performed with all its ceremony when it was raining.

'Don't be silly,' retorted the woman; 'This is England. I don't think the Royal Guard would allow the weather to interfere with their stately duties.'

Lombard peered across the room. It was dawn outside now, the morning wind driving the rain against the windows.

He sugared his coffee and swallowed it in one gulp. Deborah De Moraes would not call now.

The phone in his room rang punctually at eleven o'clock. The voice at the other end of the line was not Friedman's, but that of a man who spoke with what Lombard could only make out as a provincial English accent.

'It's about the puppy. You got the money?'

Sitting on the edge of the bed, Lombard stubbed out his cigarette in the overflowing ashtray on the beside table, eyeing his empty briefcase on the upholstered chair in front of him.

'Yeah,' he said after a moment.

'Right. What time will you be available?'

He needed to go to the bank and…

'Any time after two.'

The man gave him the address of a restaurant in St. John's Wood called Le Mercury and told him to be there at three o'clock.

'Ask for Peter.'

'Peter?'

'Peter.'

Stepping through the Métropole's front door into the renewed downpour that swept Piccadilly felt almost like a deliverance. For a fleeting moment, Lombard even became aware of the warmth gripping his nape and shoulders. He took a few deep breath of fresh air, lit a Gitane under cover of the hotel entrance and set out along the crowded pavement to stretch his legs, delaying hailing a taxi until he got to Cambridge Circus at the top of Shaftesbury Avenue. A little over an hour later, after a detour to his bank near the Angel, he was back in Essex Road, the briefcase in his hand £20,000 heavier, which, by his reckoning, left him with a quarter as much still in his safety deposit box.

As he weaved his way across the road through creeping traffic towards his front door, he wished he had not caught sight of Perkins. But Perkins had seen him and, standing in his apron behind his neon lit butcher's shop window, was gesturing eagerly for him to come in. Lombard wasn't in the mood for Perkins' customary small-talk, thought of ignoring the butcher, tried looking away, but their eyes had met and, all things considered, this was not a good time to risk offending his landlord. Thankfully, a handful of customers stood inside the shop, so whatever Perkins wished to tell him, he'd have to get on with it.

He opened the shop door without stepping inside:

'How are you, Mr. Perkins?'

'I've been better and I've been worse, ha-ha...' replied the butcher. He was chopping a joint of meat with a cleaver, looked his flushed and jolly self.

'And how are you, *Savieer*?'

Lombard grinned. He'd already made out, with some relief, that the customers in the shop were all regulars. At least Perkins would proceed without the ritual introduction he invariably launched into whenever Lombard happened to enter his shop and encounter new faces.

'This is *Monsieer Savieer Lombard*,' the butcher would declare, eyes glinting, in an all but possessive tone of voice; 'He lives upstairs. He's French. From Paris…' It had taken Lombard a while to understand the object of the exercise, until, as it went on, he realised that Perkins was exploiting him as an endorsement of his shop, or, to be more accurate, exploiting his Frenchness to promote his meat. France's reputation for food being what it is, the butcher clearly believed it was good publicity to let people know he had one of its citizens living on the premises, a Frenchman who bought meat from his shop – even if Lombard only very occasionally did so.

'Good. It's Monday and I just wanted to let you know I left a note in your letter box about what we discussed the other night,' Perkins was saying.

Lombard frowned. He couldn't remember discussing anything with him.

'You know? About the rent…'

Lombard remembered now.

'Ah…'

Perhaps oddly for a shopkeeper, Perkins found it hard to discuss money, preferring to deal with such matters in writing.

'Right. I'll have a look at it.'

'I hope it's all right,' said Perkins, smiling almost sheepishly.

Lombard was a good tenant; he paid his rent on time and was a valued member of the football team. For these reasons alone, had he not been a fair landlord, Perkins would have been reluctant to lose him. By however much the butcher had felt compelled to raise his rent, it would be by as little as he deemed necessary.

'I'm sure it is. Thank you,' said Lombard.

Perkins nodded gratefully, Lombard grinned, shut the shop door and turned to his front door, nearly colliding with an umbrella that was held by a woman in a green duffel-coat who stood there. She was looking away from him, ringing his bell, unaware of his presence, and he quickly scrutinised her. She stood tall and slim, with a determined countenance and well-defined features. A few grey strands showed in her curled blond hair but, bar the crow's feet around her eyes and the lines at the corners of her mouth, her skin was smooth, full and untouched by make-up. She was perhaps in her early forties and, judging by the battered brown handbag that hung from her shoulder, the worn wet loafers on her feet and the blue pleated skirt that swung with the wind around her strong calves, she was of modest means and strict character.

'Can I help you?' he asked.

She turned with a start, quickly looked him up and down, briefly fixed her bright blue eyes on the keys in his hand and stepped away from the door as if to let him through.

'Er... I'm sorry. I—I was looking for the *Lombard Detective Agency.*'

Whoever she was, she was not there in any official capacity, canvassing for a religious organisation or collecting for charity. Lombard knew the signs. Her nervousness, her apologetic tone of voice, the way she held her handbag tight against her coat, meant she'd probably come in the hope of hiring him, was uneasy about it and doubtless, like most people, especially those with little money, had thought long and hard before bringing herself to finally make the move.

From professional habit he glanced at her left hand clasped around her handbag. There was no wedding band, no rings of any kind on her fingers.

'I'm Mr. Lombard. What can I do for you, Miss...?' he asked, having already decided that he didn't want a new job, not at the moment anyway.

'Oh...'

She raised her brows, taken aback. Either she was surprised to have bumped into the man she'd come to see, or he didn't live up to her image of a private investigator. Still, she promptly enough regained her composure.

'Er, good afternoon, Mr. Lombard. My name is Miss Johnson. I saw your advertisement in the Yellow Pages. I—I live around the corner and today's my day off and—'

'I understand,' cut in Lombard, curtly; 'What can I do for you, Miss Johnson?'

She pulled her head back and narrowed her eyes, tight-lipped.

'You... You are the Mr. Lombard from the *Lombard Detective Agency,* aren't you?' she queried, fixing her eyes on his keys again.

He'd offended her, could see she was thinking of walking away. He contemplated letting her do so but decided against it. It would have been rude. She'd taken the trouble to come to his office, seemed a responsible woman and, if the absence of a wedding ring on her finger signified anything, she was not a suspicious wife wanting her husband followed.

He checked his watch. It was nearly half past twelve. He'd give her fifteen minutes and send her away.

'I'm sorry,' he said with a conciliatory smile; 'I would just like to know if you wish to see me in a professional capacity, Miss Johnson. I'm quite busy at the moment and...'

'Yes. I had hoped to ask you...' she began before breaking off to say: 'But if you haven't got the time I—'

'Why don't you follow me to my office, Miss Johnson,' he said, already inserting his key in the door. He pushed the door open and took a step back to let her in, half-expecting her to come up with a ready pretext for leaving. But she sent him a stony look, shook her umbrella, folded it and stepped inside.

'Thank you.'

Once upstairs, Lombard told her to take a seat at his desk and, pretending he needed a hot drink, invited her to speak while he went to the kitchen to make some coffee. With time, he'd learnt that as a rule people found it easier to say what they'd come to say if they didn't feel watched or called upon to perform. Left alone to speak, some would find it hard to begin with, but once they were going they forgot their inhibitions and got on with it. If nothing else, they wanted to fill the void around them, and free from constraints, often ended up revealing things they would have found too painful to relate in a face-to-face situation. But mostly, it saved time. Lombard's and theirs.

Miss Johnson wasn't any different. At first awkward and dithering, she soon got into her stride and, taking barely a few minutes, in a composed and concise manner, not once turning to look over her shoulder at Lombard who observed her from the kitchen, made known what had brought her to see him on her day off.

She was a nurse, had been for the past twenty years, the last four of which had seen her employed in a private ward of the Royal Free Hospital in South End Green. A few months earlier a male patient, who was a writer by profession, had been admitted to her ward after being diagnosed with a cancer of the stomach and intestine. This patient was a healthy forty-year-old and, since his illness had been caught at a relatively early stage, his future well-being was not in too much doubt. As she explained, caught early, cancers of the digestive system are comparatively easy to treat, seldom proving fatal, and in this case it had appeared to be a straightforward situation requiring removal of the cancerous tissue. However, despite three such operations in succession and intensive chemotherapy, the patient's health had continued to deteriorate, his cancer forever developing as if unchecked. In all her years of experience Miss Johnson had never seen anything like it. It was, she said, as if he was not being treated at all, as if the operations and treatment were having no effect whatsoever, and in her opinion, the patient's cancer could not have spread any faster had he just been left to die. As time had passed, however much she fought the notion, Miss Johnson had come to suspect, and finally to conclude, that this just might be what was happening – that the doctor looking after her patient was letting the man die while ostensibly endeavouring to treat him. She felt no animosity towards the doctor, she hastened to point out; on the contrary, the man was an esteemed practitioner with an impeccable record and, in the years she had known him, had never once behaved with impropriety, proving himself at all times a kind and fair man. But in the face of what was happening, she could not help but think his failure to remove her patient's cancerous tissue was wilful. It was the only explanation for the progressive deterioration of the man's health, and since the doctor was far too experienced to make such a blunder acciden-tally, especially on three consecutive occasions, Miss Johnson had to assume it was indeed intentional. She concluded by declaring that, in order to allay her doubts, she would like to hire Lombard to discreetly investigate the doctor so as to establish if he might have any motive for wishing this particular patient dead, expressing the sentiment that, if her suspicions were right, the man's actions had to be motivated by something as momentous as it was specific.

'Doctors are simply not in the habit of letting their patients die,' she stressed; 'And before you suggest it,' she went on, 'Please believe me when I tell you that I did of course consider sharing my concerns with the police, the appropriate medical authorities and the patient's relatives. But as things are, I have no evidence, only doubts, and it would be improper for me to go public with such defamatory allegations against a reputable doctor without being absolutely certain of what I suspect. It would cause too much distress. To the patient and his family. To the doctor and his family. To the hospital and to myself. If nothing else, I would most certainly never find a position as a nurse again.'

Lombard had never before been approached with such an odd story. He settled opposite her with his coffee, lit a cigarette and observed her across the desk between them. She stared at her hands clutching the handbag on her lap, looking calm and composed, except for the constant flutter of her batting eyelids.

'Tell me something, Miss Johnson?' he asked; 'Would you happen to know if your patient and his doctor are acquainted outside their doctor-patient relationship?'

She looked up:

'No, they're not.'

'Are you sure?'

'Yes. Well, if they are neither of them ever said or did anything to suggest they were.'

Lombard sighed.

'I see. So, Miss Johnson, what in your opinion might motivate a reputable doctor to...'

He broke off, thought about it, then said it anyway:

'... to murder an innocent patient?'

She looked away from him, back at her hands, batting her eyelids again.

'It stands to reason that I don't know the answer to that, Mr. Lombard,' she declared; 'I wouldn't be a nurse if I believed it made sense for doctors to murder their patients.'

He took a drag of his cigarette, asked:

'I take it the patient in question is not a friend of yours either, is that right, Miss Johnson?'

She looked up, surprised:

'No. He is not.'

Lombard nodded his imperceptible nod.

'And yet you are proposing to spend your own money to—'

'I know,' she cut in; 'I know what it looks like, Mr. Lombard.

But what if I'm right? Wouldn't you like to find out if you were right in my position? Wouldn't you have to? Well, I'm just a nurse. That's why I'm here. Perhaps someone like you might help me find out.'

Lombard refrained from asking what she thought he could do to help her. Had she already written down the name and address of the doctor for him? Was it in her handbag…?

He didn't know what to make of Miss Johnson. She might have it in for the doctor, might be serenely mad, or a most remarkable woman. He couldn't tell. He couldn't read her, could only see the obvious: that she was poor and probably lived alone in a small flat a bit like his own. And for some reason, he also guessed she'd always live alone. It was something in the way she held herself, something in her expression. She looked modest but not timid, detached but not distant, sullen but not bitter. Just self-contained. Yet she was attractive, in a cold kind of way, and had probably once been one of those tall slim young blondes who draw envy and jealousy for their looks. Even her hands were pleasant, smooth and slender with long fingers. How many of the people that she knew wondered what was wrong with her? That was often what happened to good-looking women who reached her age still living alone. People couldn't help wondering what was wrong with them. Was that why she was still only a nurse after twenty years? Because people thought there was something wrong with her?

'I'd rather not not waste your money, Miss Johnson,' he said; 'For one thing, I'm quite busy right now, for another, I'm a private detective, not the police. I don't really know what I could do for you even if I did take your money. I understand your reasons for not wanting to voice your suspicions openly and sympathise with your situation, but I'm afraid that what you propose is not something I can take on. Besides, presuming you're right and your doctor does indeed have a motive for letting his patient die, I should think it might take some time to find out what it is. And from what you say, I guess his patient hasn't got that long to live, am I right?'

She looked more saddened than disappointed, swallowed hard, composed herself and stood up.

'I should think he still has a few months to live, but anyway,' she said, somewhat loftily; 'Well, I'm sorry to have taken so much of your time, Mr. Lombard.'

'And I'm sorry I cannot be of more assistance, Miss Johnson,' he replied, standing up; 'But I tell you what,' he went on helpfully; 'If you still feel like pursuing this in a couple of weeks, or stumble onto something a little more tangible to be going on with perhaps, why don't you come back and see me then. Otherwise, of course, there are other detective agencies that might be willing to—'

He broke off as his front doorbell rang. He apologised and looked out the window. A blue Aston Martin sat double-parked in front of Perkins' shop, blocking the traffic.

'Just in time it seems,' he heard Miss Johnson say behind him.

He turned around with a frown. She was already making for the door.

'It's all right. I can find my way out, Mr. Lombard.'

'Yes. Goodbye…'

The bell rang again as she opened the door.

'Would you be kind enough to leave the door open and tell the lady downstairs to come up to the first floor when you leave, Miss Johnson?' he called after her.

'Of course,' she replied; 'Goodbye.'

Watching her tall body disappear into the stairwell, Lombard guessed he would not see her again. Was she going to try another detective? Or would she now tell herself that she had done what she could and stop worrying about her patient, convince herself that her suspicions were misguided? He still didn't know what to make of her. Or of her *Just in time it seems*. Had it been sarcasm?

His bell rang again.

'Mr. Lombard asked me to tell you to go up to the first floor,' he heard Miss Johnson's distant voice say from the stairwell.

'Oh. Right. Thank you,' replied Deborah De Moraes.

He sat at his desk and waited, listening to the sound of his visitor's heels clip-clopping against the wooden stairs, wondering what was bringing her. Out in the street, the drivers caught in the congestion caused by her car were beginning to honk their horns. Lombard raised his brows, stubbed out his cigarette and lit another as Deborah De Moraes appeared in the doorway and stopped.

Holding onto a Marks & Spencer's carrier bag, wearing pearls and dressed impeccably in a becoming pink skirt-suit, sheer stockings and black shoes, she managed to send him a cold look at the same time as giving his office a critical glance.

'How are you, Mrs. De Moraes?' he said, remaining in his chair; 'Why don't you come in?'

She eyed him, reluctantly started across the room and flung the Marks & Spencer's bag onto the desk in front of him.

'I still don't buy your story but I figured it can't do any harm to let you get on with trying to find my brother. Besides, if you do turn out to be nothing but a cheap little extortioner, we could always get the right people onto you. I trust you know who I'm talking about.'

Lombard glanced inside the bag. It contained several bundles of pristine £50 notes. He grinned and looked up. It seemed he wasn't the only one to have had a bad night. In the crude light of day from the window behind him, she looked rough under her make-up, and for the first time, Lombard noticed the dusky down shading the olive skin near her ears. But her eyes were as brazen as ever, her seemingly immovable sneer just beneath her full lips, awaiting.

'You drive a hard bargain,' he said, grinning; 'May I ask to what the change of heart is owed, Mrs. De Moraes? Did you watch the tape perhaps?'

She frowned, opened her mouth to speak, wavered and changed her mind, asking instead:

'So I take it I'm not too late…'

'Too late for what, Mrs. De Moraes?'

The sneer came out.

'What do you think? Christmas? Look, as you seem to be accepting my money, am I right in concluding you haven't yet broken contact with the Austrian you say might know something about my brother, Mr. detective?'

He frowned. After what had happened the previous evening he had better not let her steal his self-control again, voluptuous petulance or not. She just might decide to change her mind again and walk away with her money. He let his eyes linger on the pearls around her neck, sent her his most charming smile.

'I haven't yet broken contact with the Austrian, Mrs. De Moraes.'

'Good,' she said; 'So now you've got what you wanted you can go to work. I'll be waiting to hear from you.'

She left without shutting the door behind her and clip-clopped down the stairs.

He leaned back to look out of the window. Her Aston Martin had practically brought the road to a standstill. A couple of schoolboys peered in through its windows, a small gathering of onlookers across the street stared their disapproval at it and, beside it, Perkins stood talking to a couple of woman, hands on hips, the rain bouncing against his bald head and Brylcreamed lock of hair. Deborah De Moraes walked past him into the street and got into her car without a glance or a word for anyone or anything and drove off. Lombard pulled himself away from the window as Perkins turned round to look up towards his flat.

Deborah De Moraes had watched the tape. He was convinced of it. Had she watched the whole thing though?

He checked his watch. It was just after one. He hadn't got much time left. He peered at the Marks & Spencer's bag, took a drag from his cigarette, heard it hiss as he dipped it in his cold coffee, ran his hands over his face, took a deep breath and pulled a sheet of paper from his desk drawer. He would have to take a taxi to St. John's Wood, he thought, realising that this was one area of London he knew only by name, having never even driven through it.

He wrote down all he'd learnt about Friedman and Leonard and his boy, from Rhian's address to the telephone number of the woman who had put him through to the Austrian, to the name of the restaurant he was about to call at. It filled a page, which he put in an envelope addressed to Deborah De Moraes. He placed this envelope into another on which he scrawled a note for Jane:

'Dear Jane, a little favour. If I'm not back or you haven't heard from me by the time you leave for work tomorrow morning, please send the enclosed letter by express messenger. Xavier.'

He then went to lock his front door, stepped into his bedroom, pushed the wardrobe away from its corner, pulled up the carpet and, kneeling, removed the corner floorboards. The leather bag he'd put there the day he'd moved into the flat still sat between the main beams, dark and dusty. The sight of it gave him a hollow in his chest, something close to quiet anger, and he gazed at it for a moment before he could bring himself to pull it up and shake the dust from it.

He'd forgotten this was where he'd put his old leather jacket. He pulled it out and peered inside the bag. Amidst the jumble of loose French bank notes, passports, identity cards, driving licences and cartons of bullets, he couldn't see his Beretta or its silencer. He plunged his hand into the bag and felt around until his fingers met the cold metal of the handgun, then of the silencer. He checked the Beretta magazine was loaded, put it aside and, as he was about to put back the leather jacket, caught sight of his wedding band against the dark blue plastic cover of an old French passport. He hesitated, stuffed his jacket into the bag, then changed his mind and got the ring out after all.

Why did Miss Johnson come to his mind as he played with it between his fingers? Unlike the cold metal of the gun, the band of gold felt warm. In the end, still unsure, he put it on his finger, peered at it a little longer, and decided to keep it on.

At 14:50, showered, in a clean suit and carrying his briefcase, he climbed out of a black cab across the road from Le Mercury in St. John's Wood, having fed his goldfish and slid the envelope containing his letter for Deborah De Moraes under Jane's door before leaving.

Standing on the kerb in the rain he surveyed the restaurant's elegant pale green facade. Adorned with hanging flower baskets, it stood between a Pizzeria and a Turkish restaurant, indistinguishable from the many other eating places that lined the busy pavement, except perhaps by the intricate thermometer-shaped sign that climbed high above its dark windows with what appeared to be mercury steadily rising and falling in its central tube. Lombard ran his eyes over a white Mercedes parked outside its door, peered at the young man with a crew-cut who sat at the wheel reading a tabloid while absent-mindedly running a finger to and fro along his white shirt collar.

He sighed and started across the street.

'We open at six,' said the lonely barman as Lombard stepped through the door. In the dim light of the ceiling spotlights he was polishing wine glasses behind the bar.

'Peter?' said Lombard, across the empty tables.

The barman eyeballed him, then motioned to a table deep inside the room. There sat – Lombard had already seen her – the only other person present, a blond woman in a suit. She was nibbling from a plate of salad while talking into a cell-phone and she too had already seen Lombard. Without interrupting her phone conversation, she sent him a pearly white smile.

Lombard sent the barman a stony grin.

EIGHT

'Five to three. You're early…'

She had glanced at her wristwatch, and now the brown eyes which looked out at the world with blunt confidence from beneath her neat plucked brows were quietly assessing him. She must have been in her late forties, had permed dyed blond hair, and although she appeared statuesque, even sitting, her high cheekbones were the only sharp features left in what had undoubtedly at one time been a handsome if sallow face, but now had the bloated appearance that results from too much of a good time, too many late nights and a penchant for strong drink.

'Should I come back in five minutes?' he said.

She scoffed, causing her fringe and pearl drop earrings to flutter, glanced at his briefcase and gestured towards the seat across the table with a smile which, he guessed, was meant to be enticing.

'May I offer you a drink?'

'What happened to Peter?' he asked without moving.

'I am Peter.'

He frowned, nodded his nod and sat down, putting his brief-case up on the table.

'I'd like to see what I'm buying,' he declared.

She raised her brows, amused.

'*Chaque chose en son temps, Monsieur Marchand,*' she said, in a flawless accent.

With another smile she got hold of her fork and casually resumed eating her salad with smooth and easy movements.

'What about that drink?'

'No,' he said.

She raised her brows again, forked aside a piece of green lettuce, stabbed a slice of cucumber and put it between her white teeth.

'I gather we've done business with a friend of yours,' she said eventually, after swallowing.

'Have you?'

'The person who put us in touch seems to think so.'

Was that what Nathalie had told her contact?

'I don't recollect mentioning a friend,' he said.

'Really?'

She swallowed a slice of tomato, put her fork down and pushed her plate aside, dabbed her lips with a napkin, drank some mineral water, dabbed her lips again, reached for the briefcase, turned it around, opened it just enough to glimpse inside, turned it back towards him and reached for a packet of cigarettes from the table.

'Your lady friend did,' she remarked, putting a tipped cigarette between her thin lips.

He watched her light it. He was still unable to grasp all the nuances of the many English accents but was convinced hers was upper-middle-class. In any case, it suited her quiet countenance, the casualness with which she sat in her elegant grey linen suit and the simple tastefulness of her probably expensive jewellery. What was such a woman doing working for child procurers? She couldn't be one of the top people, or she wouldn't be charged with the task of handling interviews. Even crooks don't much enjoy the company of perverts, especially not those on the highest rungs of the hierarchy. Had this outwardly refined lady fallen on hard times and become an easy recruit for Friedman? If that was so, the chances were she'd started as a consumer and, like a drug addict, had drifted into the business side of things in order to support her vice. Unless of course it was simply a case of greed, the lure of gain. Whatever, she was perfect for the task. Her polished voice and manner were definitely a plus, gave the whole thing a friendly air of respectability; *one* could almost forget what *one* was talking about.

'The lady's not a friend. She's a whore,' he said deliberately, looking coldly back at her as she snapped her lighter shut; 'Someone at a special screening I attended in Paris mentioned certain goods could be got from an Austrian here in London. And not just movies. The person in question was no more a friend than the whore you just referred to.'

Her eyes scrutinised him, gleaming with detached indifference. This was just a sport for her. She was suspicious because she had to be. He could only be one of two things: a mug willing to part with good money to indulge in depravity; or a threat – some undercover operative for the cops or another gang. But he knew that unless he said the wrong thing, she'd settle for the mug, had probably already done so, especially now she'd seen Deborah De Moraes' wads of crisp £50 notes.

She glanced at the wedding band around his finger. He saw it register in her eyes. He was definitely a mug. He swallowed hard. He'd put it on for effect, but still…

'And while visiting our fair city, you decided to—' she began.

'That's right,' he cut in, saving her the trouble of finishing her sentence.

She nodded.

'An Austrian?'

'An Austrian,' he stated.

'An Austrian… Not much to go on, is it?' she remarked; 'Wouldn't it have been more sensible to get a name or contact number rather than relying on… let us say a whore to hunt around town for you?'

'Questions can amount to revelations,' he replied, showing impatience; 'As I already said, Peter or whoever you are, the person who told me about the Austrian was not a friend.'

'I understand,' she said, smiling her enticing smile again – or was it in truth more of a condescending smile; 'But, this person who happens not to be a friend, you wouldn't happen to have a name for him, by any chance?'

'It's a "her",' he replied, just to contradict her.

'Well, him or her, what does it matter? Everybody has a name.'

He sighed:

'Look, I'd hate to think I was made to come here carrying a substantial amount of money in cash in order to be subjected to a cross-examination. Last night Mr. Friedman led me to believe we had a deal. Do we? Because if we don't, I'd sooner be elsewhere than sitting here chatting with you. No offence meant.'

She frowned, slightly intrigued by his open antagonism, which was what he'd hoped for. With the exception of working prostitutes who stand at the receiving end of things, people who trade sex, from pimps to pornographers, tend to deal with a predominantly timid clientèle who, driven as they may be by the need to satisfy their lust, cannot help but feel exposed and vulnerable while acting upon it in public. Lust or not, decency, which some elect to dismiss as inhibition, can prove a resilient constant, can prove awkward and compelling, and breed the kind of shyness that allows the staff who man sex-shops, peep show venues and the like to earn a great deal more from short-changing their customers than from their wages. How many good citizens in the process of paying for their forthcoming hard-on take the trouble to check their change? And if they do, perhaps afterwards, and realise they've been conned, how many dare make a fuss or call attention to themselves? When they've got what they wanted. However, that was the lot of small fish. The big ones, the ones ready to cough up a small fortune in their quest for gratification, need not act shyly. On the contrary, it might be ill-advised, might look suspicious. Money must come with contempt, or at least self-assurance, otherwise...

Probing him, 'Peter' seemed to agree, seemed reassured...

'Will you be alone?' she asked.

'I'm sorry?'

'The merchandise,' she explained; 'Is it just for you or—'

'I'll be alone.'

'Good. Then all that is left before we can proceed is for you to allow us to make sure you're not wired to any listening or viewing devices.'

He just frowned. He'd expected something like this. And she grinned, took a drag of her cigarette, misread his silence and felt it necessary to gesture she was sorry but...

'You see, ordinarily, clients come with an endorsement that's a little more... Well, anyhow, it's just routine, really. A simple search. I know it might appear unseemly—you're the paying customer—but once this slight hindrance is out of the way, let me assure you there will be no more obstacles to worry about. You will select your merchandise and, apart from the small matter of the blindfold for your journey to—'

'What?'

She'd become blurred all of a sudden. He heard his heartbeat. He felt his numb temples, felt the blood beat against the bones beneath the skin and the void in his chest.

'You must be taken to another location,' he heard her say.

She was coming back into focus.

'Is that a problem?' she asked, peering strangely into his eyes.

He looked hard at her. He was himself again, was one with it again.

'Where are you proposing to carry out your simple search?' he asked.

'Here. And you needn't worry,' she added with a coy smile; 'It won't be myself but a man...'

He glanced at his briefcase.

'That's fine but not the blindfold part of it.'

'I beg your pardon?'

'I can't let you blindfold me.'

'It is not—'

'I can't let you blindfold me,' he reiterated.

'Well, I'm afraid—'

'Am I to be taken away from here in a car?'

'Yes...'

'Then if you like I'll lie on the floor. But there's no way I can let you blindfold me.'

She'd lived long and well enough to know not to ask why. She knew he wouldn't tell her.

'It's that or I walk away,' he said.

She nodded, thought, then explained that what he proposed might be acceptable for the car journey but not on arrival at their destination.

'It would be preferable for all concerned if you were not to know where you are to be taken, you understand? One never knows what the future may hold...'

He didn't want to do this, but he grabbed his briefcase, stood up, turned and started towards the door.

'Would a blanket over your head make any difference, Mr. Marchand?' she called after him.

He stopped, thought, turned back. He'd see his feet. He'd see the floor. He'd see something...

She was smiling again.

'What's the matter? Afraid of the dark?'

He grinned, coldly, then scowled at the barman who was

watching him with a self-important smirk while still polishing glasses. The man looked slowly away, and, turning back to the woman who was now busy dialling on her cell-phone, Lombard finally took time to survey the dining room. The tables were dressed in pale green tablecloths adorned with slender silver vessels each holding a single red rose. One of the chrome-coloured walls displayed an elaborate thermometer-shaped sign like the one outside, except that this one was more intricate, the words 'Le Mercury' twinkling on and off in a dim copper light as the mercury-like substance in its central tube rose and fell.

'It's time,' she said into her phone and, a moment later, the young man with the crew-cut he'd spotted outside in the Mercedes came through the door and led Lombard into the restaurant toilets where he asked him to undress down to his underpants and shirt. Satisfied he was clean, the man then led the way out into the street and to the white Mercedes in the back of which 'Peter' the woman was awaiting. He opened the car's rear door, motioned Lombard to get in beside her and went to settle behind the wheel. Lombard had not uttered one word to him, he had barely pronounced three sentences, and they'd each avoided the other's eyes. He was very young and this was clearly just a job to him, and not one he seemed to enjoy much at that.

'Here you are,' said the woman; 'Take your pick.'
Now clad in a fine black coat with a fur collar, she held out towards him a deck of Polaroids. Lombard peered at the solitaire on her finger, reached for the photographs and, tight-lipped, gazed at the one that was showing. A young Asian-looking boy, very much like the one he'd seen at Rhian's, looked back at him. He stood naked against a dark backdrop, the flash from the camera reflecting crudely against his bare dusky skin. A number '1' was scrawled with a felt-tip pen on the white strip beneath the print. Lombard frowned and started slowly shuffling through the rest of the deck.

In all, there were six photographs, each numbered, each showing a naked boy. Each one stood against the same dark background, docile and limp, their ages ranging from about seven to eleven, and as they unfolded before his eyes, Lombard became aware of the sweet scent worn by the woman beside him. Combined with the heady smell of the car's leather upholstery, it created a sense a well-being, and Lombard felt compelled to turn away to the life on the other side of his window.

'So this is St. John's Wood,' he said silently to himself, gazing through the rain at the frantic street outside. The shops, the restaurants, the crawling traffic and the passers-by defying the blustery weather might as well have been in Hampstead, Islington or anywhere else in North London. He gazed at a young woman struggling to fit a small Christmas tree into the trunk of her car, then at a tall bearded man who had just stepped out of a Wine Bar. He wore a fur-lined buckskin coat similar to the one Lombard owned, the one he'd bought at Jones Brothers. Had his also been described as a 'car coat'? Did his also let in water at the seams?...

'Is something wrong?' he heard the woman enquire behind him.

'Number six,' he said, handing the Polaroid's back without looking at her. He didn't want her to see the expression in his eyes. He didn't want to have to talk to her. He'd save his feelings for Friedman.

'Right,' she said; 'Let's go, John.'

A moment later, as the Mercedes pulled out into the traffic, she spoke into her cell-phone:

'Number six. We're on our way.'

After a short stop in a quiet street to allow the woman to move to the front and Lombard to lie face down on the back seat – he was too big to fit in the space between the seats – the journey went smoothly, passed in complete silence and lasted a little under an hour. Lombard didn't bother to peek or guess where he was being taken. It wasn't necessary, he didn't plan on having to retrace his steps, and, staring at the carpet behind the driver's seat, he let himself go into a thoughtless daze, lulled by the smooth motion of the car. He welcomed the rest, both mental and physical, so much so that by the time they reached their destination and, as he'd been warned would happen, a small dark blanket was thrown over his head, he no longer felt the effects of his sleepless night, felt calm, which was just as well since he might otherwise have let his displeasure at being unceremoniously grabbed by the arm and dragged out of the car get the better of him. Moreover, since he had to concentrate on keeping his eyes on his shoes, he could do without the distraction of emotion.

'Just walk,' said the man leading him forward across a wet pavement. Together with the deep voice which had come from high up, the heavy steps and the strength and size of the grip around Lombard's arm suggested a tall and muscular individual. They stepped through a door and onto a red-tiled floor, went up a small flight of steps, past what sounded like the din from a restaurant or canteen kitchen, went around one corner and along a green linoleum floor, moved through a swing door, climbed several flights of brown carpeted stairs, marched along a corridor likewise carpeted and, after turning through a doorway, finally came to a stop on a garish maroon and red patterned carpet. Lombard heard the door slam shut behind him, felt the hand around his arm release its grip and squinted in the bright glow of a neon light as the blanket was pulled from his head.

'I hope your journey wasn't too unpleasant,' said a man with piercing blue eyes sitting across a table in a dark pullover with rolled-up sleeves.

He was stocky, thick-necked and pot-bellied. His voice and accent were the same as those of the man who'd called him at the Métropole in the morning to fix the meeting with Peter. Lombard silently returned his probing glance, ran his eyes over his weather-beaten face, rested his gaze on the receding red hair combed back above his broad forehead, and turned to observe the room around him.

It was small, bleak and impersonal. The curtains were drawn. A dark wardrobe filled one corner and a washbasin another, its pedestal rising beside a metal wastepaper bin of the kind found in cheap hotels. Otherwise, bar the table and chair occupied by the pullover man, it contained only a single bed, all but dwarfed by the massive bulk of a man in a tight grey suit and black shirt who sank into rather than sat on its mustard-coloured mattress, quietly folding the small blanket which a moment earlier had been over Lombard's head. This was clearly the person with the strong grip and heavy step who had escorted him from the Mercedes, but even though Lombard had guessed he was big, he was still somewhat amazed to see how huge the man really was. Indeed, he belonged to that category of individuals one marvels at, wondering where they can possibly find clothes to fit, seeing only their bodies and eyes, the rest being somehow obliterated by their formidable bulk and the worrying dimness that burns in their eyes.

This fine specimen of manhood greeted Lombard's gaze with a stony nod and a grimace that could just about pass for a smile. He was clearly not the person to talk to.

'Where is Mr. Friedman?' asked Lombard, turning away from him.

'Mr. Friedman's otherwise engaged,' replied the pullover man. Lombard frowned.

'What happens now?'

'We conclude our transaction.'

'Do we?'

'Uh-huh.'

'No more unpleasant journeys?'

'No more unpleasant journeys.'

He grinned. This was not what he had envisaged. At this point, he was meant to have got together with Friedman, not these two. He thought, quickly, then stepped forward, put his briefcase on the table, opened it and swivelled it around towards the pullover man. It pained him to part with the money but, in the circumstance, there was not much else he could do. He had better use it to buy himself time to reassess the situation.

'I'd like to hang onto the case,' he said.

The pullover man smiled, nodded, peered at the cash, picked up a wad, pulled out one note, examined it up against the light and, satisfied, began to transfer the rest of the money onto the table, saying in a toneless voice:

'The room is yours for 24 hours. It's soundproofed, stocked up with food, drink and other things you might find useful. You can do anything you like.'

'Anything at all?'

'Anything at all,' confirmed the pullover man; 'I presume you won't want to take the boy with you when you're finished?'

Lombard didn't reply, just watched the man snap the briefcase shut and push it back towards him.

'There's a £500 fee for disposal. The boy is yours, you understand?'

He nodded, jaws clenched, then couldn't help himself:

'What if I leave him behind in a useful condition? Do I get a £500 refund?'

The man scowled, scrutinised him, broke into a grin.

'Well, we could always sort something out... *Vous êtes Français?*'

From the inflection he'd used, this one had definitely not learnt his French at school...

'Does it matter?'

The man eyeballed him again, without hostility, just curious, then smiled and casually motioned towards the giant:

'He'll take you to the boy,' he said, replacing the note he'd inspected in the wad it came from; 'Don't forget your briefcase...'

His fingers were already racing expertly through the notes, his lips already silently counting.

Lombard picked up his briefcase and followed the giant, noting the number '40' on the door in gold figures as he stepped out and into a long corridor lined on both side with yet more numbered doors.

'This way,' said the giant, turning towards a dark, rain-lashed window at one end of the corridor.

The other direction led to a stairwell, probably the one they'd used on their way up. Lombard followed on the giant's heels, past numbers 42 and 44, and stopped past number 46 as the other pulled a key from his pocket in front of number 48. A 'Do Not Disturb' sign hung from its handle and, as the giant bowed his massive frame to unlock it, Lombard saw the embossed lines of a strap across the man's back under the stretched-tight fabric of his jacket. He was wearing a holster.

'I'll lock behind you. Pick up the intercom if you need anything, all right?'

He held the door open, had moved aside and was waiting for Lombard to step inside.

Lombard peered through the door into a narrow corridor that led to another door, which was padded and shut; he looked up into the giant's vacant eyes, grinned, and stepped inside. He stopped as the door came shut behind him, listened to the sound of a key turning in the lock, waited a few seconds, lit a Gitane and made for the padded door.

First he heard the unmistakable voice of Bugs Bunny, then his eyes met the cartoon character himself on a huge flickering television screen, and then he saw the boy.

Whether or not this was boy number six, he couldn't tell. But he was a boy, he was Asian and, perched on an armchair in front of the television in a stripy T-shirt, short trousers and plimsolls, he gazed straight back at Lombard with placid eyes, his thin arms resting on his chair's armrests, looking barely eight years old in the light from the large chandelier above his head.

Standing in the doorway, a stretch of emerald green carpet between them, Lombard took a drag from his cigarette and called loudly over the sound of the television:

'Do you speak English?'

The boy just frowned.

'Français?' he tried.

The same frown suggested it was no use. He smiled, stepped inside and shut the padded door, turning his attention to the room.

The pullover man had not exaggerated when he'd said the room would be stocked with food, drink and other things he might need. Had he been a customer, Lombard would doubtless have been more than pleasantly surprised by the windowless environment that sprawled around the boy, would definitely have pushed aside any misgivings he may still have had about the money he'd just handed over. If ever a place was dedicated to sexual recreation, this was it. The walls, lined with an auburn padded fabric pined back with matching upholstered buttons, were adorned with erotic paintings and engravings and lined with shelves of pornographic videos and literature. The ceiling stretching above was one vast wall-to-wall mosaic of mirrors. There was only one bed, but it stood centre-stage, dressed in dark silk sheets and big enough to accommodate four to five people. A small bar was stocked with alcohol, soft drinks and cigarettes. A hi-fi system came with a collection of tapes and compact discs. A video camera on a tripod was rigged up to the TV and video recorder, complete with instruction manual, and, opening the double doors of a walk-in closet, Lombard found everything from a vast array of S&M paraphernalia to countless sexual aids and diligently hand-labelled bottles of aphrodisiacs, tranquillisers, pain killers and even indigestion and cold remedies. And to ensure that all of this could be enjoyed to the full, there were two doors en-suite: one led to a fully-fitted kitchen, its refrigerator loaded with fresh fruit juices, bottles of Champagne and edibles ranging from bars of chocolate to pre-packed oven-ready meals; and the other to a white tiled bathroom that doubled as a fun chamber, one end of which was fitted with a suspended iron cage and a gallows-like steel structure provided with chains, shackles and hooks.

The pullover man had most definitely not exaggerated. Still, Lombard wasn't a customer, and stubbing his Gitane into the ashtray at the bar, he ran his eyes over the mirrored ceiling. Given the nature of what was likely to take place on and around the princely bed, it wouldn't be surprising if the pleasure dome around him was to contain more than met the eye, for the walls and mirrors to conceal surveillance equipment. If nothing else, a few well-positioned cameras would make for interesting viewing which, in a sound spirit of enterprise, could also be taped, edited and peddled as yet more sordid entertainment, or even retained for blackmail purposes. Everything is recyclable, can be made profitable, not least filth…

'Bande de fumiers,' he heard himself mutter between clenched teeth.

He rejected the idea. It would be bad business for Friedman and his colleagues to compromise their wealthy and captive clientèle by turning them into unsuspecting actors, be it for profit or blackmail. The word would get around and they'd lose their reputation and, with it, their business. Paradoxically, if they wished to prosper, criminals trading kids at £20,000 a go had to vigilantly protect their good reputation, had to be perceived as thoroughly trustworthy, appear safer than safe, beyond reproach or suspicion. First and foremost, what they really provided was safety. More than trading in children, they traded safety to have children safely. That didn't mean he wasn't being watched though. Only that if he was, it was for surveillance purposes only, just in case one sick sonofabitch were to lose it completely while getting his kicks and end up doing something dumb like setting the place on fire. Still, it was a risk he'd have to take.

He looked down. The boy had not moved, was still gazing at him from his chair in front of the TV set, where a Popeye cartoon was now playing. He put his briefcase on the bar, went to fetch a chocolate bar from the kitchen, returned to the bedroom, switched off the television and, squatting in front of the boy with as reassuring a smile as he could manage, held the chocolate out to him.

The boy warily reached for it. Lombard saw his dilated pupils, realised he was sedated…

'You go in there. In there, yes?' he said, pointing towards the kitchen door.

As before, the boy just frowned.

'In there, all right? You go in the kitchen, you understand?' he said again.

The boy still didn't move, just gazed back into his eyes.

'In there. You go in there,' he tried again with no more success.

He didn't want to get hold of him and forcefully lead him away. *The only pups currently available are brown and trained,'* Friedman had said. Sedated the boy might be. For all Lombard knew he'd also been lobotomised. But still, he didn't want the boy to think that…

'In there! Okay!' he said again, more firmly this time, doing away with the smile.

The boy reacted at last. He opened his eyes wide, turned in the direction indicated by Lombard's finger, stood up, and trekked docilely towards the kitchen, through the door and out of sight, the sound of his plimsolls flapping against his bare feet still reaching Lombard for a few seconds after he'd disappeared.

Lombard sighed, straightened up and made for the kitchen doorway. The boy stood by the sink, eyeing him from under his thick black brows.

'It's all right, huh. You sit down. Sit,' he ordered, pointing at a stool.

This time the boy understood first time. He climbed onto the stool and sat without taking his eyes off Lombard.

'Good. You eat your chocolate. It's yours. You eat it,' he said, pointing at the chocolate bar in the boy's hand and making eating motions.

The boy didn't move. It didn't matter.

'You stay here and be quiet, okay,' he said; 'Shhh…' he breathed, bringing his finger to his lips.

'*Chut,*' he said, softly closing the door.

He headed for the bar, opened his briefcase, lifted its false bottom, reached for his Beretta and silencer, made for the intercom, wedged the receiver between his shoulder and ear and slotted the silencer onto the handgun's barrel.

'Yeah?' said a man's voice. It was the giant.

'There is no toilet paper,' said Lombard.

'What?'

'There is no toilet paper.'

'Right. Er, Sorry. Must be the maid… Forgot…'

'Uh-huh. I'm sure. Bring some and hurry, will you.'

He opened the padded door to the outer corridor, settled behind it and placed a Gitane between his lips.

'*Must be the maid…*'

The metal wastepaper bin, the long corridors, the numbered doors. He could only be in a hotel. Were they going to send a maid? Or was the big man himself going to show up? He peered towards the kitchen door. He checked his watch. It was 16:45…

He didn't care who showed up. It made no difference. He lit his Gitane and fixed his eyes on the cold blue steel of the gun in his hand.

He didn't wait long. The cigarette between his lips was only a quarter spent when he heard the key turn in the lock of the outer door. He moved his eyes from his gun to the edge of the padded door and stopped breathing. The giant had either decided or been told to come himself. Even the thick carpeting of the inner corridor could not muffle the thud of his heavy steps.

'Your toilet paper…' he said, stepping through the padded door with a pack of toilet rolls in his large hand.

Lombard stuck the gun's silencer into his nape and kicked the door shut behind him.

'On the bed!'

With a grunt that sounded like 'What?' the giant turned on his heels to face him but Lombard whacked him across the face with the gun and shoved him hard, sending his big frame stumbling backwards across the room towards the bed. The man dropped the toilet rolls, crashed against the bed and tumbled backwards onto the silk sheet.

'Jesus Christ…' he said, peering at Lombard with bemused eyes and blood pouring from his nose.

'I'm not interested in you, big boy. Where is Friedman?' said Lombard, making for him.

The giant sat up, felt his nose, glowered at the blood on his hand.

'You fucking—' he pronounced, starting to rise and reaching under his jacket.

Lombard sent him back down with another crack across the face and stuck the gun against his forehead, with barely a glance at the handgun that now showed in the man's exposed holster.

'Your size is playing against you here, big man,' he said; 'I'm not even going to try to beat it out of you, you understand me? So don't let your dumb brains be yet another insurmountable obstacle, huh? Where is Friedman?'

'Fuck you!' the other replied with defiant eyes.

'Come on. You're not playing with little boys now, scumbag. Where is Friedman?'

'Fuck you! You're never gonna walk out of here, man…'

Lombard glared. Either the man had never used the gun in his fancy holster or he'd become too used to dealing with little boys. He aimed at one of his knees and pulled the trigger. The man's leg jerked, fell still, and its big owner gaped at it.

'Now, once again. Where is Friedman?'

'Jee—fuck! You're mad!' the man shrieked in a falsetto squeak, staring at the blood that had begun to cascade down his grey suit trousers and onto his polished shoes; 'You're fucking mad!'

Lombard aimed at his other knee, pulled the trigger.

The giant fell silent, peered at his new wound, then looked up, incredulous. When his eyes met Lombard's, his disbelief turned into fear. Could even a man like this one see through his eyes?

'Who are you?' he asked, wide-eyed.

Now Lombard knew he had never used his gun, at least not against someone armed who'd used theirs. He could see him so clearly now. Were those blackheads around his bleeding nostrils? The scumbag was probably close to seven foot tall, dealt in little kids, wore fine suits and polished shoes and had blackheads...

'Don't worry,' he said, grimacing at the man's bleeding knees; 'It's not going to hurt for a while – and you might be dead in a while anyway. So now, where is Friedman?' he asked again, pointing the gun at his crotch.

The other instinctively brought his hands in front of his genitals.

'Jee—I don't know. He's gone! He's gone...'

Lombard slapped him.

'He's gone. I don't fucking know where, I swear... He's gone. On holiday...'

Lombard frowned, then whacked him again.

'Try again.'

'I swear, man. He's gone.'

'On holiday?'

'Yeah...'

'When did he leave?'

'This morning. He left this fucking bloody morning... Jesus, man, my knees...'

Lombard swallowed hard, then let his eyes linger on the giant who, starting to sob, now gawked at his bloody knees with his trembling hands held suspended in mid-air above them, as if wanting to touch them but too scared to do so.

He felt the hot burning tip of his cigarette near his lips, yanked it out of his mouth, angrily flicked it onto the carpet and put it out with his shoe. Friedman was gone...

'So Friedman's gone?' he asked.

'Huh? Yes—he's fucking—'

'Is Friedman Austrian?' he cut in.

'What?'

He aimed his gun at the man's crotch again.

'Is Friedman Austrian?'

'Yes. Friedman's fuckin' Austrian.'

'Who's the money man?'

'Who?'

'The pullover man who took my money?'

'Martin… He's Martin…'

'Does he know where Friedman is?'

The giant stared, then a glimmer of thought resembling hope passed through his eyes:

'I—yes… He does…'

Lombard reached into his pocket and pulled out the snapshot he'd found in Leonard's bedroom. He'd torn off the half showing Rhian so that all he put in front of the giant's eyes was the part showing Leonard standing by the mountain stream.

'Ever seen him before?'

'No… No. Never,' said the man, peering at the snapshot.

'Are you sure?'

'Yes. I swear…'

He'd get him to swear to anything now.

'What's this place?' he asked, pocketing the snapshot again; 'A hotel of some kind?'

'Yeah… A hotel.'

'What's it called?'

'The Diplomat… It's called the Diplomat.'

'Where?'

'What?'

'Where are we?'

'Er… In London.'

'Where in London?'

'Finsbury Park. We're in Finsbury Park.'

'Where are the other kids?'

'What other kids?'

'There were six on offer, you scumbag. Where are the other five?'

The giant sent him an imploring look:

'Man, they gonna kill me if—'

Lombard whacked him across the face again.

'Down—down the road! At the Ambassador... Christ...'

'The Ambassador?'

'Yeah. It's another hotel. Just down the road.'

'Where precisely in the Ambassador?'

'Man...'

He whacked him again.

'Where?'

'On the third floor. That's where—'

'You're sure?'

'Yes. You better get me out of here, man...'

'How many of you scumbags are here right now?'

'What?'

'How many of you are there in the hotel?'

'... Right now? Just me and Martin. We brought the kid over from the Ambassador... The—there's more people there... More—no, it's just me. Martin was off to the Ambassador when I came up... It's just me. Just me.'

'Just you?'

'Yeah...'

'So no one's watching us at the moment, right?'

The giant looked back, befuddled.

'Are there surveillance cameras in here?'

'Er, surv...? No...'

'What about the staff?'

'What staff?'

'Is the hotel closed?'

'Closed? No.'

'Then what about the staff, huh?'

'What about them?'

'They must be in on what's going on, no? How many of them?'

'F—five. The Wilsons and their three kids. They run the place.'

'They run the place?'

'Yeah...'

'Who for?'

'What d'you mean?'

- 174 -

'Martin? Friedman? Who's the boss?'

'Friedman is. Look man, I don't know anything. I just work for Martin, that's all. Martin knows. He knows everything. He works for Friedman. He knows…'

'And who does Friedman work for?'

'Huh? The company. We all work for the company.'

'What company?'

'I don't know. I swear I don't know, man. I work for Martin, that's all. I don't even know Friedman really, I—'

He broke off to stare at his bloody knees again, then at the pool of blood that was beginning to spread on the carpet around his feet.

'Man, you've got to get me to a d—'

'Where's my money?'

'Martin's got it. I need a doctor or—'

Lombard knocked him out with one crack of the gun against the back of his head before he could complete his sentence.

The top half of the man's sitting body slowly slumped forward, then came to stop, leaving his head hanging a few inches above his knees and his arms dangling to the side of his legs. Lombard cracked him across the head again for good measure, heaved him back up and started to search him.

Besides his gun, which he tossed away, he found amongst other things a cell-phone, a wallet, a pack of chewing gum and a bunch of keys on a BMW key ring, but not the key to the room. Only then, after opening the padded door, did Lombard realise that, expecting he was coming in only to go out again, the giant had left the door to the corridor open with the key in the lock. Luckily, no one had noticed it or, if they had, thought much of it. In any case, it had not attracted any unwanted attention. He retrieved the key, locked the door from the inside and, after securing the giant's hands and feet with handcuffs and ropes from the closet, he left him on the bed, stepped out into the corridor and, holding his gun inside his coat, made for door number 40.

No one answered when he knocked and it turned out the door was locked when he tried the handle. He considered breaking it down but it would have made too much noise and, if what the giant had told him was true, his money was probably no longer in there anyway. He would do better to ascertain where he was and look for the way out...

He made for the window at the end of the corridor. It over-looked a wide road congested with crawling traffic that stretched along a metal fence. Through the downpour and the darkness lit by the glow of car headlights and street lamps, the area behind the fence was just a dark expanse, but the sign on the front of a double-decker bus listed Finsbury Park amongst other locations, and he guessed that it was indeed a park that spread out beyond the fence.

He turned and hurried towards the stairwell at the other end, passed on his way a few closed doors from behind which came the sounds of muffled conversation and television, came to a sign reading '3rd FLOOR', proceeded down the stairs looking over the handrail towards a noisy and brightly lit area at the bottom, and eventually stopped on the landing between the first and ground floors. The stairs below him led into a lobby. From where he stood he could see only its red carpet, a green potted plant, the bottom of a door, an armchair and the lower legs and shoes of a woman standing by the reception desk; but through the sound of a television and the loud voice of a man with a slurred Irish accent who kept repeating 'I'm telling you, woman, I'll be home on Sunday', as if speaking into a telephone, he heard the voices of at least three young women quietly chatting about their upcoming Christmas plans.

He turned around and climbed back up the stairs, on his way passing a sad-looking old man with an umbrella who gave him a polite smile. He had intended to look for the way the giant had used to bring him into the hotel, which must have involved a service or back door of some kind as they had definitely not crossed the red-carpeted lobby; but recalling it had entailed passing through or near a busy kitchen, he rejected the idea. It would be safer to go through the lobby. That way, even if he was made out, it was unlikely he could be stopped from reaching the relative safety of the street. No one, especially not child traffickers, would risk blowing their cover by starting a gunfight in the lobby.

'Nom de...' he muttered on reaching the third floor.

Dark footprints on the pale brown carpet led from door 48 to

40. He peered at his shoes. They were spattered with blood. He'd stepped in the blood around the giants legs when he was searching him.

The big man was still out when he returned to the room. Lombard peered at the blood still pouring from his knees, picked up the BMW key ring, pocketed it and felt the man's pulse. It was weak. At the rate he was losing blood he would probably die within the hour.

It proved necessary to slap him several times to make him open his dazed eyes with a groan, and then to give him time to understand what was being asked of him.

'You drive a BMW?'

'Huh?'

'You drive a BMW?'

'Y—yeah…'

'What colour?'

'B—black… Jesus, my knees… They hurt.'

'You got it downstairs?'

'You're gonna take me to the hospital?…'

'Just tell me where your car is, huh?'

'Downstairs… Yeah, at the back,' he said, expectantly; 'Behind the Ambassador…'

Lombard knocked him out again, took the silencer off his gun, crossed the room picking up his briefcase on the way and opened the kitchen door.

The boy still sat on his stool, the chocolate bar in his hand untouched, looking straight at him, just as he had been when Lombard had left him, as if he'd kept his eyes fixed on the door all the time it had been shut.

This time force was the only option.

'Allez, viens!' he said, picking him up and sitting him on his arm.

He didn't need his gun, and the women who'd been chatting about their Christmas plans had gone. Partly thanks to the unwitting assistance of an embracing couple who had chosen to leave the hotel at the same time as him, and also to that of a group of young Scots who were teasingly asking directions of the pretty young receptionist who stood behind her desk bent over an *A to Z*, Lombard carried the boy unhindered past a drunk leaning against the wall, past the crowded desk, across the lobby, out through the glass door and down the rain-swept front steps to the pavement, receiving only the briefest scrutiny from the receptionist, who sent him a mechanical smile when she looked up to turn to the couple as they stopped to hand in their room key. Even so, he didn't let go of his gun until he'd put several streets between himself and the hotel and, satisfied he wasn't being followed, hugging the drenched and shivering boy firmly to his chest, he eventually stopped under cover of a newsagent's doorway in a busy shopping street.

The boy in his arms was so rigid and shaking that he'd snapped the chocolate bar between his fingers in two. Lombard peered into his wide staring eyes, smiled, and, starting to rub his back vigorously to warm him up, searched the street.

'Qu'est-ce que je vais faire de toi, hein?'

After a moment his eyes caught sight of two women in a bus-shelter across the road. They stood silently side by side, one young and laden with shopping bags, the other middle-aged and standing stiffly hugging her handbag close to her loden coat. They'd do…

He hurried across the street, put the boy down, ruffled his wet hair and turned to the women.

'Excuse me?'

The woman in the loden coat turned, sent him an instinctive smile and then frowned on seeing the shivering boy standing at his side in his plimsolls and soaked T-shirt and shorts.

He grinned:

'I just found this boy standing all alone in the rain,' he said; 'I'd be grateful if one of you would be kind enough to take him to the local police station. His parents are probably looking for him. Sorry. I'm in a hurry. Thank you.'

And he turned, hastened away into the rain, crossed the street between the traffic and made for the nearest corner, glancing back over his shoulder only when about to turn the corner.

The women at the bus-stop were talking over the boy, the

younger of the two peering through the rain after Lombard. Would either one of them think of covering the boy with her coat on realising how cold he was? Probably...

He was panting. As when he'd left the Métropole in the morning, the warmth gripping his nape and shoulders let itself be felt, for just a fleeting moment. The Diplomat was just around the next corner...

NINE

Smoking in a rainstorm requires know-how and a certain degree of desperation. Keeping a cigarette dry when one has only one hand to do the trick and the rain is falling thick and fast and is swept this way and that by a wild and unpredictable wind, is a skillful exercise mastered only after much practice and many wasted cigarettes. With time, Lombard had perfected a technique that just about allowed him to perform the feat. However, he knew that as soon as he moved his hand to bring his Gitane up to his lips to take in the much needed drag, it would be the end of it. To keep a cigarette dry in a rainstorm was one thing. To actually smoke it without getting it wet quite another. If there was a way to do it, he had yet to discover it.

He brought his Gitane to his lips, took in a deep drag and flicked it away towards the kerb in front of him. The rain put it out before it reached the water rushing along the gutter.

This was the cigarette he had lit a few minutes earlier in the lobby of the Ambassador, and now, standing in the downpour with his back to the fence that ran along Finsbury Park, midway between the Diplomat and the Ambassador which stood fifty or so yards apart across the Seven Sisters Road and its crawling late afternoon traffic, he clasped his wet fingers around the Beretta in his raincoat pocket and peered across the road towards a car that had just pulled to a stop along the kerb.

A woman and two teenage girls climbed out of its back door and hurried away towards a side street.

He sighed, flexed his fingers around the briefcase handle, let go of the gun, pulled his hand back out of his pocket, brought his watch right up to his eyes in order to see its hands through the sodden darkness – it was six o'clock – and turned to the Ambassador.

'In about a quarter of an hour...' the receptionist had said.

Ten minutes had elapsed since then. In another fifteen, if the pullover man that the giant called Martin had failed to turn up, he would return to the Ambassador and, as the receptionist had suggested, continue to wait for him inside the hotel, however many unpleasant characters were in there. Unless of course Martin had already returned, in which case there wouldn't be any more waiting to be done; from where he stood he had a clear view of both hotel entrances, could not have missed Martin if he'd returned using the front, but for all Lombard knew, just as the giant had done when taking him into the Diplomat earlier, Martin had returned via a back door…

He put his hand back in his pocket and around his gun.

So far, the giant's information had proved reliable. On leaving the boy at the bus-stop, Lombard had made his way back to the Diplomat, established that it was just one of the many non-descript hotels that lined the section of Seven Sisters Road running along Finsbury Park, and found the Ambassador further up the road past another hotel named The Park Inn.

Whereas the Diplomat was a dull modern building of five storeys with a white facade and a red neon sign spelling out its name, the Ambassador was a squat grey Victorian edifice whose front steps climbed to double glass doors set within a porch of carved columns above which its name, in large black letters, stretched against a white light-box. However, apart from their contrasting appearance, there was really nothing to chose between the two establishments, or for that matter between them and the other cheap hotels that are typically found close to London's parks; inconspicuous, uninspiring, they struck one as places of need rather than choice.

Still, from the road, through the Diplomat's glass entrance, Lombard had observed the young receptionist he'd passed on his way out. He'd found her alone behind the desk, watching TV with a bored air, which suggested he'd made no impression on her when leaving with the boy and that as yet no one had missed the giant, or if they had – although no one would have if, as he'd claimed, the big man had been the only gang member left in there – that his absence had not as yet been deemed significant. So, Lombard had gone on to look for the man's black BMW and, having found it parked in the back street where he'd been told it would be and made sure the giant's keys opened its door and started its engine, he'd retraced his steps to the Seven Sisters Road and made for the Ambassador intent on confronting Martin there and then. He didn't like it, it was dangerous, but all in all, it was the best thing to do. Whatever he'd learned thus far, Leonard Spitz's disappearance remained unexplained, and now that he'd left the injured giant in the Diplomat, he had better get to Martin sooner rather than later, or else think of another way of seeking the answer, because how long it would take before someone missed the giant's dumb company and thought of seeking it out in room 48 was anybody's guess, while what would happen after he was found, whether dead or alive, didn't leave much room for speculation; alarm bells were going to ring, and not only would he then lose the element of surprise and any chance of finding Martin unprepared but doubtless the children and any other incriminating evidence would be removed from the hotels long before the night was over. This he didn't want to happen, especially not before he got to Martin. The children, if there were children on the Ambassador's third floor – he was still not sure – had to remain just where they were. His knowledge of their presence gave him the edge he needed, would persuade Martin to co-operate, ensure that he or whoever he might be with didn't get any bad ideas. That was why he'd made for the Ambassador, why he'd felt compelled to step in there, where he'd found the receptionist, a harassed-looking grey man in a brown shirt and with nicotine-stained fingers, arguing wearily with an irate middle-aged Dutch couple who were checking out.

'This is preposterous,' the Dutchman had declared as Lombard stepped inside; 'You cannot expect to get away with charging this kind of money for a three minute call to Holland…'

'I'm sorry,' sighed the grey receptionist; 'But if you're unhappy about it you'll have to speak to the manager…'

'Unhappy? Tell me. Would it make you happy to be handed this—this… Thirty five pounds for a three minute call! Would that make you happy, huh?'

'That's not the point,' broke in the Dutch woman; 'The point is that we cannot speak to the manager, isn't that so?'

'He should be back in an hour or so...'

'We've got a train to catch in an hour or so.'

'I understand, and I'm sorry, but... I can't let you leave unless you settle your bill in full...'

'But you wouldn't mind if we missed our train?'

'Look, I only work here and...'

'What do you propose we do, huh?'

'As I already said, if you don't want to pay your—'

'We are not suggesting we shouldn't pay our bill. Only that we shouldn't be charged this ridiculous...'

'I don't have the authority to change the rates. Only the manager can...'

'Yes. I know. But the manager is not here and...'

While this was going on, Lombard had used the time to peer through the open door to a small office behind the reception desk where, in the light of a fluorescent strip, two women, who appeared to be Filipinos and wore identical cheap purple raincoats, sat silently at a table behind their handbags while a bald man in shirtsleeves with tattooed forearms reclined in an armchair beyond them browsing through a newspaper. Both women had the vacant eyes and numb posture that people in transit often instinctively adopt as a way of protecting themselves from the unfamiliar and therefore potentially threatening nature of their transient environment. The man, on the other hand, looked as if he was at home and, as he had his back to the women, also appeared to be just waiting there, killing time.

'Yes. What can I do for you?' the receptionist had eventually asked.

Lombard had glanced at him, then at the couple who now stood in silent anger, he glaring in resigned fury at his hands and she shaking her head in open disgust; they knew they'd lose this one, knew they were going to have to pay, however much they resented it – they had a train to catch, couldn't afford to miss it, and appeared too respectable to risk leaving without paying.

'Martin around?' Lombard had asked curtly, turning back to the receptionist.

The grey man had frowned, quickly looked him up and down, glanced at his briefcase, peered at his stony grin, at his wet hair, and dithered before replying:

'Er, Mr. Martin's gone to the dentist. He should be back soon. If you want to wait…'

Lombard just might have taken up his offer, but at that very moment two men, one middle-aged, in an alpaca coat and scarf, the other young, with long hair and a leather jacket, had appeared down the stairs and stepped through a side door that led into the office behind the reception desk. Seeing them, the Filipino women had stirred in their seats and the bald man got up and moved to shut the door through which Lombard had been watching them, absent-mindedly sending him a probing look as he did so.

'What do you mean by soon?' Lombard had asked, reverting his attention to the receptionist.

'Oh… Er, in about a quarter of an hour… Something like that. I don't know…'

He'd nodded.

'Thank you. I'll come back later…'

Just before stepping out of the lobby and into the rain, he'd paused to light a Gitane.

'This is scandalous. This is robbery,' the Dutchman was saying behind him; 'I'm going to do something about this. I want the owner's and the manager's names…'

A few moments later, as he settled in the spot from where he now kept watch, he'd observed the angry Dutch couple hurry down the steps with their bags and climb into a waiting taxi. Then, the two men who'd walked into the reception office had also come out and hurried through the rain to the side street he himself had taken earlier when looking for the giant's BMW. And a little later still, the white Mercedes he'd travelled in earlier had appeared and stopped to pick up the Filipino women and the bald man before pulling away again. Peter the woman was no longer in the car, only the young crew-cut driver. It was soon after watching it disappear into the rush hour traffic that Lombard had flicked his wet Gitane into the streaming gutter.

He peered across the road towards the burly silhouette of an overcoated man with an umbrella hurrying past the Diplomat; he stepped to the kerb, then stopped; it wasn't Martin, this man had dark hair, wore glasses and was heading for the Park Inn.

He took one step back, glanced at a young woman at the wheel of a small hatchback who quickly looked away as their eyes met through her sweeping windscreen wipers, then frowned, took a deep breath and gently rolled his head back to loosen his stiff neck. He was so numb with cold he no longer felt the rain rolling inside his collar, merely sensed its caressing flow across his skin as it impregnated his shirt and suit jacket. Already, his back and chest were soaked, even though he'd pulled his coat collar up in a vain attempt to keep the rain out; but still, he didn't feel cold. He knew he was cold but didn't feel it, knew his mind was too focused on the task at hand to relay the information. He also knew that, were he to remain there, in time the cold would get the better of him, only as yet, it had not, and once again he surveyed the dark pavement across the road through the bronze dazzle of the headlights crawling past him.

It might prove necessary to run but, given the opportunity, he reckoned there was time to prevent Martin reaching either of the hotels' doors. He had no idea how the man would turn up, whether he'd be on foot or in a car, alone or in company, or which side of the road he'd appear on, or even which hotel, the Diplomat or the Ambassador, he'd make for when and if he did appear. Nor did he yet know what he would do after he'd dealt with the pullover man – about Leonard Spitz and the children in the Ambassador. That would depend on what came of their meeting, and on whether he'd got to him without arousing anyone's attention. But insofar as one can ever be certain of anything, he was convinced Martin would prove helpful, however reluctantly, even if they ended up meeting inside one of the hotels with the man surrounded by a protective ring of colleagues. He'd seen his piercing eyes, seen the cogs moving behind their deep blue cast. Martin was smart. Martin had been around and survived. He wasn't a tough guy, he was the real thing, a criminal through and through. Crime was his vocation, not just a way to make an easy living or get high on fear and feelings of immortality by behaving more amorally than the next man. Lombard had made him out the moment their eyes had met, seen he'd done time, seen his scars, seen he'd fought hard and given as good as he'd got to get where he was today. In his book, he'd probably done well for himself. Today he traded kids, tomorrow who knows? Whatever paid the bills. Unlike the giant, he thought ahead, wasn't in it for the excitement or for lack of brains, and he'd know better than to challenge an armed man. And unlike the giant, he most likely knew killing was easy, often a lot easier than not killing. The smart ones live, control and die. The fools live, kill and get killed. Ordinary folks just live and die. And somewhere in between all of them, there were people like Martin and...

Lombard tightened his lips and swallowed hard. He could always kill him. Right out there in the street. He could always shoot him. It was dark, pouring with rain, the wind howling, the pavements deserted and the few people who ventured out hurrying through the puddles. No one would see. And the chances were no one would hear the Beretta's blast through the wind and the traffic. It would be a matter of just walking away. Drivers and passers-by would see the man's body slumped on the pavement, would just keep going, assume he was a drunk or something, as people do, and then someone would stop and the police would come, cordon off the area, and, in case they didn't connect his corpse to the hotels – and why should they? – a call from the phone box that stood a hundred yards away would make sure they did, and that they found whatever was in them. After all, he was only waiting for Martin because the giant had told him Martin knew where Friedman was. Yet, if everything the big man had said was true, Friedman was on holiday. If that was so, Friedman wasn't even worried about Leonard Spitz, let alone holding him captive. If that was so, Friedman had already got rid of Leonard Spitz and Martin didn't matter... But then again, maybe Martin did matter. Leonard Spitz was a worried mother's son. He had better find out as much as he could before he declared him dead...

He gazed up towards the Ambassador, ran his eyes along the third floor windows – most were dark, the few with light beyond them had their curtains drawn – and turned as the familiar high-pitched scream of a black taxi's brakes reached his right ear.

Fifteen yards away, on his side of the road, right beneath a street lamp, Martin, wearing gloves, a coat, a scarf and a hat, was climbing out of a black cab. Lombard put his finger on the trigger of his Beretta. Martin would see him before the taxi had even pulled away. All he had to do was look left, which he would inevitably do if his next move was towards the Diplomat, or the cab's front window to pay his fare. But the man didn't turn or even look to his left. Instead, he slammed the cab door shut and, between hunched shoulders, hands pushed deep in his pockets, turned to his right, made for the back of the cab, stepped off the kerb and started into the traffic across the road towards the Ambassador.

Lombard hurled himself straight across the road, weaving his way between the cars, veered right and jogged along the pavement to reach the front of the Ambassador to block Martin's way with time to spare.

Martin stopped and peered at him with a tight-lipped frown.

'How are you, Martin?' he said.

He saw the cogs moving behind the blue eyes. It took Martin a moment to place him, after all they had met only briefly, in bright light and dry conditions, but when he did, he glowered and instinctively lowered his eyes towards the pocket in which Lombard conspicuously held his gun.

'I hear you've been to the dentist,' said Lombard, peering at Martin's left cheek; from ear to chin, it was one huge swelling which twisted his mouth into a grotesque sneer.

But Martin couldn't look grotesque, not with those foxy eyes of his.

'Wisdom tooth?' asked Lombard.

Martin eyed him. He was scowling, but he didn't seem worried, pissed-off or frightened. Rather, he seemed puzzled, or curious, just as he had when they met in room 40 earlier.

'Problems?' he finally asked with a slight slur.

Lombard grinned. He'd been right. Martin was smart.

'Is my money in there?' he queried, nodding back towards the Ambassador.

And Martin wasn't going to do anything foolish either. Just as Lombard had hoped, he found the question reassuring. His eyes had narrowed into a smile. He who cares about money cares about the future. He who cares about the future isn't going to kill you out in the open like this, gun or no gun... Or so, probably, went the equation inside his skull.

Lombard sent him an icy grin which the man promptly returned, producing as much of a smile as he could command with his fixed sneer. He felt safe all right, so safe he'd already taken the equation a step further. He who cares about the future makes for easy prey, or at least, can be lured...

'Uh-huh,' he said; 'You could've waited for me inside though, rather than standing out in this terrible weather.'

Lombard nodded, gently, glanced at the rain bouncing off the man's hat.

'I thought of the kids on the third floor and all your friends in there, and reckoned I'd sooner meet you out here. Besides, if I don't make a call within fifteen minutes, the place is going to be overrun with cops. I thought I'd better catch you where you can't do anything foolish that might jeopardise your prosperity.'

The creases around Martin's eyes deepened, his lips gave up their futile attempt at a smile, and he sent Lombard a quizzical look. He didn't seem frightened, just perturbed, in a challenging sort of way and, for a moment, Lombard thought he'd misjudged him after all.

First reassurance, then threats. Lombard had learned this a long time ago. Indeed, he'd been taught it.

'... If you're the frightened guy with the gun and you want to give yourself a chance to not shoot the other guy and to take control of the situation, you better find out who you're dealing with the moment you pull your weapon out. So first reassure, then threaten. The object is to disorient, to sort out the men from the boys, the smart from the dumb, so you can figure out your options and make the right next move. Reassure then threaten. At this point the dumb guys get confused, panic, are overcome by fear, start acting hostile or else reveal what truly dangerous arseholes they are by going in for self-delusion or denial, either trying to outdo themselves with smart remarks or acting as though they're the guys with the gun and nothing can kill them. The smart guy on the other hand will instinctively act* *like someone who better buy himself some time to weigh the deal. So he'll act more friendly than he feels, or ask a pertinent question...'*

'How thoughtful,' said Martin; 'And there I was thinking you were just a pissed-off customer wanting a refund,' he went on, letting Lombard know this wasn't so by attempting a smile again; 'I don't know who you are or what your problem is but—'

Martin was trying to outdo himself.

'Right now your big friend at the Diplomat is bleeding fast, Martin,' cut in Lombard; 'My guess is he might just possibly live if he's attended to soon. And he did co-operate. Do we understand each other?'

Martin understood. Indeed, it was his turn to nod. He looked at the pocket in which Lombard held his gun again, letting his better instinct take over. Lombard had not been wrong after all. The man asked a pertinent question:

'What can I do for you?'

'Let's go,' said Lombard signalling in the direction of the nearby side street.

'What about your money?' the man asked.

In his situation, he couldn't help but have one last go at fighting.

'Let's go,' repeated Lombard.

Martin sent him a searching glance, peered towards the Ambassador's bright entrance, sighed and let his eyes speak for him. He'd chosen the sensible option, was already turning in the direction Lombard had signalled.

'You're the man in charge,' he said, checking his watch.

He had still not shown any sign of fear. He just walked through the rain, brooding all the way, too busy trying to figure out what was going on to say or try anything, which suited Lombard just fine. Oddly, only when they stopped by the giant's BMW and he saw Lombard unlock the door with its key, did something close to fear seem to dawn on him. His eyes opened wide, so spoiling his ruminative composure, and, for a moment, he looked like any other man with a swollen cheek who is afraid of the unknown. A gust of wind blew the hat off his head as Lombard ordered him into the driver's seat, but after a mere glance back over his shoulder to watch it spin away, he turned and climbed into the car. On reflection, his disquiet at that moment was perhaps not that odd after all. Until then, all Lombard had done was talk. For all Martin knew he'd been bluffing, made himself seem meaner than he really was. That he knew where to find the giant's car though, and held its keys, left little room for ambiguity. It drove the message home. Indeed, something comparable had happened to Lombard a little earlier. The giant had told him children were kept in the Ambassador. He'd believed this, but belief had become a near certainty only when he'd seen the two Filipino-looking women sitting in their purple coats with their vacant eyes in the office behind the reception desk. He knew who these women were, knew what their presence meant, what had brought them there. Just as Martin now knew that Lombard must really have hurt his big friend. How else would he have known about his car, let alone got hold of its keys…?

'Whoever you are, whatever you're after, you're making a mistake,' he said as Lombard settled on the back seat right behind him.

His head was at work again, his eyes peering into the rear-view mirror, searching across the shadows between them as Lombard put down his briefcase, reached into his pockets for his gun and the snapshot of Leonard and switched on the courtesy light above them.

'Ever seen him before?' he asked, leaning over the man's shoulder to hold the snapshot out in front of his nose.

The other squinted.

'I need my glasses,' he said dryly; 'They're in my inside pock—'

Lombard stuck the gun against the back of his head.

'Just look at the photograph, Martin.'

'Look,' said Martin with a shrug; 'I can look all you like but I can't see, all right?'

What game was he playing now?

'How come you didn't need glasses for looking at my money earlier, huh?'

Martin sniggered.

'Since you can remember that, you must also remember I held

the note away from me, don't you? I've got hyperopia.'

'What?'

'I'm long-sighted. Can't see your picture unless you let me stick it on the bloody passenger window, all right?'

Lombard frowned.

'Fine. Get your glasses. Easy does it.'

Martin sighed, pulled a pair of spectacles from his breast pocket with undue slowness, put them on and examined the snapshot. With his head just above the man's shoulder, Lombard could smell the odour of antiseptic mouthwash on his breath. He glanced at his swollen cheek. It seemed to have grown in the last few minutes. But maybe that was just an impression. He was so close to it…

'Am I supposed to know him?' asked Martin, pulling off his spectacles.

'Plain English will do, Martin,' said Lombard; 'Do you or don't you know him?'

'I don't *know* him,' replied the man; 'But since you obviously seem to think I might, it could be I've seen him. I see a lot of people. Maybe, with a frame of reference, like context and time, I might just be able to place him for you, huh?'

Was he lying or just digging, trying to find out what Lombard was after? If he needed to dig, maybe he'd never seen Leonard before. Still…

'He bought a boy of yours. About four weeks ago.'

'Clients come and go.'

'This one came back and was never seen again. I understand Friedman looked after him.'

'Friedman…'

Martin had put his spectacles back on, was scrutinising the snapshot again.

'Huh. Tell me, what am I looking at here? Some artist or pop-star of some kind?' he asked, sounding genuinely curious.

'What exactly is the problem, Martin?' said Lombard

'I just need to know. Is this person famous, or the son or brother of somebody famous or highly placed?'

Lombard frowned.

'Not really…'

'Yeah. I didn't think so,' the man said, taking his spectacles off again; 'You must be mistaken, friend. You must have understood wrong or been misled. You're knocking at the wrong door.'

'Am I now?'

'Is that what this is all about?' Martin said, deciding to ignore his question; 'You hurt one of our men and brought me here because of a missing person?'

Lombard gave him a little tap on his swollen cheek with the barrel of his gun.

'Just answer my question, Martin. What makes you say I'm knocking at the wrong door?'

'Well, if you must know... A: without wishing to sound disrespectful of your friend here, Friedman only deals directly with select customers. I handle the rabble, you see, and I can't recall seeing this individual within the last four weeks or four months. B: assuming for the sake of argument we did do business with your man, we're not in the habit of making the clientèle disappear. And C: at the risk of sounding narrow-minded, if his photograph does him justice, even allowing for the fact that appearances can be deceptive, I'd say your long-haired friend doesn't look even remotely like the sort of people we commonly deal with. I'd go further. If he's just another bum, had he come to us, I doubt we'd have given him the time of day...'

Lombard peered at the snapshot across Martin's shoulder. From what Rhian had said, it could be as much as two years old. Leonard could have cut his hair since then, put on weight even...

'Just imagine him in a suit with a short haircut, eh?' he said.

'I don't need to. I never forget a face and this is one I've never seen. And if all this excitement is really due to you trying to track down this one guy, you're most definitely making a bad mistake. Unless of course you have a particular reason to think we might be responsible for his disappearance. Have you?'

'Why are you asking?'

'Isn't it a valid question? I mean, you posing as a customer? Standing to lose twenty grand? Hurting one of our men and... Well, you must at least have probable cause, no?'

Lombard chose not to answer. He eyed the snapshot again. Martin was right, Leonard Spitz was no select customer...

'What do you mean precisely — Friedman deals only with select customers?'

'I'd have thought it was self-explanatory.'

'I'm not asking you to think, Martin.'

'What do I mean?... Well, our rates might be exclusive, but still, they're within the means of many, and we cater for the likes of you – or should I say for the likes of you were you a bona-fide customer – and then we have special people. Eminent, distinguished, high-profile mortals. These great individuals are Friedman's preserve. Everything else is passed on to me...'

Because of his slur and accent, it was hard to say, but Lombard was sure bitterness had pervaded Martin's last words.

He leaned back, pocketed the snapshot, turned off the courtesy light and searched his pocket for his cigarettes.

'Friedman's Austrian, right?'

'Why do I think you already know the answer to that? But since you're asking: yes, he is.'

'Does any other Austrian work for or with you?'

'... No.'

'Good. Then, in your opinion, Martin, how many Austrians would you say are peddling kids and snuff movies in London at any given time?' he asked, opening his packet of Gitanes.

'Are you serious or just killing time now? Because—'

'Answer me, Martin. In your opinion, how many—'

'I shouldn't think there'd be more than one,' cut in Martin; 'Or only one that I know of...'

'Right. And you know about these things, don't you?' Lombard said, sticking a Gitane between his lips.

'Christ... Are you just fishing or what?'

'No,' he said, lighting his cigarette; 'We have a problem here, Martin. I have it from a reliable source that my man bought a kid from an Austrian in London. Now, even you seem to agree that the coincidence of two Austrians selling little boys at the same time in London is just too much to consider. And yet, you also tell me that your Austrian couldn't possibly have dealt with my man. What are we to make of that, eh?'

'Look, it's your problem. Not mine. You make of it what you like. I've told you all I can tell you.'

'Then let's say I choose to believe you. How can you be so sure Friedman couldn't have dealt with my man without you knowing about it? Or are the two of you such close bedfellows you keep no secrets from each other?'

'Huh…' muttered Martin, pausing to check his watch; 'Ten minutes ago you mentioned something about making a call in fifteen minutes or else. What about it?'

Lombard frowned.

'Forget the call,' he said; 'Is it or is it not possible for Friedman to sell little boys without you knowing about it?'

'Look,' Martin grumbled; 'Unless it was just a cunning ploy to get me to behave, I've got nothing more to say to you unless you make that bloody call, all right?'

Lombard peered at the man's head, then through the darkness to the eyes watching him in the rear-view mirror. He'd sounded worried, and now Lombard could see he looked it.

'What's the matter, Martin? You're safe. You're here with m—'

'I live there!' cut in Martin; 'I fucking live there. You get my meaning?'

'… You live where?' asked Lombard, intrigued.

'The Ambassador. If the law gets to it I'll be done for whether I'm there or not, you understand what I'm saying now?'

Lombard stared in front of him for a moment, then felt his lips break into a dark grin. He'd forgotten all about the fictitious call the moment he mentioned it. But Martin obviously hadn't, must have been worried about it all the time they'd been together, and had done a good job of concealing it…

He nodded his imperceptible nod, took down a drag of his cigarette and blew out the smoke, having resolved to restore the man's confidence. He hadn't finished with him yet.

'There's no call to be made.'

'You're sure?'

'I'm sure.'

Was that a sigh of relief from Martin's mouth?

'Damn you…'

'Now, the answer to my question, Martin?'

Martin shook his head. Maybe it was just plain relief, or anger at having been deceived, or maybe, feeling heartened by the fact that Lombard had come clean about the call, he fancied the time had come to turn the situation to his advantage. Whatever it was, he suddenly turned around, fixed his eyes in Lombard's, and spoke, calm, self-assured and sinister:

'Look, I don't think you're fully aware of what you're playing with here, Mister. Whoever put you up to this either pays too well or misinformed you as to the realities of what we are about. Okay, so you know a few things and you hurt one of our people. So be it. It's upsetting but we all make mistakes. Why don't you just tell me what I can do to make you happy so I can forgive you your mistakes and we can part company in a civilised manner, eh?'

Without thinking, Lombard swung his arm and whacked the man's swollen cheek with his gun, causing his head to roll back towards the windscreen and his mouth to let out a strangled howl which seemed to last an entire minute before it turned into a lamenting wail. Evidently, the anaesthetic he'd been given at the dentist had worn off. Leaning back in his seat, smoking, glaring out the window, his fingers clasped around the Beretta on his lap, Lombard just waited. There was no point in asking any more questions until the man's pain had subsided. It did, it always does, and Martin's wailing became moaning, and the moaning soon stopped, and once again the car filled with the silence made by the rain drumming against the metal above their heads.

'Fucking…' he heard the man moan; 'There was no bloody call for—'

'I thought you were smart, Martin,' cut in Lombard, turning from the window to the man again.

He was gently feeling his swollen cheek with the tips of his fingers, softly tapping the stretched skin.

'If I were you I'd stop swearing, stop worrying about the pain, and narrow down my thoughts to speculating on whether I'm going to kill you even if you do answer my questions,' said Lombard, scowling at the back of his head.

Martin didn't say anything, but he took his hand away from his cheek and sat absolutely still, which was just as well because had he spoken or moved Lombard just might have killed him, and no doubt Martin had heard it in his voice.

'So, Martin? Do you still remember my question or do I need to repeat myself again?'

The man didn't reply immediately and while waiting for him to speak, all of a sudden, Lombard started to feel cold. He felt his wet shirt sticking to his skin. His mind had finally succumbed and begun to relay the information.

'It's possible,' declared Martin; 'Everything's possible. I don't know all of Friedman's clients but...' he trailed off and shrugged.

'So it's possible,' said Lombard; 'Good. Why don't you tell me where I might find Friedman, eh?'

Once again, Martin took a moment to reply, sighed before he spoke:

'Look, I told you you're barking up the wrong—'

'Don't,' cut in Lombard, sticking his gun against the man's head again.

Martin's eyes were back in the rear-view mirror, observing him, probing and glistening in the semi-darkness. He'd been crying, hard tears of pain and frustration.

'All right. All right. You want Friedman, eh?' he said; 'You're not gonna like it... Right now Friedman must be landing in Los Angeles. Not due back until after Christmas.'

He must have seen Lombard's frown of dismay in the mirror, because as he ever so slightly moved his head, Lombard saw the reflection of the sneer across his lips. And this wasn't just the grotesque sneer produced by his swollen cheek. It was a full and deliberate sneer. The man couldn't produce much of a smile with his bulging cheek but he sure could sneer...

'What'll you do now, eh? Fly to the US or make an appointment for New Year's Eve?' he heard him say.

Lombard stayed silent, just moved his eyes onto his gun. He saw the Beretta's barrel moving against Martin's red hair, realised his hand was trembling, felt his arm shaking, and wondered whether this was due to his feeling the cold or to the tension in his shoulders. Martin also knew what was happening. He could feel the gun moving against his head and, naturally, took it as a bad sign.

'Hey... Easy now. Easy... I swear it's the truth. Friedman took off this morning for the US,' he said, sounding as if he was more worried about Lombard's state of mind than about dying.

'Friedman lives with you at the Ambassador?' Lombard heard himself ask.

'... No. He doesn't.'

'He doesn't?'

'No...'

'Where does he live then?'

Once again, there was a slight delay before the reply came, and a resigned sigh:

'In Hampstead.'

'In Hampstead?'

'Yes. In Hampstead. Why?'

'Does he live alone?'

'What?'

'Does he live by himself?'

'He lives by himself.'

'No wife, girlfriends, children or maids?'

'No.'

'Can you drive?'

'Drive. Huh? Yes…'

Lombard had made his decision.

He pulled the Beretta away from Martin's head, found he'd mislaid the car keys, located them next to his briefcase on the seat beside him, held them out above Martin's shoulder.

'Don't jump any red lights.'

'What…'

'Friedman's.'

He whacked him across the back of the head and tossed the keys on to his lap.

'Just shut up and get driving,' he said, leaning back in his seat again. He was still shaking. It had to be the cold.

'And turn the heater on. Full…'

Martin sighed, moved in his seat, put the key into the ignition and started the engine. The car jolted backwards and stalled.

'Christ!' he cried, shifting the gear stick fitfully, searching for neutral; 'The damn thing was in reverse…'

Lombard pulled the Gitane from between his lips, wound down his window and flicked it away through the rain as the car engine caught again. It didn't jolt back this time…

It became clear from the moment he started manoeuvring the BMW out of its parking space that Martin was either unfamiliar with a manual gearbox or a lot more nervous than he'd let on. He put his incompetence down to the gearbox though, claiming he was an 'automatic man', and the way things were going he could well have been telling the truth. He over-revved, miss-clutched, stalled and cursed nearly every time he had to take off from a standstill which, in view of the fact they were travelling in rush-hour traffic, made for a lot of stopping and stalling and swearing from both Martin and the many angry drivers caught behind them. All this put Lombard on edge and at one point, as they drove up Hornsey Lane and the car began to jolt and cough, apparently unduly since they'd been progressing at a slow but steady pace on that stretch of the journey, he lost his temper and threatened to kill the man again, accusing him of deliberately driving carelessly – in the circumstances the thought that he might try to cause an accident or a situation that would allow him to slip away was excusable – but the man protested his innocence, pointing at the flashing fuel warning light on the dashboard.

'This car needs petrol...'

They were not far from Hampstead then.

'Just keep going...'

Martin had not been lying. The car ran smoothly again once they reached a level road, as smoothly as his handling of it allowed anyhow. Still, the man may have been a poor driver but he knew his way around and got them to Hampstead via a series of back ways to avoid the predictable rain-induced bottleneck of The Spaniards along Hampstead Lane – unlike Lombard almost four days ago now – and eventually pulled up at the kerb in a well-to-do residential street which, Lombard couldn't help noticing, was not only familiar but also stood less than half a mile from Templeton Road and Deborah De Moraes' house. Obviously, Mr. Friedman was doing well for himself and, like most who did well for themselves in and around North London, had succumbed to the lure of living amongst the privileged few.

The name of the road was Kidderpore Avenue. He had not seen the street sign but happened to remember it. One of his former clients lived just around the corner, the jealous French restaurateur who he'd remembered after receiving Mrs. Spitz's first call, and Martin had driven right past his house.

'There you are. Friedman's,' Martin signalled across the road towards a little white house that lay in darkness behind a gravel drive in which a car sat sheltered under a tarpaulin.

It was more of a cottage than a house, a leftover from old London, a quaint little structure standing on two floors with diamond-paned windows which time had slightly twisted and arched. The drive was edged with small trees and, to one side, between the front door and a low wall running alongside the tall hedge of the adjoining property, a wooden palisade blocked the way to a side passage.

It all looked very tranquil and, judging from the dark windows, nobody was home.

'Satisfied?' said Martin.

He'd kept the car engine running, hoping Lombard would take one look at the dark windows and decide to move on.

'Friedman's got a back garden?' asked Lombard, peering at the palisade.

'Huh? Yes. Why?'

'I take it you haven't got the house keys?'

He didn't expect a positive answer but he had to ask.

'What?'

'You don't have Friedman's keys, do you?'

'Why should I have his...?' Martin started, trailing off as the thought dawned on him; 'What's on your mind? You're not thinking of—'

Lombard didn't reply but just surveyed the house and his surroundings. The house was – or at any rate was made to appear as if it was – fitted with an alarm system; a metal siren box clung to the facade, of the type manufacturers made conspicuously ugly so as to be noticeable and deter opportunist burglars. Behind their hedges, the windows of the houses on either side were lit, as were those of the one directly opposite.

'Pull across and stop in front of the drive,' he said, reaching into his pocket for the Beretta's silencer.

'Christ...' said Martin, glancing back over his shoulder.

He saw the silencer, fell silent, gave Lombard an almost reproachful look, and turned away again.

'Christ...'

He was unhappy, but he did as he was told, stalling only once

- 199 -

before bringing the BMW to a stop in front of Friedman's drive.

'What's the fucking idea, huh?'

'Move forward a couple more yards,' ordered Lombard, winding down his window; 'Don't turn off the engine. When I say "go", you make straight for the end of the road, understand? And don't stall the car again.'

Martin understood, not only what Lombard had just said but, after peering at the house, what he was about to do.

'You're out of your mind…'

Lombard moved back from the open window, lowered himself on his seat to get a clear view of the siren box, clasped the Beretta firmly with both hands at the end of his outstretched arms and aimed, unhindered by the downpour as only the tip of the silencer jutted through the window.

He pulled the trigger twice in quick succession. The sharp clinks of the bullets piercing the metal box and its insides reached him at the same time as the muffled thuds from the gun, then all fell silent. Through the bullet holes, a few sparks lit up the inside of the box, as if its wires were short-circuiting. He took two more shots at it, sat up, moved back across the seat and wound the window up.

'Let's go.'

Martin, as if determined not to get caught, pulled away very carefully and managed not to stall. When they reached the end of the road, Lombard made him turn around, drive back and stop about 30 yards away across the road from Friedman's.

The house still lay in quiet darkness, the road was still deserted and there were no faces peering out of the neighbouring windows.

'Turn the engine off.'

'What now?'

'We wait.'

The hands of his watch showed 19:15. Fifteen minutes would be enough to establish if anyone had heard or seen anything and called the police, or if Friedman's alarm was linked to a police or security watch-centre which, even given the nature of the Austrian's occupation, was certainly not to be ruled out. If all was clear, the low wall by the palisade would offer easy enough access to the back of the house.

He swallowed hard, lit a cigarette and observed Martin who was now leaning slumped forward on the steering wheel with his face buried in his arms, too upset or perplexed to ask any more questions. From his body language, insofar as his sagging posture could indicate, and his breathing – short rapid breaths blown through his nose loudly enough to be heard above the rain hitting the car – he was upset rather than perplexed. By now he had guessed what Lombard had in mind and didn't like it. But he said nothing and gradually calmed down until his breathing was no longer discernible, and Lombard went on smoking, surveying Friedman's house while keeping the man's slumped body in sight from the corner of his eye. The car heater had warmed him up during the journey and he no longer felt so cold.

It was just a matter of time before Martin had to break the silence. Lombard knew he was going to speak the moment he heard him stir and saw him lean back in his seat and flex his shoulders.

'There are easier ways to disarm those worthless alarms,' the man said in a toneless voice.

Lombard frowned. He didn't want to talk. He'd been watching Friedman's little house, been imagining how pleasant it must look in the Spring when the trees around it were in blossom, and he'd started absent-mindedly toying with the wedding band around his finger. The sound of Martin's voice had caused him to let go of it, and he opened the window just enough to flick his cigarette away. He lit another. If nothing else, the smoke helped keep his chest warm.

'I'm puzzled,' Martin went on in the same toneless voice; 'What do you want in there? You don't really think your man's there, do you?'

Lombard ignored him, hoping he would shut up, but Martin went on:

'You sure you're just trailing your guy? Or are you really after something else? I mean, it's become obvious to me you like taking risks. Something must be eating you. Is this guy you're after a relative or a close friend or something? 'Cause if he's not, you don't make much sense.'

Lombard ran his eyes over the man's broad shoulders.

'What is it, Martin? You can't stand the silence or you just came up with something and you're trying the friendly tête-à-tête overture?'

'I'm not being friendly,' replied Martin; 'As you can imagine, I don't like you. It's like I said: I'm just puzzled. What are you hoping to achieve by breaking into Friedman's? I told you, he ain't there. You can see there's no one there. Haven't you screwed up enough as it is for one night?'

It was too late now, he'd started talking.

'Maybe my fear's greater than my common sense, Martin.'

'Your…' began Martin, trailing off, as if to think about what Lombard had said.

Lombard turned back towards the house, but Martin had already thought things over.

'You mean you disapprove of what we do, is that it?' he said.

'You sound surprised,' returned Lombard.

'Do I? I don't know you. Why should anything about you surprise me?'

'I don't know. Why don't you tell me about it, Martin? Do you approve of what you do?'

'Huh…'

Lombard felt himself grin, set his eyes on the man's back again.

'How many kids would you say Friedman's little house is worth, eh?'

Martin shrugged:

'That's just a matter of arithmetic.'

'You people are sick,' said Lombard, turning away again.

'Really?'

'Really.'

'I'd have thought a tough guy like you would know better. The sick ones are out there, friend. They make up the clientèle. Get rid of them and we're out of business.'

'Only feeding the disease, eh, Martin?'

'Money talks, bullshit walks. Everything else is just a matter of perspective. Whether you like it or not.'

'Maybe I don't like it.'

'Obviously. Just tell me one thing, though: would you like it any better if we crammed our hotels with suckers on housing benefit? The nice man we bought them from did just that. Had anything from four to eight penned up in a room, kids and all. And raked in about a quarter of a million quid of taxpayers' money a year. Tell me, would you still think we were sick if we did that, or would that be all right?'

'Are you trying to tell me something, Martin?'

'Maybe. The guy in question went around claiming he was helping the public, providing for people who'd otherwise roam the streets and frighten the middle-classes. And no one, from the great Department of Social Security to the local council or his respectable neighbours, thought the worse of him for it. It's all a matter of perspective, you see. But money talks.'

'And from what pleasant perspective does your money talk to you, Martin?'

'Well, think about it. Those who can afford our goods do their thing without upsetting anyone. Those who can't do it to kids from the street or their own family and it makes upsetting headlines.'

'I'm overcome by your public-spiritedness.'

'No you're not. But maybe you should be. Boys like the one you met today are surplus. Commodities worth a handful of notes in whatever arsehole of the world they happen to be born into. We improve some lives buying them where they're not wanted, improve still more selling them where they are. Is that too hard for you?'

Lombard clenched his jaw, considered hitting him again, but decided against it.

'You see, the possibility of raking in hundreds of grand a year for kicking a ball isn't open to all, whatever they tell you. And not everybody's born in the right place or with lucky parents. But perverts, they're everywhere. They transcend everything and every country, whatever you, I or anybody else might think about it. Mind you, if the lucky ones weren't so busy counting their good luck things might be a little different. But the lucky guys have never yet volunteered to carry the torch for humanity. There's no money in it, you see. Or fun. Once you're sitting on top of the world, humanity just looks like a vicious and ugly herd. It's much more fun, more rewarding, to give to charities, to talk about freedom, make movies about bad guys and write cookery books. So some folks are reduced to selling their kids to survive while others don't think twice about coughing up more than their parents might earn working their entire pissy lifetime to have a little fun with them. That's what freedom's all about. That's the principle of it. It's just the way it is, the way it's always been, the way it'll always be. And contrary to what you think, I'm not *just* feeding the disease, friend. I'm just feeding *off* the disease. It doesn't need me to exist. But my children do.'

Lombard frowned. The man had children... He peered at Martin but turned away without saying a word.

Martin must have known what he was thinking, felt his eyes on him. He heard him scoff.

'Uh-huh. And you can take it from me, they won't have to do what I'm doing.'

Lombard bit on his cigarette.

'You're right. You're not even sick. You're just slime.'

'Well, if I am, you find me unrepentant. I'm just the same as everyone else. I'm just like all those folks who go through life calling extermination camps concentration camps. Except that I work in one, in a manner of speaking, and don't gawk at the pictures.'

Lombard took a deep breath.

'You know what, Martin? I ought to tie you down with your old arse up in the air and advertise the hole in the middle of it to the world. Free. And hope you never die...'

'Huh... I'm sure there'd be lots of takers.'

Lombard nodded. What was there to say?

'Could someone have hurt you that bad?' he heard himself pronounce aloud as the words formed in his mind, and he briefly felt the void in his chest and cursed himself.

He shouldn't have said that. It implied too much. Martin was quick to pick up on it. He glanced at his watch.

'Aha', he heard Martin exclaim, more perversely than triumphantly; 'A believer in cause and effect. So? What is *your* story, eh?'

It wasn't time yet. They'd only been waiting eight minutes...

'Well, I tell you what,' Martin went on; 'I don't know how long you intend to keep us in here but, I'll make a deal with you.

I tell you my story in one minute if you tell me yours in one minute. How does that sound, eh? A least that way we're not going to bore each other. But then again, you never know…'

He didn't reply, didn't even turn towards the man.

'I see. What's the matter, friend? Afraid to find out we're the same? 'Cause we are, aren't we? I mean, we both know it could be me sitting back there with a gun threatening to kill, don't we? We could just swap places, couldn't we?'

'Shut up, Martin.'

'Huh. What you gonna do if I don't? Kill me? Well, go ahead then.'

Lombard frowned. The man was challenging him, enjoying himself, and, if he'd been frightened of dying before, he no longer was.

'This is intense, isn't it?' he was saying now; 'I mean, here we are. Two men stuck in a car. You at the back. Me at the front. You with a gun and ready to use it. Me defenceless and ready for you to use it. And neither of us is scared of what you might do. Doesn't that make us the same, eh? Can't you feel the great bond between us. That great intimate void? I mean, we're so close it's almost obscene. All the usual bullshit conventions that rule relationships mean nothing to us, and all the instincts that cause hatred, contempt, compassion, warmth, are just as meaningless. I mean, we hardly know each other, right? I don't like you any more than you like me. I can't even say that I dislike you. But man, just like you, if I was sitting where you are right now, I too could kill you. I tell you, we're more than the same. We're one. A big obscene fucking one. And it's scary, isn't it… *Partner?*'

Lombard didn't want to reply.

'Correction. We're different in one respect,' added Martin; 'Right now my bloody face hurts and yours don't.'

He just couldn't let this pass:

'No, Martin. It's not just your painful face that makes us different. I'm selective in who I kill and I don't have any children to help me feel good about it. Now, since you seem to enjoy talking so much, tell me, what do your kids think of what you do to make a living? Or don't you talk to them about it?'

He swallowed hard, waited for the reply, but none came. Martin had fallen silent at last, and Lombard left him alone. He wasn't interested in him, didn't care whether he'd hit home or if the man was just busy thinking up a clever reply. He had just wanted to make him shut up, and it seemed, had succeeded.

He sighed and peered into the distance towards a car stopping at the corner of the road. A man climbed out of the passenger door and ran through the rain into a public telephone box.

'Whatever, I won't go to hell. No, sir,' Martin suddenly declared, as if emerging from meditation; 'No, sir! I won't go to hell...'

Lombard could hear it in his voice. Martin had thought of something and was intent on sharing it.

'You know, Friedman's got himself a cuckoo clock in there. A genuine antique number. Late 18th century, if he's to be believed...'

Threats might have got him to keep quiet, but Lombard decided not to bother. He knew what was going on. It was all very clear now. The man was still healthy. He was not ready to die yet. Had he been unafraid of dying, he'd have opened his door, got out and quietly walked away. But he was a survivor. And right now, he needed to fill the silence to feel alive, to not think of Lombard and his gun, to ward off the wrenching inner void that Lombard had himself felt just a moment ago. So, he let him talk, let him get on with it, listening to his voice as if to music, hearing its refrain without really listening to the words. Besides, all things considered, it was preferable to have him sit there talking rather than brooding or deciding to open his door and...

' "Cuckoo! Cuckoo!" the damn thing goes... Huh. Did you ever see that movie with the famous speech about the cuckoo clock?'

Movies again. What was it with movies that everyone...

'You know, about Switzerland and centuries of democracy resulting in nothing but the bloody cuckoo clock? Well, they got it all wrong in that movie. The Swiss aren't dumb. They didn't start making their clocks because they had nothing better to do. And they didn't pick on the cuckoo to stick in their clocks by accident, for lack of choice or because of its sweet song. They know exactly what they're doing with their cuckoo clock, and it has bollocks all to do with democracy or calling up the country-side or the arrival of summer or any bullshit of the kind. It's about the way things work, and how they, the fucking Swiss, make things work for them...

'For "Cuckoo-Cuckoo", hear "Fuck You-Fuck You". That's why those Swiss bastards made their cuckoo clocks. To say "fuck you" to the world. To proclaim the world order as it really is at the top of every fucking hour. And the damn world listens only too happily. Huh! "Cuckoo!" Tell me, what do you know about the cuckoo? I mean the fucking bird itself. What does anyone know about the cuckoo except for the fact that the damn thing goes "Cuckoo", eh? I mean, have you ever seen a cuckoo? Have you ever even met somebody who's seen a cuckoo? Have you ever even met somebody who's met somebody who's seen a fucking cuckoo? I mean, unless you rub shoulders with better people than me or you've got yourself a nice country cottage, that is...'

Martin had started using a lot more swear words...

'Well, let me tell you about the cuckoo. The freaking thing is probably the worst sonofabitch in the bird kingdom. For a start, your average specimen feeds on vile hairy caterpillars that other birds won't touch. Still, some might say that's a good thing, but anyway, it's quite beside the point, so... The point, the real crux of the matter with the cuckoo, is the way it makes the rest of the bird kingdom work for it. That's the interesting part. You see, there's no *I'm gonna work hard and break my fucking back to make a home and look after my eggs and rear my young* in the cuckoo's book of good conduct. No, sir. The thought doesn't enter its head. It worked out a long time ago that the great big show is a mug's game and that everything's for the taking. That the only object of it all is survival for survival's sake, no matter what. Survival by any means, and even by means meaner than necessary...

'So come Spring and egg-laying time, the thing goes flying about in search of smaller birds' unattended nests, birds which in all likelihood don't know any more shit about cuckoos than the rest of us but which the cuckoo selects for the very reason of their small size in comparison to itself. When it finds what it's looking for, it lays just one egg and, depending on its mood, and whether it's got the time, it might or might not toss the rightful nest-owner's eggs off the side, though more often that not it will, and as a healthy cuckoo turns out about a dozen eggs a year, and repeats this exercise as many times and in as many nests, it might or might not toss over the side a hell of a lot of eggs before it's done. Quite a carnage. Anyhow, once that's over and done with, off it goes, to enjoy itself for the remainder of the good season, assured of its *descendance*. And for good reason...

'Because you see, what happens after it's left its egg in each nest goes something like this. Small bird returns home, finds it's got only one egg left or—hallelujah—one dropped from the heavens to lodge itself amongst its other eggs inside its precious little nest. Whatever, a slave to its good and natural instincts – which tell it something like *I'm gonna work hard and break my fucking back to make a home and look after my eggs and rear my young whether I only have one funny looking egg left or I'm blessed with an immaculate conception* – it sits tight and expectantly awaits hatching time. And that's when the cuckoo really comes into its own, when it leaves other parasites and sonsofbitches leagues behind. When God definitely tries to tell somebody something...

'If young cuckoo hatches to find out it's an only child, that mother has already seen to its foster parents' unborn babies, everything's cool; it lets foster mummy and daddy dote on it until it's big and fat and it's time to fly off. And the foster parents inevitably look after it. They didn't read the ugly duckling story. Worked hard building the nest and all that. And were rewarded with the happy hatching. What's a bird to do, huh?... But if mother cuckoo was sloppy, or had better things to do than get rid of its unborn foster brothers and sisters, then what happens is truly fucking remarkable. It's one thing to think of adult birds behaving like callous amoral parasites and mass murderers. But newly hatched ones? Innocent little things? Isn't the world meant to be a nice place, where only he who gets hurt misbehaves? Isn't it? Cause and effect, right? Well, if it is, somebody forgot to tell the cuckoo. Or, as I already said, God is bloody telling us something, because them young cuckoos, whatever damn purpose they're meant to fulfil other than swallowing hairy caterpillars, they sure are ungrateful merciless little shits in their hunger for life. Truly fucking amazing and despicable. Because they don't just hatch, you see. They hatch to kill. However plentiful the batch of eggs young cuckoo might find itself in, as if by magic, it will always hatch before any of the others. That gives it an edge, see – first out, first fed, first to grow – and since it already has the edge anyway by virtue of the fact mummy cleverly dropped it into a family of smaller kind-hearted birds, in no time it's strong enough to eject all its foster brothers and sisters over the side. And it does it. It's already being looked after, it's already stronger than all the other guys in there, it needn't worry about the competition, needn't kill or destroy, but it fucking does it. Truly remarkable, wouldn't you say? Truly fucking remarkable…

'Well, that's what the damn cuckoo is all about when it ain't busy eating grubs, enjoying itself or going "Cuckoo", and that's what the Swiss must have been thinking when they came up with their clock. Their clock's no accident of democracy. It's no creation of a bored and boring people. It's a fucking cock a snook at the world. A sweet "Fuck you" by a parasitic people. A clever proclamation to the world of the world order as it really is at the top of every fucking hour…

'Like the cuckoo, the Swiss sorted things out a long time ago, see? Like the cuckoo, they make the world work for them while they enjoy the good seasons. And like the fucking cuckoo at the end of the day they're probably responsible for untold slaughter…

'Think about it. For small bird and nest, think the decent world of rules and regulations designed to ensure fairness, good behaviour, love-thy-neighbour and rewards for the nice hard-working folk. For cuckoo, think of the secretive Swiss banking system. Now, by virtue of allowing anyone to hide away unlimited amounts of cash no-questions-asked, the Swiss virtually behave like the cuckoo. By providing every bad guy everywhere from bloodthirsty dictators to drug barons to crooked this or that and lucky ones who don't fancy paying their taxes with the means to conceal the fortunes there are to be made from deceit, they virtu-ally make the world work for them, virtually feed off and destroy all the good work everyone else does. Everyone says, "You must be accountable"; fucking Switzer-fucking-land says, "No you don't. Just drop us a line and let us tell you how things work". And what about the hatching part of the plot, you may ask. Well, for young cuckoo throwing his foster brothers and sisters out of the nest, think how many people are exploited and die as a result of others being provided with the means of hiding immorally acquired wealth? You follow what I'm saying? Your good Swiss breeds crime. The misery and death directly or indirectly caused by Switzerland's banking system is just not fucking quantifiable. You can't parasite on crime and deceit and not breed crime. No way. At best, leaving hard crime aside, each time a rich fucker hides his money in a Swiss coffer to avoid paying taxes someone somewhere loses out. The rich don't pay their taxes, schools, hospitals etc. aren't built, kids aren't educated, the ill don't get treatment, blah-blah-blah-blah-blah...

'See? The Swiss are just like the cuckoo. And like the fucking cuckoo, they rely on the great paradox of nature – a corrupt subsistence is determined by the goodness of others. The cuckoo depends on good-natured birds to lead its corrupt existence, the Swiss on other countries' good-natured men and laws. And like the cuckoo, they're doing very well, thank you very much. Switzerland is a fucking lump of rock. No natural resources, nothing. Yet, it's got one of the highest standards of living in the world. With banking as one of its main sources of income... "Cuckoo!" Yeah, they can go fucking "Cuckoo!" Huh! The wicked shall inherit the earth, all right. And so will I. So will I. If what I'm doing was wrong, if what I'm doing went against the world order, against God's instructions, there'd be no fucking Switzer-fucking-land. And no cuckoos. But cuckoo-bird and Switzerland are here with us, and both are prospering and merry. So I won't go to hell, friend. The cuckoo is part of humanity, just like the Swiss. The plight, hell, is for the small birds...

'No. I won't go to hell...'

Lombard nodded. The man was in his forties, just about the right age to have been one of those young men who'd held court in cafés and other public places when he himself was still a young teenager. He could just imagine him with a long mane of red hair, all piercing blue eyes and smooth pale skin, making an equally obscure and long-winded speech for the sole purpose of impressing upon an innocent young audience how bad the world was and how good drugs were. It had been fashionable then for youth to theorise about conspiracies and look down on the apparently well-ordered society of ordinary people. Perhaps it still was...

'Tell me something, Martin,' he asked, glancing at his watch – it was safe to go now; 'Did you start your criminal career peddling drugs with such enlightened speeches? Was that how you persuaded potential recruits to drop out, turn on and tune in to what you had to sell?'

'Huh... You got it wrong,' said Martin; 'It was turn on, tune in and drop out... And nah, I started long before I got to that...'

He probably had too.

'Let's get out of here,' said Lombard, opening his door.

He glanced at his briefcase, chose to leave it behind, climbed out of the car and shut the door with his eyes on Martin, who reluctantly got out of the driver's seat.

'Must you really do this?' asked the man as they stood facing each other in the rain.

His eyes had lost their sharpness. He looked merely demoralised as he tucked his hands into his coat pockets, like a child who is about to be taken for a stay with a boring relative.

Lombard motioned for him to move away from the car door and leaned inside to pull the keys from the ignition.

As he locked the car he couldn't help but realise that he felt strangely light and clear-headed all of a sudden, and he took a moment to gaze at the keys in his hand. Besides the car keys, there were two Yale keys on the giant's BMW key ring. The big man owned the keys to either two doors or two locks on the same door. Unlike Martin, he probably didn't reside at the Ambassador. Perhaps he rented a flat, just like Lombard who also had just two keys on his ring besides that of his Triumph; one opened the front door by Perkins' shop and the other his flat door...

He swallowed hard, pocketed the keys and turned towards Friedman's house.

It was a pretty house indeed, its old-fashioned charm marking it out as special, even in Hampstead, even in the dark, through winter rain and with a car concealed under a tarpaulin spoiling its front drive.

'What's up?' he heard Martin ask grumpily beside him.

He realised why he felt so light, why things looked sharp and free from unpleasant associations. It was the motion he'd just made of leaning inside the driver's door to retrieve the keys from the ignition. He'd done this well over a dozen times when teaching Aline to drive; she was so nervous of driving that when they stopped she always climbed out of the car with such relief that she invariably forgot the keys inside. Or so it had seemed, because later she'd confessed that her forgetfulness was perhaps not that unintentional, that she hated cars so much, found them such alienating machines, that she took exception to having to take any part of them into her 'real' life. And as far as she was concerned, the car keys were part of the machine…

TEN

He stepped around the man's leather slippers aligned squarely to the single wooden bed and, without thinking, lifted the bedspread.

The sheets stretched impeccably white and crease-less, but in the pillow, there was a hollow, just in the middle. He gazed at it, imagining the person who'd made the bed tossing the pillow against the headboard and automatically slapping it down, as one does after changing sheets, because it was clear they hadn't been slept in; they still smelled of fresh starch.

He let go of the bedspread and pulled open the bedside table drawer.

It held a folded white handkerchief, a hair-net, a leather-bound German bible and a brown pigskin case which, after inspection, turned out to contain a manicure set and a matchbox filled with nail clippings. He frowned. Friedman was in the habit of cutting his nails in his bedroom, and although he still had no idea what the man looked like, having failed to find any photographs anywhere in the house, he pictured the Austrian sitting on his bed, dressed in a pair of the silk pyjamas he'd just seen in the cupboard, fastidiously picking up each chip of nail after each snap of the clippers and putting it away in the matchbox. Was he in the habit of doing this in the evening, just before going to sleep? Nail-cutting, especially in one's bedroom, especially when one lives alone, wasn't really a morning occupation, rather the kind of quiet grooming that's performed in the unconstrained time between washing and getting into bed.

He replaced the manicure set in the drawer, let his eyes linger on the hair-net, wondered if the Austrian had styled hair which needed protecting at night, and reached for the bible.

Its pages were well-fingered. He put it back down, looked up, peered at the oil landscape on the wall above the bed, sighed, turned, walked across the deep carpet and switched off the light on his way out.

The monotonous ticking of the cuckoo clock in the ground floor hallway reached him as he started across the landing towards the stairs.

Exactly what he had hoped to find at the Austrian's was unclear even to him. He'd merely followed instinct, maybe needing to see for himself that Friedman really had left the country, or possibly responding to that old impulse – the beast craving for the smell of its prey. It was probably a little of both. In any case, he hadn't really expected the house would hold the answer to Leonard Spitz's disappearance, which was just as well because, the moment he'd switched on the drawing room chandelier after breaking in through the French windows from the garden, recognising the classical elegance of his surroundings (two words had come to mind as he surveyed the polished antique furniture around the padded sofas: Regency and Rococo, even though he wasn't quite sure what either actually referred to), he'd guessed the occupant was far too strict and refined an individual to bring his work home, let alone to leave clues to his criminal activities lying around.

His exploration of the house had proved him right, and also convinced him Friedman was one of those men who, whether by inclination or necessity, regards his home as a sanctuary, in this case an opulent, television-free haven of culture which possessed a strange timeless quality. Inasmuch as a house can speak for its resident, this one had suspiciously little to say, but there could be little doubt that, unless forced by circumstances, it was not the place where the Austrian would have held someone captive or, for that matter, stored his merchandise, whether it be snuff movies or doped-up little boys. The mere suggestion seemed like sacrilege.

From what Lombard had observed, Friedman was partial to fine wines – the vaulted cellar was well stocked; played the piano – a ground floor room was devoted to a grand piano, classical recordings, score-books and librettos; favoured conservative black or white summer suits which, according to mood, he wore with sober neckties or bright bow-ties; was most particular about his footwear, possibly even had a shoe-fetish – several dozen shiny pairs held taut with shoetrees were kept in a purpose-built cabinet in the mirrored changing room off his bedroom; and, if the English and German novels that lined the study and the oil paintings on the walls weren't just for show, he was also well-read and an Art enthusiast. In short, a man of vanity and sophisticated tastes, together with the means to indulge them. Yet, all that was there and, more significantly, all that wasn't there, pointed to an austere and pragmatic mind. The furniture alone could conceivably have been worth as much as the building itself, but it stood so highly-polished and bereft of clutter or personal effects that, if not for the few odd, discordant ornaments here and there – like the two rather crude statuettes of bow-and-arrowed angels which flanked the spare bedroom's heavy oak bed – most rooms could have featured in an interior decorating publication just as they were, from the pastel coloured bathroom with its gold-tapped bathtub, to the kitchen with its gleaming black Aga, sets of copper pots, round wooden table and exposed beams.

It all just seemed too tidy and formal and, oddly, given what had brought him there, reminded Lombard of Leonard Spitz's barren and impersonal Highgate apartment. Like Leonard's, Friedman's home felt hollow, perhaps even more hollow. There were no neat piles of magazines here, no messy darkroom or strange smell – Friedman's house smelt clean throughout, or rather, wholesome, a blend of wax, wood and expensive fabrics; there were no lurid photographs of girls, no address book, private letters, snapshots, flashing answering machines or dirty cereal bowls. Even the refrigerator and bathroom medicine cabinet were empty. The Austrian surely called there only infrequently; or else he had no social life, always ate out and spent his time home reading, playing the piano or contemplating his paintings while sipping his fine wine.

Or, like most men intent on living long while pursuing a criminal career, he watched his back carefully, depriving himself of anything which might help trace him if and when his day came to flee at short notice, from friends' and relatives' addresses to all those little things that make a home but also shed light on one's personal habits. People's affairs were perhaps never that complicated, but insofar as nothing is free, they were never that simple either. Even peddling little boys for vast amounts of money has its downside and, refined as he was, Friedman would be as wary of his business associates as of the authorities. In fact, it wouldn't have surprised Lombard if his Hampstead house was merely a convenient investment, a *business address*, and that the Austrian owned another place, a real home that looked and smelled like a home, one he skulked to from time to time. For a man who could speak calmly of children as trained and untrained puppies, leading a double-life was probably no more than a nuisance, a small price to pay for being allowed to sleep peacefully at night.

'Dear Maria,' began the hand-written note on the dresser by the front door. Lombard had already read it, earlier, before seeing the upstairs, but his eyes came upon it now as he crossed the hall on his way to the study and he paused to read it again. Now he'd seen the house, it somehow held more resonance.

The letters were small and neat, but fuzzed here and there, as if drafted by an occasionally shaky hand.

'Dear Maria, I will have gone by the time you arrive today and as I informed you, shall not return until December 28th. Tidy up the house as usual and do not forget the laundry (you forgot the bathroom towels last week!). While it won't be necessary for you to come during the next fortnight, I will expect you to come on the 27th to dust the place before my return. Also, if between then and now you have snow or frost here in London, I would appreciate it if you could come by and turn the heating up. It is presently set on medium to high. In case of problems (frozen, burst pipes etc.), inform Mrs. Woodcock immediately.'

It was signed with a capital 'O' followed by a full stop, and ended with a post-scriptum which simply read:

'Happy Christmas.'

Judging from the crisp sheets on Friedman's bed, Maria had come and gone and, for some reason, had left the note on the dresser. He couldn't say why, but Lombard guessed it had been left there deliberately. Anyone who could do as thorough a tidying up job as had been done in this house was unlikely to have overlooked an obsolete note sitting in full view by the front door. Had Maria disliked its tone? Or the exclamation mark after the part about the bathroom towels? Or the formality of the post-scripted seasonal good wishes? If Maria was a maid, she may have expected to be left a Christmas bonus rather than a 'Happy...'

A muffled sound of breaking glass from the direction of the kitchen interrupted Lombard's thoughts. He froze, moved his finger inside the gun's trigger guard, turned and, remaining still, peered across the hall and through the open kitchen door. There was no need for him to go in there. The dull nature of the noise pointed to its source. It came from the cellar off the kitchen, where he'd left Martin. It was the only place without windows and, although there were no keys to it, he'd secured the door by wedging the handle with a chair on which he'd balanced one of a pair of matching turquoise vases. Were he set on it, Martin could always force his way out, but not without making enough racket to be heard.

Martin was not trying to force his way out of the cellar. Apart from the sound of the rain drumming against the front door fanlight behind him, silence had returned between the crisp clicks of the cuckoo clock on the wall just beside his ear. He guessed Martin had accidentally knocked over one of Friedman's hoard of wine bottles. The man who'd had to be helped over the garden wall after proving incapable of lifting his portly body up its four foot height by himself, and who had then stood resolutely grim-faced when asked to step through the French windows, eventually driving Lombard to shove him inside, and who had then gone on brooding, standing rigidly quiet with his hands pushed deep in his pockets and his eyes fixed on the floor, was not likely to be ready to take chances. Not yet. Not while he could hear footsteps moving around the house above him.

Still, Lombard wondered if he shouldn't investigate, but then decided against it. Short of going for the door, there wasn't much Martin could do, and besides, Lombard knew what had brought about the man's sudden subdued apathy. Or he thought he knew. He'd found the explanation in Martin's fixed stare towards the floor, when he'd realised that the redheaded man wasn't brooding but was actually engrossed in dark contemplation of the wet footprints they were leaving all over Friedman's deep carpets.

Martin wasn't just grinding his teeth in angry resignation. Nor, as might have been expected, was he concerned about being killed now that it could be done discreetly; nor for that matter was he worried about what Lombard might find inside the house. It was simpler than that. Martin was scared. He was scared of Friedman. *'Martin works for Friedman,'* the giant had said, *'Friedman's the boss',* and Martin's thoughts of cuckoo clocks and hell had been all but supplanted by fear even as they stepped into the Austrian's front drive. They were breaking into his boss's retreat, profaning its immaculate tranquillity, and, judging by his bullied-schoolboy demeanour, that wasn't just a bad idea but one he knew he'd be made to pay for. Martin was so scared of what the Austrian would do when he learnt who was responsible for bringing Lombard to his house that he who had held his own in the car when faced with the possibility of being shot by a stranger had lost his voice, his nerve and the canny glint from his eyes when the time had come to violate Friedman's sanctuary.

Maybe all the time in the BMW he'd been too preoccupied with the nearness of Lombard's gun to worry about the long-term implications. But in time a four foot high wall had defeated him... There was no need to investigate. Martin must have knocked over one of Friedman's wine bottles.

Lombard let go of the trigger, took a deep breath and frowned. Even so, even now, he couldn't help finding Martin's behaviour strange. That a man should be frightened of his boss, particularly amongst child traffickers, was not in itself extraordinary. But for a seasoned criminal like Martin to react to this fear in the manner he had, was, to say the least, unexpected. Fear invariably sparks one or other of the many survival instincts, but Martin ought not to have succumbed to what in his position was possibly the most inappropriate of all instincts: the one which tells the mind to switch off and distance itself from its owner's plight, feeding it the notion that non-active participation, passive resistance, disapproval or even feelings of guilt will add up to innocence and accordingly bring salvation or absolution. Martin ought to have known better. He ought to have been relied upon to know that that particular instinct belongs to the self-preservation bag of tricks, that its sole *raison d'être* is to rescue troubled consciences, not people in perilous situations, that it shows up to make you feel good on the inside, not beautiful on the outside, and so may be of help in defeating inner demons but is of no benefit against outer, three-dimensional threats.

Since it was doubtful Martin was a believer in the merits of 'inner glow' as an instrument of survival in the face of danger, he had to be very scared of Friedman indeed to be reduced to acting as if he was. And, since Martin had already demonstrated he could handle fear, Friedman had to be very frightening indeed to have that kind of effect of him.

Cuckoo!

Lombard sprung back. The clock's small wooden bird was announcing eight o'clock. He glared at it, waiting for its song to end.

When the cuckoo had retreated behind its carved shutters which closed with a snap, and silence returned, he glanced at Maria's note again, made for the study, stopped just inside the doorway and lit a Gitane.

The dark, wood-panelled room was just as he'd left it, its heavy velvet curtains drawn, its veneered desk inlaid with a black and gold four-headed eagle scattered with the household bills and bank and credit card statements that he'd pulled from its drawers. These documents were all addressed to one Mr. Otto Gluck in Kidderpore Avenue who kept over £10,000 in a current account, held half a dozen credit cards and had below average electricity, gas and telephone bills. He had quickly glanced at the telephone bills' itemised numbers and the bank statements' recorded transactions, guessing they wouldn't have been left there if there was anything to be learnt from them. The room also contained a combination safe. It was set into the wall behind a section of wood-panelling which turned out to be a hinged screen. Lombard had hit upon it after noticing that this screen was of a slightly lighter shade than the rest of the room's panelling. However, since safecracking wasn't one of his skills and the safe was too well-built to be forced open, its contents were out of reach.

He let his eyes wander across the lamp, pen-set, old Bakelite telephone and snow-dome lining the edge of the desk – this snow-dome, a cheap plastic bauble which held an upright English bobby, was, like the angel statuettes in the spare bedroom, one of the house's discordant ornaments – then moved to the large gold-framed oil portrait which hung on the wall directly opposite the desk.

There had been no reason for him to give much thought to this particular painting when he first came across it. It was just one of many, showing a lanky man in a dark suit sitting rather stiffly with his legs crossed in front of a fireplace. Only, later, another painting in the upstairs changing room – a landscape with a windmill in a wheat field under a flaming red sky – had inexplicably held his attention. It had taken him a while to realise why, but then he'd remembered the cross-legged man, and it had struck him that the house had only one portrait among all its still lifes and landscapes.

He was right. There was a painting within the painting of the cross-legged man. Above the fireplace, just over the man's right shoulder, hung a landscape, a mere sketch of the original in the upstairs room but unmistakably the same windmill beneath its flaming sky.

That he could have noted, recollected and then placed this small detail somewhat surprised him. Had he been asked, he'd probably have been incapable of describing the man in the portrait, although, on reflection, he had spent time at the desk across the room from it, and the red sky around the windmill did stand out against the rest of the painting's predominantly pale green and dark brown shades.

The artist's signature in the bottom left corner was illegible. Lombard stuck his Gitane between his lips, reached for the painting's frame, unhooked it, turned it over to inspect the back.

Through the smoke from his cigarette, he nearly missed the small, faded caption pencilled against the grey canvas:

'WIEN, 1979'

There was no need for him to be fluent in German to know *Wien* was the German name for Vienna. This was the kind of general knowledge one acquires subliminally while going through life.

He turned the painting around again, held it at arms length and focused on the man's face. The complexion was pale, ashen almost. The hair was fair, slightly wavy, parted on one side and combed back from the round forehead. The lips were tightly shut, stretching in a thin line between the hollow cheeks beneath high cheekbones. And the slightly slanted eyes above the narrow nose were dark and intense, staring rather than looking back at the viewer. All in all, it was a handsome forty or fifty year-old face, a face one would guess belonged to a romantic or artistic soul, an impression reinforced by the man's proud pose and slender hands which lay clearly defined against the dark cloth of his suit trousers, as if both subject and artist had set out to show off their elegant distinction.

Lombard nodded. All other pointers aside, such fine hands could most definitely be those of a pianist. But if they did belong to Friedman and the date pencilled on the canvas indicated the painting's age, since the man it portrayed was at that time well into his forties, it made Friedman an old man who should now be nearing his seventieth birthday. And this without even taking into account the likelihood that the artist had flattered his subject by making him look younger than he was at the time.

The voice Lombard had heard on the phone was old, but... If the opulence of the house and its display of culture were a true reflection of his means and disposition, a seventy-year-old Friedman ought to be discovering the joys of retirement, not living dangerously and watching his back, like a young blood on his way up through the ranks.

Teeth clenched on his Gitane, he peered into the portrait's eyes. If they were Friedman's, the Austrian had to be upsetting a lot of younger men, men who were waiting for him to retire or die, hungry for promotion, greedy for power. When it comes to old age, criminals are not that different from everyone else. The Austrian had to be smart. Unless they retire early, dumb criminals don't get old. And, unless this was all a trick and the redheaded Martin had brought him to the wrong house, he was also far too wealthy not to know his business. Yet...

'Leon bought him. From an Austrian who sells little children to perverts,' he could still hear Rhian say in her soft Welsh accent.

'Aren't you glad you came, Mr. Lombard?...'

After one look at Leonard Spitz's photograph, even Martin himself had...

Things weren't getting any better. A few hours ago it had just been a matter of following a trail that pointed straight to an Austrian child procurer he was still convinced was responsible for Leonard Spitz's disappearance. Now, he'd lost Deborah De Moraes' £20,000, left a man dying in a hotel room, abducted another who at this very moment was brooding in the cellar of a house he'd broken into, and for all that, he was as far from finding out what had happened to Mrs. Spitz's son as he had been all of those few hours ago. If anything, he was further away. According to Martin, thousands of miles away. The man with the answers was in Los Angeles, had left the very morning after they'd spoken on the phone, not due back until the 28th of December, almost three weeks away...

He swallowed hard, biting on his Gitane. He had better have another chat with Martin.

The warmth from the Aga enveloped him as soon as he stepped into the kitchen and, perhaps because of that, he momentarily became aware that his sodden shirt still clung to his skin. He crossed the red-tiled floor to the cellar door, transferred the portrait into his right hand which already held the gun, with his left hand removed the vase from the chair that wedged the door closed, kicked the chair away and pulled the door open, taking a step back as he did so.

He realised something was wrong as soon as his eyes registered that there was no light in the cellar stairwell. He frowned, his hand still pulling the door open, but before he could process the information, a piercing scream rooted him to the spot. He squinted, focused into the darkness down the stairs and, in the light from the kitchen behind him, saw Martin's screaming face looming up fast out of the darkness, caught sight of the broken bottle at the end of his outstretched arm…

There was no time to get out of the way or slam the door shut. In two seconds, the broken bottle would stab him. In three, Martin's body would hurtle into his.

He let go of the door, let go of the painting, started bending his knees, started turning the gun in his right hand, moving his left arm to shield his face, moving his finger towards the trigger.

The bottle was one second away from his chest now. He saw the sharp glass still glistening with wine, felt his finger hit the cold trigger. He was nearly squatting now. His left arm hit his face. He shut his eyes, squeezed the trigger and winced.

Bang! The glass stabbed through his coat, jacket and shirt, punctured the flesh somewhere beneath his left shoulder and impacted on bones. He let himself go, let himself flow with the impact, tumbling backward, squeezing the trigger again.

Bang! The glass ripped his flesh as his body fell away from it. Martin's legs stumbled over his flying knees.

Bang! He squeezed the trigger again as his back collided with the hard floor.

The sound of breaking glass filled his ears. His head cracked against the hard tiles, his teeth clashed and Martin crashed on top of him, crushing his rib cage.

His throat contracted. A lightning bolt sliced across his head, hot and blinding, exploding against his eyelids.

He opened his eyes, winded. He was peering into silent darkness. He could not move, breath, see or hear, but he felt his heart thump, felt Martin stir on top of him. He… Martin was sitting on top of him…

He moved, spat out the Gitane still stuck between his lips, opened his mouth, let out a silent yell and freed the air stuck in his throat. Two hands closed around his neck and squeezed.

He tensed his neck muscles, heard his ears fill with Martin's scream again, watched his eyes fill with light again.

Martin's crazed eyes gazed down at him. Martin's twisted mouth yelled. He brought his right hand up, pressed the trigger and…

He froze, stared at his empty hand, felt his neck give way, tensed up again and threw his hand down.

He had to remain calm, had to pat rather than feel the ground, not too fast, taking care not to sweep the gun out of reach…

He brought up his left hand, tried pushing Martin away. It was no use. The man was too heavy, too frenzied, too high on adrenaline to be moved. Maybe… He closed his hand into a fist and struck his swollen cheek. Martin just went on screaming, just went on squeezing.

He clasped his left hand around Martin's wrist, tried pulling. It felt like rock, hard and immovable. He let go of it. He could feel his head swelling. His chest burning. His eyes bulging. And Martin's face was becoming ever more dark and distant, a sinister silhouette, starting to dance in the light of flashing and shooting stars. He was going to die unless…

He shut his eyes again. His right hand was still patting the ground, but the gun wasn't there… He was going to die.

He opened his eyes. He could still see, just. The monster's face was but a twisted and sparkling shadow, but he could still see. He focused just below the chin, until he could make sense of the lines of the neck. If…

He brought his right hand back, clasped his fingers tight with his knuckles protruding and, with all the strength he could summon, aimed for the Adam's apple…

He didn't feel his fist make contact, just lost the use of mind and sight again as tears shot from his eyes when the air locked in his chest wheezed from his mouth and his throat exploded in a fit of flesh-ripping coughs. Then, after however long – there was no way for him to tell – his mind kicked back into life, relaying the message that the monster's hands were still clasped around his neck, but no longer squeezing, merely resting on the skin.

Martin was gazing down at him. He looked shocked, his head and shoulders swaying gently to and fro while he jigged up and down in time with Lombard's coughing convulsions. Martin was choking. Lombard had obviously hit his target.

He wrenched the man's hands from his neck, grabbed hold of his lapels, heaved him up and tossed him aside with such force he sent him flying into the legs of the nearby table, then he sprang to his feet, searched for the gun, spotted it just outside the cellar door, picked it up and spun round.

Martin lay still on his side, his cheek to the floor, his hands around his own throat now. He was clearly breathing again, gasping for air, but that was all he appeared capable of doing.

Still coughing, lungs still burning, shaking now, Lombard remained where he was, eyes and gun firmly fixed on Martin.

A minute later he was again breathing softly enough to hear the hallway clock through Martin's low rasping groans. Martin had moved just once, slowly bringing his knees up to his chest, so that he now lay in a foetal position, and two pools of blood had begun to appear on the floor around him; one was small, fanning around his head, the other, growing fast, spread around his gut, over the side of his open coat.

Lombard stepped forward, stopped above him and forced him flat onto his back, pushing his shoulder down with his foot. The man sent out a plaintive cry but didn't resist. He just let his arms slump to the ground and looked up, face set in a grimace.

Lombard frowned. Martin had cracked the side of his forehead on hitting the ground. The blood around his head trickled from an open gash just beneath his hairline. He also had blood on his lips and teeth, but more significantly, his eyes had lost their pupils. They were pure blue now, as if made of dull blue liquid, like sunken seas, and although they looked straight up at Lombard, they were distant, as if they didn't really see, like the eyes of a blind man.

Martin's lips twitched; he appeared to want to speak but only managed a throaty groan and to cough a little blood.

Lombard moved his eyes to the man's chest. A soft gurgling sound seemed to come from beneath his blood-soaked pullover. He squatted and, ignoring Martin's distressed groans, yanked the bloody pullover, the shirt and vest up to his chest, which, due to the man's bulk and potbelly and weight, required both hands.

One of the shots he'd fired had entered the upper abdomen, just beneath the breastbone, and had clearly caused internal damage. The wound spat blood and hissed, indicating, amongst other things, a perforated lung.

He wiped the blood off his hands on a clean part of Martin's coat, brought the tip of the Beretta above the hissing wound, but then paused, noticing a pattern of dark intersecting lines through the blood on the man's skin. The lines ended in three triangular points which made up the lower part of a geometrical pattern partially concealed under the rolled up clothes. It took Lombard a moment, but he eventually made out what he was looking at; Martin had a Star of David tattooed across his chest…

He raised his brows, gently jabbed the wound with his gun and winced as a spatter of blood hit his face and Martin sent out a high-pitched moan:

'Damn…'

Martin was still responsive. Martin wasn't gone yet.

'Damn.'

Squatting by his side, Lombard scrutinised him. He was slowly stroking his round belly now, eyes closed.

'Damn…'

The blood from the gash on his forehead rolled down his temple, making a dark red trail through his hair, and, staring at it, Lombard found himself thinking he'd been wrong to regard Martin's hair as red. It wasn't red. It was brown-red, a colour he'd have described in police reports as Titian red, or even *vénitien blond*.

'Can you hear me, Martin?' he asked, softly.

'Damn you… Who are you?'

The voice was barely audible, a faint rasp rather than a whisper, but he could hear Lombard all right.

'Who are you working for, eh?' Martin went on.

'Can you see?'

'I… Are my eyes shut?'

'Yeah.'

'Right, then give me a moment.'

'You haven't got time, Martin. You're going to die.'

'Are you sure?'

'Yes.'

'Damn…'

Martin opened his eyes and kept them fixed on the ceiling above him. Lombard leaned over him. The irises were still liquid blue, but the pupils were there again, tiny and black but there.

'Can you see me?'

Martin gazed back at him silently, then asked:

'Did I hurt you?'

'Just tell me if you can you see me, Martin.'

'The bottle. I'm sure I got you with the bottle.'

Lombard had forgotten about the bottle. He leaned back to inspect his shoulder and stiffened. His shirt and jacket were soaked with blood, but a quick examination of the flesh under his shirt allayed his fears; the skin was cut, raw and bleeding, but it wasn't as bad as it could have been. Most of the blood on him was Martin's.

He sighed. He was lucky. Had Martin hung onto the bottle when he'd stumbled on top of him…

'Why didn't you wait just behind the door instead of halfway up the stairs?' he asked.

Was that a perplexed frown above Martin's eyes?

'You… You don't think I did right?' the man asked, turning his head slightly to face Lombard.

He could see. And not only could he see, but the cogs behind his eyes were clearly hard at work again.

'You don't think I did right? Huh?'

The possibility he may have done wrong seemed to genuinely trouble him.

'Needed the run-up, to make sure your gun wouldn't stop me,' he went on.

Lombard didn't reply.

'I almost got you, didn't I?'

'Friedman, Martin,' said Lombard; 'Save your breath to talk to me about Friedman. Where can he be contacted?'

Either Martin hadn't heard or his mind was stuck on track.

'Thought I might as well have a go,' he rasped, breaking off to cough some blood; 'You were going to bump me off anyway, weren't you?'

'Friedman, Martin! Where is Friedman?' said Lombard.

'You were, weren't you?' persisted Martin; 'You had to. You know you had to. What you did back at the hotel. Here. I'd have had to hunt you down. You knew that, didn't you…?'

It seemed that more than dying itself, Martin couldn't bear the thought of passing away as a result of an error of judgement.

Lombard sighed, stood up, went to retrieve the painting from the floor by the cellar door.

'Now,' he said, holding the portrait above Martin; 'You may be dying but there still might be time for me to make you wish you'd never turned bad. And I'd sooner not bother, okay? So don't make it hard on both of us. Are we looking at Friedman here, Martin?'

Martin gazed at the portrait, then either snarled, grimaced or grinned. It was impossible to tell. But something happened inside his head, because his pupils clearly enlarged, ate up the blue of his eyes and, briefly, he looked his cunning self again.

He wasn't so much eyeing as challenging Lombard when he spoke again:

'You were going to do me in, right?'

Lombard scowled, turned to the man's bleeding chest, raised his foot but then changed his mind. Martin had just found an angle, found a new lease on life on discovering he had something to trade. Perhaps he had better give him something to be pleased about.

'That's right, Martin,' he said; 'I was going to do you in. Now, is this Friedman?'

He'd made a mistake. Instead of answering, Martin simply looked away, rested his gaze back on the ceiling, heaved a sigh of relief and, his face so relaxed that even the swelling on his cheek seemed to have suddenly shrunk, began to cry, faintly, all the time gently rubbing his belly.

Lombard looked away, on impulse, as if there was something indecent about Martin crying, then turned back, seething:

'Do you really want to take Friedman to your grave, Martin? I didn't think you did.'

'Give me a moment,' said Martin.

'You've already asked for your moment, Martin. And you've already had it. You haven't got many moments left.'

'A dying man can do with every moment he can get,' replied Martin; 'I'm in charge of this show now, tough guy…'

He attempted what looked like a smile, coughed some more blood and shut his eyes again.

Lombard swallowed hard. Martin was right. Apart from subjecting him to pain and killing him in the process, there was nothing left to be done with him. At least he'd declared his willingness to talk. Or had he?

'Open your eyes, Martin,' he said; 'Keep your eyes open or you might just slip away.'

Martin obeyed, and Lombard mouthed a silent curse when he saw that the man's eyes were all liquid blue again.

'You're no cop, are you?' rasped Martin.

Lombard hesitated.

'No.'

'Good… I was going to go up in a hot-air balloon for my 45th birthday, you know… Have you ever been up in a hot-air balloon?'

'Damn…' cursed Lombard; 'Talk to me about Friedman, Martin.'

'The Wyatt…' groaned the man.

'What?'

'It's a hotel, in Los Angeles…'

'Los… Is that where Friedman is?'

'The Wyatt. It's a hotel in Los Angeles…'

'What? One of your hotels?'

'Huh… It's sad.'

'What is?'

'Dying without ever reaching the top,' said Martin, suddenly going off into soft rasping laughter.

Lombard scowled.

'Is the Wyatt one of your hotels, Martin? Another place were you keep kids? Is that where Friedman's gone?'

'No. It's just a hotel. But you won't catch him… You can't catch him…'

Was he talking about Friedman?'

'Why is that, Martin?'

'Because he's as sprightly as a mountain goat and as cruel as a… cuckoo… Ha! Cuckoo! I'm coming…'

This was taking too long. Martin was beginning to lose it.

'Who's the man in the painting, Martin?'

'The commandant…'

'What? Is Friedman the man in the painting, Martin?'

'No. He's at the Wyatt. His father's the commandant…'

'So the man in the painting is not Friedman. Friedman's at the Wyatt in Los Angeles and the man in the painting is someone else? Is that what you're saying, Martin?'

'No. You don't understand… Think. He can't be in two places at the same time.'

'Who?'

'No, you got it right… What did you say?'

'Never mind. What name is he travelling under?'

'The commandant?'

'No. Friedman.'

'Friedman's name.'

'Are you sure? Otto Gluck is not Friedman?'

'That's his name too… And the commandant's, right?…'

'What commandant, Martin? Are you calling Friedman the commandant because he's your boss? Is that it? Or is the commandant Friedman's boss? Who's Friedman boss, Martin?'

'No. You're—I'm confused now. You're confusing me…'

Lombard raised his brows.

'Who's the commandant, Martin?'

'Ha… That's him, the man in the painting…'

'The man in the painting is the commandant?'

'That's it.'

'And the commandant and Friedman are two different people?'

'Friedman's father's the commandant…'

'Friedman's father? The man in the painting is Friedman's father?'

'Good. We understand each other…'

'What? Friedman works for his father? Friedman's father is Friedman's boss?'

'No… Why are you saying that now?…'

'Why are you calling Friedman's father the commandant, Martin?'

'He was the commandant… In a death camp, you know…? That's where Friedman learned… You understand…? You can't catch him, see… Oh, God, it's all too complicated…'

It was useless. He was delirious.

'My father's waiting for me… I was going… Not Hell, I'm not going there…'

Lombard took a couple of steps back, peered at the painting still in his hand, tossed it away and waited for Martin to stop mumbling, which he did before long.

'Oh dear…' he said with a last sigh, and Lombard knew he'd died when he saw his bloody hands slowly slide to the ground; the moment before he had still been stroking his belly.

He lit a cigarette and stood peering at what was now Martin's corpse. The wound beneath his right shoulder had begun to burn. It struck him that Martin's coat was dark green, that like most people with red hair, or Titian red hair, Martin had worn green. It was of no significance, but the thought floated around his head for a moment, until it drifted away, and he felt the strength drain from his body. He wanted to leave the room, to get away from the bloody scene at his feet, but something kept him there, something about Martin's body. It would come to him. He knew it would come to him. But there was no point in trying to force it. This too he knew. So he stayed there, cleared his head, and immediately found himself thinking about another corpse, in another kitchen, in Paris, ten years or so earlier. Then too he'd stood alone with a dead man. The kitchen had been more modest than this one though, reeking of stale alcohol and mouldy foodstuffs, and the man, unlike Martin, had died sitting on a chair. He was a murder suspect, had shot himself through the mouth with a rifle as Lombard stood outside his front door waiting to ask him a few questions. On hearing the gun blast, he'd broken into the flat, found him dead at his kitchen table.

He'd left a suicide note, just one line:

'Men only avenge slight injuries, never serious ones.'

It was as good as a confession. The story was sad, grim and simple. The man was a self-employed computer programmer who'd developed a computer game of some kind or another in his spare time. The project had occupied him for nearly two years. He lived alone and, being of humble means, had joined forces with a more affluent, business-minded acquaintance when the time had come to try promoting his creation. His new partner had advised him to steer clear of the computer game industry, convinced him it would be more profitable for them to produce and market the game themselves, and assured him he could raise the funds required to set things up. They'd signed a contract between them which was drawn up in such a way that, for an agreed fee, the game's inventor could be made to surrender all rights and claims to his creation while retaining the right to a percentage of any net profits resulting from the sale of the game in perpetuity. The buy out fee was, relative to his income, quite substantial, or in any case substantial enough for him to trust he needn't worry about being ripped-off, and besides he was assured that such a contractual buy out clause was standard practice, that without it, it would prove impossible to attract investors and that it would, and could, only be exercised as a kind of safeguard in the unlikely event that he might one day, on a whim or as the result of a dispute, decide to bring the whole enterprise to a stop. The argument that his new partner together with potential investors required this sort of guarantee before risking their time and money in a speculative venture had seemed reasonable enough. All the more so as he had also been made to understand that financiers looked warily on poor unknown inventors who they considered eccentrics and individualists who, clever and original as they may be, could not be relied upon to appreciate the realities of the commercial world. As a poor inventor conscious of his own business illiteracy, he had not so much understood as wholeheartedly agreed with this point of view. And so, he'd entrusted his game and his future prosperity to his new partner's care. Only, six months later nothing much had happened, his partner had stopped returning his calls and in the end had taken the time to write explaining he was too busy to deal with their project and would get in touch when things changed. He waited a few more months, but eventually ran out of patience and lost faith in the other man's ability or will to champion his game, and informed him that he regarded their partnership dissolved and intended to sound out games companies. Within a week he'd received a cheque together with a solicitor's letter by which he was notified of his partner's decision to exercise his buy out option. This action, he was informed, was necessary for the long-term good of the project, and his partner hoped he would understand and wanted him to know that he was most grateful for his contribution to their work. On the face of it there was nothing sinister or unseemly about the man's decision to buy him out; his game hadn't made any headway, he wasn't sure it ever would and, after nearly a year of waiting in vain for some-thing to happen, the idea of cashing in the buy out cheque was tempting and seemed the wise thing to do. As to the future, if his ex-partner was ever to make good, there would also be his percentage of the net profits. He could have taken the money, probably would have, but the word 'contribution' had stuck. It was his game. It was two years of his life, two years of work carried out on faith alone. To no avail, he had returned the cheque, protested and approached solicitors, but the contract was binding and, choosing the lesser of two evils, he'd resigned himself to taking his buy out fee and using it to devise a new game. He never completed it. Within a few months, his old game had appeared in the stores, renamed, partially redesigned, licensed to an established corporation and accredited to his ex-partner along with another person he'd never heard of. Later still, it had begun to sell world-wide. By then, he'd taken to drinking which, as it turned out, signalled the onset of a mental break-down which had led him to purchase the rifle with which he'd killed first his ex-partner's wife and child and, later on, himself. Sometime between his game appearing in the stores and his suicide, he'd tried and failed to legally reinstate his name as its creator, and as for his percentage of the net profits from sales in perpetuity, he found out that net profit was but an abstract concept which, as administered by his ex-partner's creative accountant, meant he would never receive any money, however many games were sold.

The day that he had stepped into the dead man's kitchen, Lombard knew next to nothing about any of this. He found out later, in a detailed newspaper article in which, he remembered, the journalist had speculated at some length as to the man's thinking in sparing his ex-partner but killing the man's wife and child. The same journalist had then found it necessary to conclude his article by declaring it ironic that a man naive – or was the word foolish? – enough to sign away his work to an acquaintance should have died quoting Machiavelli.

It had been news to Lombard, and to his colleagues, that the man's one line note about avenging injuries was not original. In any event, they'd failed to share the journalist's sense of irony. Nor had they found it necessary to speculate on the man's thinking in murdering the ex-partner's loved ones. It was fairly obvious. And not very ironic either. It was just sad, grim and…

He frowned. It was Martin's tattoo, the Star of David across his chest. A thin thread from Martin's tattoo spun a web that linked Leonard, the old Spitzes and Friedman. He scowled at the portrait laying on the floor. Unless Martin's claims were merely delirious dying words, he was looking at Friedman's father, who had been a death camp commandant. Martin hadn't said anything about place or time, but the nationality and age of the painting's subject, now taking into account artistic flattery, accepting that the painting did indeed date from 1979, could place him in a Nazi extermination camp. If that was the father, Friedman was the son of a Nazi officer. And Leonard Spitz, a man who kept books about the holocaust on his shelves, was the son of a Jewish couple involved with a group of Nazi hunters. Could it be just coincidence?…

Lombard slowly blew out his cigarette smoke. It had to be coincidence. With or without recommendation, the worried Mrs. Spitz wouldn't have hired an unknown private detective to find her son if she'd suspected his disappearance was connected to her own covert activities. Moreover, according to Moreau, the old couple no longer got their hands dirty. And Leon had spoken to Rhian only of kids and snuff movies, not…

He flicked his cigarette into the ceramic sink, gazed once more at Martin's tattooed chest and returned to the study.

He called International Directory Enquiries, and then the Wyatt in Los Angeles.

'The Wyatt. Good afternoon. How can I help you?' answered an eager young man's voice.

'Yes. Hello,' he said in his best French accent; 'This is *L'hôtel Georges Cinq* in Paris. We have a letter for a Mister Friedman who was staying with us until two days ago and left your hotel as a forwarding address. I would just like to confirm this.'

'Of course. Er, what name did you say again?'

'Mr. Friedman.'

'Just a moment.'

Lombard peered at the bobby in his snow-dome, wondering if Friedman had taken his call from this very same telephone the previous evening. After all, if he was due to catch a plane in the early hours of the morning, he could have been at home packing.

'I'm afraid we do not have any guest by that name. Are y—'

'Oh. I'm terribly sorry. My mistake. I was looking at the wrong name. Mr. Gluck. Mr. Otto Gluck is the name…'

'Right… That's right. Mr. Otto Gluck. We do have a guest by that name. But I'm afraid he hasn't checked in yet. We are expecting him today.'

'Good. Would you be kind enough to give me his room number so—'

'Oh. You needn't worry about the room number. Just forward the mail to his name care of the Wyatt, Sunset Boulevard…'

Lombard didn't insist. It was standard policy for hotel's not to reveal their guest's room numbers.

He went quickly around the house wiping surfaces for finger-prints, remembered to collect his Gitanes stubs, turned off all the lights, left the way he'd got in through the drawing room French windows and drove away in the BMW. It ran out of petrol some-where along the Holloway Road and he left it at the kerb, walk-ing the last mile home on foot. Covered in blood as he was, he couldn't quite have stopped at a petrol station, but it was safe to walk the dark pavements through the blustery rain. No one gave him a second glance.

It was 21:15 when he finally stepped into his office. He called Deborah De Moraes, who was home, then Nathalie, who wasn't, and then an airline company to check if he could book a morn-ing flight for Los Angeles. He could, but didn't. He examined his wounded shoulder and took a long hot shower.

He hoped Mrs. De Moraes wasn't going to change her mind about calling the police…

ELEVEN

He stood by his desk, lighting a Gitane.

'Thank you for coming, Mrs. De Moraes. Step inside and close the door, will you?'

She looked so alluring in her scarlet beaded cocktail dress, fur coat and pearls that he could have felt indebted to her for simply being there. But she would not have allowed any such pleasant effect to materialise. As earlier in the day, when she'd turned up unannounced with her money, she remained in the doorway and coldly ran her eyes over his bare chest.

'Last night you upset my sleep. Tonight my social life. We have two minutes. My dinner guests are waiting,' she declared, pausing to scowl at the towel wrapped around his waist; 'On reflection, I could give you another minute to put something on.'

He'd given her an hour to show up but she'd made it within forty five minutes, barely giving him time to dress his wound.

He ran his eyes over her, put his pack of Gitanes down on the desk, grabbed the Marks & Spencer bag and tossed it towards her.

'Here.'

She didn't attempt to catch it, just stepped back to watch it land on the floor with a thump.

'It may not look as good as yours but I guess you won't mind,' he said, sitting down; 'You'll find everything I know inside the envelope, including the location of your brother's boy.'

She glared. The envelope together with a few bank notes had spilled out of the bag and now lay in front of her rain speckled high-heeled shoes.

'What is this?'

'I wouldn't want you to think of me as a cheap little extortioner,' he said.

She just went on glaring at the mixed banknotes at her feet, uneasy, as if wondering what had happened to her crisp bundles of £50 notes, then understood and looked up again, brazen eyed:

'You lost my money?'

'You could say that. And Friedman left this morning for Los Angeles.'

'Who?'

'The man who sold the boy to your brother.'

She barely took a moment to think:

'I'm impressed. That information could have cost me £20,000.'

'Well, I found out a little more than that. Let me put it this way: last night I thought your brother might be dead, tonight I'm convinced he is,' he said, deliberately using her own syntax – he wasn't retaliating, merely making sure he appeared true to type; 'That said, I have no evidence of it. But in light of what I now know, I must advise you to contact the police.'

Her dark eyes filled with such contempt that had he not known her better he'd have thought she was offended by the cold way in which he'd just declared her brother dead. But she quickly enough regained her icy dignity, pursed her lips, took a deep breath, and, without thinking, he found himself glancing at her cleavage as her breasts heaved up.

'Do you mean to say you made me come here to tell me you want to quit your job, Mr. Lombard?' he heard her summon.

He nodded his imperceptible nod; as expected, she wasn't going to go for it.

'Is that it, Mr. Lombard?' she insisted.

'Your parents hired me to track down your brother, Mrs. De Moraes,' he said, calmly; 'As it happens, after nearly four days looking, I've become convinced he's dead. It would be easy for me to waste your time and spend the next days or weeks living at your expense, only, it wouldn't be right. Then again, I could be mistaken, Leonard could still be alive – on the run or hiding some place – but if that is so, besides wasting your time, I'd be playing with his life if I didn't urge you to contact the authorities. At the risk of repeating myself, your brother got himself involved with some very bad people, Mrs. De Moraes. If they've killed him, you're looking at a murder investigation. If they haven't, possibly a rescue operation. Either way, from here on the job might be best left to experts. I trust I needn't remind you I'm just a small-time private detective.'

She was no longer looking at him. As he spoke, her eyes had moved from his mouth to his shoulder. There was no need for him to turn his head to know what she was looking at; he could see from the corner of his eye that some spots of red had begun to appear on the dressing covering his wound. It was still bleeding.

'What happened?' she sneered; 'Someone frightened you?'

He felt his body tense up, clenched his jaw and just about managed to contain his anger as she rooted her eyes back into his, chin up, not quite finished yet.

'Last night I couldn't fire you. Tonight you expect me to accept your resignation. Huh! And fickleness is said to be a woman's trait.'

He grinned, not because he felt like it but on automatic, as a way to calm himself down. She'd had to hit him back with it, had to return the gibe. She'd just been told her brother was probably dead and...

'I believe my two minutes are up,' he said between his teeth.

'And I believe you want my brother dead,' she returned, indignant; 'Still. Your advice is duly noted. All the same, it's as we said when we hired you, Mr. Lombard: no police.'

He considered taking the opportunity that presented itself: last night she'd fired him, tonight... It was idiotic. He merely sent her a stony stare.

'No police, Mr. Lombard,' she repeated; 'You talk of strange and unpleasant things. You found a loathsome tape. Perhaps even a poor little boy. But as yet, you have not found my brother, have no idea where he is or, if I understand correctly, any evidence to back up what really amounts to nothing more than morbid speculation. Tell me, Mr. Lombard, presuming your story about my brother is true, have you even got any evidence that he did set out on—how did you put it again yesterday? A second shopping expedition? Is that it? Have you any evidence of that, Mr. Lombard?'

This had occurred to him, of course.

'Wouldn't he have staggered back to the nest by now?' he said, recalling one of her previous remarks.

'Have you got any evidence Leon went back to see your Mr.

Friedman, Mr. Lombard?' she insisted.

'No.'

'Right. When you have, we'll ascertain whether or not to involve the police and break my parents' hearts with the news that their son is involved with... pornographers. Your Mr. Friedman could shed some light on the matter, you say. Well, find him. Didn't I hear you say he was in Los Angeles?'

He didn't reply, just said 'yes' with his eyes.

'Good. Then you know what to do. Are we understood?'

She was ready to leave, and he was tempted to let her go, but...

He peered at the envelope at her feet. It wasn't the one he'd put under Jane's door earlier. Jane was out and that one was out of reach. This one contained a blank A4 sheet. He could have written down his information again but hadn't, guessing it wouldn't be required. Still, had she decided to follow his advice and contact the police he'd have had to tell her all he knew, he'd have had to ask her not to reveal where she'd got it, have had to tell her about Martin and the giant. Would she have turned out to be helpful or...

'You watched the tape?'

She frowned. He'd already asked her that in the morning. She'd also frowned then, had parted her lips as if to reply, but said nothing, and left him convinced she had watched it.

'*Sleeping Beauty*? Did you watch it, Mrs. De Moraes?'

She appeared to brood over some thought, then condescended to reply. After all, she wanted him to stay on the job now...

'What if I did? Whatever else, it didn't show me my brother dead, did it?'

Now it was his turn to frown. She was even tougher than her act, or... Had he not witnessed her distress the previous night, he'd have been inclined to believe that far from being motivated by concern for her brother, she was following up on this with her own agenda, seeking to satisfy morbid curiosity or some dark perversion. Then again, she seemed so consumed with hatred, perhaps she was simply high from having smelled blood, had become desensitised, was moving in for the kill, pouncing on her chance to once and for all disgrace her brother, in spite of her 'break my parents hearts with the news that...'.

'Nor, for that matter, did it provide an explanation for how it ended up at his place, if that is indeed where it came from,' her mouth pronounced as he gazed into her eyes.

There was another possibility of course. She could be hostage to those voluptuous looks and easy wealth of hers, felt compelled to live up to them, to be their equal, to stand as proud as her beauty and as cold as her money...

He felt himself grin, then quickly looked away as fear flashed across her face, realising he'd become so rapt in contemplation of her eyes' impenetrable brazen darkness that he'd unwittingly allowed her to see inside his own eyes.

'Friedman and his people don't just peddle little kids and nasty videotapes, Mrs. De Moraes,' he stated, facing her again; 'They're in the import-export business. They run hotels, here in London and most probably in various other cities across the world. They use them as warehouses and ports of call for their merchandise. You understand?'

She raised her brows, baffled but still wary.

'I just want you to know who we're dealing with. In case you're not quite aware of it,' he went on; 'The hotels are capital investments. The kids liquid assets. My guess is that they also own travel agencies specialising in flights from the third world and might even have holdings in charter airlines.'

Now she sent him a sceptical look.

'Minimises the risks,' he explained; 'Children can be moved safely from one country to the next through reliable businesses which, besides providing money-laundering fronts, can also be used to move drugs, women and currencies. However much money there is to be made from children, it makes economic sense to combine their trade with other activities. Kids might be peddled as sexual toys, sold for adoption or as slave labour, auctioned to pornographers and pimps, or even cut into pieces and retailed as organ donors, but any organisation that included hotels etc. would be dumb and doomed if it relied on just one source of income.'

He had her attention now. She looked back at him with a mixture of incredulity and curiosity, and he just couldn't help it, he felt a cruel grin forming across his lips again as he said:

'The pursuit of money can be a slimy business, Mrs. De

Moraes. Would it surprise you to know that the kiddie porn industry alone is estimated to generate larger yearly profits than the entire American film industry?'

'Why are you telling me all this, Mr. Lombard?' she asked, half-angry, half-troubled.

He looked away, stamped out his half-burnt cigarette. He'd let her get to him again…

'Why are you telling me all this?' she asked again, more firmly this time; 'I'm concerned with my brother, not the lurid business of… of kiddie porn, to use your terminology. Anyhow,' she went on after a short pause; 'For a small-time detective, you seem rather well informed on the subject. Or are just you ad-libbing? Still trying to talk yourself out of the job?'

She wasn't upset anymore, or angry or wary, just her familiar haughty self.

He grinned, sombrely this time, and lit a new cigarette.

'You're sure about the police?' he asked, leaning back in his seat.

She let out an exasperated sigh:

'Quite sure.'

'Fine. This has become dangerous. I'll have to increase my fee.'

She peered back at him, a rueful smile slowly forming across her lips. She'd already guessed what he had in mind.

'I see…'

'It's your call,' he said.

'And there I was,' she sniggered, 'starting to believe the pursuit of money was a slimy business.'

He stayed silent as she turned to glance at the bag at her feet.

When she looked up again, she focused on the dressing on his shoulder, curled her lips and proceeded to let her eyes wander over his bruised chest and throat…

'You drive a hard bargain, Mr. Lombard.'

'Do I?'

'It's all right,' she snarled, batting her eyelashes; 'My end is easy. All I have to do is tell myself my £20,000 actually bought me something. You're left with the burden of delivering it. And you better come up with something this time, I might not feel so munificent next time. Now, as we seem to have covered everything, can I expect you to set out for Los Angeles in the near future?'

He smiled.

'Good,' she said, turning to leave; 'Let me know where you're staying when you get there. Just in case Leon does stagger back to the nest. I wouldn't want you to spend more money than necessary.'

'Not quite so fast, Mrs. De Moraes,' he called as she was already halfway across the landing; 'As I'm still on the job, I need to ask you a few questions.'

She stopped, turned on her heels.

'What?' her voice echoed in the stairwell behind her.

'It won't take a moment,' he said; 'When did you last see your brother, Mrs. De—'

She sighed:

'Is this really necessary?'

He smiled again.

She sighed again:

'About two months ago. He came to the house to see my mother who was visiting.'

'Did he still have long hair?'

'Pardon?'

'Did he still—'

'Yes.'

'Right. In your opinion, how would you say he feels about the apartment your parents bought him?'

She narrowed her eyes ominously. He'd meant to ask Rhian this, but since he had her there...

'I gather he's been living there for nearly two years,' he explained; 'Yet the place is almost bare of furniture, personal effects or clothes, as if he wasn't really intending to stay there.'

'I thought I'd already told you I've never set foot in Leon's, Mr. Lombard. I wouldn't know anything about his taste in interior decorating. All right!'

'He never spoke to you about his feelings—'

'I'm not interested in his feelings, Mr. Lombard.'

'I'm sure. But what I was asking is—'

'I understood what you were asking,' she cut in; 'Whatever feelings he may have, Leon knows better than to make me privy to them. And I'd have thought a discerning man like yourself would have guessed that much by now. Or haven't I made my dislike of him plain enough yet?'

'He's your brother. You must—'

She interrupted him again:

'I'm unaware of Leon's feelings about his apartment, Mr. Lombard.'

He nodded:

'Okay. Then perhaps you could tell me what he was like as a child.'

She just stared, incensed.

'You did live together when you were children?' he asked; 'Or didn't you?'

She just went on staring.

'How was he, Mrs. De Moraes?' he queried, regardless; 'Austere? Wild? Would you say he was untidy or—'

'Why—' she cried in a high-pitched voice, breaking off to clear her throat; 'If you're not simply intent on spoiling my evening more than you already have, would you mind telling me what the exact purpose of this ludicrous line of questioning is?'

'I'm only trying to understand who your brother is, Mrs. De Moraes,' he said; 'It helps to know who one is looking for, and I'm not sure who Leonard is yet. You see, the information I'm getting doesn't quite add up. He's held to be confused and emotional, yet he keeps his home so tidy and barren it could be a monk's cell. Your mother describes him as contented, but his employer portrays him as suicidal. Both you and your father appear convinced he hasn't got it within him to turn his back on drugs, yet your mother and his ex-lover are adamant he has. The only thing that's become clear so far is that, in the words of a waitress he worked with and photographed, he is a little weird. Considering he's decided to take on child traffickers, if not strictly speaking confusing, this one truth is not exactly helpful.'

She almost laughed:

'But to know why he keeps an empty apartment or wardrobe would be?'

He grinned.

'How was Leonard as a child, Mrs. De Moraes? Austere? Wild? Or—'

'What he was then bares little relation to what he has become, Mr. Lombard,' she cut in.

He succumbed again:

'Could that mean you liked him then?'

Once more, she narrowed her eyes, ready to sting, but perhaps because she was in a hurry to go, thought better of it:

'He was not what I would call austere,' she stated.

'Then what was he like, Mrs. De Moraes?'

He watched her chest heave up again as she sent out a heavy sigh. She hesitated, grudging and derisive, but answered:

'He was a child, Mr. Lombard. He laughed. He cried. He sulked. He dreamed. He sparkled. And he didn't always eat all his supper or wash behind his ears, and he never made his bed. Mind you, we had staff to deal with such chores as bed-making.'

He took a drag from his cigarette, surprised by the simplicity if not the grace of her depiction of her young brother, even if she'd had to spoil it with her last sentence.

'What—' he started.

'Drugs,' she cut in, reading his mind.

He went along with that.

'Why?'

'Huh! Why? *Nothing can permanently please which does not contain in itself the reason why it is so, and not otherwise,* Mr. Lombard.'

She scoffed as he paused for thought.

'Coleridge,' she declared; 'If the name means anything to you...'

It didn't, but he nodded.

'How much does your brother know about your parents' Nazi hunting activities, Mrs. De Moraes?'

'What has this...?'

'It might be important.'

For once, she appeared concerned, afraid even, her eyes asking questions rather than fighting.

'I cannot be sure of the information yet,' he said, deciding he might as well let her know what was on his mind, partly to encourage her, partly to see her reaction; 'However, it would appear that the Austrian who sold your brother his boy is the son of a former Nazi. If true, it would make for an extraordinary encounter, don't you think? It could simply be coincidence, but I can't help finding it intriguing.'

He observed her as she took time to make the connections,

absorb the implications of what he was suggesting. The fear didn't quite evaporate from her eyes, but her concern did.

'I can assure you there is nothing to look for there,' she declared eventually; 'Leon scarcely knows anything about that side of our parents' life. As a matter of fact, since you so cleverly managed to dig up the information from somewhere, and I won't ask how or where, I wouldn't be surprised if you actually knew more about it than he does.'

'Leonard's got quite a few books about the holocaust though.'

'Yes?'

'Well?...'

'He's Jewish,' she stated, impatient.

He considered asking her if she too read books about the holocaust, thought he better not...

'I need an answer, Mrs. De Moraes. How much exactly does Leonard know?'

She cast him one of her looks, her clenched fist nervously tapping against the side of her coat, then glanced at her watch and spoke:

'My parents are old, Mr. Lombard. They've been expecting to die for quite a few years now. About ten years ago, they decided to tell us of their association with the people you know about. They wanted us to hear it from their own mouths, to spare us finding out after their deaths. Things of that nature have an uncanny way of coming to light after people die, you see, and getting distorted. It took five minutes. They spoke their piece, made us promise never to bring up the subject again, and we never did. So you see, if Leon met up with a Nazi's son, it can only be coincidental. Unfortunate, extraordinary, troubling and, coming from Leon, dare I say it, characteristic, but coincidental. Most definitely, it could not be, nor is it, connected with my parents' affairs.'

Five minutes ten years ago... She had to be lying. As he recalled, her memory hadn't needed refreshing when he'd brought up the topic the previous night. Still, her resolute poise suggested she'd said all she would about the matter.

'I recall you mentioned Leonard went to university and tried a career in music...'

'Yes?' she snapped.

'I take it therefore that he didn't always lead a secluded existence. He had friends once…'

'I hate to remind you, Mr. Lombard, but my dinner guests are still waiting.'

'I won't be long now, Mrs. De Moraes. Just a couple more questions. So, your brother had friends once.'

'Huh. If that's what you want to call the people he hung around with, yes, he had friends.'

'You wouldn't happen to know any of them by name, would you?'

'Leon's friends?'

'Yes.'

'No, Mr. Lombard.'

'You're sure?'

She was, and reminded him he had just asked his couple of questions.

'Okay,' he smiled; 'Well, if by chance you do come to remember any names from Leonard's past on your way home, give me a call, will you? You see, I don't think your brother was alone when he purchased the boy. I think someone helped him. Possibly someone with whom he'd recently renewed contact. I just don't know. But if I'm right, it could be that at this very moment Leonard is with that someone. Which of course is not to say that they might not be dead together.'

She looked back at him sullenly.

'What are you on about now, Mr. Lombard?'

'One thing I learned tonight is that Friedman is not just any child procurer, Mrs. De Moraes. If you think of his operation as a multinational, he is the equivalent of a national branch manager. As such, he confines his services to select customers.'

'Does he now?'

'He does. And the fact is, whatever he may be, your brother doesn't quite belong to that category of customer, Mrs. De Moraes. Even supposing he could have made his way into the branch all by himself, there's just no way he'd have been served by the manager. Yet, somehow, he was. The only way I can start making it make sense is if I give him a partner. Someone who knows the ropes. Someone with the right credentials and a direct line to Friedman. Then, it can begin to work. And perhaps also begin to explain how come Leonard felt brave enough to take on Friedman's operation instead of running to the police when he found out about it. It's just an idea, it raises new questions, still doesn't explain where your brother found the money to bankroll his crusade, but at least it fits better than a lone Leonard does. Anyway…' he concluded, rising to his feet; 'If you do think of any old friends of his, especially well-off ones, do call. I expect I won't be leaving for Los Angeles until sometime tomorrow.'

She eyed him for a moment, grim and pensive.

'A partner?'

'I know,' he conceded, guessing what she was thinking; 'Who in their right mind would get involved with your brother in such a venture? I don't know. It's like I said, it raises new questions.'

'Yes,' she nodded; 'Indeed… Well, the more you say, the more it looks like you better have that chat with your Mr. Friedman, Nazi's son or not.'

He returned her frosty stare, was about to bid her goodbye, then remembered:

'Oh. One other thing, Mrs. De Moraes. If you wanted to safely hide away a very large amount of cash, where would you take it?'

She frowned, thought, found the idea amusing, delighted in her reply:

'I myself buy jewels, Mr. Lombard.'

He glanced automatically at the pearls against the olive skin above her décolleté:

'I'm sure. But imagining you preferred ready cash to jewels, Mrs. De Moraes. Where would you take it? Switzerland?'

She smiled, glanced at the bag and money on the floor across the threshold in front of her, shook her head:

'You're out of date, Mr. Lombard,' she declared, derisively; 'Switzerland is not what it used to be. Banks no longer offer clients the right to open anonymous accounts there. This being Britain, I'd recommend Gibraltar, the Channel Isles or, if you want to mix business with pleasure, some warm British Caribbean Island, like Montserrat or Anguilla. Your money would be as safe from prying eyes there as it would in Switzerland.'

And she turned away.

'By the way,' he called a moment later, listening to her heels clicking against the stairs; 'Did I mention that Mr. Friedman lives just around the corner from you?'

The stairwell fell silent, then, a couple of seconds later, her clip-clopping resumed, the street door downstairs slammed shut and, trembling, he stamped his Gitane in the ashtray, at long last allowing his body to shiver. Her refusal to step inside and shut the door had left him exposed to the icy draught between the landing and the window behind his desk. He could have moved, or told her he was cold and insisted on making her close the door, but, without quite knowing why, he'd chosen instead to endure the cold...

He picked up the phone and dialled.

'I'm not here,' announced Nathalie's voice after a few rings; 'Leave a message or call later.'

He slammed down the receiver, glared at the goldfish in their aquarium, made for the door, kicked it shut after picking up the bag, money and envelope from the floor and stiffened as Deborah De Moraes' Aston Martin roared into life outside his window. She revved a few times before pulling away and speeding into the distance, leaving behind her an all enveloping silence to which his ears only gradually readjusted until he could once again perceive the monotonous drone of the rain pounding the street.

'I myself buy jewels,' he heard her voice echo inside his forehead as he turned to the kitchen.

He considered going to make some coffee, having it in front of the television, just to warm up and rest for a few minutes. Apart from reaching Nathalie, he had still to contact Rhian and Moreau, book his flight and decide what to do about the hotels in Seven Sisters Road.

'Switzer-fucking-land,' rumbled Martin's voice now.

He frowned, wondered why he was hearing voices, then clenched his jaw as the boy he'd left at the bus-stop flashed across his mind together with the realisation that French citizens need a visa to enter the United States.

'What sort of puppies are you looking for?' Friedman now asked.

Switzerland… That was it. Before Martin, Moreau had also mentioned Switzerland when talking about the Spitzes' Nazi hunting. Something about their victims being mostly affluent German and Swiss citizens.

'People need guilt in order to accept the bad things in life,' whispered a man's voice.

A dark hallucination, Bill, the pet shop owner, standing tall and walking his new black and white puppy, strolled across his office.

'Guilt is a bit like a rubber ring,' the tall man said with a proud smile, fading away to be replaced by the two women in purple coats from the Ambassador. And, gazing at their ghostly faces, he heard his own voice instruct that he had better check the name in the British passport he kept in the bag under his bedroom floorboards before booking his flight.

'Merde! Qu'est-ce qu'on va foutre du marmot, Laurent?' one of the purple women said, turning to him.

He gazed at her. Why was she speaking French? Speaking Moreau's words? And what were these two doing there anyway? Why were they sitting in front of their handbags, just like they had at the Ambassador, numb and vacant-eyed? But they were alone now, enveloped in shadow, their faces lit from beneath by a vaporous purple light that emanated from their coats, looking like cheap gaudy madonnas.

He shut his eyes, opened them again hoping they'd gone, and they had, but were already re-emerging in front of his kitchen door, and now, the one who'd spoken in Moreau's voice moved her lips again. This time she spoke English with a German accent:

'Pups. Bitches. From three to twelve months. Trained and untrained ones. White and brown ones. You understand?'

'Yeah,' he replied on automatic, swallowing hard. And he understood what was happening. He was not only cold and tired but also hungry. He'd not eaten or drunk anything all day, not since leaving the Métropole in the morning, and because he'd also lost a fair amount of blood, he…

'Would you like some more coffee?' a young blonde asked with a sensual smile.

It took some time for him to make her out, but her handsome

smile, the frilled apron on her slim body and the mug of coffee in her hands…

Something tickled his chest, and he looked down. The dressing on his shoulder was all blood now. A red pearl flowed leisurely along his bare skin down the side of his stomach and sank into the porous fabric of the towel around his waist.

'*No thank you. We're only passing…*'

Of course. That's why the purple women were there. It was their vacant eyes and numb postures, their people-in-transit demeanour. Soon, he'd be just like them, be just another person in transit, without… He didn't want to leave London. He didn't want to leave England. He didn't want… He'd never been to America. Never thought he would.

He felt faint, looked up again, saw nothing but whirling shadows, as if his eyes could no longer focus.

'*Baton Rouge… La Nouvelle Orléans… Le Pays Cajun…*' said a strangely familiar man's voice as the outline of the women slowly reformed out of the moving shadow. The smiley waitress had gone, but the other two, the gaudy ones… Were they nodding at him?

He scowled.

'*La Louisiane? Baton Rouge, hein?*' articulated one of them in the same man's voice.

Could it really…? This all belonged to the past. He remembered now. The voice and the words. That was it. It all belonged to his old history teacher. That was it. But… What? Briefly, a heady elation took hold of him, just like when, still just a Paris kid, he'd heard the sound of those names for the first time.

Baton Rouge. La Louisiane… Yes, the Far-West, wild and French.

'*Ah. Mais les Anglo-Saxons…*'

The teacher himself had seemed disappointed to be telling the class that no less a man than Napoléon had ended up selling all those names to the Anglo-Saxon Americans. But by then…

The women dissolved as the distant sound of a key turning in a lock reached his ears. Jane was stepping into the downstairs hallway. The door slammed shut behind her and all went quiet again, as if she'd stopped to check her mail or, as was her habit when she carried one, paused to shake her wet umbrella over the large doormat by the door. He thought, quickly. She was going to climb up the stairs and past his door, find his envelope on opening her own door and probably feel compelled to climb back down at once.

He'd eat later. He turned his back to the kitchen, flicked the light switch, stepped across the darkness towards the light from his bedroom and quietly shut the door behind him before flinging the bag with the cash onto his bed and making for the bathroom, ripping the bloody dressing from his shoulder.

Soon afterwards, back in the shower, allowing the warm water to do its soothing work, he thought he heard what sounded like three loud knocks, and imagined Jane standing in the draughty stairwell outside his door, and then climbing back up to her floor, the eager eyes in her rain-flushed face peering inquisitively at the envelope. Then again, she might have healthier preoccupations than his envelope tonight, could have found herself a new boyfriend. That was unlikely though. It was Monday, and if things were still anything like when he was her age, Mondays don't breed new passions…

The last days' rains had turned the stack of newspapers on his Triumph passenger seat into a sodden cake. The drips from the sunroof continued to drum against it, but instead of being soaked up, they now merely added to the water that trickled down the edge of the seat onto the carpeting. As a result, the flooded floor of the car reflected the street-lamp glow and inside the steamed-up windows the stale air was clammy and smelled of wet cigarette ash; but still, a sense of relief came over Lombard when he settled behind the wheel. His Triumph, leaking and damp though it may be, was the only place he truly held to be his own, from where his eyes beheld no threats, and tonight was no exception, even though he still felt too fragile to turn on the ignition and drive away. Moreover, he didn't know where to head for. He hadn't had time to think about it yet. The nausea that had struck a quarter of an hour earlier following his booking of a seat on a morning flight to Los Angeles was still with him. Deep within. Together with the feeling of weightlessness that had come with it.

He took a deep breath, then another, let his back sink into the familiar contours of his seat, searched his pockets for his Gitanes and lighter, brought a cigarette up to his mouth and glared at his windscreen.

He'd just fled from his flat. Like a thief. Hurtled down the stairs as if bolting from the devil. As if...

'Putain...'

What was he doing? His lighter flame fluttered half way up his cigarette, burning the white paper.

He wound down his window, flung the cigarette out and lit a new one, smoothly this time.

'Bon sang!'

It wasn't like him to indulge in self-deception. But that's exactly what he'd done when, hanging up the phone after making his reservation, he'd looked up from his desk to find his flat changed. It was as if, all of a sudden, the moment his trip had got that much closer to becoming a certainty, the well-known objects and spaces around him had grown odd and remote, still clearly recognisable and well-defined but distant, as they might have looked if viewed in a mirror or through a window.

'Connard...'

There was nothing he could have done about this altered perception. That, it so happened, was outside his control, just like the nausea. But even so, to yield to playing mind-games, to dismiss it as a panic attack...

'Hein!'

To conveniently blame some deep-seated fear of travelling for his little crisis was contemptible. To justify it by reminding himself that, after all, this was his first trip abroad in a long time, indeed his first trip since he'd arrived in London, was weak. And then to explain it away by holding himself to be a creature of habit who was only reacting normally to his impending deprivation of routine was, to say the least, pitiable. Still...

If that was bad, what could be said about crowning it all by coming up with the idea of using Jane to steady his nerves, eh? What did that make him?

'Connard.'

He already knew. Of course he already knew. Even before he'd started up the stairs towards Jane's he'd known what was going on. It was more painless to pretend he didn't though, even to smile when Jane opened her door.

'Savieer…'

She was surprised. It was nearly ten. He'd never been up to her flat so late. Perhaps it was even the first time he'd knocked at her door after dark. He couldn't remember.

'How are you, Jane?'

The sitting room behind her was messy, stuffy and smelled of sweet tinned soup. A comedy show punctuated by canned laughter flickered on the television set. And, he'd noticed it right away, she was barefoot, her toenails painted pink.

She must have come in from the rain with wet shoes and…

'I left an envelope under your door this morning and…'

'Oh. Right. I came down earlier but…'

Youthful, self-absorbed Jane. There was no danger of her seeing through his deceit. Not even in his sorry state. Not tonight, not ever. The impish mouth under her upturned nose had beamed when he consented to step inside while she went to fetch the precious envelope. She'd put it in the kitchen by her kettle, she explained, to make sure she wouldn't forget it in the morning…

'What's going on? Are you in some kind of danger or…'

'Salop.'

He could have taken the envelope and left, but he'd lingered, feeding from her warmth, her mess and her sounds, evading her questions while letting her know he would be leaving in the morning. It was just for a few days. Three or four perhaps. Did she mind feeding his fish while he was away?

'Your fish… Sure. Where are you going?'

Dependable Jane. Had her curiosity made him feel better? Made him feel he would be missed perhaps?

'Salop.'

'Where are you going?'

'Los Angeles.'

She was impressed.

'Wow…'

'I'll leave a key in your letter box, okay?'

'What?'

He was improvising.

'So you can get in. For the fish.'

'Right. What… This is sudden. What's in LA, eh?'

Had he smiled?

'Work.'

Had she uttered another 'Wow' before proclaiming he was lucky?

'Lucky you.'

He knew he hadn't smiled then, merely grumbled:

'Yeah…'

'Well. Er, this calls for… What about…'

'Ordure…'

He had. He really had hesitated before turning down her offer of a drink, and probably would have gone for it had he not thought she'd served her purpose, that he was better, that it was safe to… Or had he still enough of a sense of decency?

'Thank you, Jane. But…'

He'd started back down the stairs, leaving her alone with her disappointment. Only, Jane hadn't finished with him yet. It wasn't in her to let go so easily.

'What about your accounts, *Savieer*? Have you signed them yet? If you're leaving tomorrow it would be…'

He hadn't even looked at them but…

'I'll sign them and put them in your letter box with the key.'

'Ah. Okay… Oh, by the way, I hope you didn't mind me letting that woman into your flat yesterday. I didn't know who…'

Neither did he. He'd forgotten she'd met Nathalie. In truth, at that very moment he'd forgotten everything about as long ago as…

'Yesterday?'

'Yes… When I woke you, you know? You were at your desk and… Don't you remember? She was French, wasn't she?'

Healthy, innocent, prying Jane. Hungry for life, she'd brought his sorry game to an end, caused him to stop outside his open door, stiff, afraid of what awaited on the…

If he'd had his keys and his coat, if he'd not felt so sheepish, he'd have made straight for the street.

'It's all right. I was expecting her.'

'Ah. Right. I thought I might have screwed up, you know?

Anyway, who was she, eh? She was pretty.'

'She...'

'Pauvre con.'

'She used to...'

Any port in a storm. Break the mirror if you can't stand...

'She's my girlfriend, Jane.'

How long had it then taken him to run for his door, slam it shut and then grab his coat, keys and cigarettes while steering clear of what his eyes saw before escaping back out, down the stairs, into the street and through the rain to the safety of his Triumph? Five minutes? Or was it only two? No. It couldn't have been two. He'd headed the wrong way once on the pavement, hurried past Perkins' shop while still getting into his coat and only then remembered he'd left his Triumph in a side street in the opposite direction.

It might have been only three, though. He hadn't even waited to make sure Jane had left the stairwell before stepping back out of his flat.

'Pauvre con...'

He smiled, wryly, realising he didn't know the English for what had brought about his nausea. Anguish? Maybe. Whatever, it was nothing more than a mere *coup de cafard*, of the kind he thought he'd become immune to. There perhaps lay the explanation for his pathetic conduct, his stab at Jane when... He thought he was safe from such experiences. It wasn't supposed to happen anymore. His well-honed defence mechanism was meant to protect him, meant to keep him impregnable, like an island. Yet, somehow, tonight it had failed, detached itself from its moorings and left him behind to face what he in turn was about to leave behind now he was going away. And all his eyes had seen was an unforgiving, all implicating emptiness...

It would never have happened had he not been...

'Nom—' he muttered; *'Nom de Dieu!'*

Now he was in danger of searching for absolution...

'Tu déconnes, Laurent. Tu déconnes!' he screamed, flicking his Gitane stub away.

He wound up his window, turned on his engine, wiped the steam from the windscreen with his sleeve, pulled away from the kerb and took a turn into Essex Road, slamming on his breaks just in time to avoid being rammed by a flashing police car which had swerved into his lane to avoid a cyclist. He cursed after the police, glared at the cyclist's dark silhouette, engaged first gear again.

By the time he got into second, the adrenaline rush had cleared his head. By the time he cruised through a red light on reaching the Angel his mind was back at work. And by the time he drove past Sadler's Wells and took a right into Roseberry Avenue, he knew where he was going, only to realise it was still only a quarter past ten, much too early to expect Nathalie to be at the Brewer Street brasserie, for, given the choice, she shunned the evening crowds, seldom appearing in public before midnight when they could be relied upon to have begun to disperse after their end-of-day revelries.

'*Merde!*'

A frown and a sigh later, he cursed again. He'd hoped to call Rhian and Moreau from the brasserie and, more urgently, to sit in front of a hot meal, which he had better do soon if he intended to get through the night without further crisis. Instead, he found himself heading in the direction of Nathalie's Knightsbridge flat. He'd tried calling her again before booking his flight, but got her machine. He wasn't supposed to know where she lived, and it was possibly still too soon to worry, but as it was, he did know where she lived, he was worried, and he knew her well enough to suspect she could be at home ignoring calls, stoned out of her head and feeling good for feeling bad, which tonight of all nights, she had better not be, and not just because of his concern for her well-being.

He'd rejected the idea of getting the Seven Sisters Road hotels raided, an option he'd considered pursuing through his one contact in the local police, a hatchet-faced Metropolitan police inspector named John Fitzpatrick who Moreau had introduced him to a few years back. The man was cordial and helpful enough, the police being a great family that sticks together, but they'd never taken to each other, as much because of personality as cultural differences, and Lombard tended to avoid him, using him only on occasion with minor requests, car registration checks and the like. In any case, his decision to leave the hotels alone had nothing to do with his feelings for the hard-faced man, or the questions the latter would inevitably ask on finding out what was involved. It was simpler than that. The fact was that making more ripples at this point could only prove counterproductive. By now, Martin's disappearance was guaranteed to have raised the alarm, the alarm to have led to the giant's corpse and that in turn to the removal of the kids from the Ambassador. Whether Friedman already knew or still had to hear, it made for bad news, but it was unlikely to cause a man of his experience undue worry or fear for his personal safety. As things stood, unless the Austrian was psychic, there was no way for him to figure out the who's and why's or to make the right connections. Apart from Nathalie, the two people who could tip him off were dead and, unless his cautious disposition led him to dispatch someone to his Hampstead house before Lombard made it to Los Angeles, for all he knew Martin was merely missing and the troublesome Frenchman a loose cannon. A lost kid, a dead employee, a missing colleague and a Frenchman on the loose made for upsetting news indeed, but not upsetting enough to lead him to pack up, retire and never be heard of again. Or it shouldn't, because apart from anything else, the man ought to feel secure in the knowledge that it was only a matter of time before his London people got their hands on Lombard, or found out who he was, which ultimately came to the same thing. Inasmuch as logic dictated, that's how a situation such as this ought to end. And, insofar as Nathalie could be trusted, that's how it would end if they got to question her. Nathalie was not Leonard Spitz. She wasn't going to die for the cause, let alone to protect him or anyone else. She'd talk. Everybody talks. And then, if they let her live, she'd just go on slowly killing herself...

Her flat lay on the second floor of a white three-storey house in a quiet residential street a few blocks from Harrods department store. Whether her upstairs and downstairs neighbours knew her, Lombard didn't know, but since all the windows of the house were dark, it was of no importance.

He cruised past the house a couple of times, inspecting the

cars on either side of the street, and, satisfied no one was staking out the place, parked around the corner.

There was no answer when he pressed the lit-up button next to the name 'DUTOIT'. Trying the others proved equally futile. He gazed at the door, contemplated breaking in, then pushed all the bells again, stepped back and looked up, shielding his eyes from the rain with his hand.

Nothing appeared to be moving beyond any of the windows. He had to try:

'Nathalie! Ouvre la putain de porte si t'es là, nom de Dieu!'

As he waited, hoping against hope for something to happen, the rain pelting his lips made him realise he was thirsty. He glanced at his watch, had another look at the door, turned around and trekked back to his car.

Midnight was but an hour away. It would be even nearer by the time he got to the brasserie. Failing Nathalie turning up there by one, he'd return and break in. And failing to reach her by two, Fitzpatrick would get a call after all. There would be no flight to Los Angeles, he'd never get to meet Friedman, or tell Mrs. Spitz what had happened to her son, but at least Fitzpatrick would keep the Austrian's London people occupied and give him a chance to try to locate Nathalie. It was strange, but apart from her flat and the Brewer Street brasserie, he had no idea where to look for her. That's how much they shared. Tonight, because it was inconvenient, Lombard found it strange.

The barman, a tall Belgian he knew by sight, shook his head when asked if Nathalie had been in, then gave a laconic shrug when asked if she was expected. Lombard ordered a Perrier, a steak, with express orders that the chef be told to cook it *bleu* and not rare, and turned to the pay-phone by the door to the lavatories.

'Le Perrier. On a plus de petit, ce soir. Que des grandes bouteilles...' started the barman behind him.

'Eh bien dans ce cas là donnez m'en un grand, okay?' he cut in without stopping, reaching for his wallet.

'Hello. My name is Xavier Lombard. I'm...'

Rhian's sister had been asleep. Yes, she knew who he was. Yes, everything was all right. Yes, she did mind driving to Rhian's at this hour. Was it really necessary? They had snow falling there and…

'It is. How long will it take you to get back with her?'

'Christ. Can't she just call you from a public…'

'I can't be reached at the moment. How long?'

'I don't know… Half an hour. No. Forty…'

Replacing her number in his wallet, he tried Nathalie again, glared at the lavatories door as what sounded like a woman's shriek reach him from the other side, then returned to the dining room.

It felt good to sit down, to see and hear people, and to sip cold sparkling water in the warm atmosphere pervaded with the smells of food and alcohol. He was thirstier than he'd thought, swallowed three glasses of water, slowly, because his bruised throat hurt with each gulp, and then lit a cigarette and surveyed the room around him. Most tables were deserted, awaiting the nocturnal clientèle, but the place did not feel empty. A young couple sat over coffee near the door, holding hands across the table. Another couple, older and nearer Lombard, ate in silence without looking at each other. By the bar, a distinguished-looking old man sat by himself, reading a newspaper over a glass of wine. And, at the far end of the room, a party of about a dozen men and women in bright paper hats sat laughing, drinking and talking all at once. From their high-spirits, it was obvious that some amongst them had drunk more than they were accustomed to, and their paper hats, educated voices, conservative clothing and relative youth suggested they were fellow office workers having an early Christmas celebration rather than friends on a night out.

As his steak arrived, Lombard had determined they worked in advertising.

'The chef said don't hesitate to send it back if it's not perfect,' said the waiter.

'Thank you. I won't. And I'd like another bottle of water, please.'

A moment later, putting out his Gitane, his eyes caught sight of a ruddy-faced young man who'd just appeared from the direction of the lavatories. He was heading towards the noisy table, stuffing his shirt into his trousers with a huge grin.

'Paul? Your presence is requested!' he called loudly, still halfway there.

'My God! She's not!' cried a high-pitched female voice.

'Yes! Hooray for Georgina!' a male voice bawled as the entire table erupted into a mixture of laughter, shrieks and amused cursing.

The young couple holding hands exchanged an amused look.

The steak was perfect. Watching the man who'd caused all the commotion around the noisy table of paper-hatted revellers help another two pull a seemingly reluctant Paul from his chair, Lombard became convinced his theory about Leonard having had help to buy his boy was right, whatever Deborah De Moraes thought about it.

TWELVE

The first thing he saw was her smile. It was the same curious smile as the one that had made her look strangely vulnerable in his flat the previous day. It threw him somewhat, but not enough to prevent him guessing from her stance that she must have been standing in the doorway observing him for some time. He'd only just caught sight of her because, freeing his mind from his screaming chest wound, he'd looked around for the waiter to order another coffee.

Their eyes met, she reclaimed her smile, briefly watched him watch her, started towards him and called towards the bar:

'Bring us a cappuccino and an espresso, Robert.'

He scowled. She knew. She had to, or else she'd never have allowed the two of them to…

'You look worse each time I see you, Xavier,' she said, putting her handbag down on his table; 'Aren't you pleased to see me?'

Without waiting for a reply or another look in his direction, she took off her coat, folded it over the chair directly across from him, sat to his left and lit a Marlboro.

'That's right,' she announced, evidently aware of his searching stare; 'I got word they're looking for me.'

He just went on probing her profile, not knowing how to react yet. Given that she had to be aware of the gravity of the situation, she seemed remarkably calm. Not only had she come to the brasserie as though this was any normal evening but, finding him there, she'd smiled, as if amused. Or had she expected him to be there?

At least she appeared lucid. Her eyes were alert, her movements smooth, graceful even, and as always, she was impeccably dressed, tonight wearing a long black skirt with a sky-blue silk shirt and dark patterned scarf-cravat which concealed most of her proud neck.

'You really ought to get yourself one of those cell-phones,' she declared, snapping her lighter shut; 'If nothing else, it would help you look the part. Anyway, I thought I'd find you here.'

So she had been...

'Tu me cherchais?' he asked.

She didn't answer, just turned to the bar:

'Forget that cappuccino, Robert. Make it two espressos.'

'Tu me cherchais, Nathalie?'

She grinned:

'How bad is it?'

'What did you hear?'

'How bad is it, Xavier?'

He let his eyes rest on the brooch against her breast, an elegant leaping cat mounted on a silver pin. He knew it well...

'I suggest you spend the night at my place and leave first thing in the morning for a long vacation. You choose the destination, I pay. That's how bad.'

She showed no emotion, just took a drag from her cigarette, slowly blew out the smoke and brooded over some thought.

'Your place, eh,' she said eventually; 'So it's you they want?'

He grimaced, fought back the pain in his chest.

'Your friend—' he started, breaking off to correct himself; 'Your contact called with what I needed and things got a bit messy. But you're right, they don't know who I am.'

'Things got a bit messy?'

'That's what I said.'

'Messy?' she repeated, in a mild challenging tone.

'What did you hear, Nathalie?' he asked again.

She gently shook her head, thought for a moment, and at long last turned to face him.

He read her thoughts. It was easy, because unlike her ordinary silent gazes, this one was clearly not meant to draw him into one of her moments of suspension. Rather, she was silently talking to him, and he could almost hear her voice: *Now, what exactly are you worried about, Xavier? My well-being or my mouth?* Or those were the words he lent her, because, had she spoken, she'd probably have said it differently, been more incisive, or cruel. Still, surprisingly, there was no reproach in her eyes, just a hint of teasing, as though she was trying to provoke him, hoping to lead him into saying something dumb perhaps, something like 'I'm sorry'.

Somewhat irritated, he sent her a 'you'd-rather-not-know' look and reached for his cigarettes.

'Did you at least get to your Austrian?' he heard her ask.

He frowned.

'No...' he conceded, lighting a Gitane before quickly going on to add what sounded to his own ears like a desperate 'Not yet', which warranted a cynical riposte.

It didn't come, which was just as well because, the way he felt, he might have stooped as low as to remind her he'd only wanted a name from her, that it had been her decision to compromise herself by volunteering to...

There was no need for further preamble:

'Will £5,000 do, Nathalie?'

'I'm sorry?'

'For your enforced vacation. Will £5,000 do?'

She probed his face, made as if to speak but broke into a sneer as the waiter turned up at their table.

'Thank you,' she said, as the man put their espressos in front of them.

They observed each other as he picked up Lombard's empty cup and changed the ashtray, then both turned to watch him stroll away with his tray.

Whatever Nathalie had intended to say before the interruption, she no longer planned on sharing it. In a familiar gesture, she brought her cup up to her mouth and, holding it close to her lips with both hands, with her cigarette smoking between her fingers, softly blew on the hot coffee.

Manifestly, his suggestion had gone down badly. Or she was haggling. He had better...

'Okay. Why don't you just tell me what and how much it will take, Nathalie?'

'What and how much have you got to offer, Xavier?'

He sighed:

'If you don't mind, I'd sooner skip the cat and mouse games.'

'Who's playing?'

'Come on. Just say what it is you want, okay? I promise I'll do my best to meet it.'

In that her face didn't move, strictly speaking she didn't laugh. But her eyes laughed.

He didn't like it.

'I find you quite furtive tonight, Nathalie,' he said, trying to sound calm, growing more irritated by the second, already sensing he was wasting his time; 'You're not normally one for foreplay. What's the matter? Did you lose your killer instinct or are you at long last trying to surprise me? I hate to be a spoilsport, but this isn't the time or the place. Tell me, how many people know to find you here at this hour?'

She sent him a sideways glance, let her dark eyes linger on his hand, raised her eyebrows – so reminding him that he was still wearing his wedding band – then glanced at his coffee, brought her cup to her mouth and drank.

'Your coffee's getting cold, Xavier. But if you want to talk money, you still owe me £500. And I understand you charged your room at the Métropole to my account.'

Perhaps it was the way she'd spoken, but she'd just made him think of Deborah De Moraes, and the thought used up what little goodwill and patience he had left:

'Right. Let's make it ten thousand. No. Fifteen. It doesn't leave me much room for negotiation but I'm hoping even you might find that enough to buy a pleasant time and still have change to afford the odd fix now and then. Or have I got that the wrong way round?'

'*Eh bien,*' she said, softly, as if to herself; 'How comforting it is to know you can be generous…'

He nodded his nod, ignored the latest stab from his wound, clenched his teeth and turned away to stare at the burning cigarette between his fingers.

He'd been wrong. It had clearly been wishful thinking to hope that, with her life at stake, she'd be anything other than her perverse and stubborn self. Still, he'd prepared for this, knew what to do, even if…

He had already tried and failed before her arrival, but once again he scoured his mind, searching for some kind of sensible threat with which to hit her. Again, none came, none that would work on her anyway…

'Okay, Nathalie,' he said, taking in the information that the hands of his watch pointed to twenty four past midnight before rooting his eyes back on his cigarette; 'Presuming a man with a gun doesn't walk through the door in the next five minutes, unless you let me help you help us, I'll give the Austrian and his set-up to the cops. After that, it's every man for himself. Maybe we'll both live. Maybe we'll both die. Maybe you don't care. Maybe you're already dead. Whatever, it should buy you some time.'

She didn't say a word, but he heard the soft rustling of her scarf and shirt as she turned his way, and then felt her glare. It took a lot of restraint not to face her, almost as much as it took to keep his cigarette in front of his eyes and not bring it to his lips, for his throat had grown so sore by now, the nicotine hit wasn't worth the pain of taking it in. Be that as it may, he could do with some caffeine, needed it almost as much as he needed to do something in order not to yield and look at her. Without knowing why, he was set on avoiding eye contact. Maybe he just didn't want her to know what he was thinking.

He got hold of his espresso and drained it in one go, screwing up his face as he swallowed. It was that or groaning.

'Let me put to you a hypothetical situation, Xavier,' he heard her voice as he brought his cup down; 'Let's say some sucker hires you to shadow his or her spouse,' she went on, sounding unexpectedly amenable; 'Let's say you catch the spouse in the act but by then you've assessed that the sinner is only having a little harmless fun or that, say, there are mitigating circumstances and that, all in all, you're really dealing with a troubled but sweet little couple here, one whose marriage isn't worth breaking. What do you do?'

He just kept his eyes on his cigarette, puzzled, trying to figure out where she was trying to take him.

'Come on. It's simple enough. What do you do, Xavier?'

He hesitated. Whatever she was after, he didn't need to answer this. She knew him well enough to know the answer.

'Why don't you just tell me what you think I ought to do, Nathalie?'

'Come on. Your watch is ticking,' she returned; 'What do you do?'

He nodded, reluctantly decided he might as well…

Le client est roi, Nathalie.'

He heard her scoff, in assent from the sound of it.

'What if the sinner makes you out, begs, cries, promises never to do it again and offers to buy your silence?'

Le client est roi,' he simply repeated.

'The offer is one you can't afford to refuse.'

Le client est toujours roi.'

'So much so that you'd pointlessly break his heart and marriage?'

Le client est roi,' he said again, bearing it, still trying to figure out what this was all leading to.

The answer, if that's what it was, came after a short silence, and when it reached him, he spun his head, ready to...

'So, you too are just a whore...'

He could have slapped her, but instead, the moment she came into his field of vision, in spite of himself, he merely gazed at her, or more exactly, he gazed at her smile. Once again, she was watching him with that uncanny new smile of hers, adrift, and before he knew it, just as had happened in his flat, he found himself trying but failing to interpret it. It was too healthy, too sensual and too pure to be given meaning. As before, it simply curved her lips, put light into her eyes, softened her face, making her look fresh and brittle. And this time, because he was so near to it perhaps, it touched him, roused his protective instinct. Willing, he let it stir into life, swell in his blood, breath into his skin and numb his pains. And before long her scent reached him through all of the dining room smells, he felt himself break into a smile and...

The warmth living in his nape and shoulders made itself felt, his temples became numb and heavy, his blood surged against the bones beneath his skin, his chest screamed.

He killed his smile with a grimace. He couldn't...

'What's that damn smile about, Nathalie?' he snapped, not thinking.

Her smile vanished, her face hardened and her eyes darkened with hatred.

'Right,' she said, turning away to give herself a moment to

gather her thoughts; 'Thanks for the offer but I didn't bring my passport. In any case, I don't need your help. I made a few calls when I heard who was looking for me and it's being looked after. My only problem is you. I don't know what your plans are but it won't matter whether I take a holiday or who or what favours I call upon if they find out ours is anything more than a client-whore relationship, you understand?'

He did, let her know it with a scowl, angry, letting his eyes ask why she'd waited until now to tell him this, why she'd let him…

She cut him off with a sneer:

'Now. What do you think, Xavier? Should I trust you, or ask what and how much it will take to send you packing?'

He didn't reply. No words came. She'd turned the tables, humbled him and let him off the hook all at once. He grinned, unable to contain his admiration, and then let her eyes draw him onto more familiar ground, their ground, where words were superfluous.

A few seconds later, as they silently agreed to agree, he wondered whether she felt as frightened as he did. His wasn't an unpleasant fear though, merely the kind which occurs when one makes a momentous decision which one believes to be wrong. Because what they were agreeing to was wrong. To consent to link their lives like this, to charge each other with the burden of responsibility for the other, was unquestionably wrong. They were opting for the easy way out. It was frightening, but still, not altogether unpleasant…

'Good,' she said, turning to stub out her cigarette; 'Just in case, I know you as Pierre Marchand. You come to London about once a month to pick up artworks at auctions for a private French collector. We met at the Métropole bar a couple of years back, I sold you a hard-on, you've come back for more on each of your stopovers since. It won't hold water if they find out the true nature of your occupation, but that's another story. Okay?'

He watched her light a new cigarette, reach for her coat, thought she was about to leave.

'If you don't mind my asking, Nathalie – what makes you so sure they'll buy it even now? Or for that matter leave you alone?'

'My credentials, Xavier,' she retorted, starting to search

through her coat pockets; 'Those same credentials that made you come to me in your hour of need.'

'They're that good?'

She grinned:

'Don't worry. As long as I can keep my credibility, they'll leave me alone whether they buy it or not. As it happens, assholes who have to get up in the morning to peddle kids for a living don't run the show. They can be told what to do, what not to do, what to believe and what not to believe by bigger and smarter assholes.'

'The company of whom you keep?'

'Huh. When you look as good and know men as well as I do, it comes with the territory,' she said, pulling a small folded piece of paper from her coat; 'But we don't want to speak about me, remember?'

She folded her coat back over the chair, grabbed her handbag and rose to her feet.

'I have to make a call,' she said, turning away slinging her bag over her shoulder.

Grim, he watched her stride through the dining room tables without a glance right or left, her long black hair wafting gently over her narrow shoulders with each of her steps. She stopped briefly, as if remembering something, then moved on and out of view along the corridor to the lavatories.

He felt the Gitane between his fingers snap. He stared at the two pieces, tossed them into the ashtray and turned to the bar.

'*Un expresso et un cappuccino,*' he called towards the tall barman.

'*Non,*' he corrected himself as the man nodded; '*Faites-nous deux expressos.*'

It was sad and idiotic, but he hoped that, on finding a drink waiting for her when she returned, she would stay, if indeed it was her intention to leave.

She didn't say a word when she came back, but she sat down, lit yet another cigarette, brought her coffee up to her mouth, leaned back and started softly blowing on it, her eyes surveying the tables in front of her.

Toying with a new Gitane, he loosened up, immediately thinking about her smile again. He still wanted an explanation for it, wondered how to broach the subject, but as seconds and then minutes went by, her contemplative stillness took over. Perhaps it was her way of dealing with the situation, but sitting beside him as she was, whether by design or not, she created a welcome sense of normality. They could have been at the Parliament Hill café, performing one of their Friday morning rituals, and coming after the events of the last days, the illusion simply felt too comfortable to risk shattering with uninvited questions. So, he joined her in her quiet contemplation of their surroundings, hoping she wouldn't speak or leave too soon. He was too weary to think about what his eyes saw, but it didn't matter, was perhaps even preferable, he'd done so much thinking lately. Soon, his pains mellowed and, inasmuch as there was nothing left for him to do until morning and he well knew that he wouldn't be able to sleep, he felt thankful for the opportunity to kill time sitting with her.

He'd spoken to Rhian. She had met some of Leonard's old music friends in the days when he had played in a band, but could only recall a few first names, had no idea what had happened to them since or even where they may have lived at the time. Nor could she remember Leonard mentioning anything specific about the man he'd called the Austrian, about his age or his looks.

He'd also called Paris, and left a message on Moreau's answer-phone asking him to see if he could dig up information about an Otto Gluck. He'd kept the details to himself, let on only that the man he was concerned with was possibly Austrian, a former Nazi or, as the case may be, a former Nazi's son. It seemed wise not to let his friend know about the child trafficking angle; there was no way of knowing how he'd react.

Nathalie eventually broke the silence. Peering at the dining room's fake nicotine-stained wallpaper, Lombard had just decided that, when the time came, he'd drive to Heathrow airport. That way, he'd avoid the crowded tube train's brew of aftershave, perfume and other morning smells which tended to give him a migraine, as well as save himself the expense of taxis to and from Heathrow, which, he guessed, would probably exceed the airport's parking fee for the few days he would be away.

'Earlier on I watched TV,' Nathalie said; 'A programme about Mozart. And then one of those nature documentaries, you know? Do you know anything about Mozart, Xavier?'

'No.'

'Well, Einstein described him as a guest amongst mankind. *C'est joli, tu ne trouves pas?*'

He frowned…

'Ouais…'

'Later on, in the nature documentary,' she went on after a moment, 'the commentator explained that ninety percent of the planet consists of boiling matter, and went on to say that we and everything else living on its thin crust are really just lucky guests…'

He waited for the punch line. There was always a punch line when Nathalie spoke more than a few unprompted words.

'That too is a nice thought. Only, looking at Georgina over there, I think he ought to have said *lucky accidents.* Whose guest could our Georgina possibly be, eh?'

He turned to the big table at the end of the room. Its dozen or so occupants were still there, still paper-hatted, merry and looking too hot now. Amid the more tranquil night creatures who had gradually filled the other tables, they provided a rather incongruous spectacle, like an unwelcome reminder of daytime life, even if by now some among them had grown tired and quiet. The woman in Nathalie's sights, the one named Georgina, was by far the quietest of the group. Arms crossed, as if cold, she sat in her coat at one end of the table, her head resting on another woman's shoulder, smoking, with dark rings under her shining eyes – a glum, wasted figure. Earlier on, still eating and alone, Lombard had watched the men from her table follow each other to the lavatories, each returning after a few minutes with a '—, your presence is requested!', which, inevitably, had on each occasion given rise to cries of *'Hooray for Georgina'* and high-pitched giggles and shrieks of astonishment. Eventually, some time after the last man's return, Georgina had at long last appeared from the direction of the lavatories. She was a tall, slim young woman, with short fair hair, a pale complexion, tight thin lips and bulging, dreamy eyes, which all combined, even now, to give her a permanently ungrateful air. At first, she'd joined in the general merriment. There had been light-hearted arguments about a bet as it wasn't clear who should honour it, men only or both men and women. After much discussion, Georgina had collected IOU's and cheques from everyone at the table, and then gradually grown quieter and more jaded, reserving her smiles, grins or words for the times when one or other of the men around her raised his glass with a 'Hooray for Georgina', which with time had become a kind of loud punctuation, the last of which Lombard had heard only a few minutes earlier without paying it any attention.

Nathalie had not witnessed any of this. There was no way she could possibly know what had happened. Yet somehow, reading the signs on Georgina's face, the shine in her wasted eyes perhaps, and the 'Hoorays for Georgina', she seemed to have guessed.

He opted not to say anything, trusting Nathalie would come up with something soon enough.

'Well,' she pronounced in due time; 'I suppose the city's welfare and prosperity hinges on her and her friends sacrifices.'

'Do you know a woman called Peter?' he asked.

'A woman called Peter?'

'She works for the Austrian.'

'No.'

He nodded, finally gave in and lit his Gitane. The pain in his throat was just about manageable. The hit soothing.

'You wouldn't have any sleeping pills?' he queried, peering at her handbag.

She chose to misinterpret the request, to read something sinister into it, let it be known with a scoff.

'I need sleep, Nathalie.'

'Oh… That's all.'

'It's a lot when you haven't slept for a couple of nights.'

Again, they surrounded themselves in silence, watched the

dining room, until Nathalie rose to her feet, put on her coat and, standing, began to search her bag.

She produced two tiny blue pills from a small silver casket and put them on the table.

'I can only spare a couple. Still, don't take them both at once.'

He agreed.

'One would do.'

'Have two,' she said; 'And don't forget my money on Friday. You know what they say about settling one's debts.'

'I might not be here on Friday. I'm going away. Just a few days but I don't know for how long...'

She probed his eyes, understood.

'I'll let you know if—' he started.

'I don't want to know anything, Xavier,' she cut in; 'And by the way, if the fancy takes you to pay me a visit again, don't ring the neighbours' bells or yell under my windows, will you?'

He scowled, but...

He drove home ten minutes later, leaving the brasserie at the same time as Georgina and company. By three, he'd tidied up his flat. By four, freshly shaven and dressed, he'd packed a change of suit and his sponge bag, fed his goldfish, signed his accounts and read the note Perkins had left in his letter box the previous morning; the butcher was giving official notice that his rent would go up by five pounds a week as from the first of the following month, which made it New Year's day. Soon after five, he left Leonard Spitz's flat, having returned the missing man's video player and wiped Rhian's messages from the answer-phone.

Dawn was just about breaking when he finally reached Heathrow and pulled into the airport car-park. He spent a few minutes tidying up his Triumph, replacing the wet newspapers from the front seat with dry ones from the trunk, in the process coming across his sodden road map which, somehow, had made its way down onto the wet floor behind the passenger seat since his journey to Wales. The sodden pages were stuck together. He considered throwing it away, but then changed his mind, shook the water off it and, taking it to the trunk, pulled it open to find the contact sheet on which he'd written the names of the villages near Rhian's cottage. It clung to the page. He peeled it off, peered at the sequence of shots of the angry trudging tramp laden with plastic bags who had clearly not taken kindly to being photographed by Leonard, and put it into the trunk with the road map before picking up his suitcase.

'I booked a seat last night for the 10:30 flight to Los Angeles,' he said, smiling at the uniformed check-in girl; 'My name is Paul Lamont…'

He spent the next two hours drinking coffee in the departure lounge, thinking about nothing, except, briefly, about the fact that, bar a snag, he would be talking to Friedman in just a few hours time. When the tannoy called, he swallowed down one of Nathalie's blue pills.

'In the entertainment business, sir?'

Lombard glanced at the young taxi driver in the front of the car. He found the question odd, almost as odd as the suburban landscape unrolling outside his window. The sky was blue, the sun dazzling, there were palm trees along the broad avenues, but the pavements were dusty and empty and the buildings uniformly dull. Then again, perhaps they were still in the famous city's outskirts. After all, it wasn't long since they'd passed the oil fields outside the airport. The sight of the grasshopper-like pumps moving up and down across the desert sands had also struck Lombard; he had no idea oil was produced around Los Angeles.

'No,' he said, squinting in the harsh light.

'Oh… Right. So where you from, sir? Europe?'

'What?'

'You come from Europe?'

'Yes…' he said, after musing over it; 'I'm from Europe.'

'First time in Los Angeles?'

'Uh-huh.'

'All right! Then let me tell you, you made an excellent choice, sir. The Wyatt's a great hotel. One of the…'

He talked too much.

'Thank you,' Lombard cut in, peering into the rear-view mirror to catch the confident piggy eyes of the gum-chewing man; 'But why don't you focus on your driving and leave me to worry about your tip, eh?'

The driver pulled a face and Lombard gazed down at his shoes.

His feet were hot and his head groggy. He'd slept the whole flight, until the air hostess had shaken him awake to tell him to fasten his seat belt as they were about to land.

'Are there any hotels near the Wyatt?' he asked.

'I'm sorry?'

'Are there any hotels near the Wyatt?'

'Yes, sir.'

'In Sunset Boulevard?'

'Yes.'

'Stop when we get within sight of the Wyatt, all right.'

And, turning back to the window, he absent-mindedly began to finger his wedding band. For no particular reason, he'd chosen to keep it on before leaving London, and now, in contrast to the dreary sunlit scenery outside, the gold band felt comfortingly cool and clean.

The Delaunay was a theme hotel. Its decor of abstract geometric patterns echoed the work of the artist after whom it was named – who, besides being news to Lombard, also turned out to be French – and its complimentary matchbook proclaimed simply: *Delaunay, Hotel de Grande Classe*.

Whether or not this was a statement of fact, it happened to be conveniently situated across Sunset Boulevard from the Wyatt, not directly opposite but near enough for Lombard to have a good view from his fifth floor window of the rows of balconies lining the sunlit facade of Friedman's hotel. Friedman was not there, but he was still in town and Lombard now knew his room number. To obtain it had been easy, called for a simple ploy he'd learned a long time ago which rarely failed when dealing with inexperienced hotel staff. And these days, most hotel reception staff were just that.

'Can I have room 405?' he'd called the Wyatt shortly after

stepping into his room, which was numbered 504. He was put through, a woman answered, declared she didn't know any Gluck and he'd called reception again.

'You put me through to the wrong room. I asked for room 405. Mr. Otto Gluck's room. Can you try again and get it right this time.'

Doubtless as keen to please as to transfer the blame, the person at the other end had readily informed him that the mistake was his. Mr. Gluck was not staying in room 405 but 337. Did he still want to be put through?

There'd been no reply from room 337, which suited Lombard fine.

He surveyed the Wyatt's third floor windows, observed the uniformed doorman and a capped chauffeur who stood chatting by a stretch limousine in the shade of the hotel's covered forecourt, and then followed the twisting line of Sunset Boulevard as it meandered up and away across the sprawling city towards some distant hills half-concealed in smog. For all its fame, Sunset Boulevard, or at least the section of it visible from his window, looked fairly ordinary. It was possibly sprucer than what he'd seen of the city so far, but even here, the pavements were dusty and deserted, as if they served no other purpose than that of demarcation zones between buildings and traffic lanes. Indeed, lofty hotels aside, it just about managed to compare favourably with any dual carriageway on the outskirts of London. Only, this wasn't London. The sparse traffic under his window moved smoothly, the Wyatt stood against a steep dry bushy hill and the sun dazzled the eyes.

He lit a Gitane with a match from the hotel matchbook, flicked the burnt match out the window, sat on the bed, reached for the phone, dialled and, with the handset wedged between his neck and shoulder, started to untie his shoelaces. Whatever had brought Friedman to Los Angeles, whether or not he'd heard the news from London, he clearly felt safe, or else he wouldn't be staying at the Wyatt; hotels, especially sizeable ones, were arguably the most unsafe of places.

'The Wyatt. Good Afternoon...'

'Good afternoon. This is Mr. Gluck, room 337. I'm expecting delivery of a parcel in the next hour or so,' he said, formally, in a slight German accent; 'Could you see to it that it is taken to my room immediately when it arrives.'

'No problem, Mr. Gluck. We'll keep a look out for it. Anything else?'

'No. That will be all. Thank you.'

He took his shoes off and felt his socks.

They were damp. And his shirt and trousers were creased and the vest against his skin warm and sweaty. He pulled his watch from his wrist, reset it against the time on the digital clock on the bedside table, opened his suitcase and begun to undress. It was nearing three o'clock. The time difference between London and Los Angeles had gained him eight hours. Fortunately, thanks to Nathalie's pill, he'd slept them off, and now that his head had cleared, felt much better for it. For one thing, his chest wound no longer twitched and screamed uncontrollably, even if it required a change of dressing. The one he had on was caked with dry blood and sweat.

He hadn't thought of packing any, and called the lobby for some to be brought up.

'Er, what kind of dressing do you mean, Mr. Lamont?'

'Some gauze and a roll of adhesive plaster. Oh. And also some antiseptic cream...' he said, deciding he'd better shave on feeling the stubble around his chin.

The Delaunay's lobby store stocked boxes of luxury chocolates and sunglasses. Lombard selected the cheapest type of each, and, after telling the tall brunette behind the counter that he'd be paying cash in reply to her query, asked for the chocolates to be gift-wrapped. This did not present any problem, earned him a knowing smile even, but his request for a label and the loan of a pen proved more troublesome.

'We have packs of ten labels for $2.40 and pens at...' the brunette declared, all square grin and self-assured stare, as if it went without saying that he ought to buy ten labels and a pen.

He sent her a smile and, after a moment's thought, she offered to lend him a pen but remained adamant about the labels. He bought a pack of ten, paid, scribbled 'O. Gluck, The Wyatt, Room 337' on one label, pocketed the other nine and left her to finish wrapping the chocolates.

'Could you kindly stick the label on when you've finished and ask reception to deliver it to the Wyatt at once. Thank you.'

About fifteen minutes elapsed between his stepping out of the store and into Friedman's room. He paused outside the Delaunay to put on his sunglasses, moved into the sun, made across Sunset Boulevard, acknowledged the burly Wyatt doorman's genial 'Hi, there!' with a grin, walked through the lobby to the lifts, as expected found room 337 on the third floor, knocked to ensure no one was in, took cover in a nearby corridor, heard the lift door open a couple of times, after the third time caught sight of a young porter heading towards Friedman's door with the wrapped box of chocolates, let him knock, let him unlock the door, then moved after him as soon as he disappeared inside.

The porter was already heading back out when Lombard walked in the door, and stopped in his tracks on finding his way out blocked.

'Oh. Hi there,' he said.

Lombard sent him a silent grin. Given that Friedman had only been there a day, it was unlikely the porter knew what he looked like, but still…

'Mr. Gluck?' the other asked.

'Uh-huh.'

'Right. That packet just came for you, sir. I was told to bring it up to your room.'

He'd moved back against the wall, was signalling towards a coffee table in the room behind him.

Lombard glanced at the chocolates.

'That's right. Thank you,' he said, not forgetting to sound German, and dipping his hand into his pocket.

He pulled out the $5 bill he had ready, tipped the porter and took a step back to let him leave, which the other did, bowing and grinning.

'Thank you, sir. Have a nice day…'

He shut the door, took off his sunglasses and frowned. Either, even so far from home, Friedman was concerned about his safety and used the hotel merely as a contact address, or he'd left in a hurry without notifying reception. In any case, his room was plainly unoccupied. Not merely tidy and formal after the maid's daily visit, but vacant. From bedside table to bathroom shelves, there were no personal effects anywhere. Still, there could be no doubt Friedman had been there, for, in the wardrobe, together with a Heathrow Duty Free bag holding a sealed bottle of Armagnac, was a small travelling bag with a Virgin Airways tag containing a pair of man's leather slippers almost identical to the ones Lombard had seen sitting square to the bed back in the Austrian's Hampstead cottage.

A quick inspection of the sole and lining told him they'd been worn and, mulling over them, Lombard came up with two likely explanations for their presence – Friedman had indeed left and had forgotten them, or these were simply his travelling slippers. Quite a few people took their shoes off on long flights, and if the riches of the Austrian's London shoe cabinet signified anything, it was that he was fussy about his feet. He would be just the type to fly shoeless and, concerned about soiling his socks, to carry around a pair of special travelling slippers.

After thinking about it further, Lombard decided this had to be the right explanation. The Austrian was too fastidious to have left without his slippers, let alone without having checked out. These were his travelling slippers. That's why they had a bag all of their own – so they could accompany him on the plane – and why they were at the hotel; wherever Friedman was staying, they were superfluous to his needs until his next flight.

Lombard stuffed them back into their bag somewhat comforted by their presence. At least, presuming he was right, and instinct told him he was, Friedman was around. Under the circumstances, it was heartening news, for the fact that the man was not using his hotel room meant he might be with friends, and apart from what that implied, it also spelt a longer stay in Los Angeles than Lombard had hoped for. It no longer seemed reasonable to trust coming face to face with the man today.

Still, on the plus side, the room overlooked Sunset Boulevard, and after peering out trying unsuccessfully to locate his room along the Delaunay's fifth floor, Lombard propped up a bright hotel brochure against the window, drew the curtain against it, put his sunglasses back on and left leaving a 'Do Not Disturb' sign on the door.

'How are you?' the doorman greeted him this time around as he stepped out into the forecourt.

He grinned, pressed on, but then turned to ask if there was somewhere near to rent a car.

The uniformed man knew just the place one block down the road. 'Tell them Jack from the Wyatt sent you. They'll treat you nice,' he said with an encouraging wink, presuming Lombard was staying at the hotel or hoping for a tip. Or both perhaps.

He made do with another grin. Lombard crossed the boulevard towards the Delaunay, scanned the Wyatt's third floor for his brochure, found it resting in the fourth window from the right, clearly visible against the dark curtain behind it, and, the only person in sight walking under the sun, trekked the short distance down to the car-rental place, which turned out to be a timber structure in the middle of a car pound behind a chain-link fence.

It really could have been a London suburb…

He was greeted with a combined 'Hi there—How are you?', made no mention of Jack, was disappointed that all the vehicles on offer were automatic but satisfied that they bore no exterior signs or logos to broadcast they were rented and quickly settled for an unassuming blue Ford. Then, the formalities over with, recalling the taxi driver's 'In the entertainment business, sir?', he asked directions for the nearest working-class Hispanic neighbourhood, letting on he was in town working as a location scout for a Franco-English film production company.

They kindly gave him a map and directions for the San José precinct.

Taking a turn in Los Angeles' broad avenues turned out to be a game of anticipation. There were no roundabouts. It was all about getting into lane in good time, or else missing the turn altogether or angering the locals by stopping and indicating at the turn itself in the hope of being allowed through. However, the story about American drivers being polite because they never knew whether the next driver was carrying a gun proved fairly accurate, and after a few hiccups and some time readjusting to driving on the right, moving in the city's flowing traffic became simple enough.

The streets of San José were shabby, rough and dusty. Many buildings looked in need of repair, stores hid behind security screens, people walked the pavements and the air was thick with a sharp dry smell that at long last conveyed a sense of city, stirred the senses and braced them for challenges, unlike the Sunset Boulevard area where the only smell Lombard had noticed reminded him of a holiday resort. This was probably due to the nearness of the Pacific Ocean, which he knew was somewhere around but had yet to see.

Cruising along the streets peering out of his open window, he soon found what he was looking for. At an intersection, a gang of five Hispanic men and boys loitered in front of a liquor store. As he steered slowly past eyeing them, one of the five immediately made him out. Wearing jeans, a sleeveless T-shirt and a tight woolly hat, he looked to be in his mid-twenties and had small probing eyes. From behind his sunglasses, Lombard watched him, searching his face, and then observed him in his mirror as the other went on looking over his car as he drove away.

Unlike the self-assured stares, toothy smiles, 'Sirs' and 'Hi theres' he'd sampled up to now, this was recognisable territory. Woolly-hat's face spoke, and he knew what it was saying.

He locked his door, did a U-turn, headed back toward the intersection and pulled up at the kerb with his engine running.

Woolly-hat had clearly had a word with the others because, before Lombard even came to a stop, like a pack of wolves, their backs to the liquor store, the five had stopped whatever it was they were doing to eyeball him suspiciously from behind their dark eyes.

'Hi there. How are you?' he called, pulling off his sunglasses to let them see his eyes.

Not one replied. They were still too busy trying to place him, had yet to pick an attitude.

He grinned, focused across the pavement on Woolly-hat who, he now saw, had bloodshot eyes, a tiny cross tattooed on the side of his neck and a cigarette lighter clenched in his fist. He leant against the store's metal screen, gauging him, his thin lips set in a smile. Clearly, he'd already worked out from his accent and pale skin that Lombard was from out of town, and was working hard to match him with a type fitting his set of references.

'What's the matter, motherfucker? You take a wrong turn?'

This had come from the youngest of the gang, a swaggering, sniggering fourteen-year-old wearing a studded belt and cowboy boots.

'No, no, no, no' said the next one in line, a lanky figure with a budding moustache and icy eyes; 'I think the mother's looking for thrills. I think the mother's brought his ass over looking for action. And I think the mother might just find it if he doesn't get the fuck outta my sun spot.'

'Huh…'

'You guys think dumb,' Woolly-hat spoke at last, keeping his eyes on Lombard; 'What we have here my friends is a mother cruising for nookie. This mother's queer and fancies my ass.'

This led to some laughter, some comments about him being in the wrong part of town, and then to the greasy-faced tubby one amongst them speaking from behind his Budweiser T-shirt. He looked well past thirty years old.

'That why you keepin' your ass in your nice automobile, cock-sucker? Hey? You into asses? Come on. Get outta there and show us what a manly tight little ass you got yourself, huh!'

'That's right, cock-sucker. Get your ass out here. I'll show you some pussy,' the young one gibed, grabbing his crotch with a 'Huh!' when Lombard scowled at him.

Lombard nodded his nod, turned to Woolly-hat:

'I don't wish to offend you, but I'm only really looking for a handgun,' he said; 'I want it quick and don't care what it is or where it comes from as long as it works.'

A mixture of disbelief and mirth rippled across the five faces.

'Motherfuck—'

'What's this guy…'

'This cock-sucker…'

'I'll pay $250. $500 for one with a silencer,' he announced, trusting this would shut them up.

It did. They shut up, thinking now. He'd heard that as little as $40 bought one a gun in Los Angeles, and from the frowns and glances they exchanged, they obviously thought they were onto something. Too much perhaps...

'So you want a gun?' queried Woolly-hat, eyes probing again.

Lombard nodded, grinning.

'The man wants a gun,' Woolly-hat said, nodding at his friends with a shrug; 'He doesn't want pussy. He wants a fucking gun... Where you from?' he asked, turning back to Lombard.

'Out of town, which is why I'm feeling so generous.'

'Where about from outta town?'

'Europe.'

'Europe?'

'That's right. Now, are you good for it or should I take my custom elsewhere?'

Woolly-hat scowled:

'Huh. What makes you so sure we want your custom, eh?'

He grinned again:

'My money.'

Woolly-hat snarled, pinched his bony nose, scratched his chin, glanced at the others again. He wasn't sure...

'What the fuck are you, huh?'

Lombard stayed silent, waiting.

'What says you ain't no cop with a funny act, eh?'

'What says a cop would bother to put on an act to hit you big boys?' returned Lombard calmly, running his eyes over the five faces; 'Or are some of you smarter than you look?' he went on, deliberately provoking them. They were not going to do anything now; he was easy money...

Woolly-hat scowled again, exchanged yet another glance with his friends and they silently agreed they had better confer out of his earshot.

'Sit tight, Europe,' Woolly-hat said, signalling for the others to follow him.

They huddled together like a bunch of mischievous school-kids about ten yards away, came back a mere thirty seconds later and reassumed their position in front of the liquor store.

'Okay,' said Woolly-hat, breaking off to let an old man with a grocery bag walk between them and away; 'Suppose we get the thing, we take five hundred, seven fifty. You want the piece quick and silencers are fuck to come by.'

Lombard lit a Gitane. He wouldn't have expected them to behave any other way.

'When?' he asked.

'You got the money?'

'You have the gun?'

'Right. One hour. You know where we are.'

'For that price I expect the shells thrown in. And I want more than one round, okay?' he said, pulling away.

'Yeah. And don't you get into trouble. And don't get fucking lost, cock-sucker,' one of them shouted behind him.

It was the young one with the cowboy boots. He was all smile. Easy money…

He spent the next hour in a burger bar car-park a few blocks away, eating a cheeseburger, drinking coffee and smoking, observing three teenage girls perched on swings in a playground across the road through his windscreen. Like him, they were killing time, looking as bored as only teenage girls can, now still, now gently rocking, mostly gazing vacantly at the passing traffic. In time, they decided they needed a change, and dragged their feet fifty yards away into the shade of a basketball court stuck between two apartment blocks where they were soon joined by another couple of girls…

When he stopped again by the liquor store, two of the gang moved to the front of his car, two to the back, and Woolly-hat asked to get into the passenger seat. The brown paper bag he handed Lombard held a 9 millimetre Browning, a silencer and two dozen or so loose shells. For a handgun it was heavy, its serial number had been filed down, but it was clean and the silencer was easy to mount and lock onto the barrel lug. Lombard loaded the magazine with eight rounds, opened his door just enough to point the gun at the tarmac and pulled the trigger, revving his engine hard to mask the thud of the shot. It worked, and

Woolly-hat got out of the car thinking he was crazy but smiling for being seven hundred and fifty easy dollars richer.

'For some guy from outta town, you ain't doin' too bad, Europe,' he said, standing in the open door.

Lombard didn't understand.

'In this shithole buses are for losers, you get me? In this shit-hole, the green bill rules. You got enough of it, the town is yours.'

Lombard frowned.

'It's much the same everywhere else.'

'Yeah?'

'Yeah.'

Woolly-hat shook his head:

'You don't say. Well, all the same. And if you need any more favours, and I'm talking pussy too, you know where your friends are, eh...'

The brochure was still in Friedman's window when he got back to his room at the Delaunay, clearly visible in the deep crimson glow of the setting sun. It was a little past six o'clock, but the city looked ablaze, a scarlet and black world sprinkled with millions of electric lights which spread forever into the horizon. The sight held Lombard in wonder long enough for him to notice that the distant sky was also home to an endless stream of passenger aircraft, their great number and dark, gliding silhouettes contributing to the eeriness of the sight; they might have been ravens flying across the flames of a huge bonfire.

He leant out the window to search for his hire-car. He'd left it at the end of the steep side street that ran between the hotel and an adjoining patch of scrubby wasteland, preferring that to using the hotel's underground car-park. It wasn't visible from his window and he made for the bed, tossed the gun in its brown paper bag into his open suitcase, took off his jacket and shoes, lay down, lit a cigarette and reached for the phone.

'Reception. What can we do for you, Mr. Lamont?'

'I need to make a call to London. Can you give me the code...'

'Would that be London, England?'

'Er... Yes.'
'Right. You need to dial...'

He'd expected to hear the voice of Lawrence the butler; instead he immediately recognised the suave Brazilian accent of Deborah De Moraes' husband.

'Hello?'

'How are you, Mr. De Moraes?' he said, dredging up from deep in his mind that the man was called Carlos; 'Mr. Lombard here.'

'Oh. Mr. Lombard. Yes. Wait. I think you better speak to my wife. Just a moment. I'll see if she is still awake.'

He peered at his watch. He'd not thought of the time difference. It was two in the morning in London. It was too late though. The Brazilian was gone.

'Mr. Lombard?'

'How are you, Mrs. De Moraes? I hope I didn't wake you up.'

'Er... No, it's all right... Where are you?'

He scowled at the hotel matchbook in his hand. This hesitant, amenable woman didn't sound like the one he knew. Either her husband had got her out of bed and she was groggy with sleep, or she wasn't well...

'In Los Angeles. Have you got a pen?' he asked.

'Just a moment... Right. Go ahead.'

'The Delaunay, room 504. The phone number is...'

She noted it, her slow breathing reaching his ear.

'Right. Did you... Have you spoken to him yet?'

She definitely didn't sound like herself.

'Are you all right, Mrs. De Moraes?'

'I'm sorry?'

'Are you all right?'

'Yes... You... It's the middle of the night here. I'm tired. Have you spoken to your man?'

He frowned:

'No. The hotel where I'd hoped to find him turns out to be little more than a contact address. I'll give it twenty four hours though. He just might show up.'

She stayed silent, and he heard her breathing again.

'I see. What will you do if he doesn't...'

He'd already thought about it, already decided, but there was no point in telling her.

'I take it there's no news from your brother?'

'Leon? No.'

'If you need to reach me, ask for Mr. Lamont. Paul Lamont, all right?'

'Paul Lamont...?'

'Yeah. Goodnight, Mrs. De Moraes.'

He hung up, kept his eyes on the matchbook in his fingers for a while, then dialled Nathalie's number. He just couldn't resist. At least, she was unlikely to be asleep...

'I'm not here. Leave a message or...'

A moment later he got through to the brasserie in Brewer Street. Nathalie had been and left half an hour earlier.

That was all he wanted to know...

The evening hours saw a steady stream of limousines pulling into the Wyatt's forecourt, and also of crowds making for the doors of a night-club next door to it. At one time, nearly all the windows behind the hotel's balconies were lit up, became alive with people moving in the rooms beyond them, and then, as the traffic along the boulevard all but stopped, the night-club emptied, curtains were drawn and lights turned off. The Wyatt's windows fell into darkness and night set in.

He did not sleep, he couldn't, but nothing, no thoughts, disturbed his night. Now standing at his window, now lying on the bed with the flickering silent TV screen for company, sometimes eyes closed, sometimes not, he spent the hours smoking and waiting. He might have dozed off at the first light of dawn, but a shuffling sound near the door pulled him wide awake again. A newspaper, *USA Today*, had been pushed onto the carpet underneath his door, and soon after, any hope he may still have entertained of catching some sleep vanished with the arrival in the boulevard below of a couple of road sweepers. He watched them from his window as, with masks over their mouths and whirring air blowers strapped to their backs, they proceeded to blast the dust from the hotels' entrances and pavements. Los Angeles was waking up, the brochure had not moved from Friedman's dark window and now he knew why Sunset Boulevard's pavements were not as dusty as San Jose's.

THIRTEEN

'I'm sorry, sir. A coffee and…?'

'A coffee and a couple of croissants.'

'Crow what?'

'Croissants,' Lombard repeated, squinting in the sunlight.

The waiter sent him a perplexed grin:

'I'm really sorry, sir. But, could you try that again?'

Lombard scowled. Already, he'd been asked to sit out on the terrace by the pool when he'd stepped into the hotel restaurant with a cigarette burning between his lips. It was not that he minded being outside, but he'd left his sunglasses in his room, had not felt like going back up for them.

'Croissants. Like that,' he said, motioning towards a basket on a couple's table.

'Oh! You want some coffee a couple of *crescents*?'

Lombard looked him up and down. He was young, probably gay and all grinning blue eyes and dimples above the pot of coffee he held in his fine manicured hands.

'Those things are called croissants,' he remarked.

'Not in America, sir,' the other returned with a self-satisfied smile; 'So, one coffee and a couple of *crescents*. I'll be right back.'

He strutted away, stopped at the couple's table and, beaming, refilled their cups.

Lombard nodded his nod, turned back to his newspaper, decided it was too bright to read.

'So, Ian, Steve tells me you made a documentary about car safety, eh? Sounds great…' said a voice behind him.

There was no ashtray on his table, and after wondering what to do with his Gitane stub, he flicked it away, aiming for a potted palm tree alongside the pool.

He missed. The cigarette overshot pot and palm tree, landed in the blue water with a hiss.

'That's right,' declared another man at his back, sounding as if his mouth was full; 'I had fun with it. It wasn't about car safety, though. Rather, about the car safety industry. And it's not as boring as...'

By the time he left the restaurant to make his way back to his room, he'd learned that apparently deceased children were used in crash simulation tests because dummies just couldn't give an accurate picture of what happened to childlike bodies in a car accident, and that since the introduction of airbags many crash victims, although ostensibly unhurt thanks to the device, had been found to go into unexplained coma. This latter fact, in the words of the documentary director, who'd thought nothing of chewing and speaking loudly at the same time for a good ten minutes, had left airbag manufacturers, physicians and scientists alike baffled. But long and costly research into the matter had eventually cleared up the mystery. The airbags, located in front of people as they were, formed an effective safeguard against injuries, but were of no avail against violent lateral swings of the head, which, it turned out, led to coma. This finding had sprung from the study of baboons rendered comatose by way of being knocked on the skull. First, it was found that coma could only be induced if the knock was delivered so as to produce a sharp sideways jerk of the baboons' heads – as opposed to a forward or backward motion – and then that this was due to the brain hemispheres squeezing together and then bouncing apart inside the skull, causing the connections between them to inflame and malfunction; all of which, according to the munching man behind Lombard, had made for a controversial documentary.

'... Apart from annoying a few folks by showing secret footage of dead kids used in test crashes, and suggesting airbags would be more useful if fitted at the sides as well as the front of cars, we didn't make many friends pointing out the stupidity involved in wasting millions of dollars playing around with baboons in order to come up with the great discovery that blows to the side of the head are a bad thing. We came up with the idea of closing the film in a New York boxing gym, see? Got the guys in there to talk about sideways blows. That was cool. From fourteen year-olds onward, they all said the same thing. I mean, for Christ's sake, how do you spot a boxer? Broken nose and scarred eyebrow! Why? Because these guys who punch each other senseless for a living know to shield their chins and the sides of their heads, not their noses and eyes. Hit me in the face all you like, but you're only gonna take me out with a swing to the side or an uppercut to the chin. Huh! One trip to a boxing gym or one hour watching a boxing video could have saved a lot of people a lot of money and possibly quite a few more from coma. Yeah, it didn't go down too well. But it was fun. Bad news for baboons though…'

Baboons…

The word hovered in Lombard's mind as he scanned the Wyatt's facade from his window. He'd asked the operator to confirm Mr. Gluck was still staying at the hotel, was waiting for him to get back on the line.

'Hello?'

'Yeah.'

'Right, sir. Yes, Mr. Gluck is indeed still a guest at the hotel. However, he doesn't appear to be here at the moment. Would you like to leave a message for his attention perhaps?'

He scowled at the brochure on Friedman's window.

'I would indeed. But could you check he actually calls for his messages? This is important. I tried him all day yesterday and he seems to be forever out.'

'Uh… Just a moment, sir. Let me see what…'

He peered down. A sun-glassed blonde in a low-cut top at the wheel of a gleaming black convertible was pulling into the Wyatt's forecourt. The doorman – not the burly one from the previous day, this one was lanky and too thin for his uniform – together with a hotel porter, were already hurrying towards the spot where she would come to a stop. Five storeys and the width of the boulevard away, the beaming grins in their tanned faces were plain to see.

'Absolutely, sir,' came back the operator; 'As a matter of fact he called early this morning.'

He nodded his nod, swallowed hard:

'Right. Next time Mr. Gluck calls can you make sure he gets told that he is going to get a call between eight this evening and the same time tomorrow. He better be there if he cares at all about the puppies he left in England…'

'Sorry. Did you say puppies, sir?'

'Yeah.'

Down below, the blonde was getting out of her convertible, flashing her teeth at the lanky doorman who held her door open.

'Right… puppies left in England… Is that it?'

'Uh-huh.'

'Okay! Let me check this with you, sir…' said the operator, starting to read back what he had taken down as the blonde exchanged a few quick words with the porter and started for the hotel entrance, all curves and mini skirt above her long bronzed legs on stiletto heels.

'And who shall I say the message is from, sir?'

'A friend of Martin's,' he replied after a moment's thought, watching the blonde's legs slither out of view through the door.

'A friend of Martin's?'

'That's right. Thank you,' he said, hanging up, now eyeing the two men the blonde had left behind with her car.

They were peering towards the hotel door, clearly still watching her, then turned to face each other, exchanged a slap of the hand, clenched their fists, howled up to the sky, and the porter hopped into the convertible and revved away for the hotel car-park leaving the doorman to crouch in the sunshine and brush the tip of his shoe with his uniform cuff. He was still beaming.

Lombard smiled, checked his watch – it was 9:30 – turned away from the window, took off his jacket and went to hang it in the wardrobe.

A moment later, stretched out on the bed, he lit a Gitane and reached for his newspaper. If the Austrian wouldn't come to his hotel, the only thing to do was try to bring him to it. This was his answer to Deborah De Moraes' 'What would you do if?'. He hadn't waited a full 24 hours, but…

There was a knock at the door through the telephone's ringing. He frowned, realised he'd dozed off, opened his eyes, sat upright and gazed at the blurry numbers on the digital clock on the bedside table until they began to make sense.

It was nearly 2 o'clock in the afternoon. He scowled at the telephone, then towards the door from where another three knocks came, glanced at the blue sky outside the window, pushed the crumpled newspaper off his lap, cleared his throat and got to his feet grabbing the handset to bring the ringing to an end.

'I'll be with you in a moment.'

'Mr. Lombard. Mrs. De—' he heard Deborah De Moraes' voice before putting the handset down and making for the door running his fingers through his hair.

The person behind it was knocking again.

'What is it?'

'Mr. Lamont?'

'Yeah.'

'This is the hotel supervisor, Mr. Lamont. I'm sorry to disturb you but we're checking the rooms' fire extinguishers are all in good order. If it's not inconvenient we...'

'You're checking what?'

'The fire extinguishers. It shouldn't take more than a...'

He scowled again, rubbed his neck, looked back into the room searching for a fire extinguisher, focused on the handset off the hook near the bed, decided he might as well...

Two men, both dark, one tall, holding a clipboard against his white shirt, the other small, in a T-shirt, jeans and carrying a small bag, grinned back at him.

'Thank you, Mr. Lamont,' the tall one said as he frowned at the other one.

He just about found time to process the information that the T-shirt man's stare was too direct, his grin too rigid, his shoulders too stiff, but before he could act on it, his white-shirted counterpart had already stepped forward.

He caught sight of the stun-gun emerging from behind his clipboard, watched it nearing his chest, understood what was about to happen.

He felt nothing, merely heard a crackle as his body ruptured and...

He was alive. His voice was telling him he was alive. He couldn't feel or see anything but he could clearly hear his voice:

'Friedman...?'

Did he say that?

'Imbecile!'

This... The accent...

'Who is paying you, imbecile?'

This was the puppy man's... This was... Friedman was there, very near, somewhere just above him by the sound of it and...

'Friedman?'

His Gitanes... He could smell...

'Who are you working for, you dog?'

He recalled the two men now, the small one's grin, the other's clipboard, the stun-gun... He... He had to be still in his hotel room. The stale smell of Gitanes. Had to come from the ashtray next to the bedside table. It was full. He'd noticed it just before... from the door, beside the handset off the hook...

A hand had just slapped his face, bringing feelings back. He became aware of his mouth now, it was dry and moving. He opened his eyes...

'What have you idiots done to him?' Friedman spoke again; 'What is this blood on his shirt? Didn't I tell you not to injure him if this was to be done inside the hotel?'

Ah... Good. That was good. If the Austrian didn't want him injured it could only mean...

'It's nothing to do with us,' said another voice, an American one this time, coming from the opposite direction to Friedman's; 'Looks like someone had fun with him. He's bleeding from some kinda chest wound. And if you take a look at his neck you'll see he was strangled or something. Or maybe tried hanging himself...'

'Huh!'

Why couldn't he see? His eyes were definitely open but...

He was... His blood surged against his temples. They'd taped his eyes. A piece of tape covered his...

He held his breath, summoned his hands to rip the tape off, and his arms yanked and tugged but wouldn't obey, instead caused his legs to jerk and his whole body to bounce up and down...

'There. He's moving, see? He's okay...'

And he understood. He was on his bed, lying on his side, hands tied to his ankles behind his back, his head close to the ashtray on the bedside table...

He took in a deep breath, tried not to panic...

'Friedman?' he called.

'Friedman! Friedman! Is that all you can say? One more time, dog: who sent you after me?'

'Take the tape off my eyes.'

'Pardon?'

'Take the damn tape off my eyes.'

'Huh!'

A throat clearing sound reached his ear and... Something warm and soft landed on his cheek...

'Imbecile! Stupid little amateur! For the last time, who sent you, eh?'

He clenched his teeth:

'That... That's not the way it is, you scum. If you want to talk you better...'

A hand slapped him again. He felt it this time.

'You are dead, you understand? This is not bargaining time! You are going to die like the rabid dog you are! All that is left for you to think about is whether you want me or your death alone to convey my message to the fool who thought of sending an amateur after me. Do you understand? You were badly misled if you were told you could cause me trouble and get away with it. Unless of course you are just mad. A mad stupid rabid dog! Whatever. It is all the same to me. Now, what is it going to be? You have five seconds. Will you talk or is your last achievement going to be acting like a good and stupid faithful dog to its paymaster?'

He couldn't think clearly, couldn't quite work it out, but Friedman's words weren't making sense. Something... Besides, his taped eyes, the man's concern about him being injured... He was bluffing. Had to be...

'Go to hell,' he heard himself say; 'You—'

Another slap cut him off.

'Right. I have no time for this. Get rid of the dog. Now. Just get rid of him. Now!' Friedman commanded.

And it all happened very fast, too fast for him to manage to speak again. Two hands grabbed his shoulders, flung him on his chest and pinned him down, driving his face hard into the bedding while someone else got hold of his arm and...

He tried yelling as he felt the stab in the flesh somewhere around his elbow, but his lips were buried too deep and too hard into the bedding to move. He tensed his body, hoping to…

It was too late. A warm numbness was travelling rapidly up his arm, reaching his shoulder. The stab… He'd been injected…

'Nonnnn…' his distant cry echoed inside his head, just as a flash of radiant white light hit his eyes.

'Non…' he heard himself cry again, noting how soft the blanket against his skin felt…

Thump… Thump…

'Good. Untie him and…'

Was that angry voice speaking through his throbbing heartbeat Friedman's?

'… Take that thing off his face. Anyway, why did you blindfold him?'

It was Friedman. Something had gone wrong…

'I didn't like the look in his eyes when he let us in…'

'What?'

'Didn't know how long you'd be and…'

Huh… Baboons ate crescents and went into coma… That's why it had gone wrong. This was America… It didn't matter now. Nothing mattered now. He was going home…

Thump… Thump… Thump…

What were all these glum swirling faces? And why were their eyes spinning? And their eyebrows frowning? He was fine. It wasn't that bad. Not that unpleasant at all, really…

Thump…

Ah. That's why it was so peaceful… His heart was no longer with him. It throbbed somewhere outside his chest now… Outside, with the birds and the swirling, frowning…

Thump…

Yes. He knows. The grass is too long. But, hey, there's so much of it, it would take a lawnmower to…

Thump…

'He's still not responding…'

Not responding? Not responding to what? Couldn't those

glum faces at least try to be coherent instead of swirling talking nonsense and looking like – what was it? – Oh yes, a stormy grey sky, they were swirling into a stormy grey sky above…

'I don't think this one wants to come back… We're going to need adrenaline…'

Huh. There was no need for that. Frankly, looking so glum was, to say the least, overreacting slightly. It's only grass. Sure it needs cutting, but even so, it looks fine. Couldn't they see the violets and… What were those small yellow flowers called again? Well, never mind. They'll all be gone once it's mowed. Anyway, the birds didn't mind. They sang and…

Can't you hear the birds, you fools…?

Thump…

'I think… We…'

Oh no… It was so peaceful and now…

'Yes! We got him back.'

What was the matter with them? What were they… He was not a gardener. There was no need for them to put his heart back inside his rib cage like this. Someone else could cut the grass if they were that…

Thump…

'Yes… We've got a beat…'

Couldn't they leave him alone. Couldn't they… He couldn't hear the birds anymore…

'Vous auriez pu au moins venir m'en parler avant de faire ça. Vraiment? C'est la moindre des politesses. Enfin, quoi qu'il en soit, c'est pas bon du tout, tout ça. Pas bon du tout. J'insiste que vous remettez tout comme c'était, hein! Sinon, c'est la guerre. C'est comme il vous plaira, d'accord!'

What…?

'C'est comme il vous plaira!'

Who was speaking?

Thump…

What was that spade doing thumping the grass…

Stomp…

Oh… Someone's gumboot had just…

Thump; the spade again…

Oh non! Non! Not…

Thump…

'Right. We better give him—'

Non... They were doing it all wrong. He didn't want to be here. It wasn't right. It wasn't time. They had to take his heart back out. They had to... Didn't they know where he was? Hadn't they seen the spade? It wasn't right. They had to take his heart back out again. Until later. Until he was elsewhere. Anywhere but...

Thump...

'Okay. It's all right now. He's all right...'

No. It wasn't all right. This was not all right at all. Soon his neck would hurt if... Damn! Didn't they know it? They had to know it. They were in the sky. They were the damn sky. They had to know everything. See everything from up...

Please...

Thump...

Oh no... The spade again...

Stomp...

Damn! Where were they? They... Where had they gone? They couldn't leave him to trample the grass like this. He was heading for the cottage across the field. Couldn't they see? Damn...

Come back! Come back, you cruel...

'Enfin, j'insiste que vous remettez tout comme c'était, hein!'

Damn he was angry. It had seemed such a good idea to buy the old cottage perched on its hillside overlooking the distant sea. It was cheap. It was perfect. Thyme, lavender, even old olive and orange trees blessed its four acres of wild ground. And with the ocean commanding the horizon, offering plenty of opportunity for sailing...

'Sinon, c'est la guerre...'

He flung his spade forward...

Thump...

Trekked past it...

Stomp...

Like an angry schoolboy, looking down at his feet, which is exactly how he felt.

Damn Mr. Théo and his *'J'insiste que...'* He'd stood, no, towered, above the grey little man in his loose cardigan and wet slippers. It would have been so easy to... instead of feeling sorry for him, instead of letting him get away with it, turning around to walk away just to avoid doing something he knew he'd regret.

Really? How pathetic! How petty! What harm could a little water do to the neat little garden the man kept down the hill from the access track to the cottage? Didn't the water end up down there anyway? Had the fool not heard of gravity? The first heavy rain, the first time the track ruts had overflowed with water, the first time he'd stepped outside the boundaries of his land to break up the track's grassy sides to let the trapped water run and the man had to rush out in his slippers, accuse him of flooding his property and threaten to…

Damn he was angry.

Thump…

Huh. The cottage was getting closer now, and… Perhaps… Perhaps if he tried hard enough, perhaps he could keep it to that, would be able to start again, right back at the beginning. If only he could call the glum faces again, beg them to…

There was no trace of them in the stormy sky anymore, just black and grey…

Thump…

Oh well, he already knew, it might not be so hard…

Thump…

Yes! He was moving on, but…

Damn! He didn't need this. Were he someone else, he'd say it wasn't fair. Not fair at all. A man called Friedman – or was it Gluck? – well, a man who owned a nice little house in a trendy part of the world and possibly had nice neighbours had just killed him. Wasn't that bad enough? Did he really need to go on, to step through the cottage doors again. Had he not stepped in there time enough already? Couldn't he be spared this? There was no sense to it. No purpose. Absolutely none whatsoever. Surely…

Clang…

Yes. Yes. The spade he'd just hurled hit the wall, crashed against the flagstone floor.

Stomp…

Well, fine, but he wasn't going to take off his muddy gumboots. Not this time. This was just some bad dying trip; what would a few muddy footprints on the new floor matter? Not this time. Besides, the grass had probably brushed away most if not all of the mud caught between the ribs of the sole, so…

The door grated, reminding him he had still not oiled the hinges, and... There he was, taking his boots off before stepping in, examining their soles to see if...

He was right, not a trace of mud...

Huh! He swallowed hard, slammed the door and called on his way to the kitchen. Like with the boots, he couldn't help it. It had happened that way, and even though he knew what awaited, even though he was going through it all again with the benefit of hindsight, it appeared he couldn't fight it, couldn't rewrite the script.

Never mind. It wouldn't feel that bad this time. It couldn't. He was ready for it... Damn, his neck was already hurting, so...

'Aline! Devine un peu ce que notre bon voisin Monsieur Théo vient de...'

'La revanche est un plat qui se mange froid, Inspecteur Delfosse.'

'This is unnecessary. I'm dead,' he tried to say to the smartly-dressed bespectacled man sitting at the kitchen table; 'I'm dead, you understand...'

Instead, of course, he followed the script, found himself frowning at the stranger, wondering how he and the other three standing around the kitchen had got there without passing him on the track. And just as when it had really happened, the answer came to him right away; the woodland behind the cottage, it climbed over the brow of the hill, to the village road across the...

That's right... He was inspecting their shoes, seeing the mud, the marks they'd left all over the floor, and in a moment, when he looks up, he'll see their guns, but he won't...

Damn... He was. Why? Why had his mouth dried up all of a sudden? Why the nausea? He—It wasn't right. It wasn't fair...

'Who—who are you? What...?'

'Qui suis-je? Eh bien, tu ne te rapelles plus de José, Inspecteur? I know I only wrote you a short note but...'

Nine years. Nine years had gone by, but it took a mere second to remember the name, a second during which, looking beyond the man, he also saw the three dirty hessian bags hanging heavily from the living room beams...

For God's sake, he wasn't going to start shuddering now! Was he...?

Damn! He knew the script, but did he really need to feel, to suffer again? Couldn't he just go through the motions? Couldn't this just be like a movie seen a hundred times. Damn! He'd seen it a hundred times...

'Perhaps you remember my wife? You're a man, you must remember her. Or at least her eyes. They were turquoise, the colour of jade. And you sent them into darkness for eternity. Have you forgotten them, Inspecteur?'

The words meant nothing, but... Bloody bags. He couldn't take his eyes off them. He knew what they were. There were six of them. He owned them. They'd come with the cottage. Came from the barn. Huge dirty old things, which had probably once served to haul coal or hay...

'I see you noticed we decided to have a little bag party,' floated José's voice; *'Don't look so worried, Inspecteur. We didn't forget you. In fact, you're going to be our guest of honour. And I, merely the master of ceremonies...'*

'Où sont...?'

Why was he asking? Even then, even on that dark Easter holiday afternoon as he'd stood gazing at the bags, he'd known where they were. Weren't the bags moving? Wasn't what was inside them stirring? Wasn't his neck already... Hadn't the poison struck?

'Ma femme? Mes enfants? Où...'

Damn. Why was he crying? He shouldn't cry. Not anymore. Not him. He was dying. He was dead... Surely...

'I'm glad you're asking,' said José, *'Because, you see, I kind of forgot myself. Yes, you guessed right. They're hanging back there, but who's in which bag? Well... Your guess is as good as mine, especially since they can't help us as their mouths are...'*

Oh God! Why was he crying again staring at José, why was he trying again to recognise him from the picture he'd once seen of him. What good could it do? What good could it have done then, apart perhaps from helping him to make it make sense? The glasses, the big brown eyes with their strangely long lashes behind the lenses, the deep furrows around the proud mouth, none of it had any meaning. It would, later, on another day, but not now...

Oh God! Why were his ears humming? He was about to throw himself on José. Maybe, if...

Could that be why he was back? Why he was there again?

Maybe, if he could leap back towards the bedroom behind him this time. If he could get hold of his gun in… Yes, he might just get there in time. They'd have to shoot him. He'd see to it. Might even take one or two down with him before…

'Sorry about that,' said José's grin…

Damn! It was useless. He couldn't even make himself think of the gun in the bedroom. He should have, though. He should bloody well have! Aline had argued against him bringing it, threatened him with an 'It's me or…' as they sat in the car all packed and ready to leave Paris. He'd pretended to give in, to take it back up to the flat, and ever since felt somewhat guilty for deceiving her and bringing it anyway. How could he not have thought of the gun in…

'Sorry about that…'

Sorry about that! Sorry about that! Words did mean…

Okay! Okay! To hell with this. It was just a last bad trip. He'd never really thought about it but he never imagined he'd go in peace anyway, so. And besides, he'd already hurt all he could. This too could not be undone. He might as well. He might as well go ahead and do it. He might as well choke the fucker, the disease, the sick degenerate slime. He'll trip. Like a clown he'll trip on the chair before even getting within arm's length of the slime and his 'Sorry about that', but so what? He couldn't just do nothing, it was not possible to just do nothing. Not possible at all.

Ahhhh…

Yes. That's right. They could hit and kick. It didn't hurt. So what if he was raw and bloody? So what if he could barely see out of his tearful swollen eyes or take air into the lungs inside his broken ribs. In a moment, once the battering ceases, they'll tie what's left of his ailing hands and it will take the four of them to stuff his limp body into the darkness of the bag and to heave and hang him in the living room beside… In a moment, he'll wish to die, but anger, pain and hatred will refuse to let him go… That's when… He had better try to get ready for it.

Thump…

What was that?…

Thump…

Ah… The glum faces. They were back…

'Okay. Clear everybody…'

Clear what…?

Swishh…

What—? They… He'd gone blind… What were they doing…?

'No response. Clear…'

Swishh…

'Okay, Inspecteur, this is not quite what I had in mind but since you seem so ill-disposed…'

Why was he blind? Was he already inside the bag…?

'Still no response. Stand by…'

Swishh…

Ah! The glum faces had come back, not to help but to torture him. He could no longer see but…

Can't you leave me alone!

'This is how it goes. You killed one of mine, I'm going to take away one of yours. But before you thank me for being so fair, I'm afraid that first you're going to have to sacrifice one of your loved ones. Think of it as interest. You killed one, repay with two. But at least, I'm going to give you a choice…'

'Okay! Again. Clear…'

'Now, we can play the game three ways. As you know, we split your little family into three bags. One, two, three…'

Swishh…

La revanche est un plat qui… Fucking José! He'd really loved his woman. Could slime like him really—

'Plan one: you give me a number between one and three, we kill whoever is in the corresponding bag, of the two left I leave with the younger one. Plan two: we forget the bags, you give me a name, again I leave with the youngest one left. Plan three: you decline to play, we kill your wife, your eldest kid, which I gather is the pretty little girl with the chestnut eyes, and I take the boy…'

'Right. We've got a beat… He's back!'

Back! Of course he was back. Heartless fools! He'd never left. Where could he have gone? Blind, bloody, benumbed, crumpled on himself upside down inside a hessian bag, ears humming, and his nape and shoulder… Where was there to go, huh? Didn't they know he was too busy trying to understand? Then trying not to understand? Trying to stop crying. Then trying to cry again. Didn't they know that soon he would no longer be able to try anything? That his head would just hum and his neck burn and his eyes dry out forever, once he'd grown weary of the sickly banter of the slime outside his dank hot humming darkness. Damn! He'll even stop feeling the cold water and punches they occasionally throw at him to make sure he's still conscious...

'We're going to sell one of your kids to —. You know what they do with kids over there? Use them as jockeys in camel races. They starve them to keep them light, flog them daily to keep them alert and strap them to camels on race days. The lighter the kids, the more terrified they are and the louder they scream, the faster the dumb camels run...'

'That's what we might do if we end up with the boy. I'm afraid your girl's already too old to... Beside, I'm not sure they allow girls to ride...'

'Well, unless he makes us kill him, the boy we shall have. He's the youngest, isn't he...?'

'That's right. But just in case, what do you think we should do with the girl if we end up with her, eh, José?'

'The girl? I don't know. She's pretty. She could... But then again. She looks very healthy. If all her organs can be sold, she might be worth more cut into pieces than...'

'What do you think, Inspecteur? How would you like it if your girl could be made to bring some happiness into this miserable world? Huh? Just imagine how many dying folks in bad need of spare organs she could help. Imagine their happiness. And that of their fathers and mothers, sons and daughters, brothers and sisters...'

'Yeah. Not to mention lovers...'

'Did you ever imagine your little girl would give so much to so many? Did you, Inspecteur?'

Scum! Aline, Pierre and Josianne had to have heard every sick word. Had the children understood? Pierre was only six, but Josianne nearly ten and...

'You won't get away with it. You won't, you slime.'

It wasn't time yet, but he said it anyway. Apart from begging them to kill him, these were the only words he'd say: 'You won't get away with it...'

'Oh no? And who's gonna stop us? Aromatherapists? Baldness patch researchers? Come on now, Inspecteur. You just called us slime, *did you not? You ought to know nothing sticks to slime. We'll get away with it, and you'll spend what's left of your sorry life a cripple, wondering what we did to one of your kids, crying for having sacrificed the other or your wife, or, as will happen if you go on playing dumb, for having sacrificed the other and your wife. That's why I'm not going to kill you, Laurent Delfosse. You're going to be a broken man. A cripple. Just another sad and sorry cripple who might just about have enough strength left to kill himself one day. And do you know what saddens me the most about all this, Inspecteur? Do you? No? Well, it is that my wife is not here to see what I'm about to do to the man who killed her. Tell me, Inspecteur, did she die quick or did her beautiful eyes stare at you a little after you shot her?...'*

Oh God! There he was again. There he was again. Thinking about it. Working out all the permutations, trying to understand. How was it? Yes. Pierre was lost. Whatever he did, little Pierre was lost. But Aline and Josianne... If he named Pierre, they'd take Josianne, and Aline would... If he named Josianne, they'd take Pierre, and Aline would... If he named Aline, they'd also take Pierre, and Josianne would...

So it could only be Josianne or...

Josianne? Could he...? She was so young, so... Yes, but apart from all that, what was she? She hadn't gone through the pain of growing up yet, had not yet invested in... While Aline... What about Aline? He couldn't think about Aline. She was his life, she...

Nom de...

How could he? How... What was becoming of him inside his bag, eh? Had he really already discarded Pierre? Was he really considering...? Sure, there was a rational way to proceed. Sure it was normal to think about it. Wasn't it? For God's sake! He had only two options, didn't he? To condemn one or condemn two. It was obvious. He had to think about it. He couldn't simply...

'Aline! Les Enfants. Je vous aime...'

Oh. He'd forgotten he'd said that too, wailed it against the coarse jute fabric cutting into his skin.

A number. Be brave and pick a number. For them. For whoever... It's easy. One—two—three. It ought to be easy. It had to be easy. One. Two. Three. They'd forgive him. They'd understand... It wasn't for him. It was... He'd die anyway.

One, two…

'So, what will it be, Inspecteur? A number, a name, or bye-bye to all?'

Nom de…

What was becoming of him… What was… The script! Remember the damn script and stop thinking! There was no decision to make. No names or numbers. Just the script. Within an hour, or a day, or two or three days – you never worked that out – José will lose patience, grow tired and…

You know. Through the hum inside your head, the numbness inside your skin, your nape and shoulder so hot you will no longer be able to care, you will hear a few meaningless whimpers, two meaningless shots, meaningless words and then the hum again, just the hum…

If only the damn bag had not been so old? If only they'd not thrown water at it – or was it your sweat and blood which had softened the fabric? – your weight would probably never have ruptured it…

Bang! One… Bang! And two…

Right, so that's where we are… Good. You see? You don't feel a thing. You don't even know anyone died yet. You don't even remember what's outside your bag. Perhaps there's nothing outside, perhaps it's all darkness now, and you just don't care. You… It's only later, remember? Later, when crawling along the invisible floor somewhere outside your swollen crusted eyes, when your fingers will feel the cold but soft skin, interpret the familiar contour of her…

'Nonnn…'

'Hey! It's all right. I'm only trying to clean you up, Mister—'

'Non! You mustn't…'

It couldn't be. She was… pulling his hands. She was pulling his… This wasn't right. She couldn't be. She—they were both…

'Non!'

'Calm down now, Mister. Don't worry, all right? I'll put your ring back on when I'm finished, all right? I've got no need for it. See? I got one of my own…'

'What? You don't understand? You mustn't touch my hands. Nobody must touch my hands. You're dead. You're both dead.'

'Oh. I see. I'm dead. I and someone else are dead. Is that right?'

'Yes.'

'Right. And how about you? Are you dead too?'

'Huh?'

'What about you, Mister? How are you? Are you dead too?'

'I... I wouldn't be talking to you if I was dead.'

'Okay. Now that makes sense.'

'Thank you.'

'You're welcome. But, if you don't mind my asking, if you ain't dead 'cause you're talking to me, could you tell me how come I'm dead although I'm talking to you?'

'You...'

Huh! Was that... a big black face looming in the darkness above him. She didn't look like... Aline. Where was Aline?'

'I—I'm... I thought you were someone else.'

'Really?'

'Yes. I thought you were dead. She... They have to be dead, you see? I killed a lot of people because they died... Six, Moreau told me. Some newspapers claimed it was nine but they were wrong.'

'Well. That's a lot of dead people. Are you sure you haven't left anyone out?'

'Anyone out? Er... No, José, his two brothers and their women makes six. Doesn't it?'

'Their women?'

'Yes.'

'Did they have only one woman each?'

'Yes. They were in a restaurant. Three couples. That makes six, doesn't it?'

'Yes, I guess three couples make six.'

'Yes, six. I didn't mean to kill them all but José wouldn't tell me what happened to Pierre until I shot one... You see, he told me then, and... He didn't believe I would, you see? He laughed. There were witnesses and he didn't believe... I might only have killed him if... But... You know?'

'Yes. I know. That's all right. I'm sure you didn't intend to kill everybody. Now, do you think it's safe for me to remove your ring while I wash your hand or will you get angry and declare me dead again?'

He nodded his nod at the white eyes in the face above him. Whoever they belonged to, they looked safe…

'Yes. Thank you…'

'Good. Now…'

Ah. This felt better. It was nice to talk with a nice soul… He could go now… It was better now. No more José and—

He was alive! Something cool and damp caressed his skin. He was… How? Again?

'Excuse me? Are we really not dead?'

'Unless you know things I don't, I'm happy to say that's right, Mister. We sure ain't dead.'

He peered hard through the darkness again, saw the face again. It was smiling. Not at him, but at his hands. He was with an angel. An angel was cleaning his hands and smiling…

He was dead. He would rest now…

Waking, feeling warm and relaxed against the soft cotton under his cheek, he thought at first he was still in his hotel room, still waiting for Friedman. Then, little by little, things fell into place. First, the clean smells and sounds that reached him made him realise he was somewhere else. Next, he remembered what had happened, that he was meant to be dead, wondered why this was not so, what the Austrian had done wrong. And then, opening his eyes onto a harsh metallic and white world, finding himself gazing at an intravenous drip tube linking a couple of infusion bags to a needle taped to the back of his hand, he understood he was in a hospital, that he was safe, and shut his eyes again wondering how long he'd been unconscious. It was pointless to attempt to sit up, let alone get to his feet to try to find out; his neck was burning, his drowsiness too comfortable, and besides, a nurse or doctor was bound to come around with the answer before long. Still, he brooded over it, spent time and effort trying to place himself in space, worked out he'd landed in Los Angeles on a Tuesday, which meant Friedman had happened on the Wednesday, and, from the way he felt, guessed he'd been out for at least a day or two, that it was now possibly Friday or Saturday.

His thoughts then moved to his belongings. He worried about his money and passport, wondered whether Friedman had got hold of them or if they were still at the Delaunay, or had been brought to the hospital. If they were lost, he'd have to get Jane to forward some of the money from his flat, and Moreau to send him an English passport so he could get out of the country. That would entail posting a photograph of himself to Paris, but that would be all right, would be simple, in any case simpler than working out how the Austrian had tracked him down, how the fox had turned into the hound. Because, without thinking about it, he knew this should never have happened, and that it wasn't going to be easy to come up with why it had. No one apart from Deborah De Moraes knew about the Delaunay, his borrowed name or room number. Only, aside from the question of why or how Mrs. De Moraes would have tipped off the Austrian, something else already suggested Friedman's information was unlikely to have come from her; the man wouldn't have bothered to ask the name of his employer if it had, especially as he'd seemed in such a hurry to get rid of him. That left Nathalie. Nathalie could have spoken. But again, Nathalie didn't know where he was, could only have given away his London address, and since he himself hadn't known of the Delaunay before leaving, there couldn't possibly be any clue there that pointed to it. Of course, there was the envelope, the one holding the information about Leonard and his boy – he'd left it in his desk – but again, had Friedman's men got hold of that, they'd have known about Deborah De Moraes, and again, the man would have skipped the question about his employer. Yet...

Soon, he dozed off again, lulled into sleep by his wandering thoughts. He pictured Nathalie waiting for him at the Parliament Hill café on Friday morning, sitting in her coat on the cold terrace and smoking her cigarettes. Would she wait long? Would she worry? And then, what about Perkins and the rest of the football team in the evening? It was the first time he'd fail to turn up without...

It was Sunday, the sun outside his window sent spears of warm light across the bed, he was in Los Angeles Grand City Hospital, had been there since Wednesday, and Doctor Brunswick – tall, bald and beaky – peered down in marked disapproval as he spoke.

'I could tell you you're lucky to be alive, but it would be truer to say you ought to be dead. That you are not, is really down to your heart. You have a most amazing heart, Mr. Lamont. As a matter of fact, it's a bit of a marvel. Do you know anything about your heart, Mr. Lamont?'

His head resting against his pillow, Lombard grinned. There was no point in contradicting the good doctor who had just explained how he'd ended up at the hospital and pulled through four cardiac arrests in the short span of twenty four hours. The way Lombard saw it though, his heart, marvel or not, had only done its job, and if he owed his life to anything or anyone, from what he'd just heard it was to his would-be killer's caution, and to the hotel maid who'd raised the alarm on finding him senseless on his bed beside a hypodermic needle and what turned out to be a gram of neat heroin.

It appeared that, concerned he might have been caught on a hotel surveillance camera, Friedman had chosen to cover his tracks by making his death look like a mishap, guessing that the demise of a lonely tourist who'd injected better quality junk than he'd bargained for in the privacy of his hotel room would attract little more attention than a traffic argument. And so far, apart from the fact that Lombard was alive, the Austrian appeared to have been right. As yet, the doctor had not mentioned the police and, if the man's feelings matched his manner and begrudging eyes, he was there himself only reluctantly. For it was clear the doctor didn't think much of his patient. And perhaps that was understandable. Putting time and resources into nursing drug addicts back from death could not be very satisfying. Still, at least now Friedman's worry about not injuring him made sense.

'Well,' the doctor spoke again, returning Lombard's grin with a frown; 'That heart of yours is very big and robust, Mr. Lamont. And more impressively, rates around thirty six beats per minute. That's fourteen beats below low-low average. In other words, that thing in your chest is just the kind of wonder athletes would die for, if you can forgive the turn of phrase.'

'That's all right, Doctor,' Lombard said, looking at the man's hands clasped around his clipboard. He had long but plump fingers, so much so that they looked swollen and boneless.

Perhaps they were swollen. Perhaps the man was on some kind of drug…

'May I ask what it is you do for a living, Mr. Lamont?'

He thought for a moment, then:

'I'm a restaurateur.'

'A restaurateur,' echoed the doctor, nodding to himself with a sad grin; 'Well…'

'I do play football now and again, though,' Lombard said, just to placate him; 'I believe you call it soccer over here. Anyhow, if you don't mind moving on to more practical matters than my heart, Doctor Brunswick, would you happen to know if my belongings followed me here or whether they're still at my hotel?'

'Your belongings?'

'My clothes and—'

'Are you intending to leave, Mr. Lamont?' cut in the doctor.

Lombard grinned again. He'd already tried getting up, had found his legs too weak to carry him, but given a few hours, a day at most…

'Not right at this moment,' he said; 'But I need my things. And to get to a phone. For one thing, you might as well know I have no medical insurance. However, since I'd sooner show my gratitude for your hospital's good work by settling my bill before leaving rather than sneaking away the moment I can make it through the door, I'd very much like to get hold of some money. Only, to do that, I need my things. And to get my things, unless of course they're here, I need a telephone. But that said, I need a telephone whatever. A few people must be wondering where I am. Not least my wife back in England.'

The lips above him puckered, the eyes above them narrowed, moved to his hands resting against the blanket on either side of his body, searched for and found his wedding band, then turned to the clipboard and read.

'It says here you're from the United Kingdom. Don't you have any kind of medical insu—'

'No,' Lombard cut him off; 'I rely on the National Health Service.'

The man scowled, peered at his clipboard again, turning over some thought in his mind.

Lombard pre-empted him. His accent...

'French mother.'

'Ha... I thought I recognised the accent,' the doctor said, tucking his clipboard under his arm to bury his hands in his white coat pockets with a sigh; 'Right. I'll see what can be done about locating your belongings and about a phone, Mr. Lamont. Meanwhile, my advice to you is to take it easy and rest as much as humanly possible. We cannot keep you here against your will if you're set on leaving, but if I were you I'd wait at least a few days. If nothing else, it might make us feel we haven't wasted our time. However, it's your life. But if you care about it at all, you better be good to it. We found just the one needle mark on you, which suggests you don't do this kind of thing every day. However, and I can't stress this enough, considering what you injected, it's a minor miracle you came through. I'm not going to ask about your lifestyle, but take it from me, even with your heart, you're not immortal. Now, have you got any questions?'

'Yes. Just one. What about the police?'

The doctor raised his brows, perplexed.

'Wasn't I found in possession of narcotics?'

'Oh. I see. Well, that's up to your hotel, Mr. Lamont. Our business is to fix people, not to punish them. Besides, I don't know how things are back in England, but this is Los Angeles. If we reported everyone who ended up here through drug abuse, our corridors would see an endless procession of police officers. I believe we all really have better things to do.'

Lombard nodded:

'Thank you.'

'You're welcome,' snarled the doctor, returning his nod dryly; 'Oh yes. And one more thing, Mr. Lamont. I won't ask how you sustained the bruises around your neck or the cut on your chest, but you might like to know that we retrieved glass from the cut. Green glass...'

He let his head sink into his pillow the moment the doctor left, clasped his chest between his arms and closed his eyes to find relief from the spears of sunlight. He was aching all over. His ears hummed. His mouth was dry and his throat burned with the taste of sour tobacco. But he felt rested and his mind was clear, bar for the three names that, just like before the doctor had interrupted them, like a poisonous chant at once resumed turning inside his forehead: *Leonard Spitz—Friedman—Deborah De Moraes. Leonard Spitz—Friedman…*

Could he have made a mistake? Could he have overlooked something? He had to. He had better think. Start right back at the beginning. Right back at…

An hour or so later a male nurse brought a telephone and informed him that the only things of his at the hospital were the clothes he'd been brought in.

'No jacket?'

'Just your trousers, shirt and…'

His wallet was in the inside pocket of his jacket. He could recall hanging it up in the hotel room wardrobe. And Rhian's sister's number was in his wallet…

'You can't dial direct outside calls from this extension,' said the nurse, plugging the telephone cable into a socket beside the bed; 'So you'll have to go through the hospital exchange.'

'Thank you.'

'Uh, I'm afraid it's hospital policy to charge for calls. Would you like to see our tariffs before—'

'No. What time is it?'

The nurse bent his knees and stretched his neck to peer out the door:

'… Five past one.'

That made five past eight evening time in London. And it was Sunday…

'Would it be possible to get a drink? Like a coffee,' he asked, pushing hard on the mattress to heave himself up to a sitting position.

'A coffee? Absolutely not…'

He settled for a glass of water. And yes, later, he'd love to have some chicken and leek soup. It was futile to ask if he could smoke.

FOURTEEN

Some of the news was good: his passport and other belongings were at the Delaunay and Nathalie was alive and well. Some was as expected: Friedman had checked out of the Wyatt and Nathalie claimed not to have spoken to anyone. Some was possibly bad: the Delaunay consented to despatch his belongings to the hospital but insisted on holding onto his passport until he was well enough to collect it in person. Some was plain bad: his flat had been broken into and the only thing missing appeared to be the envelope with its information about Leonard Spitz. And then, some was heavy with implications: Rhian and the boy were fine and Leonard's whereabouts were no longer a matter of speculation.

Mrs. Spitz's son had made the news, albeit the 'News in Brief' column of one of the national papers back home. Lombard had heard it first from Rhian's sister, but now, clutching the telephone handset, sweating, wrestling with the pain while pacing slowly around the intravenous drip stand as far as the tube stuck to his hand would allow, he listened to Rhian's congested voice as she read the newspaper item, sniffing and fighting back sneezes.

She had obviously caught a bad cold.

' "The body of Leonard Spitz, 31, was found hanging from a tree by a man walking his dog north of High Beach in Epping Forest, Essex, yesterday. The body was in an advanced state of decay. High Beach police are treating the death as suicide. Mr. Spitz, of Highgate, North London, was single and unemployed". There. That's all,' the Welsh girl concluded, finally yielding to a sneeze.

'Sorry. I'm sorry. I have a terrible cold,' she whimpered before blowing her nose.

'Your sister said this came out in the Friday paper,' he remarked after a moment's thought; 'Is that so?'

'Yes. Actually, she came across it. I don't buy the papers. But I don't understand. How come you didn't know? Didn't Leon's family tell you?'

He grinned, a wry grin:

'I've had to go away.'

'Ah. What... Jeee—'

She exploded in yet another sneeze.

'God. Sorry,' she apologised again.

'Are you in a state to talk or do you want me to call later? Perhaps you should make yourself a hot drink.'

'No. No. I'm fine. Anyway. I don't buy it, Mr. Lombard. Suicide? No way. Leon wouldn't have killed himself. Not now. Not like this. I just don't believe it.'

He nodded, used his hospital pyjama sleeve to mop up the beads of sweat that clung to his forehead.

'How's the boy doing?'

'Shiva? Fine. He's fine.'

'Who's looking after him right now?'

'My sister. She stayed at my place with the children so I could come here to get your call.'

'Good. Now listen, Rhian. You needn't worry because there's probably nothing to worry about. But when you get back home, I want you to pack a bag and take your daughter and the boy somewhere safe. By that I mean somewhere where no one might think of looking for you. It won't be for long. Two or three days at most. Do you think you can do that?'

She didn't speak immediately. She couldn't, she had to sneeze again.

'I... Why?' she queried; 'What's happening?...'

'Nothing. It's just a precaution. I know it's a nuisance, but I need you to do it. All right?'

'I don't understand. I mean, Leon's dead and... Is it... Is it the Austrian?'

'No. You needn't be concerned about the Austrian. Let's just say that like you I'm not convinced Leonard killed himself. Now, can I count on you to do what I asked?'

'You found him? The Austrian? You—'

'Will you just do it, Rhian?' he cut in, firmly.

All of a sudden, there was only silence on the line. No more sniffs or sneezes. Just silence.

'Rhian?'

'Yes. I'm here. I… Listen, Mr. Lombard, apart from the fact that you *have* got me worried, where do you think I might go with Shiva. I mean, it's not as if I can just sit him in my van and ask him to behave like a normal child. Or tell people he's mine. Is it?'

He frowned. She was right, the boy was likely to draw unwelcome attention. He'd been so wrapped up in other considerations, he hadn't thought about that. Another thing he'd overlooked.

He pictured her stone cottage in its wilderness, its rocky stream, the track from the road, the flooded footpath, her drenched brothers with their crowbars and cricket bats…

'What about your brothers? Can you stay with them?'

'My brothers? I suppose so. But they still live at our parents old place. It's barely a mile across the valley. I wouldn't say it's what you'd call safe…'

'Is it on the phone?'

'No.'

'Never mind. It will have to do. Take the children to your parents, make sure as many of your brothers as possible stick around at all times and keep your eyes and ears open. If you notice anything or anyone suspicious, don't even think of confronting them, you hear? It's important. Make at once for the police with the boy and tell them everything you know. Can I trust you on this?'

'But—'

'No buts, Rhian. Just do it, all right?'

'I… Yes. Okay. But aren't you even—'

'Thank you. Now,' he said, quickly, to move on to other matters; 'I need to ask you some questions. It won't take long. The night Leonard turned up at your place with the boy, you told me you pleaded with him to go to the police but he refused. Can you remember exactly what he said?'

She'd gone quiet again.

'What did Leonard say, Rhian?' he asked again, guessing the reason for her silence.

'I'm sorry, Mr. Lombard. I know you're telling me not to—'

'Don't worry, Rhian,' he interrupted her, impatient; 'If I

thought you were in serious danger I'd have sent the police to you by now. Are you with me?'

She was, muttered a dubious 'Okay', blew her nose, and he repeated his question:

'What did Leonard—?'

'Um… Yes. I'm sorry. My head's a little…'

'Take your time.'

She sniffed for about five seconds.

'Well, I can't remember his every word. But he just wouldn't have anything to do with the police. As I think I told you when we met, he said he couldn't.'

'When we spoke you told me he said he had good reasons not to. You remember?'

'Yes. That's right.'

'Good reasons. Those were his words?'

'Yes. But… I mean, that's not all he said. We talked a lot. But you're right, that seemed to be the main thing. He said he couldn't go to the police.'

'And he didn't tell you why that was?'

'No. He apologised about it but—'

She broke off to let out another sneeze, cursed and apologised.

'What did you think?'

'About what?'

'What his good reasons could be?'

'Oh… I can't tell. With Leon it could have been anything, you know. But to tell you the truth, I think he was scared he'd get into trouble. After all, he'd just bought Shiva, hadn't he? I mean, there was no way to know how the police would react, what they'd do with him. But on the other hand, he was so excited, it could be that he just wanted… You know, to just keep it all to himself. He'd found something to do…'

'His crusade?'

'Yes. That's right.'

He nodded his nod:

'Okay. I want you to think carefully about this, Rhian; can you remember if at any point that night Leonard said "We" instead of "I" while telling you how he got the boy? Do you understand?'

She did, and more:

'My God! You think... He... Somebody helped him?'

'Maybe. Did he say "We" at any time?'

'God! Shiva would know...'

That, he'd thought about, only...

'You think you could get it out of him?' he asked.

She took a moment to think, replied as expected:

'No. I'm afraid not. I wouldn't know how... I can barely communicate with him as it is and—'

'Let's stick to Leonard then. Did he say "We" at any point, or for that matter say anything that might suggest he was involved with someone else?'

This time she took longer to answer:

'I'm not sure. I was in quite a state. But, I'd say no. I mean, he kept saying "I". "I saved him." "I bought him." You know? He just said "I". It's all—'

She sneezed, blew her nose, and he mopped his forehead again.

'It's all I can remember,' she went on where she'd left off; 'He just said "I" all the time.'

'That's fine. Am I right in recalling the money Leonard gave you for the boy was cash?'

'Yes.'

'Three thousand pounds?'

'Yes. I've hardly—'

'Did he mention anything to you about a forthcoming exhibition of his work?'

'Leon?'

'Uh-huh. It needn't be that night. It could have been some time in the preceding weeks. Did you see a lot of him in the weeks before?...'

'No. Not really. But we talked on the phone. We always did. But he didn't say anything about an exhibition...'

'You're sure?'

'Oh yes. I'd remember.'

'Would you?'

'Yes.'

'Perhaps he just didn't tell you about it?'

'I don't think that is possible, Mr. Lombard. All Leon had going for him was his photography. That's almost all he ever talked about. Or maybe I should say moaned about. He was getting nowhere, you see. In fact, he was so depressed about his work he'd just started to put together a new portfolio. Er, new material—'

'I know what a portfolio is, Rhian.'

'Ah. Right. Well, he'd decided to change direction, try something new. Street-realism. London life – documentary stuff, you know? In fact, his cheek was quite badly bruised the night he brought Shiva over. He said he'd been hit by a market trader who'd got mad when he took some shots of his stall... Huh. Poor Leon. He hit the guy back and ended up in the nick for it. Aggravating behaviour or something. Anyway, it cost him a night in Finsbury Park police station. So, you see, I doubt he...'

Coming to a standstill, he stopped hearing her. An undefined thought, dark, distant but meaningless, like a dark cloud, had just taken hold of his mind and, rigid, glaring at the sunlit tiled floor in front of his bare feet, he tried to give it shape...

'Mr. Lombard?' he heard through the cloud.

'Mr. Lombard?'

'Huh?' he responded, on automatic.

'You're... Is everything all right?'

He didn't reply, stayed with the cloud a little longer, failing to give it meaning, attempted to shake it off by resuming his pacing, didn't quite manage to free himself completely but cleared enough space in his forehead to rejoin his train of thought.

'So, I understand, you don't think Leonard could have had an exhibition lined up?'

'No.'

'Did he ever talk to you about his sister?'

'Deborah?'

He scowled:

'You know her?'

'No. We never met. I only know her through Leon.'

'I see. He spoke of her often?'

'Oh yes. Well, he used to. Not so much lately but—'

'Did he ever tell you about the hostility between them?'

He thought he heard her scoff. But perhaps the sound she'd made was simply her swallowing another sneeze.

'You must mean her hostility towards him,' she eventually said.

'Must I?'

'Well, Leon never had any bad feelings towards his sister, Mr. Lombard. Although maybe he should've had. But he was just too fond of her.'

'Too fond of her?'

'Yes. It didn't matter how much pain she caused him, he just couldn't bring himself to think badly of her. They used to be very close, you see? And he never gave up hoping that one day they might be close again.'

'What do you mean, "They used to be very close"?'

'It's... How can I put it?... Leon always came up with the same phrase whenever he talked of their childhood. I heard it so many times I can still hear him say it: "Our world was so cold and old, we shone for one another, like handsome young lovers..." Jeee—'

As she sneezed and blew her nose, he recalled the words Deborah De Moraes had used to depict her young brother: *'He laughed. He cried. He dreamed. He—'*

'Fuck... Sorry,' Rhian broke in.

'That's all right,' he said; 'Leonard's words are very nice. But what does it mean?'

'Well, it might sound weird, but I'd say his sister was really his one true love. And, if Leon was to be believed, also the only person who understood him. They spent their childhood more or less alone in their parents' secluded Scottish mansion, you see. Surrounded with old nannies and servants. Never had friends, had private live-in tutors. As for the parents, they were much too busy looking after their businesses to spend much time at home. But even when they did, it made little difference. You see, they were already well into their forties when Leon and his sister were born. Children and parents never really connected. They were like two tribes. Leon always referred to them as "The old truants". Anyway, as a result, he and his sister grew up in their own world, depending on each other for love and friendship. They even spent their holidays together. Right up to their late twenties.'

'What happened then?'

'The sister got married. Leon took it hard, got into drugs, and she turned against him.'

He had to wipe the sweat from his forehead again.

'Because of his taking drugs?'

'No. I mean, sorry; I didn't explain it right. The drug thing came afterwards. He was still at university studying history at that time. It was only when he dropped out soon after and got into music that the drugs really became a problem.'

'Then what caused his sister to turn against him?'

She blew her nose before answering:

'Well, you better ask her that. Leon never really understood. She just turned against him. That's all.'

'No reason at all?'

'Not as far as I know. Although, because it happened soon after she married, in his good heart, Leon chose to believe it was because she didn't have any children; that she was hurt and bitter about it, needed to take it out on someone, decided it might as well be him because they'd been so happy together. You know, kill the thing you love... Anyway, I don't really know the whole story, but personally I never bought it. From what Leon said, his sister just sounds like a bitch, if you can forgive my saying so. She sounds so straight and arrogant, I think she just disapproved of him. Became ashamed of him. Leon, though, would not look at it like that.'

He thought, briefly, then:

'Did Leonard know why she had no children?'

'No.'

'Had he any particular reason to believe she wanted them?'

'Only that she had always wanted a family. It seems she grew up yearning for just one thing – marry the most handsome man and have his even more beautiful children. Huh!'

'Well, at least she got her man,' he mumbled to himself, then, realising that the husband he'd met might not be...

'When you say she married, do you mean to her present husband?'

'I... Is she still with a Brazilian?'

'Uh-huh.'

'Yes. That must be him then.'

'What did Leonard think of him?'

'The husband?'

'Yeah. Did he like him?'

'Like him? I wouldn't say so. But he didn't dislike him either. Leon didn't really have it in him to dislike anybody, Mr. Lombard. All he ever said about him was that he comes from a banking family and spends all his time and money racing cars and playing golf.'

'Racing cars and playing golf?'

'That's what Leon said.'

'I don't suppose he told you if he was any good at it?' he queried.

'Sorry? Who is good at what?'

'The husband. Racing cars and playing golf.'

'Oh. No...'

He looked up at his drip-bags hanging from their stand. There were only two more questions for him to ask:

'When we met you said Leonard had turned up with the boy four weeks earlier. Are you absolutely sure about that? It couldn't have been three weeks?'

'Er... We met last week, right?'

'Last Saturday.'

He heard her mumble to herself through her sniffing for a while, as if she was counting.

'Yes,' she eventually declared; 'Last Saturday was the eighth. Shiva had been with me for almost exactly one month. I remember because they turned up the evening after Guy Fawkes night. We had a bonfire still going outside the house.'

He nodded:

'Did you contact Leonard's family since reading of his death?'

'No. I thought of it but then—'

'Don't,' he said, bringing his pacing to an end to take in a deep breath, then, grimacing as his rising ribcage felt as if it was about to crack open:

'Thank you, Rhian. Do what we said earlier and keep in touch with your sister. I'll call her very soon. And look after your cold...'

'Does that mean—'

He hung up.

He'd gripped the handset so hard his fingers were white and ridged with lines. He kept his eyes on his hand as the blood slowly returned, restoring colour and levelling the skin, but he wasn't really watching. Gazing at his hand was just something to do, a way to keep his eyes occupied while trying to remain calm. For, through the cloud that still obscured his thoughts, his head was all anger. He could almost feel it churning inside, battering his skull and pounding his temples. He'd screwed up. There were no other words for it. He'd screwed up. Friedman had seemed so good an answer he'd passed over all the questions. Like a novice. An amateur. He'd let Leonard's Austrian blot out the horizon. Lost sight of the questions. And now…

Teeth clenched, he swallowed hard. He had better get back to Jane before jumping to any more conclusions. By now she ought to be able to confirm whether his envelope was truly missing. Over an hour had elapsed since they'd talked…

It hardly hurt when he yanked the intravenous needle from his hand, and then, reaching the window, it felt good to see Los Angeles sprawling six or seven storeys below. The sun, almost directly in front of him, burned his skin, bruised his eyes, caused the beads of sweat clinging to his hairline to melt and run down his face and neck. But these were minor discomforts well worth putting up with, because the sight of the traffic and even of the odd pedestrian moving along the boulevards that carved the palm-treed city before his eyes, like a tonic, promptly helped ease his anger and invigorate his aching limbs. Without realising it, with his view restricted to the confines of his room and the flawless patch of seemingly stationary blue sky outside his window, too hot, without escape from the aseptic hospital smell, he'd felt harassed, a hostage to sickness and death…

'Yeah. It's me again,' he said to the hospital operator whose voice had by now become familiar; 'I need another London number. 0171…'

Waiting for the connection, peering into the middle-distance through the sunlight, he thought he recognised the square lines of the top of the Wyatt tower against the backdrop of the bushy hill that he recalled climbed behind it. If he was right, it explained how come his suitcase had turned up so soon after his call to the Delaunay; the building he was looking at stood no more than a mile or so away...

Jane answered her phone on the first ring:
'Hello?'
'How are you, Jane?'
'*Savieer.* Yes, I can't find your envelope. I'm really sorry.'
He merely frowned.
'I'm really sorry, *Savieer,*' Jane repeated.
'You looked everywhere?'
'Oh yes. I went through all your papers, searched all the rooms. But it's not there. I don't know what to say. I feel terrible. I still can't believe I could have left your door open. It's just not like me to...'
He wiped the sweat from around his mouth and stopped listening to her. He'd already heard what she had to say, already tried reason, told her not to blame herself, pointing out that it would have been the television or perhaps the answering machine that would be gone instead of his envelope if an opportunist burglar had got into his flat as a result of her leaving the door open after feeding his fish. But as neither his door nor windows bore traces of a break-in she...
It was not that he was in a charitable mood, only, he needed her, and all things considered, would rather have her feeling calm than emotional.
'What's the matter, Jane?' he cut her off; 'You want me to blame you?'
'What?'
'Do you want me to blame you?'
'... No. I don't.'
'Then shut up and I won't, okay!'
It appeared to work; she shut up.
'Thank you,' he said; 'Now, while looking through my things, did you come across a small black address book? It was in the top drawer of my desk, but since you say all my papers were in a mess it—'
'Is it leather-bound?'

'Yeah.'

'Yes. I saw it. It's—'

'Fine. If you don't mind...'

Jane, ever so keen to help, possibly as a result of her misplaced guilt – or was she just thrilled at being called upon at long last? – went to fetch the address book, diligently read him every name in it, and many long minutes later pledged to call the list of two dozen names he'd selected the very next day; it was too late in the evening in London for her to get on with it now.

'Say you're my secretary, all right?' he told her, once satisfied she'd understood what he wanted her to do.

'Your secretary, huh?' she returned, challenging.

The imp was back, self-possessed and uninhibited by guilt.

'It sounds better than next door neighbour,' he commented.

'Maybe. But what's wrong with assistant?'

'If it pleases you, nothing.'

'It pleases me.'

'Fine. I'll call tomorrow. If I don't, it will probably be because I'm on my way back...'

'Oh. *Savieer*. I forgot. Perkins is looking for you. He was at my bloody door at seven in the morning yesterday asking if I knew where you were. And he wasn't looking happy.'

He almost smiled. Yesterday was Saturday, the day after the match...

'And?'

'Well, apart from the fact that I was pissed off at getting woken so early, I didn't know what to tell him. I didn't know if you—'

'What did you say, Jane?'

'I lied. I don't know why, but I just lied. I said I didn't know where you were.'

Now he smiled:

'You told him about the break-in?'

'Er, no. I...'

'Good girl.'

A moment later, peering into the outwardly uncomplicated world down below towards a lengthening line of cars at a red light intersection, he reckoned that the decision to keep him on the bench for the next game or two had already been made.

'… Or is the job too formidable for you, Mr. Lombard,' he muttered then, remembering one of Deborah De Moraes' cutting remarks.

The task he'd given Jane was something he ought to have done before now, something he'd intended to do, but again something he'd neglected once Friedman had appeared on the horizon – checking whether one or other of his clients could recall recommending his services to Mrs. Spitz or anyone else in the recent past. It could have waited until his return to London, but the way things were turning out he didn't feel like waiting. How and why the well-connected Mrs. Spitz had come to call his number when worried about her son's whereabouts had troubled him right from the beginning. Perhaps there was nothing in it. It was just as Deborah De Moraes had claimed: convinced that Leonard was off on one of his drug binges, the family had deemed it surplus to requirements to call on their expert friends, settled instead on a small-time detective who came with an endorsement.

It was possible; only, now, everything was possible. Aside from the fact that he'd lost the Austrian, all that Lombard still felt reasonably sure of added up to just three things: Friedman's information had not come from Nathalie, or else she'd be dead – had the Austrian's people got to her after all, not only would she have been made to talk but they wouldn't have let her live to lie about it later; if Friedman had made his way back home and found Martin in his kitchen then he was as good as gone forever; and the old Spitzes' concern for their son had been genuine – this, more than in what had been said the day he'd met the old folks, he'd seen in their eyes, and worried parent's eyes rarely lie…

Still, at least the Spitz family's social standing had allowed him to narrow Jane's list down to his most affluent clients, most of whom were London-based French businessmen. If indeed Mrs. Spitz had hired him on someone's recommendation, she'd have had to consider that someone trustworthy, and by and large people who've done well for themselves trust only other people who've done well for themselves, often simply because in the end these are the only people they know, the only people they can associate with without fear of being used, or as the case may be, guilt.

Reckoning that if he was well enough to walk around his room he was well enough to travel, he made just one more call, to book a seat on a noon flight to London the next day, and then, stripping off his damp pyjama top, brooding over the story of Leonard's exhibition, he turned away from the window and made for the door.

Until now, he hadn't given much thought to Deborah's husband's story about the visit Leonard had made to their Hampstead house shortly before disappearing. It had seemed straightforward enough. Leonard had gone to his sister to borrow money, come upon his brother-in-law, walked away with a £2000 loan. As it had happened just before he'd gone missing, he could conceivably have been raising funds for his new-found crusade, even though the feasibility of anyone, let alone Leonard Spitz, raising the sums involved by going around extracting loans from family and friends was questionable. Still, for want of a better explanation or for that matter any evidence against the exhibition, that was as much as Lombard had made of it before forgetting all about Mr. De Moraes' story. Only…

'Shiva had been with me for almost exactly one month,' Rhian had said, counting from the previous Saturday.

'We were hoping to ask you to look for our son,' Mr. Spitz had said, in his soft even voice on the Friday; 'He's been missing for two weeks…'

Mrs. Spitz had not seen Leonard for six weeks but said he had stopped at his sister's 'a few days before we realised he was missing.'

'To borrow money. I wasn't here. But he got to Carlos,' Deborah De Moraes had made it known.

'That's right,' her husband had confirmed; 'I gave him a couple of thousand pounds. He said he needed it to get some of his photographs printed for an exhibition he had coming up…'

What had Deborah said then? He couldn't remember her words. Only that she'd looked at her husband with contempt, called him stupid, that the husband had apologised, protesting he couldn't know Leonard did his own printing.

'Wouldn't want anyone to interfere with his Art, you understand,' Deborah had then declared for Lombard's benefit.

Presuming Rhian could be relied upon, Deborah De Moraes had been right – there was no exhibition; but more significantly, the day Leonard had turned up at his sister's intent on borrowing money, he'd already bought his boy and left him in Wales with £3,000. And this all of a week earlier – even if one stretched Mrs. Spitz's 'a few days before he went missing' to as much as a week. Of course, Leonard was intent on rescuing a second kid, but...

He stopped in his doorway and, rolling his pyjama top into a ball, glared into the room directly across the corridor. A young nurse in a plastic apron was tending a bedridden patient who lay concealed behind the huge bulk of his or her covered belly. From the size of the feet sticking up under the blanket, Lombard, without thinking about it, guessed the belly belonged to a man, and using his rolled-up pyjama top to wipe his sweaty face and neck, called:
'Excuse me?'
The nurse turned, saw him, frowned.
'I know I've been told my air-conditioning is on maximum,' he said, smiling back at the nurse; 'But if that happens to be the case, it must be faulty. I wonder if someone could check...'

He'd forgotten he was meant to be lying down, feeding from his intravenous drip, found himself ordered back to bed by the scathing nurse who swiftly proceeded to reattach him to the drip and then left taking his telephone, insisting the air-conditioning was in perfect working order.

The remaining hours of daylight passed uneventfully, with Lombard lying on his bed, sombre and meditative behind his sunglasses which the Delaunay had thoughtfully returned together with his Gitanes and lighter in a small bag that had come with his suitcase. The lure of his cigarettes proved almost too strong, but he withstood it, partly to avoid inciting the wrath of the hospital staff, partly because the sour nicotine taste he'd woken with still burnt his throat.

At sunset, eating his second helping of soup in one day, a brief shimmer of light broke through the cloud that Rhian's story about Leonard's bruise and his night in Finsbury Park police station had borne.

'*Le clodo*,' he murmured to himself, having just told the nurse to inform the people concerned to prepare his bill and asked to be woken at seven the next morning if he was sleeping as he was due at the airport.

'Leonard's tramp…'

It was the mention of the airport. It had called up the contact sheet he'd come across while tidying up his Triumph at Heathrow, and for some unknown reason the recollection had attached itself to the cloud.

He spent the time it took to swallow his soup trying to connect the two, visualising what he could remember of the shots on the contact sheet, but in the end, weary, he put his plate aside, dismissing the memory as merely circumstantial. Like the stall-holder Rhian had spoken of, Leonard's bag-ladden tramp had not taken well to being photographed, and the moment Lombard put him out of his mind, the cloud darkened again, as soon did the world outside his eyes.

His last conscious thoughts were of the Delaunay and the police. The hotel, it seemed, had held onto more than his passport. The Browning in its paper bag was no longer in his suitcase. Naturally, his first thought had been to impute its loss to Friedman or to either one of his colleagues. But people who steal guns don't usually leave easy money behind, and his money was still all there. So, the hotel management made a likelier candidate, and if that was the case, it didn't bode well, suggested they might call the police the moment he turned up to collect his passport even though they'd claimed to be holding it only because they couldn't despatch such a document without proper authorisation; but then again, if that was their intent, they really ought to have sent a couple of local cops together with his suitcase after his 'I'm alive' call.

Were he not in a hurry to get back to London, he'd wait the few days it would take Moreau to get him another passport. But he was in a hurry, and, if it came to it, wasn't unduly concerned about confronting the local police. If need be, if it happened, he'd talk, he'd tell them, and like Moreau, like Fitzpatrick and every cop he'd ever meet, they'd let him go once they knew who he was. The police is a great family. Minor offences such as possession of narcotics or an unlicensed weapon were not going to make them feel compelled to detain him, or extradite him back to France. But then again, this was America...

He woke twice in the night's darkness, reacting to his dreams. The first time, at the Delaunay, José, speaking in Friedman's voice, had just put a bullet through his heart after letting him know he'd been seen on his way in and out of Friedman's Wyatt room. He was followed back to his hotel and... He found sleep again after rejecting the scenario. The Austrian would have asked questions, if need be tortured him to know who he was. No one, especially not the likes of Friedman, would kill a stranger merely for breaking into his hotel room.

The second time, Martin, dressed in the dark suit of the man in the portrait hanging in Friedman's London office, but his foxy-eyed self, shot him in the gut as he lay on his hospital bed, having come to finish him off on behalf of his boss. This left Lombard staring into the shadows, perplexed, before sleep claimed him again. Why had Friedman not followed up on his spoiled murder attempt? It was sloppy. Not what was expected of the cautious man who lived in Hampstead. And what about Martin? Shouldn't the Austrian have asked about the red-haired man? Or had he already known Martin lay dead in his kitchen? Could that be why he was in a hurry...?

Later, he woke again. It was Aline this time. She came to claim him. He found his wedding band around his finger, but sleep did not return...

A hotel's business is to make money, and to make money it's a hotel's business to avoid bad publicity. This explains how come people are caught every day doing all sorts of bad things in all sorts of places but hardly ever in hotels, as if nothing bad ever occurred behind their windows.

Had he not been so absorbed in other matters, Lombard would have remembered this, knowing from experience that, given the choice, hotel managers preferred dealing with bad situations quietly.

The Delaunay's manageress was no different. Slim, pale, dark, with placid eyes and breasts that appeared too heavy for her narrow shoulders, she looked too young for her responsibilities and too fresh for her sober blue suit. Still, she knew her job, greeted Lombard in her office with the right mix of deterrence – an athletic golden-tanned character stood guard by her side; encouragement – his passport and brown paper bag sat prominently on her desk in front of her clasped hands; and authority – she didn't bother to invite him to sit down.

'We did not expect to see you so soon after your call yesterday, Mr. Lamont. However, on behalf of the hotel, I'd like to let you know that we're pleased you survived your misadventure.'

Lombard grinned. She'd spoken in a birdlike voice, with barely a flicker of a smile.

'It's very kind of you,' he acknowledged.

'Yes. Well…' she returned, tight-lipped, before re-summoning her managerial voice with a glance down at her desk; 'As you can see, together with your passport, we took the liberty of holding onto the weapon we found in your room. We intended to pass both onto the police along with details of the circumstances in which they came into our possession. However, after coming to the opinion that it would serve little purpose other than to turn what is for you a bad situation into something possibly worse, we concluded it would be better for everybody if last Wednesday's unfortunate incident were laid to rest. So, if this is acceptable to you, you're welcome to your property. Of course, it goes without saying that we do not expect you to remain a guest of this hotel. At present or at any time in the future.'

He nodded, peering into her well-practised professional gaze. Whatever she was thinking, only she knew, but he was in no doubt that, as she'd put it, she was indeed pleased he'd 'survived his misadventure'. Had things turned out differently, there'd have been no alternative but for her to speak to the police…

'It's fine with me,' he said, before going on to ask, perversely: 'May I ask what happened to the drug I understand was found in my room?'

She scowled, batted her eyelashes, momentarily exposing the young girl that hid behind her mature bearing, but her training quickly came to the rescue:

'It was handed over to the paramedics. To help them to determine what they were dealing with.'

'I see. What about telephone calls? Did anyone try to—'

'You had two calls,' she pre-empted him; 'Both times the people hung up when asked if they were relations.'

'Did they?'

'Indeed they did.'

'Men? Women?'

'One of each,' she answered.

He frowned. Not only did she know her job, she'd also done her homework…

'One of each,' he echoed, reckoning the woman had to be Deborah De Moraes, the man possibly Friedman. And he turned to grin into the narrow, noncommittal blue eyes of the bronzed character who stood by her side, moved to reach for the paper bag, checked inside for the Browning, silencer and spare rounds, picked up his passport, bade goodbye to the young woman with a nod and made for the door.

'Thank you. I'll stop at reception to settle—'

'You needn't worry about your bill, Mr. Lamont,' the birdlike voice said behind him; 'You were never here.'

It was still only 8:30 in the morning. He could have got into the taxi waiting for him in the shade of the hotel forecourt, made for the airport and waited there for his noon flight. He could have, and had he not paused outside the hotel entrance to put on his sunglasses and light a Gitane, he would have. Only, snapping his lighter shut to peer once more across Sunset Boulevard towards the Wyatt, his eyes met the hotel's uniformed doorman standing in the early morning sunshine slanting across the covered forecourt, and instead, Lombard tossed the paper bag and its Browning onto the back seat of the taxi, told the driver to hang on and set off into the sunshine across the Boulevard.

He'd just had a thought. It was a long shot, probably a waste of time, but the brevity of his stop at the Delaunay meant he had time to waste, aside from which his stiff body and limbs could do with a stroll.

The doorman made him out as he was still halfway there, let it be known with a grin. He was the burly one, the one with the genial 'Hi there' who'd called himself Jack.

'Hi there,' the man greeted him as he reached the forecourt.

'How are you?' Lombard returned, stopping a few feet away from him.

'It's a beautiful day,' the other returned; 'So? You got your car?'

'Yeah,' Lombard grinned.

Across the boulevard, his hired Ford was still in the side street where he'd left it, together with three parking tickets stuck on the windscreen. It seemed it was parked pointing the wrong way against the wrong kerb; he hadn't known it, but the Los Angeles Highway Code made it an offence to park against the flow of the lane.

'Great,' said the doorman; 'You told them Jack sent you and they treated you nice?'

'Yeah. They treated me nice,' Lombard replied, probing the man's grinning eyes.

There may as well have been no soul behind them. Just another pair of Los Angeles eyes, hard, self-assured and impenetrable. Unrecognisable territory. Trying to play or second-guess them would be futile. Still, it couldn't really do any harm to show one was making an effort; nobody likes to feel like easy prey.

'Tell me,' he asked, peering at the sky; 'Does the sun never stop shining around here?'

'At this time of year, it can do. But you're lucky.'

'Am I?' he pronounced, keeping his eyes on the sky, struggling to come up with more small-talk.

'So, how about the ocean?' he thought of asking; 'I still haven't seen it but I can smell it. How far is it from here?'

'Oh. About four miles. If you follow Sunset all the way down you'll get right to it. Can't miss it,' he heard the doorman say; 'It's worth a detour. Anyhow, in LA for long?'

'I shouldn't think so,' Lombard replied, peering down Sunset Boulevard; 'Although, that said, it might depend on you. Would you be interested in making an easy $50?'

As the doorman didn't answer, he turned back to face him, met with a cagey grin…

'An easy $50?'

'Uh-huh.'

'Well, I don't know what's on your mind, but $50 is merely tip money, Mister,' the man said with an amused shrug.

'Is it now?'

'Yeah.'

'Right. So you're not interested?'

'That depends. What do you think?'

Lombard nodded. If the man wanted to be tried, he'd better try him.

'I don't suppose you were on duty last Wednesday afternoon?'

'Wednesday afternoon? No.'

'That's what I thought. I recall a lanky man standing here in your uniform on Wednesday morning. You know who that might be?'

'Go on.'

'Well, one of your hotel guests checked out that afternoon. Mr. Otto Gluck. I'm not sure what he looks like. Possibly tall, thin, with dark eyes, black or grey hair. What I do know is that he's over fifty, is a careful dresser and speaks with a German accent. Also, he was away on Tuesday night, which means he actually got here sometime on Wednesday, possibly stayed just long enough to settle his bill and pick up a small leather bag with a Virgin Airways tag. It's not much to go on, but I wonder if you could ask your lanky colleague if it rings a bell. And if it does, if he can recall whether the man left alone or in company, in a private vehicle or a taxi. And if it was a taxi, from what outfit, and would he know how to reach the driver to ask where he delivered his fare.'

He'd finished, but the burly doorman just went on grinning, as if waiting for more, and, noticing the lines around his squinting eyes, Lombard realised that Jack was a lot older than he'd thought. From a distance, his tan, white teeth, black hair and round face allowed him to pass for thirty, thirty-five; close-up and grinning in the full glare of the sun, he looked nearer to fifty.

'I've finished,' Lombard said; 'I don't know how things work in this part of the world, but where I come from, what sorts out the good from the useless guys in your line of work is sharp eyes and ears, a knack for faces and an extensive knowledge of the street and what goes on in it. Do you think your lanky colleague is any good or is he just earning a living?'

'Woaw…' Jack declared, chuckling.

'Yes, woaw,' Lombard returned, frowning; 'So? How are we doing? Is it worth my spending $50 to get you to call your colleague? And by the way, I'm in a hurry. It would have to be done now.'

'Wednesday afternoon, eh?' Jack spoke at last; 'Say, it wouldn't by any chance have something to do with the guy who left the Delaunay on a stretcher, would it?'

Lombard stayed silent, took a drag from his Gitane, ignoring the doorman's self-satisfied nod.

'Huh. I thought you looked a little pale,' the other remarked; 'Anyhow, I suppose it's not on to ask what your business is or what's with the German speaking guy?'

'What will it be?' Lombard ignored him.

'Well, I like you. But my lanky coll—'

'Tell him there's $50 in it for him too if he's got something worth listening to,' he declared, guessing where Jack was leading.

'$50?'

He sighed:

'Okay. If you deliver something, fifty for him, a hundred for you.'

The doorman showed this was more to his liking by wiping the grin off his face to replace it with a frown:

'Right… Right. Leave it to me, Mister. But it might take a while, especially if you want us to go hunting after a cab—'

'I've got one hour,' cut in Lombard, lying – his flight was not due to leave for another three hours, the airport was a forty minute drive away, but…

'Fine,' said Jack, moving towards a stretch-limousine pulling into the forecourt; 'Leave it to me. I'll see you in one hour…'

The doorman went to exchange a few words with the capped driver sitting behind the limousine window and made for the hotel doors with a last 'See you in one hour'.

Alone with the limousine, Lombard peered across the boulevard towards his Ford, took a last drag from his Gitane, flicked it away, made his way back to the Delaunay, let his taxi go and moved his suitcase and the Browning into the hired Ford.

Soon afterwards, with the Ford now cleared of tickets and lawfully parked, he was back on Sunset Boulevard and stepping through the door of a train-wagon converted into a coffee bar a few hundred yards from the Wyatt. The place was empty but for a rough young woman in a sleeveless T-shirt breast-feeding a baby, and he decided to take his coffee to one of two tables outside the wagon. Sitting in the sun, he watched the passing traffic, and soon unbuttoned his shirt collar. He was too hot again, and anyway, he'd only buttoned it to conceal Martin's work. The red-haired man's finger marks on his lower neck had turned deep purple during his stay at the hospital.

At noon, his plane left without him. By then, having changed his booking for a flight leaving at the same time the next day, he was driving his Ford along the San Bernardino Freeway out of Los Angeles and towards the town of Barstow 130 miles away.

Jack had delivered, even if it wasn't quite what he'd expected.

'The German accent and the small bag with the Virgin Airways tag did it,' the doorman had said; 'But I don't know if the news is gonna be much good to you.'

Neither did Lombard, even now that he'd committed himself.

'Your man did leave on Wednesday afternoon. The thing is though, he took no taxi. My lanky colleague saw him get into a car with two other guys. That said, he also remembers seeing him turn up an hour earlier. And this is possibly the interesting part. On his way in, your man was in a taxi, and not just any taxi. The thing had 'Yellow Cab Co. Barstow' written all over it. My colleague could not help but notice it because as it happens it's not often that we get to see anything from over there over here. In fact, we never do.'

'See anything from where?' Lombard had asked.

'Barstow. It's a small desert town about a hundred miles North-east. Towards Nevada. Dead in the middle of military country.'

'Military country?'

'Uh-huh. This is Southern California. The military need space for war games. And space comes cheap out there. Anyhow, could be you're only interested in finding where your man went, but how would you like to know where he was picked up?'

'You can find out?'

'That might depend on how friendly them Barstow folks are. And it might cost you. But, as I said, it's a small town. Barstow Yellow Cab Co. can't be a very large outfit. You want me to follow up on it or—'

'If money's mentioned, it's $50 top. And tell the people concerned I need to hear something worth my making the trip to deliver it…'

It had taken Jack just over two hours to track down Friedman's taxi driver, and after hearing what the latter had to say, less than a minute for Lombard to make up his mind, even if there was no guarantee his trip would lead to where the Austrian had been prior to – or better still, returned to after – checking out of the Wyatt. According to Jack, the Yellow Cab Co. driver had not picked Friedman up. Rather, Friedman had turned up in a dirty four-wheel drive vehicle at his Barstow taxi rank and asked to be taken to Los Angeles. They'd agreed a fare, the Austrian had got into the cab, the four-wheel drive had left and the taxi driver made for a petrol station to fill up. Only later, cruising across the Mojave desert, the driver had caught up with the four-wheel drive again to see it turn off the main road onto an old dusty track leading into the sands, which he'd found somewhat odd since, to his knowledge as a local man, the said track led nowhere but to an abandoned Second World War detention camp for Japanese Americans.

That was as much as Jack had learnt because, intent on getting his $50, the driver had kept the location of the track to himself. If Lombard was interested, he could call him when he got to Barstow.

'How come he's so sure the four-wheel drive was one and the same?' Lombard had queried.

'That's what he said. Apparently it's a foreign car. They tend to stick out in Jeep country. And also it had tinted windows and was covered with dust and dry mud, which points to it being used off-road, as those things are meant to be but so rarely are these days,' was Jack's reply.

One thing was plain. Whether or not Friedman was to be found at the end of that track, whatever the giant may have claimed back in London, the sophisticated Austrian was unlikely to have come to America for a vacation. Not to Barstow, a small desert town dead in the middle of military country.

'And, Mister,' Jack had called as Lombard turned to leave; 'When you get back to wherever you come from, don't forget to tell the guys in our line of work over there how we do things over here. Do you think they'd have pulled this off for you, eh?'

It hadn't been his intention, but his little speech had clearly got to the doorman. Had he proved so helpful only as a result of hurt professional pride? Or was it the $100?

The town of Barstow matched the doorman's description. It was small and, judging by the road and shop signs, depended for its existence on the nearby military installations – from Air Force bases to Marine Corps bases, Naval Weapons Centres and Fort Reservations – and lay stretched beneath the sun in the middle of a yellow-grey desert. A two-hour drive had led Lombard to its centre, a journey which had taken him first through the sprawling suburbs of Los Angeles, then across mile upon mile of rich green fields scattered with sprinklers until, leaving San Bernadino behind to cruise along Freeway 15, the scenery had changed into a desert landscape of rocks and sands broken only by high never-ending chain-link fences displaying military warnings and 'CLOSED TO THE PUBLIC' signs. Fences and signs had eventually ended as he got within twenty miles of the town, where he stopped at a bar, arranged to meet with the Yellow Cab Co. driver at another bar, freshened up and ordered a cold beer. They had no mineral water.

'Which way you get here, Mister?' the taxi driver asked, with his eyes on the beer bottle that sat on the bar between his hands.

He wore faded jeans, a chequered shirt and a cowboy hat above his sun-dried leathery face. It was hard to give him an age.

Forty perhaps…

'Freeway 15,' Lombard said.

'Right. Get back onto it. About fifteen miles outta town you'll find the Red Mountain Bar-Motel. You carry on for another two miles or so. You'll see what you're looking for on your right. It's got an old Closed To Public sign.'

'A track on the right side of the road? Is it the only one on that side past the motel?'

'Nah. But it's the only one within two miles of the Red Mountain motel.'

'How far down it is the old Japanese detention camp?'

'No idea. Never had cause to find out. Okay? And, whatever your business, if anyone asks, it'd be most appreciated if you didn't mention our talk…'

The man picked up the $50 from the bar and strolled away towards an ongoing game of pool.

There were fresh tyre marks in the sand, from several vehicles by the look of it, but that's all there was. As far as the eye could see, all was sky, rocks, dust and sand, with here and there a few hills and crater-like holes. The only sign that there was life in this lunar landscape was the track with its tyre marks, which led into it in a straight line until, in the far distance, it appeared to vanish behind a ridge.

Frowning behind his sunglasses at the wheel of the purring Ford by the side of the empty Freeway, Lombard didn't like it at all. There was nowhere to conceal the car. It would be noticed if he left it along the road, and taking it down the track would allow no escape were he to come across a vehicle.

He peered at the weather-beaten 'CLOSED TO THE PUBLIC' sign outside his window, looked back in his mirror in the direction of the Red Mountain Bar-Motel, but decided that was no good either. Apart from leaving him with a two mile walk just to get back, it might be a bad idea. Presuming the track led to something other than a disused war detention camp, it was hard to imagine the motel folks weren't in on it, or at least aware of it…

He lit a Gitane and got the Ford into gear. Half a minute later he pulled off the road to drive fifty yards across the sands into a shallow depression. He threw sand over the car and walked back into the sun towards the road with the Browning in his pocket, having checked that it was loaded and in good working order.

The Ford's dusty roof was visible from the Freeway, but only if one looked for it, and he flicked his Gitane away and checked the time on reaching the Closed To The Public sign at the entrance to the track.

His watch showed 13:40. His feet felt hard tarmac beneath the dust blanketing the track. His eyes noted there were now a few clouds in the sky; white, round and still, they hung in the azure expanse like puffs of cotton wool.

He was already feeling the heat.

FIFTEEN

The sun kept on beating down and the tyre trail kept on vanishing beyond the next ridge. Soon, the track started to wind its way around dry river beds, depressions and rocky hills, never visible for more than a few hundred yards ahead.

Two hours after leaving the road, covered in dust, sweating and parched, Lombard considered turning back to get his car. Only, the prospect of retracing his steps with the trail's end possibly close at hand kept him moving forward. And so he trekked on, at a slow but steady pace, keeping his eyes on the ground and his mind clear to conserve energy. Summoning to mind his Scout's survival training, he also tucked his trousers into his socks, buttoned his suit jacket over his loosened shirt and refrained from wiping the sweat from his face. If his memory served him right – he couldn't be sure as he never before had cause to call upon this particular store of long-buried information – sweat acted as a coolant, hence mopping it up would only lead to more being produced and so to yet more fluid-loss and possible dehydration; layers of loose clothing offered protection against sunburn and provided insulation by trapping air next to the body, thus helping to minimise perspiration; and the desert could hide scorpions or snakes, hence his tucked-in trousers. He ought also to have covered his head, but short of using his jacket for the purpose, there was little he could do about that. Nevertheless, for want of anything better, he turned up his collar to afford his nape some protection from the sun.

An hour on, the winding trail was still drawing him deeper into the barren grey-yellow landscape. By now, his salty sweat burned his eyes, his dried lips were caked with dust, the first signs of heat cramps and exhaustion were beginning to threaten his progress and, rubbing against his clinging, sweat-soaked clothing, his skin was sore. But turning back was no longer an option. He'd gone too far, and anyhow, the sun was heading towards the horizon and the sky turning lilac, announcing the approaching relief of evening. To keep on going without slowing down or yielding to cramp, he resorted to counting his steps to time his stride, focusing on walking and walking alone, with sunset his target. Only then, were the tyre trail to go on, would he rest in the cover of dusk and turn around. But if it came to that, he'd come back. Driving this time. And if need be, keep on going all night. Whether or not it was a waste of time. Whether or not it would cost him his next day's flight.

Never mind London. Never mind the heat, the aches or the impending cramp. Never mind his parched mouth, sore skin or burning eyes. By now, there was only the tyre trail and his shoes throwing up dust with his every step. And at the end of it, hopefully, more than a deserted second world-war detention camp for Japanese Americans...

'... *Quatre-vingt-dix-neuf. Cent. Un. Deux...*'

And the Austrian perhaps. Friedman. Or Gluck. Or whatever his name was...

'... *Soixante-dix. Soixante et onze. Soixante-douze...*'

Soon, although by then 'soon' had lost all meaning, he at long last came across an encouraging sign. It wasn't much. Just a derelict cabin standing in the sands. It had no door, no roof or window. The track took the tyre trail past it to vanish beyond yet another crop of rocks in the sweltering near-distance. But a bright black and red warning sign hung against its old wooden wall:

'PRIVATE LAND. DO NOT PASS BEYOND THIS POINT'

It wasn't much indeed. But in the circumstances, it was encouraging. Or at least the warning sign was. Clearly it did not belong to the cabin and the sharp colours betrayed its newness, or in any case that it could not have lain exposed to the sun for very long. On the other hand, there was also its wording. This seemed to confirm what Lombard had already guessed on the grounds that the track would have shown evidence of heavy use or been kept clear of the blanket of dust that was here and there thin enough to reveal the tarmac beneath – he was not trespassing on nor heading towards a military installation. Still, encouragement or not, aware that a rest would lead his body to give in to exhaustion and cramp, he quickly moved on after barely pausing to wipe the salt from around his eyes and inspect the cabin, which turned out to be empty, apart from an old table and what appeared to be a rifle rack, suggesting it might once have been a guardhouse.

'*Un...*' he resumed counting, nearing the next crop of rocks.

The track took him past another abandoned cabin, then alongside a rusty hangar of corrugated-iron filled with oil drums, and over the rim and down the steep incline of a vast, searing crater where his skin dried up and his breaths began to wheeze as soon as he reached the thin hot air hanging over the plain at the bottom.

Treading on the outer edge of his right foot to spare what he suspected was a blistered big toe, he started to limp. Too jaded to speak, he took to counting his strides silently, now and then glancing ahead towards the facing cliff of the crater which, no matter how much ground he covered, for a long time remained forever in the distance. Yet, after nearly an hour, he got there, thanks to the setting sun which dyed the sky crimson, sunk beyond the crater's lip and left the plain in deep shadow. The air around him grew cooler, his wheezing stopped and he started sweating again long before the track took him back up the crater's side into the red and purple twilight above.

He would have rested and headed back for his car. That was the plan. Having got this far, he had only dragged himself out of the crater to see what lay beyond. Only, in the gentle evening breeze that now swept the unbroken expanse of dusky landscape outside the crater, he found himself taking off his sunglasses to stare at a high chain-link fence similar to those he'd seen along the Barstow road. It stretched across the flats in the near-distance, spanning the entire horizon. And the track made straight for it, through a closed gate, and on into the shadows beyond. Two signs were fixed to the gate, but they were too far to make out.

Lombard put his sunglasses away in the breast pocket of his jacket and moved to within thirty yards of the gate.

'PRIVATE LAND. DO NOT PASS BEYOND THIS POINT', read one sign, echoing the warning on the cabin across the crater; 'RESTRICTED AREA. KEEP OUT', cautioned the other. And if that wasn't enough to deter intruders, the gate was also topped with razor-wire, fitted with an intercom, guarded by a surveillance camera in a glass box perched on a high post and flanked with spotlights. Also, its top and bottom were set in sliding rails connected to two small motors by way of a system of chains and pulleys. Clearly, it could be operated remotely. And setting off just beyond it, a trail of electricity poles spanned their lines of cables away into the distance.

Lombard ran his eyes over the cables. Presumably, one linked the camera to a monitor. The field of electronics wasn't one of his strong points but, without knowing where he'd picked up the information, he recalled something about video signals carried by cables fading rapidly over a fairly short distance. If that was right, whatever lay behind the fence couldn't be very far. But then again, there existed such things as boosters and relays, and his information could be out of date, or even, the camera inoperative, serving merely as a deterrent. But then again, it could be running, even as he was looking up at it, although in the rapidly fading light…

The hands of his watch showed 18:20. Leaving aside time for a rest, that put the road and the Ford over four hours behind him.

He opted to give his theory on video signals the benefit of the doubt, decided he'd better steer clear of the gate in case it was screened by a sensor that would trigger the spotlights or an alarm, pulled the Browning from his pocket, left the track and followed the fence across the rugged ground at a distance until, a hundred or so yards on, he closed the gap to reach it.

The spotlights at the gate remained dark. He gently tapped the metal screen with the tip of the Browning. It wasn't electrified. He studied the fence. It was rusty but sound, taut, and towered above him with its bottom edge flush with the ground. To climb over it was out – not in his state – but the ground beneath his feet looked possible.

He pocketed the Browning, got out of his jacket, took off his watch, removed his wedding band, pulled his trousers out of his socks and up, and kneeled down.

It took time and a sharp-edged stone, cost a few chipped nails and grazed fingers to break up the ground and tunnel his way to the other side. It also got dark. But he got through, dusted himself off, put his watch and wedding band back on, stuck an unlit Gitane between his lips – just for the taste, he was too parched to smoke – flung his jacket over his shoulder and rejoined the track.

The thin crescent of the moon behind him now lit the tyre marks and up to six or seven poles ahead before darkness immersed all.

A new pole stood by the track every seventy strides, with one more forever looming out of the shadows ahead, questioning the soundness of his theory about cables and video signals. However, Lombard wasn't unduly concerned. He almost felt good now. His legs moved unaided, effortlessly. His thirst, his aches and sores no longer seemed so serious and, without realising it, he'd even stopped limping. Partly, darkness had brought comfort, the refreshing breeze strength. Essentially, he was high. He'd passed his exhaustion threshold. The chemicals inside had kicked in, were rushing, which was where physical exertion held the upper hand over its mental counterpart. When the head starts struggling, hurting or failing, there's no back-up system and bad things will happen. When the body nears breakdown point, the brain comes to the rescue, takes over, wipes the slate clean, and euphoria or rapture follows. Lombard knew it only bought time though. Was nothing more than a pleasant illusion. Merely nature's way of clinging to life but no substitute for it. He was still tired. He could still collapse. Only, it wouldn't hurt. He wouldn't see it coming. Perhaps this was nature's way of dealing with pain. It simply shut off, turned off the switch. Still, right now, even the back of his neck felt light and relaxed. He could even feel the cool breeze brushing against it.

'Invincibilité,' he whispered in the darkness, despite himself.

That's what the high was. Physical exertion brought a sense of invincibility. The best rush of all...

He glared. The best rush of all didn't require physical exertion. He'd been there. And it had nothing to do with a chemically induced illusion or trance. Hadn't he felt it in his cub scout's uniform? And later in his French army conscript's uniform? Wasn't that also why he'd joined the police? And unashamedly pursued Aline for two years before she'd said 'Yes'. What had she made him feel but invincible? And what had his police badge done but make him feel...

He glared again. He almost felt good. Almost. He had better keep it to just that.

Watching another pole loom from the shadows ahead, he thought about his suitcase in the Ford. It was a good thing he'd brought it with him. He'd be able to change before heading back to Los Angeles. His only other suit was also dirty and creased, he'd worn it on his way from London, but at least it would be dry and presentable, unlike the sweat-soaked one he had on at the moment...

First, he sensed it. The breeze brushing against his face suddenly became much cooler, moist, and he could have sworn smelt of fresh water. Next, he heard it. Drifting across the silence, a soft whirr invaded the night, faint at first, then growing as he marched on. And then he saw it. A dim light shone out of the night ahead, like a crystal dome radiating from the ground. The trail of electricity poles disappeared into it.

He was reaching his journey's end. And he was no longer alone in the dark wilderness. His ears now picked up music through the enveloping whirr, faint and distant but audible enough for him to make out it was rock music. Without breaking his stride, he got back into his jacket and locked the silencer onto the Browning barrel.

What he'd thought of as a whirr was the sound made by sprinklers spraying their water over pasture land.

He'd reached the edge of a plateau overlooking what appeared to be a ranch. All of a sudden the land mass dropped down one sharp fifty foot step, leaving the track to descend by a man-made ramp into the watered plain below, where it carried on across the darkness for about three hundred yards to end in the front yard of a large two storey house ringed with outbuildings, paddocks and vegetation.

Light shone from most windows of the main house. Dwarfed by two great satellite dishes, six vehicles – all four-wheel drives – and a few pick-up trucks sat in the front drive. Inside a couple of open French windows which gave onto a spot-lit swimming pool flanked with tables, parasols and sun-chairs, people were dancing. There also appeared to be people moving in one of the outbuildings behind the house, a long bungalow-like structure near a pen in which a few horses stood in the light from its windows. And in the more remote darkness, a faint glow hinted at yet another occupied building. Otherwise, all seemed quiet. There were no fences or guards. And probing the shadows for dogs, Lombard also discerned what he guessed was the old war detention camp the Barstow taxi driver had mentioned. Rows of barracks cut three sides of a square in the darkness beyond the sprinklers. Doubtless, like the ranch which had followed it there, it owed its location to a nearby source of water.

Water... He started down the ramp.

He threw his jacket onto the ground, placed the contents of his trouser pockets together with his watch and the Browning on it, took off his shoes, peeled the socks from his sore feet and turned towards the sprinklers. The grass under his bare feet felt good.

He didn't drink immediately on stepping into the swirling spray of water, just paused, mouth shut, eyes closed, to allow the mask of dirt and sweat on his face to wash away. And it felt good.

He opened his eyes and lips, tasted the water. It felt cool and clean and so he sat down and, slowly, sipped two palmfuls of it.

And this was good too.

He undid his shirt, checked his chest, saw that the hospital dressing on his wound still clung tightly to the skin.

'*Ah…*' he let out, softly, running his fingers through his hair, gazing at his feet at the end of his outstretched legs.

'*Ah…*'

He wondered briefly about scorpions and snakes, drank a little more and lay down, stretching his arms along the wet grass, looking up through the sparkling canopy of swirling water above him. And this felt good too.

Many stars had appeared since he'd last surveyed the sky, and for a while he just watched, steadily catching sight of more and more stars, unsure whether they were emerging out of the darkness or if it was simply his eyes adjusting to their brilliance.

'*Merde,*' he breathed, softly.

If he could have thought of a reason for it, he just might have cried. He just might have. But he had not come here to cry. Merely to…

And he sighed and turned his head towards the lit-up house across his dark watery shelter. And he frowned as he caught sight of it beyond the satellite dishes and cars.

Whether the Austrian was somewhere behind one of the shining windows, he didn't know. But that a godforsaken place that hid behind fences and an Austrian who got up in the morning to peddle children for a living could only add up to bad news, that much he did know.

No. He couldn't think of a reason to cry. Besides, it wouldn't be appropriate.

'… *Invincibilité,*' he murmured, silently.

Thump… Thump…
'*Hein… Trente-six battements par minute…*'

'… Yeah. Well, 2.5 litres, 161 bhp, 24 valve V6 engine sure sounds like great stuff. But if it ain't made in the US of A, I ain't interested.'

'You forgot the leather seats, ABS, cruise control, veneer trimmings and CD player.'

'Still not interested.'

'Really? What's so great about cars made in the great US of A, huh?'

'What's great about them? Well, you ex-commie bastard fiend, they're made for fucking American roads. That's what. Unlike all your German and Japanese...'

Crouching in the shadows half-listening to the conversation of the eight people sitting around dinner through the open window just above him, Lombard scowled across the front drive towards a dusty Landrover – pick-up trucks aside, all the other vehicles were Jeeps, which suggested this was the foreign car Friedman had turned up in at Barstow and the taxi driver had later spotted turning off the main road.

He swallowed hard, noted that one of the Jeeps had military plates and shifted his weight onto his left foot to brush off the pricking stone chips and dirt embedded in the sole of his right foot. Finding his feet swollen and tender after his long rest, he'd decided not to put his shoes back on, left them with his socks by the sprinklers.

'Personally, I think Italian cars are the most beautiful,' a voice was saying in the room behind him.

It was decision time. Sidling and ducking across the shadows, he'd already gone around the ranch and seen all he needed to see. The outbuildings consisted of stables, sheds, storerooms and a pigsty with about a dozen animals. The faint glow in the darkness far from the main house had turned out to be a night-light above the door of a concrete shelter housing stacks of oil drums and the generator that supplied electricity to the compound. The long structure alongside the horse pen wasn't a bungalow but two rows of three mobile homes set back to back on concrete blocks; one was fitted out as an up-to-date surgery/operating theatre, four as dormitories/living quarters and the last as a kitchen/dining hall. He'd also come across a water tower connected to a well via a pump. And stealing from window to window around the house, he'd found amongst other things an office, a small screening theatre and a vast empty lounge complete with a full-length bar and a couple of stuffed tigers. As for people, he'd counted over thirty of them, but none who resembled the portrait in Friedman's Hampstead cottage or either of the two characters he'd let into his room at the Delaunay. There were the eight sitting around dinner, between twelve and fifteen more in the room by the swimming pool, another three with four children in one of the mobile homes, a couple in the screening theatre and five more in the kitchen of the main house – a cook, two women in maid outfits and a weather-beaten old man in cowboy boots chatting over a meal with a younger Hispanic man carrying a gun in the shoulder holster over his shirt. However, more people appeared to be moving inside the first floor windows and Lombard wouldn't have been surprised if the Austrian was among them because, had he doubted it before, he was now sure the ranch was what had brought Friedman to this part of the world. Pigs and horses aside, the place was most definitely the man's territory.

Apart from three men in casual dress, all the people dancing, drinking and chatting around billiard tables and gaming machines to the music pounding from a jukebox in the room by the pool were young girls. They looked rough. Some were pretty and some not. The youngest was about fifteen, the eldest perhaps twenty-five, but all were scantily dressed, clearly strung out on dope and exhibiting various stages of pregnancy. The same applied to the three girls watching television with the children in the mobile homes, except these were heavily pregnant, distinctly close to giving birth, which probably explained why they were baby-sitting instead of partaking of the fun by the pool.

Since the ranch could not be mistaken for a private clinic, and the girls were plainly not overly concerned for their health or that of the babies they were carrying, Lombard had a good idea of what was going on. Friedman, pregnant women and a secluded ranch equipped with a surgery and satellite communication dishes didn't really leave much room for speculation.

He tensed his finger on the Browning's trigger as the sounds of laughter, shrieks and splashing reached him through the loud music from the house. Some of the revellers had clearly decided to move the party outside, were jumping into the pool and enjoying it.

He glared, fixing on the corner from around which the noise

came. He'd shoot. If anyone showed he'd just shoot. Man, woman or girl. He'd just shoot...

No one showed and, reckoning he'd better find a safer place to appraise the situation, he slipped away across the front yard towards the ramp after peering one more time into the dining-room window.

The eight discussing the merits of cars over dinner under a massive wooden chandelier in the shape of a cartwheel made a rather odd gathering. The hosts were an elderly American couple informally dressed in jeans and chequered shirts; both very tanned, he had long wavy white hair and she wore a bandanna around hers, which was dyed jet black. Two men with crew-cuts, one in his twenties, the other nearer fifty, wore military uniforms. They too were Americans and sat on either side of a dark and elegant woman in a suit who, from her accent and bearing, was either French or Swiss. The last three had their backs to the window, were all male and also Europeans. One, in a brown suit and cream polo-neck jumper, spoke softly with an Italian accent. The other two sounded like Russians, were loud, possibly drunk and had short blond hair, muscular backs and identical white shirts showing sweat rings around their armpits. From the back, sitting side by side, they looked identical, as if they might be twins.

The group had gone on chatting as Lombard observed them.

'Well, I myself drive a Volkswagen Diesel,' the elegant woman with the French accent had said; 'And I am very pleased with it.'

'Diesel, huh!' returned one of the military men.

'What do you mean, "Diesel, huh"?'

'Nothing. Just that diesel's good... for trucks and busses! Ha-ha...'

'I think they make very good diesel cars these days,' remarked the Italian; 'It is true they used to be sluggish. But not anymore.'

'You don't say? Well, if women like them, I guess they must be all right for women. At least they're cheap.'

'Cheap! *Oh non*. Not cheap,' the woman objected; 'As a matter of fact, my car is not cheap at all. If you must know, it is actually the costliest model of the range.'

'Sorry? The cost what?' asked one of the Russians.

'The costliest,' returned the woman; '*Heu*, don't I say it right? Costliest, yes?'

'No. You pronounced it very well,' intervened the hostess in her bandanna; 'Costliest.'

'She did?' said the Russian; 'Then what is it? A word?'

'*Hein. Mais bien sûr c'est...* Of course it is a word,' returned the woman; 'What else do you think it is?'

'I don't know,' the Russian replied; 'Could be the sound of jewellery hitting a parquet floor, huh?'

'Ha-ha...'

Ha-ha... Lombard had left them laughing.

It was nearing nine o'clock when he got back to the perimeter fence. He sat down in the dark just inside the gate, put his shoes and the Browning down beside him, lit a Gitane and waited, gazing at the stars. His wet clothes clung to his skin and, sitting still in the breezy night air, he began to feel cold. The refrain from one of the songs he'd heard at the ranch kept echoing in his head. It was annoying but he was too tired to fight it. And he'd also started to feel hungry, doubtless from having stood at the dining-room window long enough to see a joint of roast meat brought to the table. The warm meaty smell was still with him.

'*Ooh baby I love yoooo, what more can I say...*' sang the voice in his head.

His plan was simple. Presuming anybody left the ranch tonight, the gate was the one place they'd have to slow down or even come to a stop. He'd force his way into the car, make the driver drive on through, away from the camera and down into the cover of the nearby crater. If on the other hand no one was to show up, come midnight he'd head back to the ranch, wait for things to quieten down and then find a way to ask somebody about Friedman. If the Austrian turned out not to be there, he'd just have to make sure whoever he spoke to couldn't raise the alarm before he'd trekked back to the road. If Friedman was there, then he'd improvise.

He flicked away his Gitane and glumly watched it land on the track in a spray of sparks. Whatever had brought the pregnant women and girls to the ranch, strung-out though they may be, they most certainly didn't behave like prisoners. But then again…

'Ooh baby I need yoooo…'

His hand made for the Browning and he sprang to his feet when, without warning, the electric motors behind him purred into life and the gate started sliding open with a low grating noise. Searching the darkness, he at first thought a car had approached with its headlights switched off but then quickly realised he'd have heard it coming if this was so. Which left only two possible explanations – the gate was malfunctioning, had just engaged by itself, or it had been activated from the ranch to allow a car through.

He caught sight of the answer far away in the direction of the ranch: two headlights had suddenly appeared in the darkness.

'Nom de—'

He'd miscalculated. The driver was going to pass through the gate without having to slow down or come to a stop. It was a question of letting him go or…

He could wait, fire from where he stood, only, whoever had opened the gate was probably watching the monitor, waiting to see the car through the gate before shutting it again.

He turned to the spotlights. They were dark. There was no way the camera would pick him up if…

He looked back towards the car. It was approaching fast but he still couldn't hear its engine. There might just be time. He grabbed his shoes and started running, through the gate and along the track beyond, searching the darkness ahead for the lip of the crater.

He'd recalled it was near but, running as fast as he could, he was still searching for it as the sound of the car behind him quickly grew louder. Thinking he was about to be caught in its headlights, he nearly dived to the side of the track, but before he knew it, found himself scampering down into the crater, got to the plain at the bottom and turned in time to see the car appear over the brink of the slope above him. Still holding his shoes in his left hand, he raised the Browning at the end of his right arm and squinted when the car's dazzling headlights hit his eyes.

It was coming down fast, roaring, invisible behind its headlights. He couldn't see its front tyres and so aimed in the direction of the windscreen on the driver's side, fired six quick shots, leapt back to let it roar past and, for good measure, fired four more times towards its rear tyres. Only then, watching the vehicle rumble away at great speed, did he remark it was the Jeep with army plates.

At first, it looked as if he'd missed both driver and rear tyres. The Jeep just went on in a straight line along the track. Then, without warning, it suddenly swerved sharply, toppled onto its side and glided along the ground for about forty yards before coming to a stop, engine running and lights still on.

Lombard, already reloading his Browning, headed towards it, hoping the driver, if he or she was alone in the car, was still alive…

The smell of new leather enveloped him the moment he flung open the front passenger door and, squatting on top of the capsized Jeep, ready to shoot, peered into the dark cabin below in the glow of his cigarette lighter. Two men lay in a heap between the steering wheel and front seat. They were the two in military uniform he'd last seen sitting around the ranch dining table. The one buried deepest, against the driver's door, the youngest of the two, was clearly dead, his crushed skull a glistening pulp. The other was still breathing and gazed up with scared eyes, gargling as he tried to speak, bleeding from a neck wound. He was either hit or had been injured when the car tipped over. There was nothing to be done for or with him. He couldn't have more than a minute left to live.

'*Testa di cazzo,*' a soft murmur reached him through the purr of the idling engine.

Lombard immediately recognised the soft voice. It too belonged to one of the dinner guests. He spun the Browning, moved his lighter towards the back of the car and froze, uneasy, the moment he met the dark eyes in the stony face of the polo-necked Italian. The man lay upside down on the back seat, his head against the broken rear window, one hand clasped around the driver's seat, looking straight up at Lombard. Not only was he unhurt but plainly in full control of his thoughts and emotions, showing nothing more than icy irritation, his forty year-old eyes probing like a wounded bird of prey.

'What is going on? I am an Italian citizen' he said, quietly, in his smooth soft voice.

Lombard stayed silent. There was something chilling and familiar about the man's quiet composure, about the cold self-assured glint in his eyes. This one was no giant, no Martin nor even a Friedman. Given the situation, he was too calm and confident to be a mere criminal, child trafficker or, for that matter, a customer or honest man. Lombard knew him though, had come across him many times. Briefly, he wondered if he could be a cop. Only he was just too composed and, in his fine polo-neck jumper, sober well-cut suit and gleaming shoes, with his neat moustache, goatee and manicured nails, perhaps also too refined for that, even for an Italian cop. No. This one was well-groomed, had no fears or uncertainties, was used to getting his way, as if born with influence and a sense of self-importance. People of that kind don't enlist in the police force. He had to belong to the privileged classes, was more likely to be a judge or...

The thought stuck the moment it took shape in Lombard's head. The man was a lawyer. That is what was familiar about him. The quiet contempt and ascendency in his eyes. That was the way some lawyers, especially affluent ones, looked at both cops and criminals, victims and offenders – as if at meal-tickets. Lombard had come across enough of them to know. And this one was as phlegmatic and arrogant as they came. The car he was travelling in had just been shot at, he came from a place crowded with doped-up pregnant girls, the two men with him were dead or dying, for all he knew he was about to be killed and yet he showed nothing more than icy irritation. And he probed, sized Lombard up, like a momentarily cowed killer assessing his conqueror, annoyed, thwarted but unafraid.

He was a lawyer all right. And judging by his self-assured

gaze, for want of imagination or anything approaching fear or compassion, he could not be very good at his job. He probably made much better slime, albeit slime with clean hands.

Even if he was armed, which was unlikely, there was nothing to fear from him.

'Okay, scumbag. Turn off the ignition and come out of there,' Lombard said, letting his lighter flame die.

He leapt off the car, took three steps back, lit a cigarette, saw his hand was trembling, cursed between his teeth and pocketed his Gitane pack as the car engine died and silence returned.

The vehicle's tail and headlights were still on, illuminating the immediate darkness.

The first thing the Italian did after climbing out of the rear door was to survey his surroundings from the top of the Jeep. From his frown, he'd have preferred it if Lombard hadn't been alone, if several dozen men in police uniforms had been there to welcome him. 'I'm a lawyer,' he could have declared, indignant, before restating his citizenship. Still, he wasn't ruffled, glanced stonily at Lombard's gun, then at his bare feet, sighed, clambered down onto the ground and proceeded to dust himself with little flicks of the hands.

'You have killed two US army officers,' he softly hummed rather than said, inspecting his suit; 'I guess you don't belong to any law enforcement agency, do you?'

Lombard waited to speak until the man looked at him and, meeting his eyes again, found himself almost wishing the other would refuse to co-operate. But perhaps this was because he already knew the chances of that were remote. If he could help it, the man would talk. This one was too proud to be brave. And besides, unprotected by the law and the apparatuses of their profession, lawyers always talked. Partly because they were good at it. Partly because, better than most, they knew that talking bought time and time could always bring opportunities. Even in hopeless situations.

'I'm only going to ask this once. Where is Gluck?'

The other thought, then:

'Who?'

Lombard scowled. If the Austrian had left the ranch, the man might conceivably not know of him. But…

'I'm sorry,' the Italian went on after a moment; 'I'm not familiar with the name.'

'The Austrian,' Lombard said; 'Friedman.'

This name he was familiar with, didn't even try to conceal it. He simply narrowed his eyes into two thin slits, grinned within his goatee and nodded, brooding.

'*Figlio di puttana…*' he breathed, almost inaudibly; 'You must be the Frenchman on his trail. Well. You can't trust anybody. He was supposed to have looked after you.'

Lombard nodded his nod. So, he not only knew Friedman but also…

'I asked you where Friedman is.'

'*Tu devrais—*' began the other.

He broke off as, in one movement, Lombard made for him and slapped him across the face.

'Just answer the question. You have three seconds,' he said, stepping back to press the Browning's silencer against the man's forehead.

The other just looked back, angry but still showing no fear.

'One,' Lombard pronounced, becoming aware of the man's expensive musky scent at the same time as noticing his soft lips. Was that why he wore a goatee? To conceal his…

'Two.'

His own feelings scared him when the trigger started to give under his finger. The Browning felt heavy and solid in his hand. A premature, unexpected, unreasonable heady sense of satisfaction was taking him over, as if revulsion made it pleasant to contemplate…

He wasn't sure whether he'd actually have squeezed the trigger. A tenth of a second later, the Italian might have died. However, before it came to finding out, the other's soft lips moved:

'Friedman returned to London. He left last week,' they let out, quietly, humming again.

'What?'

'Friedman left last week for London.'

'When last week?'

'Mmmm… Wednesday.'

Wednesday… It figured. Or at least was feasible. Wednesday was the day the Austrian had appeared with his friends at the Delaunay.

Lombard slackened his grip on the trigger, took a drag of the Gitane burning in the corner of his mouth and found himself wondering whether the hollow he now felt inside his chest was due to the fact that he had not shot the man or the disappointing news about the Austrian which, in truth, was not entirely unexpected.

The other eyeballed him now, still probing but waiting, shrewd enough to stay quiet, doubtless guessing that nothing he could say would help if Lombard was intent on killing him. On the contrary. Yet, he still showed no fear, or even anger, only irritation and displeasure, even pursed his lips to show it.

Lombard slapped him again, shoved him hard back against the car and proceeded to search him.

'Are any more of you expected to leave the place tonight or are you it?'

'I wouldn't know,' the man answered.

'What about the other dinner guests. The woman and the two Russians? They're staying the night?'

'I think so.'

He didn't carry any weapon, but Lombard found a wallet and a cell-phone on him.

'You think so?' he said, pocketing the cell-phone and moving into the Jeep's headlights with the wallet.

'They're staying there for the night,' the Italian conceded.

'Right. What about you? From what I've seen they seem to have enough spare beds,' Lombard went on, opening the wallet to find inside a snapshot under a plastic sheet.

'I prefer the privacy of my hotel.'

'Do you now? And where would that be? Barstow?'

The snapshot showed a pretty woman hugging two young children on the sunny lawn of an opulent house. They were all smiling, the woman was young, the children had gaps in their teeth. One was a boy, the other a girl; she squeezed an Alsatian puppy against her chest, clumsily, like children do.

'Yes,' the Italian was replying; 'In Barstow.'

Lombard nodded. A quick search through the wallet revealed

three charge and credit cards and a Rome-issued driving licence with a photograph of the man. Presuming it and the cards were real, the Italian was called Gianluca, Gianluca Del Piero.

'Are you going to kill me?' the soft voice asked, smooth as ever while Lombard inspected the snapshot again.

He pocketed the wallet, flicked his cigarette away, stepped up to the man, peered at his hand, saw he wore a wedding band, clenched his teeth and whacked him across the face with the Browning.

'I haven't decided yet what I'm going to do with you, scumbag,' he said; 'But since you ask, yes, I just might kill you. Now, why don't you tell me how you came to know about me, eh?'

The other glowered, pawed his cut cheek, gazed at the blood on his fingers, muttered inside his goatee and pulled a white handkerchief from his pocket.

'There is no call for needless violence,' he said, diligently starting to wipe the blood from his fingers; '*In ogni caso…* The answer to your question is no one pulls a stunt like the one you pulled back in London or here tonight and expects to get away with it. I'm afraid it upsets people. It's wrong. And someone somewhere always knows something and wants to talk about it. And it always gets around. In this case this is what happened. Friedman's London associates got a call.'

Lombard stayed silent, waiting. The Italian understood he had better come up with something a little less abstract and shrugged:

'A call. An anonymous call,' he said in his unchanging soft humming voice; 'Makes you wonder how many people know what you're up to, eh, *Francese di merda?*'

Maybe he thought it was safe to swear in his native tongue, or he simply didn't care, was a lot more angry than he let on, had found it beyond him to contain himself any longer. Maybe.

Lombard whacked him with the gun again, grabbed him by the collar and pulled him right up close.

At last, he saw something close to hatred burning in the man's eyes, probably as much as burnt in his.

'Perhaps precious self-loving scum like you might, but not even the likes of Friedman would go to the trouble of trying to kill a stranger on the strength of one anonymous call. Now try again, and this time be polite, or I'm going to do much worse than be needlessly violent.'

And he shoved him back against the Jeep.

'Who tipped Friedman off?'

The Italian cleared his throat, spat what looked like blood, felt the teeth inside his mouth, folded his handkerchief and began to pat the cut on his cheek with it, gently, as delicately as a nurse tending a child might have done.

'I can only tell you what Friedman told us. I'm sorry if you don't like it,' he said, breaking off to spit again; 'Some man left a message in London to say the Frenchman posing as a customer who'd got in touch with him the night before he left was in Los Angeles looking to kill him. He said you were a hitman, had been contracted by an annoyed client, gave your name and address and hung up. Friedman did his sums and decided to take the call seriously.'

A hitman…?

'What sums?' asked Lombard, already thinking so hard the Italian in front of him was turning into a hazy silhouette as he spoke.

'Well, from what I understand, you left two dead men back in England. He didn't need your confession…'

He nodded, looking at the man but no longer seeing him, just darkness. Something was… If the other was telling the truth, if Friedman had told him the truth, the Austrian had been led to believe he was a hitman. It…

'… *or is your last achievement going to be acting like a good and stupid faithful dog to its paymaster?*' he recalled Friedman saying as he lay blindfolded in his hotel room. The Austrian's words hadn't made much sense then. Nor had his impatience, his hurry to get rid of him, which he felt sure was uncharacteristic of the man. But in light of…

He sighed.

'… *left two dead man back in England,*' the Italian had said.

'Who told you about the two dead men?'

'Well, Friedman…'

'When?'

'What do you mean?'

'Before or after he went back home?'

'Before.'

So the Austrian had known about Martin when...

'And you're sure he said the call came from a man?'

'Yes, Mr. Lamont. That's what he said he was told,' replied the other.

It... A man had called Friedman's people in London, described him as a hitman and now the Italian called him *Lamont*...

'Lamont. That's what Friedman told you my name was?'

'Yes. But I think he guessed this might just be an alias. Hitmen don't go around using their real names, do they?'

He was right. But informants don't usually conceal their target's identity. Unless of course they don't know it, or...

Deborah De Moraes emerged out of the darkness in front of his eyes, all sneer, jewels, impeccable and becoming pink skirt-suit, sheer stockings and black shoes. She might have spoken had the Italian not called, his voice dull and distant.

'If I may ask, just out of curiosity, how is it you're alive? Friedman assured us...'

He swallowed hard, took a second or two to free himself from the sneering woman and got the Italian back into focus.

How come he was alive? Friedman had left on the Wednesday, was on his way to... Martin. He had to owe his life to Martin. Friedman was on his way to London the day he'd stopped at the Delaunay to kill him. That's probably why the Austrian had been sloppy. He was in a hurry. Martin had been found in his kitchen. Yes, that had to be it. He could just imagine the cautious and fastidious Austrian being upset by the news, frantic to get back home to deal with the mess, panicking almost. Yes. Following the anonymous tip-off, hearing a hitman was after him, he must have thought of sending someone to check his Hampstead cottage and... A missing kid and a dead giant in one of his hotels hadn't concerned him enough to precipitate his departure. But that a hitman had got into his quaint cottage and...

'I guess Friedman lied,' he said, satisfied the Austrian had now disappeared for good.

'Evidently,' the other returned; 'And now I guess he'll die. And you too.'

'Is that so?'

'I'm afraid so. It may not be what you intended, but you turned him into a liability, you see? The news that he had a hitman on his tail had already not gone down too well. However, he promised to look after things. But after tonight, well…'

'Maybe he should have sent you to look after things, eh?' Lombard said, glaring at the man's soft lips.

He was being derisive, tried grinning, but his feelings just didn't let him, so he went on speaking:

'I suppose I ought to do him a favour. And one to myself at the same time.'

The Italian understood, shook his head, slowly, like everything else he did.

'Yes. You could kill me,' he said, his calm smooth self; 'But it won't help either of you, really.'

'Really?'

'I'm afraid not. This is bad. Very bad. There are two dead men in the car. You might not know it, but their uniforms are genuine. This is going to lead to a lot of trouble. A lot of questions are going to be asked. A lot of people will be asking *them*. And as I think I already said, someone somewhere always knows something. Somehow, someone somewhere will place you here, Mr. Lamont, or whoever you are. Killing me won't change this. It might buy you a little time. But save you and Friedman? I don't think so…'

Unable to grin, Lombard grimaced. Was that the other's way of begging for life? *'Killing me won't change this…'* Was that really all he was prepared to do or say to save his skin? Too proud to be brave. Too vain to beg or even fight…

Still patting his cheek with his handkerchief, the Italian looked away, all goatee, composed irritation and hatred. Perhaps, since he believed Lombard was a hitman, he was convinced he was about to die, whatever he said or did. Conceivably, dying meant little to him. He could easily be one of those men so arrogant they don't concern themselves with death, shut it out, their own or that of others. He looked fit, lean and strong though, probably exercised regularly, jogged and watched his diet as diligently as he dressed. Could he like himself even more than life? Could he…? He probably did, possibly now and then even indulged in feeling fragile, just so he could like himself that little bit more. People without feelings like to feel fragile, it saves them from having to take a close look at what they are. After all, he carried a photograph of a young woman and two smiling children in his wallet. Had he planned on looking at them later tonight, after having had dinner with people who kept pregnant girls in…?

He still didn't know what to do with him. He…

'Take your shoes and socks off,' he eventually said, running his eyes over the Jeep lying on its side behind the man.

'What?'

There was no way, even with the Italian willing, the two of them could put the heavy vehicle back on its wheels.

'You heard me. Shoes and socks off, scumbag,' Lombard repeated, checking his watch.

It was nearly midnight. Bar a mishap, he could be back in the Ford by five and in Los Angeles with time to spare to catch his flight.

'And hurry up,' he said as the Italian reluctantly squatted down.

The other did what he was told, folded his socks, put them inside his shoes and straightened up.

'Now what?'

It was subtle, but Lombard discerned the change in his voice. Still soft, humming and plaintive almost, it was just that little bit harder than it had been until now. Guessing why was easy. The man felt safe. One doesn't ask a man one is about to kill to take his shoes off, does one?

He was right.

Before he could move – had the Italian thought of moving – Lombard aimed the Browning at his bare right foot and squeezed the trigger.

'Stay here,' he said, turning to walk away from the man who was now minus one big toe.

He wouldn't try running now, nor would he slow him down too much.

No one was coming from the direction of the ranch; peering through the dark from the crater's lip, Lombard found the gate in the fence shut again. He picked up his shoes on his way back to the Jeep and found the Italian sitting on the ground where he'd left him, looking a little shaken but nothing like enough to panic or make a nuisance of himself. His pragmatic self, he was pulling his sock over his injured foot, which he'd also bandaged with his handkerchief.

'Get up and start walking.'

'I believe there's a First-Aid kit in the—'

'Get up, start walking and shut up.'

'I might bleed to…'

He thought better of it, broke off, rose to his feet, followed Lombard's silent signal and started along the track, hobbling, in pain but too proud or smart to moan or groan.

Lombard gave him about a dozen yards headway and started after him, shoes in one hand, Browning in the other.

Under the night sky's stars, they walked in silence, left behind the crater, the hangar and the two cabins. Lombard kept his distance from the Italian who soon enough got used to missing a toe and, treading on his heel, settled into a steady pace. At some time the evening breeze died down and the sounds of their breathing and footsteps became the only life in the hushed open landscape.

Lombard didn't feel good. Exhaustion had come back. Limping, sweating, thirsty and feeling hungry again, he was straining to keep up with the lame Italian. But rather than make the other slow down, focusing on his back, he used him as a pacemaker. The sooner they reached the road the better, for his mind had also started to play tricks on him, or rather, was stuck with Deborah De Moraes. He had only himself to blame for this. Walking away from the Jeep, he'd conjured her back, to run and rerun every conversation they'd ever had, until satisfied he'd found all there was to be found in her words. Only, when he'd finished with her, she'd refused to go, not quite commandeering his mind but clinging to the background, forbidding him to relax and focus on nothing but following the Italian, which in his state was proving testing. Now he could see her, voluptuous and threatening, and now hear her, petulant and scornful. And more significantly perhaps, a particular set of her words, like a haunting refrain, kept turning in his head, words he'd first recalled the previous day while still in Grand City Hospital.

'... or is the job too formidable for you, Mr. Lombard...?'

He didn't want to, had no wish to hear the Italian's soft humming voice again, liked him just as he was, a silent, faceless, meaningless hobbling figure in a suit setting the pace. But Deborah De Moraes...

'What's going on back there?'

The Italian stayed silent.

'You heard me, scumbag.'

'I heard you,' the man's soft voice drifted across the silent sands.

'So? What's with the pregnant girls? You people have decided to do away with shipping kids from Central America? Is that it? You breed them now?'

'I...' the other pronounced after a long silence; 'We're both a long way from home, *Francese*. What you saw back there has nothing to do with me.'

'You mean you and Friedman came here for the peace and sunshine, is that it?'

'No. But it still has nothing to do with me. Or Friedman. You can always go back and ask *thm* if you don't believe me.'

Lombard frowned.

'Ask who?'

'The people running things back there.'

'I'm asking you.'

Again, the Italian took some time before replying:

'I'm here as a guest.'

'A guest?'

'Yes.'

'What kind of a guest?'

Now the other sighed. He heard him all of twelve yards away.

'What kind of a guest?' he repeated.

'An observer.'

'What?'

'What you saw back there is a kind of pilot scheme,' said the other reluctantly; 'Friedman, myself and others have been invited to observe what they are doing.'

Glaring, Lombard nodded his nod, understanding.

'Go on.'

'It's an interesting idea,' the Italian said.

'You think so?'

'Yes and no. Bringing third-world children to where the money is can be expensive and hazardous. It makes the idea of producing the supply where the demand is an interesting proposition. But as I told *thm*, it's not really feasible in Europe. In America and Russia, perhaps. But not in Europe. We don't have space like here. And also, our country people talk.'

Lombard thought of the pregnant girls, the surgery, the satellite dishes in the sands far beyond him now. The ranch probably had its own in-house doctor or surgeon, kept in communication with a select network of doctors and lawyers, men like the hobbling Italian in front of him.

'What's with the military? They're selling protection?'

'What else? And they also come to fuck the girls.'

'How convenient.'

'No one's complaining.'

'No. Least of all the girls, I guess, eh?' Lombard said.

'They're happy.'

'Is that why they're being kept doped-up?'

'You sound offended,' the other said; 'Anyway, they're not encouraged to take drugs. And it would be better if they didn't. They're bored, that's all. But they're happy,' he repeated; 'And why not? They're getting well-paid for very little work.'

'You mean they choose to be there?'

'I mean, between having to fuck clients every night and being looked after for nine months, what would you choose?'

'Is that the choice?'

'They're whores. I believe, for *thm* it is, yes...'

Thm. The Italian spoke as good English as Lombard, his accent was possibly even less pronounced but, not for the first time now, he had swallowed the 'e' in the word 'them', as if he'd been taught to pronounce it like that. Or was it just an affectation? Like his soft, humming nauseating voice? *Thm*...

He clenched his teeth. Did the man find it so easy to talk about all this because he believed Lombard was a hitman, earned his living killing, therefore couldn't possibly care? Or was this just his normal self?

'So what are you? Friedman's slimy Italian counterpart?'

'No. I have nothing to do with Friedman. And I'm certainly not his counterpart…'

Lombard nodded, believing him. He was a lawyer, dealt with a different clientele. Friedman supplied perverts, he…

'No. You're a failed lawyer, right? Yours is the adoption business, is that it?'

The Italian remained silent again and, although he could only see his back, Lombard knew the man was thinking, wondering how he'd guessed. Something in his wallet, he probably told himself. The *Francese* had seen something in his wallet…

'You're a lawyer, aren't you?'

'Yes. I'm a lawyer…'

Of course he was. He found children for desperate childless Italian couples. A lawyer, he knew the ropes, knew at which doors to knock, how to fix the paperwork. Or was he into unearthing organ donors for the unscrupulous wealthy? Or immoral surgeons? On any one day, how many thousands of people awaited a replacement organ? Awaited what would turn a certain death or a life of discomfort into just life? Lombard had once known the figures, once known the price of a kidney or a heart or a liver graft. Right now though, he could only remember that the demand far exceeded the supply. But what did it matter? What did numbers amount to anyway? They were meaningless. Just like the amount of money the wealthy were prepared to pay for life and comfort. Or what they were prepared to look away from when it came to saving themselves. The desire to live can make everything meaningless, everything disappear. As can the desire to die. Or that of having children when you can't have them. The Italian was a lawyer. A middleman. A businessman. Just a soup merchant, really. Although he didn't sell soup. But Like Friedman, like José, he…

'*Che cosa c'e? Mamma e Papa non ti hanno lasciato abbastanza soldi quando morirono? O stai ancora aspettando l'eredità?*'

How much time elapsed before the Italian replied, Lombard couldn't tell. And didn't care. All of a sudden he no longer felt tired, no longer felt anything, just the heat in his nape, and his right arm and hand. This, he knew, was only because of the weight of the Browning. Like his nape, the gun's grip felt hot.

And clammy, with sweat. Yes. He no longer felt anything. He didn't quite understand why it should occur now, but recognised what was happening. In a moment…

'*Parli bene Italiano,*' the man said; 'And ask a lot of questions for a man who earns a living killing people… I'm a businessman, *Francese*. What are you, eh?'

'You'd rather not know what I am,' he heard himself say.

'Why?' he heard the other ask; 'Aren't you like everybody else?'

'And what is that?'

'What do you think?'

'You'd rather not know what I think.'

'Yes. Maybe you're right…'

This one wasn't even going to try to defend or justify himself. This one, unlike the Martins and Josés who perhaps had had to work hard to become what they were, had no worries or qualms. There was nothing wrong with what he did. That was it. Huh… There where many more questions he ought to ask him. Did he and Friedman belong to the same organisation? Who were they? Was the ranch part of it? What happened to the girls once they'd delivered their babies? Were they let loose or…

But he could guess all that. And what if he was wrong? What did it matter? It didn't mean anything. Nothing meant anything. Not even the life of the man hobbling under the starlight in front of him.

'Money—money—money…' the other's soft voice hummed across the silence.

'What?'

'Life's not like in the movies. Money. We all do what we must for money…'

He was too proud to be brave. And he wasn't even a cripple, like…

It happened just like when José, sitting at his restaurant table with the other five, told him what they'd done to little Pierre. He stopped hearing. Stopped thinking. Stopped questioning. Everything was flat…

He raised his arm. The Browning felt very heavy. The head in front of him moved left and right, up and down, as the body below it hobbled, and he trained his gun onto it, until the two became one, inextricable.

Thump…

He walked past the body lying across the track without looking at it, already counting his strides.

'Six. Sept…'

Movies. The movies again… *'Life's not like in the movies,'* the Italian had said. What else was he supposed to have done? What would he have done if this was a movie, eh? Headed back to the ranch? Killed all the bad guys? Saved all the good guys? Yeah…

'Quatorze. Quinze. Seize…'

He had not called Jane yet.

'Dix-neuf. Vingt…'

News of three dead men and a secluded ranch full of pregnant girls appeared to have little if any effect on the Los Angeles cop on night duty at the other end of the line. The man most certainly didn't sound impressed, let alone amazed. Suspicious, dismissive, resentful? Perhaps. Concerned? Hardly.

'I hear you, Mister,' the man said; 'But you don't seem to hear me too well, so I'll say it again: Barstow and its vicinity is outside LAPD jurisdiction. So, unless you're just a funny guy with a bad sense of humour, call the Barstow police, all right? Otherwise go to bed.'

Lombard sighed, noting the road sign which had just appeared in his headlights on the road ahead. 'LOS ANGELES, 110 MILES', it read.

He'd already told the man, but still…

'Maybe you hear me right, but you seem to have a problem with processing the information,' he said, wedging the Italian's cell-phone in the crook of his neck to light a cigarette; 'So here it is again. Since these people enjoy the protection of the local military, there's a strong possibility they might enjoy the same of the local police. I'm not saying they do, but it's a possibility.'

'Is it now? A possibility, eh? Well,' the police officer replied, blasé; 'In that case why don't you call the FBI? Or is there a possibility they too might be involved?'

Frowning, Lombard pocketed his lighter.

'Okay,' he declared; 'Whether or not you follow up on this is your problem. You know where to find the ranch and the Jeep. If you move on it before dawn you might just catch them unawares. If you don't, they'll probably clear out within an hour of discovering their dead soldier friends. Either way, it's all the same to me.'

And he cut-off the communication, cursed between his teeth and tossed the cell-phone out the car window.

A few minutes later, driving past yet another seemingly endless chain-link fence, he also threw out the Browning and the Italian's passport. The Los Angeles cop would probably pass on his story to the Barstow police who, in turn, may or may not bother to send a patrol car to check out the track to the ranch...

'Merde,' he muttered, biting on his Gitane; 'Merde...'

At least he'd changed suit. At least he was dry, no longer sweating. And driving was easy, even if his shoes felt too tight on his sore feet. He'd tried driving barefoot but found it too awkward.

Just before reaching San Bernardino, he stopped to fill up at a petrol station and could have picked up two young girl hitchhikers.

'Excuse me,' they accosted him as he made his way back to the Ford; 'We're on our way to LA and...'

A moment earlier, paying for his fuel, he'd noticed them climbing out of a truck. They were young, carried rucksacks, wore Jeans and hiking boots. The one who'd spoken had red hair and freckles. The other was a tall blonde with big shoulders. Lombard had peered into their sparkling country eyes, gazed at their friendly smiles, guessed they were on their way to the big city in search of adventure or decadence perhaps. They would have made for light and pleasant company but...

'I'm sorry. I'm stopping just about a mile from here,' he lied.

Driving away, watching them make for the station shop in his rear-view mirror, he recalled he still had one of Nathalie's blue sleeping pills. At least he'd sleep on his flight back to London...

SIXTEEN

Patrick Walton was in his thirties, tubby, with hooked finger-nails, hairy ears and vacant but keen eyes which, unless he frowned, gave him the air of a self-indulgent adolescent. Speaking in an even and cordial middle-class voice, he also had a fondness for the word 'incredible' – or variations of it – which somehow found its way into nearly every sentence that came out of his small round mouth. Still, unusual nails and hairy ears aside, he was one of those men one hardly notices and who, on first meeting, one would be hard-pressed to dislike. He might talk too much but came across as too earnest and benevolent to be thought of as anything other than perhaps a nuisance. He was born and bred in England but his mother, in her occupation as a cosmetic surgeon, had moved to Los Angeles where he'd just spent a couple of weeks 'convalescing' after causing the death of a young woman cyclist in a road accident somewhere in the Cornish countryside. The incident had occurred six weeks earlier. Coming out of a sharp bend in his Rover, he'd found himself confronted with an oncoming lane-straggling coach on one side and the cyclist on the other. He had not been speeding but, in his own words, his only choice had been between a head-on collision with the coach or getting out of its way. He hadn't really thought about it, simply swerved away from the coach and hit the bike with fateful consequences. The coach driver, possibly unaware of what had happened, had not stopped, leaving him alone to deal with the situation and the police who, like everyone else, had proved 'incredibly' kind and understanding. Still, the experience had left him badly shaken, haunted by the picture of the dead woman as well as racked with guilt. Why had he veered so easily towards the cyclist? He'd only followed instinct, of course, for there had been no time to make a conscious decision. But why had he not even hesitated? What did it say about him? For all he knew, had he kept his cool, he just might have managed to squeeze between both coach and cyclist. He just might. But he'd never know, knew only that, fearing for his life, he'd swerved and killed a young woman. Accordingly, he'd stopped sleeping, been put on tranquillisers, taken time off work and, after a couple of gloomy weeks at home, decided he had better get away to stay at his mother's in Los Angeles. Whether the trip had done him much good was hard to say. Perhaps it had, perhaps it hadn't. In any case, sitting on the plane next to a tired but polite Lombard, he appeared to be heavily sedated, was undeniably troubled and talked non-stop, eventually revealing that, after his time away from home, he wasn't really looking forward to going back, for it turned out that, as he rather modestly put it, there were 'long-standing problems with the wife there', problems made all the more awkward by the fact that he loved their two young children dearly. So, everything considered, he himself wasn't too sure whether his prevailing distress had more to do with his road accident or the prospect of going back to his wife. And what did that say about him?

All this apart, waiting for Nathalie's sleeping pill to take effect, Lombard also found out that Patrick Walton was in television but really thought of himself as a music video director, that his wife was a GP and that, after what had happened, the man doubted he'd ever be able to sit behind a steering wheel again, which, if nothing else, wouldn't improve things, least of all his married life.

No. Patrick Walton wasn't the sort of man one should easily dislike. He'd accidentally caused the death of a young woman, was tormented by it and returning home to a troubled marriage. Maybe, in the circumstances, he was doing the best he could. Most likely, soon, he'd find a way of coming to terms with his accident, start driving again, just because he would simply have to, merely to go on living, in order not to make complicated things more complicated, so he could go on loving and looking after his children. And why not? He didn't deserve to suffer. The most remarkable things about him were his hooked fingernails and hairy ears. What good could suffering bring him?

He bade Lombard a friendly goodbye as they got off the plane into the cold rain falling over Heathrow.

'And good luck,' he said.

'Yeah. The same to you.'

At 16:30, the sky over England was already dark, yet everything looked sharp and crisp to Lombard, as things sometimes do when one steps back into the world following a few days in bed with the flu. Perhaps it was because he'd slept, or perhaps, in an odd way, Patrick Walton had helped him relax. Then again, it could simply be that he was home again. And it was raining.

Once safely through customs, he took off the tie he'd put on in order to look respectable before leaving the plane, unbuttoned his shirt collar, called Rhian's sister, welcomed the news that all was well in Wales, would have tried Jane but remembered it was Tuesday and she didn't usually get back from work until seven, remained in the airport lounge long enough to buy ten packs of Gitanes and a coffee, made for the car-park and, having retrieved Leonard Spitz's contact sheet from the trunk of his Triumph, put away his suitcase and started towards the driver's door.

The 8 by 10 sheet of photographic paper in his hand was still damp, had curled since he'd last held it, but almost at once, examining its six strips of 35 millimetre shots in the dim light of the concrete car-park, he realised why the photographs of the tramp had inexplicably come back to haunt him while, still in his Los Angeles hospital bed, he had tried and failed to figure out why Rhian's mention of Leonard's bruise had left him so perturbed.

'Nom de...' he muttered, unable to contain himself, stopping at the Triumph's door.

It was no wonder that, lacking the contact sheet, he'd failed to give its recollection meaning. Not knowing what to make of it or what to look for, he'd focused on the tramp. It had been a mistake. As it happened, the poor man was of no significance, while the same could not be said of his location. The photographs showed the well wrapped up, bag-ladden vagrant trudging on the grass just inside a park boundary fence along a busy road. It called for verification, but trusting memory, Lombard felt sure Mrs. Spitz's son had come across his tramp in no other place than Finsbury Park. It was the fence along which the man was plodding. He knew it. Chest-high, made of ornate black cast-iron stakes, it looked just like the one he himself had stood by the night he'd waited across the road from the Ambassador for Martin to return from the dentist. It was only a park fence perhaps, as such could have belonged to any one of London's parks, but he was familiar enough with the city to know there weren't many Victorian fences like it left around London, and besides, now that he looked closely, the wide thoroughfare beyond it could easily pass for that stretch of Seven Sisters Road where Friedman's hotels stood. Just like it, this was lined with large detached buildings, a clash of the new and the old, one of which also bore a large sign above its entrance. The something 'CREST' or something 'CROSS HOTEL' it read; the letters were out of focus and too small to be made out with certainty, but some of them distinctly spelt the word 'HOTEL'.

Clearly, yet again too engrossed with Friedman, looking but not observing, he had failed to see any of this when he'd last held the contact sheet. Yet, clearly, his subconscious had proved more discerning, despite himself had registered and stored the familiar scenery beyond the tramp.

Would it have remained buried undisturbed inside his mind had Rhian not mentioned Leonard's bruise and his subsequent overnight stay in Finsbury Park police station?

'*Hein!*' he let out, then swallowed hard before unlocking the Triumph door.

The car's interior was still clammy, still reeked of stale cigarette ash, but settling behind the steering wheel, he hardly noticed, or cared. He tossed the contact sheet onto the pile of newspapers on the passenger seat, wound down his window, switched on the ignition and, as the engine roared into life, glaring, reached into his pockets for his cigarettes and lighter.

Leonard had turned up to deliver his boy with a bruise on his cheek, Rhian had said. He'd been taking pictures in a market, been hit by an angry stall-holder, retaliated and ended up in Finsbury Park police station. This suggested two things: Leonard's market spat had taken place in the Finsbury Park area and, given that his bruise was still showing when he got to Wales, had to have occurred not long before he'd purchased his boy.

How long did a bruise take to come and go? A week? Two

perhaps? Whatever. Not long enough. It just…

'*Hein!*' he growled, clenching his fist around his lighter after lighting a Gitane.

There was no way Leonard could have brought himself to snap happily away at stall holders and tramps in Finsbury Park or indeed anywhere else if at the time he'd known about Friedman and his trade, let alone his connection with the area. Nor would he have allowed himself to get into trouble with the police by getting into a fight while 'little-boys-for-sale' churned inside his mind. Never. Not Mrs. Spitz's susceptible, emotional and reclusive son. Not he who on finding out about such things had felt bound to embark on a reckless if not suicidal rescue mission. It was just not on, not feasible, and so raised the question: could Leonard Spitz really have learned of, contacted and convinced Friedman to sell him a boy and then raised the cash to complete the transaction in the matter of a few days, or a week or two, or anyway in less time than it takes for a bruise to come and go?

Scowling through his windscreen, Lombard nodded his nod. He didn't buy it. It was just as he'd suspected before he left for America, and tallied with the only way what had happened since and all the pieces of the puzzle could be made to add up to something that made sense, however many pieces were still missing. Leonard had lied to Rhian. He'd known of the Austrian and got his hands on one of his boys all right, but he'd probably never met the former and never paid for the latter. He'd got the boy some other way. Through somebody else. Just as…

Lombard sighed, turned to the passenger seat. All the time, right inside his car, almost right under his nose, had he looked a little harder he just might have…

He reached angrily for the contact sheet, flicked on his lighter to have another look at the six strips of six photographs in the glow of the flame dancing in the cold damp car-park air wafting in through his open window. The top three rows showed bleak park landscapes. The tramp made his first appearance in the middle of the fourth strip, trudged along the fence until the last shot of the last strip where, aware of the photographer, he swore towards the camera, still walking. If Leonard had taken these shots around the same time as he acquired his bruise, if the road behind the fence was indeed the Seven Sisters Road…

Without warning, fear and rage briefly shattered his thoughts. Together. It was intuition. He'd just recalled how come he'd ended up with the contact sheet, how, searching for something to write on while on the phone in Leonard's darkroom, he'd picked it up from a nearby pile of more of the same, a pile amongst many other piles.

'… *Or is the job too formidable for you, Mr. Lombard,*' the voice echoed inside his forehead.

A moment later, he let his lighter go out, flicked his half-burnt cigarette out the window and checked his watch. It was still set to Los Angeles time.

He glared towards his dashboard and reset it against the car's clock. It was 17:10.

Just over two hours after leaving Heathrow to make his way across town in the early evening rush hour, he pulled up in front of Friedman's Hampstead cottage and left his engine running. There was no need for him to get out. Through the rain, the quaint little house sat in darkness. Its front driveway where once a car had sat under a tarpaulin was empty. The curtains that had hung in the windows and the alarm box he'd shot at on the facade were also gone. Friedman had made off, decided to call it a day. This was no surprise, but that the Austrian had bothered to clear the place out was more unexpected. Yet, judging by the missing curtains, in the four days since returning from Los Angeles, that's exactly what the man had done. However Martin's body had been disposed of – then again it could still be lying somewhere inside the house – he'd packed up, called the removers and cleared the place out. Either he'd been loath to forsake his precious furniture and paintings or, ever cautious, was bent on leaving nothing incriminating behind.

Briefly, surveying the nearby houses' lit-up windows, Lombard considered stepping out into the rain to knock at a few doors. In such a quiet and well-to-do street, the emptying of the cottage could not have gone unnoticed. One or more of the neighbours had probably watched with suspicious eyes and, just in case, asked questions or made a note of the removal firm's name, for it was likely Friedman had called professionals to do the job. Apart from ensuring the proper handling of his valued possessions, it would have reassured the neighbourhood; nothing causes alarm amongst the well-off like the presence of an unmarked van in their streets, let alone an unmarked van being filled with the contents of a house. Still, following up on it was bound to prove a waste of time. Even in a hurry, Friedman would have made certain he couldn't be tracked down through the removers. His furniture and paintings were probably in storage, under a bogus name and contact address.

Friedman had disappeared for good.

A couple of minutes after pulling away from Friedman's, as it was so near and as finding the cottage empty had made him realise that, however unlikely, others might also decide to pack up, Lombard turned into Templeton Road and cruised slowly past the De Moraes' residence, searching the long bleak two-storey building perched on the sloping lawn behind its open gate.

Someone was home. Light shone from most of the windows and, although Deborah De Moraes' Aston Martin was nowhere to be seen along the gravel drive lined with potted trees, the red Ferrari which had been there on his first visit sat by the flight of steps leading up to the house.

At 19:45, crawling with the traffic along the Seven Sisters Road, he steered past the Diplomat and the Ambassador. Both hotels were closed, their windows and signs lying in darkness. He hadn't really thought about it before but, since Friedman had found it necessary to leave in a hurry, it wasn't surprising that whoever was now in charge of business had decided to shut the hotels down. As for the park boundary fence across the road from their lifeless facades, it was the one along which Leonard Spitz had followed his tramp all right – a hundred or so yards past the Ambassador, a bright blue and white neon sign gleaming in the rain read 'BLUE CROSS HOTEL'.

Lombard drove straight past it, intent on turning left towards Balls Pond and Essex Road at the junction with Blackstock Road near the Finsbury Park bus terminal. However, he recalled that, on his way to Heathrow a week earlier, he'd made a detour via Highgate to return Leonard's video player and to wipe Rhian's messages from the answer-phone. Leonard's keys were still in the Triumph's glove compartment, which was just as well, because he'd sooner not go home. Not yet. Not until he'd finished what he'd come back to do.

The penthouse apartment still lay heavy with the smell of developing chemicals, its air was hot and stifling and a thick layer of condensation misted every window. The central heating had been turned right up again. Somebody, clearly sensitive to the cold, had been there since his last visit and begun packing Leonard's life away into cardboard boxes. The shelves that had held books, compact discs, videotapes and cassettes were empty, most surfaces had been cleared and the walls were bare, the grim girlie pictures which had hung everywhere now sitting in a neat pile near the front door in the parqueted hallway, as if the person in charge of the packing, disapproving of them perhaps, had found it proper to mark them for first removal. Still, apart from stripping down the previously blacked-out windows, he or she had not started on the darkroom yet. It was just as Lombard had left it – a clutter of camera and printing equipment and the floor littered with sweet wrappers, negatives and photographic paper. And, of course, everywhere, piles of photographs and contact sheets.

It took no time at all. He found what he was looking for amongst the pile of contact sheets within arm's reach of the wall-mounted telephone just inside the darkroom door. Arranging the dozen or so relevant sheets in chronological order proved simple, merely a matter of allowing the strips of prints to tell their story, which revealed that Leonard had indeed come across his tramp the day after his night in police custody.

An autumn sun had shone over London the previous day, which was possibly what had led Mrs. Spitz's son to go on the prowl with his camera. Whether by chance or design, he'd found himself in Hackney, snapping away at the crowds and stalls in Ridley Road market. Then, walking, he'd headed for Stoke

Newington and Clissold Park, taking more pictures along the way, mostly of women with shopping bags and babies. At one of Clissold Park's two small lakes, a grey-bearded fisherman in a leather cap with fur flaps had caught his attention; over two dozen shots taken from various angles showed the stony-faced man sitting on a stool in front of a couple of rods stretching over the water, ostensibly indifferent to being photographed. Satisfied he was done with the fisherman, Leonard had moved on, returned to the streets to snap yet more Londoners and also bus queues and shop fronts, eventually winding up in Blackstock Road, as indicated by the road sign on the rundown facade of an abandoned fishmonger's shop he'd felt merited recording. It was there, or thereabouts, that he'd met with trouble, although Rhian had got one detail wrong. The man he'd upset was not a market stall-holder but a street-trader selling vegetables from an old canopied wooden cart stationed in front of a pub. A couple of wide-angle shots showed the gloved and scarfed middle-aged man reading a newspaper beside his cart in the late afternoon sunlight; another three close-ups focused on his attractive display of vegetables and then, as if Leonard had moved or been jostled while triggering his camera, one shot was just a blur, and led to a shot showing the front steps and door of Finsbury Park police station in dull grey light.

The poor light in this and the following shots leading up to the tramp's appearance suggested they had been taken the next day and – judging by the calm demeanour of the pedestrians and the moderate volume of traffic on the road – at some time after the morning rush-hour. On being released, Leonard had stopped outside the police station, for whatever perverse reason taken a shot of it, then rejoined the street to once again stroll about snapping away at whatever took his fancy, finally ending up with the tramp in Finsbury Park where, doubtless the wiser after his last experience, he'd left the man alone after being sworn at. The vagrant was nowhere to be seen on any other contact sheet, but Lombard had found the next in the sequence. It was easy, because after letting go of the vagrant, Leonard had gone on taking pictures along the fence. Here he'd captured an old lady walking a small dog wearing a coat. There, a few shots of an overflowing park garbage bin. And then, still inside the park fence but almost right opposite the Ambassador's windows, he'd taken several shots of a clamped car being lifted onto the back of a double-parked tow-truck that had created severe traffic congestion…

'Hello?' Jane's voice echoed in the receiver.

'How are you, Jane?' Lombard said, scowling at shots of the clamped car on the contact sheet he held under his eyes.

'*Savieer!* Hi. What happened? I was waiting for you to call yesterday. What…'

'I was busy. Did you do what—'

'Yes. Where are you? Still in Los Angeles?'

'No. I'm in London. So? Did you makes the calls?'

'Er, yes. But I'm afraid I didn't do too well. It's not my fault though. About half the names you gave me simply refused to talk to me. They said—'

He could guess what they'd said, cut her off:

'Just tell me what those who talked said, if they said anything.'

'Right. Only one could remember recommending you to a friend of his. Wait, I've got it all written down. Just a moment.'

He put an unlit Gitane between his lips, listening to what sounded like papers being shuffled at the other end of the line.

'Yeah. Here,' Jane came back; 'He's called Pierre Dreyer. He said he had dinner with a friend of his about a month ago who asked him if he knew of—'

'If you don't mind, I'm only interested in the friend's name, Jane,' he cut in, softly.

'Right. His name is Carlos *De Morays*. Apparently he's Brazilian and a racing car driver. I asked the guy called Pierre Dreyer how well…'

Lombard stopped listening, closed his eyes and nodded. He might have guessed, if nothing else when at long last he'd worked out from Los Angeles that Leonard had already delivered his boy to Wales by the time Deborah De Moraes' husband had claimed he'd turned up in Hampstead to borrow money for an exhibition…

It could have been so easy. Too easy perhaps. And what's more, Pierre Dreyer was the London-based general manager of a French company that made racing car engines.

'*Savieer?*'

'Yeah?'

'So? Is that helpful to you at all?'

'Yes Jane,' he said; 'It's helpful to me. Thank you. I'll see you later.'

She started speaking but he hung up, searching for something positive to think about. It soon came. It wasn't much but it was something; at least now it was safe to think the old Spitzes weren't involved in their son's murder. He didn't know why, but it made him feel better. Perhaps it was because of what he'd made of Mrs. Spitz's worried mother's eyes; he wouldn't have liked to have been wrong about that too. He'd made enough mistakes.

He took one last long look at the contact sheet in his hand. Half way along the second row, just after the shots of the clamped car being lifted onto the tow-truck, was the first of a series of medium and close-up shots of a blue Aston Martin DB5 parked along a kerb. Its number-plate read 'DDM 5'. Lombard had not paid any attention to the plate on Deborah De Moraes' car, but how many blue Aston Martin DB5s could there be in London? And what where the odds against any blue Aston Martin DB5 owner other than Mrs. Deborah De Moraes also having a select number-plate displaying what happened to be her initials? And if it wasn't his sister's car, why had Leonard Spitz stopped to take so many photographs of it? Judging by his other photographs, cars were not his thing.

Lombard lit the Gitane still between his lips, folded the contact sheet and pocketed it. The Aston Martin could only be Deborah's. Leonard had caught sight of it while looking through his camera towards the tow-truck, had left the park and crossed the Seven Sisters Road towards it, to make sure perhaps. Once there, he'd stood too close to his sister's car for it to be possible to guess its location from the photographs alone, but examining the preceding shots, it had been just possible to make out its singular shape earlier; it was parked just around the corner from the Ambassador, in a narrow side street, access to which lay a mere few yards from the car being lifted off the road, and doubtless it would have remained hidden by passing traffic had the tow truck not obstructed the road and kept the lane in front of it clear. Using one of Leonard's magnifying blocks, one could also just about make out its distinct number-plate.

Leonard had recognised his sister's Aston Martin and for some reason decided to hang around it, killing time photographing its handsome lines. Had he been waiting for his sister to return? The contact sheet gave no clue. The last shot was of the car. Perhaps Leonard had run out of film or, simply tired, had decided to call it a day and gone home.

Before leaving, Lombard stopped in the kitchen, flicked his cigarette into the sink, filled a coffee mug with tap water and drank, slowly. The apartment's dry, stifling air had caused him to feel parched. He thought of turning down the central heating, but remembered he didn't know where the thermostat was.

It was 20:20.

'I'm afraid Mr. De Moraes is away in Brazil until tomorrow and Mrs. De Moraes is out and not expected back until nine-thirty,' said Lawrence, standing stiffly in the doorway.

As usual, the butler made no effort to conceal the fact he wasn't pleased to see him, the frown above the indifferent eyes on either side of his long nose making him look almost angry.

'Is that so?' said Lombard, standing in the rain outside the front door; 'Well, that's strange, because your mistress was expecting me here at eight-thirty. I suppose I might as well wait.'

The butler looked him up and down, peered towards the gravel drive, as if searching for his car. Only the Ferrari was there.

'I left the car out in the street,' Lombard let him know, with a dry grin; 'Now, are you going to let me in or leave me out here in the rain?'

'I'm sorry, but I do not recall Mrs. De Moraes mentioning anything about expecting you, Mr. Lombard.'

'Well, then she must have forgotten. Or maybe she just didn't get around to telling you about it. But I had her on the phone a couple of hours ago and I can assure you that...'

He was improvising. Seeing the Ferrari, he'd assumed someone was home. He could have gone to wait in his car until Deborah's return, but he didn't feel like being alone with his thoughts. Besides, he'd just had an idea.

The butler dithered, clearly would rather have not allowed

him in, but eventually did just that. After all, what reason could Lombard have for lying about an appointment?

'Would you mind wiping your feet, sir,' he said, reluctantly standing aside to let Lombard through the door.

'Thank you.'

For the third time since they'd become acquainted, he followed the butler across the vast white marble hall, past its curving staircase, abstract paintings and tubular sculptures and, just as had happened on the two previous occasions, the man opened the door to the drawing room, stood aside and gestured for him to step in.

'Would you like a drink while you wait, Mr. Lombard?'

'No. Thank you. I'll just read a magazine if its all right with you,' Lombard said, moving past the butler before turning around to face him; 'By the way, Lawrence, were you here the last time your mistress's brother came over? You know, just before he disappeared?'

The man sent him one of his looks:

'I work here, sir. I'm here most of the time.'

'Yes, I know, someone's got to open doors. You wouldn't recall if the brothers-in-law left together on that occasion, would you?'

'You will have to ask Mr. De Moraes that, sir,' came the reply, crisp and icy.

'I see. Then perhaps you could tell me if you recall whether Leonard had a bruise on his face that day?'

The man sighed, thought for a second, decided it was all right for him to answer that particular question.

'Yes. I believe he did.'

'I see. Oh well, poor Leonard. I suppose Mrs. De Moraes must have taken it hard, eh?'

The man sent him a blank look.

'I'm sorry, sir. I don't understand.'

'Her brother's death, Lawrence. I'm talking about her brother's death. Haven't you heard about it?'

Lawrence decided this deserved nothing more than an icy stare, turned away and closed the door, pronouncing:

'You may dial 0–0–0 on the telephone if you happen to change your mind about the drink, sir.'

Moments later, Lombard stepped back into the empty hall. From somewhere behind a half-open door at the end of a long corridor, the butler could be heard chatting with an old woman over what sounded like kitchen activities, too far off for Lombard to make much of his faint words.

He checked his watch – it was 20:50 – carefully shut the drawing room door, crept across the hall's marble floor and up the curving staircase.

The two-storey house was surprisingly larger than its dull modern exterior suggested. The stairway emerged central to an extensive square landing. As many as twelve doors, evenly spaced around the four white walls, each flanked with abstract paintings of equal size and set in identical black metal frames, made for perfect symmetry, so that each face of the square mirrored the other three.

Lombard paused briefly at the top of the stairs to scowl at his surroundings and, moving quickly, proceeded from door to door, glancing into each room along the way until he found what he took to be the De Moraeses' bedroom.

He walked in leaving the door open behind him.

He'd guessed wrong, spent hardly any time there. With its pastel green carpet, metal ornaments, glass surfaces, television set and double-bed dressed in black sheets, it proved to be the bedroom of the man of the house. As it turned out, Carlos and Deborah De Moraes slept in separate connecting bedrooms, each equally spacious and with its own en-suite bathroom. But that was where the similarity ended. Amidst the cold, expensive modern decor that characterised the house, Mrs. De Moraes' room was a world unto itself, all flamboyance and old opulence. The predominant colour was red, the fabrics rich and velvet, the bed a canopied four-poster of carved wood. Surveying the antique furniture, the rugs on the floor, the oil landscapes on the walls, Lombard, concerned though he was with other matters, couldn't help but ask himself how someone with such taste could have contributed to the overall look of the rest of the house, let alone enjoy it. Then again, perhaps Mrs. De Moraes didn't care, was only interested in her own private chamber, glad to surrender every other corner of her abode to interior designers, or to her husband's taste perhaps.

He settled for the interior designers after catching sight of the gold-framed oil portrait that hung opposite her bed. The largest painting in the room, it showed Deborah De Moraes from the hips up standing in a tight black sleeveless dress against a dark background. Bejewelled, she gazed at the world, all poise, pearls, curves and brazen sensuality. The painter had done her looks justice while being true to his subject – which given its nature was perhaps not so difficult – even faithfully reproducing the dusky down shading the olive skin near her ears. Admiring her, while also ruling out the possibility of her allowing her husband to impose his taste on their home, Lombard, who with reason had thought he remembered her well, realised he'd actually forgotten what a striking sight she was and, before turning away to concentrate on her room, he swallowed hard, teeth clenched.

Soon afterwards, when he made his way back to the drawing room, he had a clearer idea of what hid behind her handsome looks. Nothing he'd learned upstairs had come as much of a surprise, or, bar one thing perhaps, was in itself very significant. Mainly, a few suspicions had been confirmed. Still, reduced as he was to trusting instinct and making speculations based on circumstantial evidence, every little thing that bolstered his theory was welcome.

Deborah De Moraes both smoked and drank in bed; a clean ashtray, a glass and a half-empty bottle of Gin sat beside a small radio on her bedside table, along with a few packs of cigarettes, paper tissues, earplugs, headache and toothache medicines and various labelled bottle of pills. Some of the names on the labels were unknown to Lombard, but those he recognised, *Temazepan*, *Nitrazepam* and *Diazepam*, he knew to be tranquillisers and sleeping pills.

A search through the drawers of a dressing table, buried beneath a wealth of cosmetics and perfumes, had revealed yet more cosmetics and several silver caskets and trays of jewellery items, as well as many Fabergé eggs. Also, one of the drawers – which for a few seconds had left Lombard wondering just what he was looking at – turned out to be crammed with hundreds if not thousands of lipsticks, encompassing, if this was at all possible, as many shades of red. The bedroom boasted two walk-in closets. The largest was devoted to coats, shoes, dresses, suits and shirts. The other, smaller but still the size of an average bedroom, was filled on one side with jumpers, socks and tights, and, the length of the other, with lingerie, a lot of it, some which could be called plain and utilitarian, most which could only be termed seductive. The items were either white or black and many had clearly never been worn, still bore their shop and price tags. Peering into a few shopping bags on the floor, Lombard came across yet more, and then ended his search in the en-suite bathroom which, considering the size of the closets, had turned out to be unexpectedly plain and narrow and was fitted with a small hip bath such as he'd not seen since leaving Paris. Water droplets on its white enamel and a damp red towel laying over the side suggested it had been used fairly recently. The tile floor was also sprinkled with a white powder, which he guessed came from the talcum shaker standing on the rim of the washbasin. The medicine cabinet had turned out to contain the usual everyday medicines and remedies, including, somewhat oddly, many different brands of cough syrup. Then, pulling open the drawers of a low commode next to the toilet bowl, Lombard had eventually come across boxes of tampons and panty liners, stood gazing at them for a moment, and then decided it was time to make his way back downstairs.

'Clunk' went the door when he pulled it shut it behind him.

He lit a Gitane, snapped his lighter shut and pocketed it, slowly running his eyes over the drawing room in front of him. He didn't really look at the black marble walls, the strange metal and leather furnishings or the weird sculpture of gleaming tubes that hung from the dark ceiling with its tiny star-like spotlights. He merely gazed across it all, until his eyes found the flames that swayed softly in the fireplace beyond the glass table he'd sat at with the old Spitzes less than two weeks earlier.

Against the wall to his left hung a photograph of Carlos De Moraes. He knew. He couldn't see it from where he stood but remembered it was there. Mr. De Moraes was smiling – no, beaming; a beautiful, healthy and triumphant dark Adonis on a podium, garland of flowers around his strong neck, Magnum of Champagne in his tanned hand. He was tempted, yet resisted going to have a look at him, just kept staring into the dancing flames, until Adonis left his mind and he found himself pondering whether the fire was the room's only source of heat. He decided it was unlikely, that there was too much money here not to have pipes of hot water or some similar device running beneath the floors or inside the walls, and, starting across the immaculate white carpet, he reflected on the extravagance of keeping the fireplace flames burning with no one at home.

He picked up the ashtray from the glass table, grabbed one of the metal chairs, moved to the window overlooking the driveway and sat down. Something stabbed his spine and he turned to inspect the chair's tortuous back, remembered the same thing had happened before, that there was nothing wrong with the chair, that it was just badly designed, and he turned around again, settled on the edge of the seat, placed the ashtray on his lap and stared at the cigarette burning in his hand, suddenly feeling very, very tired. The silence around him was buzzing. Or could it be his ears? His nape was burning. His bruised neck, grazed fingers and chest were hurting. And his sore feet and legs were aching. As for his heart – that big and slow-beating heart of his that the American doctor whose name he could not recall had enthused about – it felt like a stone, heavy and pounding inside his chest. Was it really only yesterday that he'd trudged into the sands and come upon the ranch? Was it only yesterday that...

He peered at his watch, on automatic, for the time hardly mattered; it was 21:04.

What had Lawrence said? Oh yes, Mrs. De Moraes wasn't expected until nine-thirty. And Mr. De Moraes was in Brazil, would be back tomorrow though...

Lawrence was already outside waiting for her with his umbrella when she parked her Aston Martin beside the Ferrari in the drive. She handed the butler several department store shopping bags, climbed out of the car holding a few more herself and started for the stairs to the front door under the shelter of the umbrella. She wore a black coat, sunglasses, a new hairstyle with a fringe that concealed most of her forehead and, although he couldn't see her eyes, Lombard imagined her worried look when, merely a few steps from the car, she came to a sudden stop and turned to Lawrence.

'What?' he thought he saw her lips ask. Or could it be 'Who?'

The butler had clearly just informed her of the visitor he'd let in, was now being made to explain himself. His mistress listened, rigid, then they both stood still under the butler's umbrella for a while, until she spoke again and started up the stairs, head down, thinking hard.

Lombard felt disappointed that neither had thought of looking up towards him; he wouldn't have minded Mrs. De Moraes seeing him peering at her from inside her drawing room window.

As she stepped out of sight, he noted she was wearing trousers. They were dark and broad, what is known as bell-bottom, the fabric swaying wildly with her every step. He wasn't sure, but he guessed it was the first time he'd seen her wearing trousers.

'DDM 5' he read, eyeing her Aston Martin's number-plate through the rain.

He put the Gitane he'd lit a moment before her arrival out in the ashtray still on his lap, shuffled on the edge of his seat and sighed.

He understood that he wouldn't attempt to deceive her the moment he heard her heels move quickly across the hall's marble floor. Contrary to what he'd planned, there would be no ruse, no lies about having spoken to Friedman or Leonard's boy.

A second or two later, turning from the window to see her standing stiffly in her black coat in the doorway, Harrods shopping bags in one hand, a small leather handbag in the other, he just sent her a stony grin.

He wasn't going to play. He wasn't going to cheat, lie or...
He'd just break her. It was wrong of course, but he didn't care
and, anyway, he just couldn't help it.

'How are you, Mrs. De Moraes?'
'Mr. Lombard... When did you get back?'
'Why don't you ask me when I left the Delaunay?' he said, still
grinning.

He could have said something else, something like 'Why don't
you ask me how come I'm alive?'. But it would have left her too
little room for doubt. She might have closed in upon herself. As
it was, the mention of the Delaunay did the trick, was ambiguous
enough to inflict the desired damage while at the same time
giving her hope. For it hit home all right. Her eyes might have
been safe behind her sunglasses but her proud red lips were out
in the open. And he saw them twitch. Just once. And that was it.
She didn't speak, didn't try to retaliate, nor, as she might have,
did she attempt to feign bemusement. Given her temperament,
it could only mean one thing.
He swallowed his grin, just went on looking into her
sunglasses as she stood in the door trying to think of something
to say. Was she regretting not having taken time to prepare
herself in the safety of the hall? He'd expected her to. He was
meant to be dead. Since he wasn't she must have wondered
whether he'd spoken with Friedman, how much he knew, what
he'd come there for. Yet, she'd made straight to the drawing
room, high heels resounding against the hall's marble floor. Had
it been anger, fear or merely arrogance that had driven her to act
so rashly?
'I...' she eventually pronounced, her husky voice so low it was
barely audible.
She left it at that, realising caution was in order, that she had
better buy some time to compose herself. And that's what she
did, stepping over the threshold, shutting the door and, after a
moment's hesitation, opting to move as far away from him as
possible towards the glass table at the other end of the room,
leaving a trail of wet footprints on the white carpet behind her.
Clearly, she'd neglected to wipe her feet, and Lawrence hadn't

dared to remind her.

'I was going to phone you. I'm sorry. We have…' she began with her back to him, breaking off to put her bags on the table.

He stayed silent, waiting for her to resume where she'd left off, but she didn't, nor did she turn to face him. Instead, she pulled a pack of Marlboro from her coat pocket, lit a cigarette, took a deep drag and, standing rigid, slowly exhaled the smoke, loudly enough for him to hear her breath.

Still, he went on waiting for her to speak, out of curiosity, to see what she'd come up with. Doubtless she was weighing her options, wondering how to proceed, trying to decide what to make of his remark about the Delaunay. And part of him was enjoying the moment. She didn't know it yet, but it hardly mattered what she would say or do. His mind was filled with too much ugliness. No matter what, he'd bite, try hurting her. The only question was whether she was going to make it easy or challenging. Knowing her though, he guessed there'd be no contrition speech. She'd fight. However, he was curious…

She signalled she'd made her mind up by burying her pack of cigarettes back in her coat pocket and reaching for her handbag.

'Leon is dead,' she announced, straining to sound impassive; 'He hung himself. They found his body in Epping Forest five days ago.'

There. Peering at her stiff back as she rummaged through her handbag, Lombard nodded his nod. She wouldn't let herself down. She'd fight. After all, as she'd just pointed out, her brother was conveniently dead. What was there for her to worry about? Whatever he may know, there was nothing he could do to her.

'Yes. I heard about it,' he declared.

'Ah. You did… Well, I can't say it came as much of a surprise. Still, things are never quite as one… One can't help feeling… Anyway. I'm sorry no one called to let you know,' she said, putting her handbag back down, at long last turning to face him.

At once, he saw the chequebook and pen in her hand and scowled.

'You must have come for your money of course,' she declared with a taut smile; 'I'm afraid you've caught me at a bad time. I don't have any cash. I'll have to write you a cheque, if that's all right.'

He didn't reply, simply ran his eyes over her. She'd had to let herself down after all. It could have been challenging and ugly, instead it would be easy and ugly. Money. She'd decided the best thing would be to get rid of him and was offering money. That was what the time he'd allowed her for thought had borne. The great fix-all. The great safeguard of the powerful and privileged few. *'You must have come for your money of course'.* And, of course, he was not to remind her of the £20,000 she'd already given him. That would be bad taste…

'I'm really sorry you were not called,' she said again.

He sneered. He'd thought she was too far away to see the cruel glimmer he knew burnt bright in his eyes, but she was aware of it all right. She was jittering nervously in her wet shoes.

'I intended to call but—'

'You're repeating yourself, Mrs. De Moraes,' he interrupted her.

'I'm sorry?'

'You've now apologised three times for not calling me.'

'Have I? Well, we're burying Leon tomorrow morning and…' Her brother's death's again.

'What did you do with *Sleeping Beauty*?'

'What?'

'Your brother's nauseating videotape, Mrs. De Moraes. What did you do with it?'

'The… I—I threw it away.'

'You threw it away?'

'Yes. Look, I wish I had more time, but it's late and with the funeral tomorrow…'

He grinned, a sour grin.

'Aren't you curious to know what I found out about Friedman?'

Ruffled she may have been, but it took her no time at all to come up with a pertinent reply, complete with a fittingly offended tone of voice:

'If you don't mind, I do not think he matters very much any more. I… It turned out to be as we thought; Leon was weak. There's no point in delving further into his sad life. Now, will you please tell me how much we owe you?' she concluded, turning to make her way around the table.

She reached the other side, pulled up a chair, sat down facing him, pushed aside the Harrods bags, put her chequebook down, opened it and began filling in a cheque, all without looking his way even once.

'Should I make the cheque out to your name or would you prefer that I leave the payee's name blank?'

Silent, he just went on watching her, briefly fixing his eyes on the pearl necklace that hung against the black sweater beneath her open coat. She held herself so stiff that it jerked above her breast with each of her movements as she drew her pen along the chequebook. Gleaming pearls and red lipstick aside though, she was all in black, and it struck him that, with her sunglasses and new dark fringe, she looked just like those images of rich grieving widows one from time to time comes across in magazines. Only, she was no widow. Had only lost her brother. A man she outwardly reviled. And on the eve of his funeral, judging from the many bags she'd handed the butler outside and the two on the table beside her, she had spent the afternoon and early evening shopping.

He swallowed hard, peered at the cigarette burning in her hand, picked up the ashtray from his lap and rose to his feet.

'Right, Mr. Lombard. What amount shall I make it?' she asked, looking up as he started towards her.

'Black suits you,' he remarked.

'Sorry?'

'Nice hair style,' he went on; 'Goes well with the glasses. What does your husband think of it?'

She opened her mouth but no sound came out.

'What are you hiding? Sisterly grief? Your husband's handi-work? Tell me? What's in the shopping bags? Lacy underwear? Is it to turn your husband on or for your own recreation? I wonder—what colour are you wearing today under your seemly mourning outfit, Mrs. De Moraes? Black or white? Or don't you actually wear any underwear? Just buy it. After all, you can afford to buy things, can't you? How does it feel to be able to afford anything and everything, Mrs. De Moraes? Does dreaming lies come a little harder when everything is just a question of money? When everything is within such easy reach? When everything is at hand? I mean, most people fool themselves by dreaming of how much better things would be if they had money. How much braver and better they'd be. But can one dream when one has money to throw away? Tell me, Mrs. De Moraes: does having money actually make one immune even to delusions? Is that why you buy so much expensive underwear? Do numbers actually help? Or is it just something you do to kill time? Not to think of what you are?'

'You…' she started.

She broke off, lost for words as he stopped across the table from her, glaring into her sunglasses.

'How come such a handsome couple as you and your husband sleep in separate beds, Mrs. De Moraes? Is it because he does it with little children? Or is it the other way around? The children are needed because you can't satisfy him?'

'You—' she let out again.

'Here,' he sneered, pushing the ashtray towards her; 'Your cigarette, Mrs. De Moraes. We wouldn't want you to sully your expensive furniture.'

It was like pushing a button. She looked down to the cigarette burning between her fingers, then quickly looked up again.

'Huh!' he scoffed, picking out her eyes behind her dark lenses.

They were wide open, staring, but he couldn't see enough of them to tell if she was more startled or afraid. She wasn't angry though. Not yet. She couldn't be. She had just heard that he knew about her husband's appetite for little children, of their sleeping arrangements and of her taste for lingerie. And if that wasn't enough, it had all come out vulgarly, his manner nothing short of obnoxious. It was a lot to take in all at once. Too much for her to be angry yet. She wasn't used to men talking to her like that. Or women for that matter. Or anybody.

He glanced at the cheque between her hands. She'd filled in the date and his name, and signed it. Now though, she held onto her pen so hard, she was unwittingly burying its tip in the cheque pad.

'Huh!' he scoffed again, looking back into her sunglasses.

In a moment, she'd become angry, her imperious, indignant and scornful self. Right now though, she could only stare, tight-lipped, and, briefly, he found himself contemplating her mouth, realising what made it so appealing. It was the contrast between the maturity of her firm proud lips and the soft fullness of the flesh around them, where her olive skin was still rounded with youthful plumpness. Tenderness and hardness. Innocence and experience. Sensuousness and bestiality. It was all there. Exquisitely gathered in a fine specimen of a woman's mouth.

'Who helped you break into my office, Deborah? Ladies of your standing don't learn to pick locks between shopping trips,' he said.

Her lips parted, but only to gape up at him.

'Come on, Deborah! Looking dumb doesn't suit you! Who knew I'd found dirt on your brother, huh? Who knew it was all written down inside an envelope? Who turned down the opportunity to get hold of that envelope because at the time she was much more interested in sending me after Friedman? Eh, Deborah? A few days later though, taking me for dead, you realised your mistake, didn't you? Decided you'd better see to it that it didn't fall into the wrong hands. No. We couldn't risk that, could we, Deborah?'

There. She'd recovered. In a second or two she'd be all cold indignation, as befits a woman of her looks and standing. But she wouldn't be angry yet. He guessed it from the calm manner in which she turned away to stub out her cigarette in the ashtray, the way she then faced him again and started rising from her chair.

'You're out of order, Mr. Lombard. I—'

He didn't want to, hadn't planned on shouting, but...

'YOU WHAT, MRS. DE MORAES? YOU WHAT?'

He thought she was going to topple over. She fell back into her chair so heavily that it started to tip backwards. Still, just in time, she managed to grab hold of the table, in so doing saving them both from the embarrassment of what would have been a most undignified situation, although, all things considered, he may not have minded.

'You're mad,' she muttered between her teeth.

'Mad?' he returned; 'No, Deborah. I have had and am having a very unpleasant time. I'm also tired. And angry. But mad? Not yet. Now, why didn't you tell your husband where your brother's boy was after you got hold of my envelope, eh?'

She didn't reply, just bit her lower lip, flicking her hair away from her face.

'I spoke to the girl who's looking after him earlier today. They're both fine. Why didn't you tell your husband where the boy was, Deborah?'

It had to happen. At last, a familiar snigger appeared across her lips:

'Why... I haven't the faintest idea what you're talking about. Your impudence is nothing new but if you—'

'Why did you save the boy's life, Deborah?' he cut in.

'I don't know what you're talking about,' she reiterated.

'Huh! You do, Deborah. Just like you know that your husband would have had the boy killed if he'd known where to find him, don't you? Tell me, does a conscience still burn somewhere inside your sore mind? Or is it just cold expediency? Could the boy perhaps come in useful when and if the day ever comes for you to face up to the man you married?'

She shook her head, turned away with another sneer:

'Have you finished?'

He hadn't.

'When did you learn about his taste for kids, eh? On your honeymoon? Or was it later, when bitterness set in and you turned against your beloved but weak little brother and abandoned him to face the world all by himself? How did you find out you'd married a sick man, Mrs. De Moraes? Did he confess? Try to convert you perhaps? Or was it just a woman's intuition? Something about the way he fucked you? Or didn't, as the case may be?'

There. It was easy and ugly and getting easier and uglier, as always happens when things become vile. As if the words 'fucked you' were just too much for her ears, she finally let anger get hold of her, leapt rather than stood up from her chair, didn't fall back this time, but whipped off her sunglasses and fixed her eyes in his.

He had expected to find fear or at least some sign of it in her dark brazen eyes. Instead, he found only hatred. Calm, controlled, haughty hatred.

'You do have a vivid imagination Mr. Lombard. I only wish you'd use it fruitfully instead of in being abhorrent,' the words lashed out of her mouth; 'I fail to understand your immediate purpose in this. Still, as it seems you need reminding of it, you were hired to find my brother and he has now been found. This puts you out of a job and means you have no business being here. So, if the reason you stopped by is to collect whatever money you might feel you're owed, I'd be more than happy to clear up the matter. If not, I must ask you to leave. At once. All right?'

He frowned, not in reaction to her words but because of the bruise he could just make out above her right eye. Had there been more than a table width between them, he'd never have spotted it. For one thing, her fringe concealed most of it. For another, what her new hairstyle couldn't hide – that is the skin between her eyebrow and eyelashes – was so expertly made up as to all but disguise it. But it was there all right.

'I guess the news you'd sent me after Friedman didn't go down too well, eh?' he said.

She eyeballed him, her lips trembling, and he thought she was going to slap him, asked himself if he'd strike back if she did.

'Did it happen before or after you called me in Los Angeles?' he asked, wilfully trying to provoke her; 'You sounded nervous. It's not like you to sound nervous, Deborah. Bitter, resentful, but not nervous.'

'Huh. You're sick,' she said, deciding to turn away to reach down for her chequebook and pen.

'Why did you send me after Friedman when I offered to quit, Deborah?'

She sneered.

'Why did you send me after Friedman, Deborah?'

'Whatever the reason, I'm sorry I did. Goodbye, Mr. Lombard. I believe you know your way out,' she said, tossing her sunglasses, pen and chequebook into her handbag.

'You knew he had nothing to do with your brother's disappearance, didn't you?'

'Huh! Don't you recall convincing me he had? You should learn to live with your mistakes, Mr. Lombard. There's some merit in it,' she returned, snapping her bag shut.

'I take it you learnt to live with yours then. Take it all the mind-dulling pills in your bedside drawer are surplus to your well-being?'

She let go of her bag, fixed her eyes in his again:

'You've already made it abundantly clear that you let yourself into my bedroom, Mr. Lombard. You obviously had fun. Now, I suggest you get out before I call the police.'

'The police?'

'That's what I said.'

'Why don't you go ahead,' he grinned, snatching her handbag from the table.

He took a couple of steps back, snapped it open, started searching through it.

'What—' he heard her mutter.

There was little in the bag apart from the items she'd just tossed into it – keys, purse, filofax and, of course, make-up and lipstick. He didn't see what he was looking for, but went on rummaging longer than necessary, trusting she was feeling defiled. If what she wanted was more sport, more ugliness...

'Will you give me—' she started.

She fell silent as he looked back up, swallowed nervously when he snarled, caught the bag when he tossed it straight back at her.

'Why haven't you got any children, Deborah?' he asked.

There. Her dark pupils dilated. She was ready now, even if her eyes were still consumed with hatred. He'd hit a soft spot, perhaps her only soft spot. She swallowed again, briefly looked away, hoping to conceal her disarray.

'You don't seem to have any contraceptives,' he went on; 'In your bag or in your bedroom. What's the problem? Can't you have kids, Mrs. De Moraes?'

Her lips had started trembling again. She tried to speak but seemed unable to open her mouth and so went on swallowing, several times, in quick succession, as if she couldn't breathe or perhaps was about to throw up.

He grinned, a callous grin:

'It must be tough being married to Adonis and end up sleeping alone every night. Is that why sleep is so hard coming, Deborah? What's harder, eh? The thought of the fine litter you two handsome folks could have bred if? Or imagining what he does with his little boys?'

She was ready to speak again, opened her mouth but, again, no sound came out. He first thought she couldn't think what to say, but then realised she'd made a conscious decision to hold back, as if at long last understanding and accepting that he hadn't come to exact money or merely to be rude. Alarm, or was it dread, was finding its way through the hatred in her eyes.

The time had come to show her the contact sheet he'd picked up at Leonard's. He pulled it out of his pocket, unfolded it, stepped back towards the table, flattened it against the glass surface, turned it round and pushed it towards her.

'I stopped by Leonard's on my way here and look what I came across, Deborah.'

He gave her time, wanted her to fully appreciate what she was looking at, watched her eyes as she frowned at the shots of her Aston Martin, mystified.

'What were you satisfying? Morbid curiosity? Was it gratifying?'

She looked up, peered strangely at him, as if in a daze, not really seeing him, then looked down again.

'What happened, Deborah? Revulsion turned into obsession? And obsession into some kind of turn-on? Where you watching the hotel windows? Is that what you were doing there – imagining what he was doing? What it would be like to partake in the fun perhaps?'

'No,' she whispered between her lips, shaking her head; 'No…'

'Tell me, did he kill his little victims too?'

There. She broke, like a twig; the tough ones always break, that's all they can do.

'No!' she cried, turning back towards him, horrified.

He nodded, silent, peering into her staring eyes, aware she was not really looking at him but lost in her own thoughts, realising she'd just slipped.

It was odd. He'd imagined he would delight in the moment. He should have. Instead, he almost felt sorry for her, and bad about what he'd just done. There was something painful, indecent almost, in the sight of her looking so helpless. It wasn't right. She still held onto her handbag, clasping it against her coat, like a shield. Her eyes had lost all their usual brazenness, looked dazed and afraid. And it did not suit her, did not go with her looks and fine clothes, and for the first time, he realised how small she was, even if he immediately corrected himself, for really it was wrong to think of her as small. Average was a fairer way to describe her height, although it was irrelevant; she was one of those women whose height was meaningless, who would perhaps have looked too intimidating and that much less attractive if she'd been taller. It was just that, until now, he'd never noticed she was smaller than himself. In fact, he'd never thought about her height. But neither had he yet seen her looking so fragile…

He had better not let her grow too tall again:

'What do you mean, "No", Mrs. De Moraes?'

'My brother hung himself,' she said, staring right through him.

SEVENTEEN

'Does the name Pierre Dreyer mean anything to you? He's a client of mine and a friend of your husband.'

'Leon hung himself,' she said again, staring in front of her, as if not listening to him.

Lombard frowned. She had to have heard him. She wasn't the kind to seek refuge in what Americans conveniently call denial. There were too many tranquillisers in her bedside table for that. This was a woman consumed with inner battles, a woman who knew too much of bitterness and self-loathing. More likely, suddenly stripped of her veneer, of the cover of deceit behind which she was so accustomed to hiding, she was temporarily adrift, desperately trying to latch back onto what until a few moments ago afforded her safety: lies, scorn and, of course, money.

'Adonis thought your brother's body would be found reasonably quickly when he hung it in Epping Forest, didn't he?' he continued; 'Seemed like a good idea. An ex-junkie obsessed with death. The perfect candidate for suicide. What happened? Adonis picked too secluded a spot? Or is it simpler than that – he merely overlooked the fact that forest ramblers are rather scarce during your average blustery English November. An Englishman might have thought of that, but a Brazilian…'

'Leon hung himself…'

'Leonard's not found, your parents worry, talk of hiring help to find him, even mention putting their man-hunter friends on his trail perhaps… and Adonis panics, decides he better take control, brings me in, recommendation and all, reckoning a small-time detective is unlikely to dig up anything awkward, not before Leonard's found anyhow. He must have kicked himself when he learned I'd exceeded his expectations.'

'Leon hung himself,' she persisted, a puzzled frown forming

above her eyes.

Could she be wondering how he knew all this? He wasn't supposed to, was he? *'Or is the job too formidable for you, Mr. Lombard...'*

Huh!

'Leonard didn't hang himself, Deborah. Your husband killed him and made it look like suicide. How did he go about it, eh? Strangulation? Is that why the tree stunt? Or was it drugs? No doubt an autopsy will tell.'

She stayed silent this time. He knew why. Could see why. Her mind had just kicked back into gear, and if her scowl was anything to go by, she didn't like what it was telling her.

He grinned:

'What's the matter, Deborah? Don't you want an autopsy performed on your brother? Don't you want his death looked into? Did you really hate him that much?'

'Maybe...' she started, batting her lashes nervously, clearly struggling to put her thoughts into order; 'Maybe, if Leon didn't hang himself, maybe Friedman killed him. Maybe... Maybe he has your envelope...'

He peered hard at her, somewhat astonished. She couldn't help it. Had to fight. Perhaps that was all she knew, had always been combative. Even long before...

'Your brother was left hanging from a tree in a public place by someone who wanted his body found, Deborah. Someone who knew enough of his history to guess his suicide wouldn't cause much eyebrow raising. Now, how would Friedman have known of your brother's inclinations? And why should he have wanted his body found, eh?'

She tried but failed to come up with a reply.

'That's right,' he agreed; 'Friedman and Leonard never met. Friedman didn't even know of your brother's existence. And had Friedman killed him, he wouldn't have bothered to disguise his murder as suicide, or risked hauling his corpse across London and all the way to Epping Forest. Not Friedman. He'd have dumped his body anywhere convenient or, more likely, there'd have been no body to find – not Leonard's nor those of the boy and his keeper. Because they too would be dead if Friedman had got his hands on your brother, Deborah. You can bet on it. He'd have seen to it. This is his turf. He had plenty of time to torture him, and he'd have done it, and got him to sing if need be. As for my envelope, had Friedman known where to search for it, he wouldn't have mistaken me for a hitman called Lamont when we met in Los Angeles.'

She didn't think, just let the words fly out of her mouth:

'You spoke to him? You spoke to Friedman?'

Stony-faced, he let her probe his eyes, wilfully kept her waiting, wondering whether to lie. It would have been so easy to throw her into utter panic. One word. That was all it required. A 'Yes'. He'd already resolved not to play with her, earlier, on hearing her cross the hallway, yet, now the opportunity was there, peering into her dark and scared eyes, it was tempting to…

'Not in the strict sense of the word, no,' he decided on; 'He was in too much of a hurry to kill me when we got within greeting distance. And then he sensibly packed up before I could catch up with him again back here.'

She made no attempt to conceal her relief, let out a heavy sigh.

'Yes. That's right. You and Adonis are safe. From him anyhow. He not only swallowed the bait but it seems also chose to go into retirement. Tell me? Was the hitman story your or Adonis's idea?'

She just gazed at him, expressionless now.

'I must say, it wasn't bad. Quite desperate and rather chancy but considering your options not bad at all. It didn't work as well as you'd hoped in that I'm still alive but at least Friedman and I never had our chat. I wonder, who would you have been most scared of if we'd traded information, eh? Me, after I'd learnt he'd never heard of your brother? Or the man himself, once he'd learnt who I was working for? No doubt the two of us would have put together an interesting story. Big trouble would have come home all right. I can just imagine how Friedman might have taken the news I'd been hired by the family of one of his regular and doubtless most trustworthy clients. What do you think, eh? What might he have done after finding out that your husband had compromised him and his operation by passing on one of his boys to his emotional brother-in-law? Would he have merely disciplined Adonis? Or might he have felt justified in resorting to something nastier? Seen to the rest of his family?'

She was still looking straight at him, but again, her eyes seemed unfocused, glazed, as if she wasn't hearing him.

'Your brother stumbled upon Adonis's little secret, didn't he? And traded his silence for a kid and some spare cash for his upkeep. And Adonis fell for it, bought him his kid, sent him away and then panicked and killed him when he came back for more. Leonard didn't come here to borrow money for prints, Deborah. By that time, he'd already got his boy, already left him in Wales. I doubt photography was at the forefront of his mind. No. He came here to extort a second kid's life. Your flunkey let him in, so his visit couldn't be concealed, hence the exhibition story. But there was no exhibition. Just as you said. Remember, Deborah? *"Leon does his own prints. Wouldn't want anyone to interfere with his Art"*. I should have paid more attention to your words. But then again, there's something about the way you say them that, well…'

He paused, clenched his fists as she turned away from him and gazed at the contact sheet on the table between them.

'Yes,' he went on; 'I should have paid you more attention. You and everything else. Damn it! Your brother purchasing kids at £15,000 a go never made sense. He just didn't have access to that kind of money, and I trust was too fainthearted and honest to steal it. Yet, he'd not only got hold of one boy but was confident he'd get another. If he couldn't pay, it had to be blackmail. I should have thought of that. Blackmail is a repeatable exercise. If it works once, the odds are it will work twice. Unless the blackmailed party decides to kill the blackmailer, of course.'

'How…' she pronounced, searching the shots on the contact sheet; 'How… If you didn't speak with Friedman and… It's my car in the photographs. How… Why don't you accuse me of being the one who… Why don't you accuse me of killing my brother?' she asked, looking up again.

He found himself searching her face. Something had just changed. Something he didn't understand. Fear had left her eyes. She looked very calm all of a sudden. And sad. Either she'd wrestled herself back under control, was scheming and about to bite, or…

Could she be about to cry?

'Kids are not your thing, Deborah,' he told her; 'You'd have been ready for me when I turned up with *Sleeping Beauty*. Then too I should have paid you more attention. "Not Leon," you said. Do you remember that? *"Not Leon!"* It struck me at the time, but obviously not hard enough. You didn't say "My God!", or whatever else well-bred ladies squeak on hearing that Uncle Henry misbehaved. "Not Leon". Who then? Eh? And then, sacking me to rehire me the very next day. That too should have told me something. These were the actions of a confused woman. A woman who knew something, though. But there I was. Focused so hard on Friedman I'd stopped thinking. Stopped looking. Tell me, did you have a good laugh at my expense when you left my office the evening I told you Leonard had to have a partner? That there was no way he could have got to and then duped Friedman into selling him a kid all by himself. That someone with credentials and a direct line to Friedman had to have helped him. Did you laugh, Deborah? Or did I scare you? Cause you a few anxious moments by being so close to the truth? Damn! You sure were right about one thing, even if you tactfully put it as a question – the job was too formidable for me. It sure was. Your parents hiring someone like me. You, your venom and neurotic demeanour. Adonis and his dumb exhibition story. Friedman living right around the corner. Huh! I might as well have been deaf, dumb and blind. Having found your brother's boy, all that was required was for me to do a little thinking, ask a few obvious questions and look at what was there to see. That's it. A couple of days. Within a couple of days I could have made all the connections. Instead, I had to nearly die before I could start thinking straight. Yes. You sure were right. Tell me, did the fact I'd proved so dumb help ease your conscience when the time came to offer me to Friedman? Or would that be giving you too much credit? There is no conscience burning inside your sore mind. What I see is all there is; a cold rich lady who buys fancy underwear at the first sign of anxiety.'

Reproach. She looked back at him with reproach now. She wasn't crying yet, but was about to. There could be no doubt about it. It was in her tight lips, the way she held her eyes wide and still; but more, her complexion had changed colour, lost its warm olive tinge, become pale grey-green, and it gleamed, markedly around her cheekbones, where it almost matched her pearl necklace.

She had to make an effort to pull her lips apart in order to speak:

'I—I didn't decide anything,' she protested, sounding sorry for herself, and tears finally materialised in the corners of her eyes.

Teeth clenched, he scowled. He didn't want her tears. Had no use for them. This was too unpleasant and ugly for tears. This was just a sick story. The pathetic domestic story of a cowardly wife, her diseased husband and her weak brother. It wasn't even tragic. Just downright sick and sad. It didn't deserve tears. Or at any rate not hers. He'd rather have her fighting. He'd rather…

He should have lied about having met Friedman. It was too late for it now, but if he had, at least she…

She spoke again, her voice feeble, her tears coming thick and fast now:

'Leon could still have hung himself,' she said, as if attempting to convince herself of it now.

'Damn—' he cursed inside his teeth, breaking off as her eyes filled with dread.

Standing frozen, freeing himself from her alarmed gaze, he realised what was happening. He was leaning above the table between them, his fist raised, suspended in mid-air at shoulder level.

Could he really have…

He cursed himself, backed a couple of steps away from the table, let his arm fall to his side, took a deep breath to compose himself and buried his clenched fists in his coat pockets.

Even in ugliness, even crying, she still…

'No, Deborah. Leon did not hang himself. Your brother had at long last found a mission. If he didn't kill himself when he was a confused and drifting poor little rich boy, he wasn't going to do it when glory beckoned in the shape of all those little boys in need of rescuing. Your husband killed him, Deborah. And I guess, since Leonard kept what he knew about Adonis a secret, since he didn't speak of him even to the woman he entrusted with looking after the boy, he probably died because of you. Sweet and weak, he decided to protect you when he found out what Adonis was up to. Horrified, he could have gone to the police. I bet he thought of it. He wasn't exactly the daring type, was he? Only, he must have realised exposing Adonis would expose you. It couldn't be helped. The publicity, the fallout would have hurt you. And he didn't want that to happen to his big sister. In spite of the contempt you showed him, he loved you. Probably still thought of you as the sunny little girl he'd grown up with. Still hoped that one day you might forgive him for having caused him so much pain. And so, ill-equipped as he was, doubtless scared, but unable to simply look the other way or seek comfort in mind-numbing drugs, he turned himself into a blackmailer. And why not? It was an opportunity to do some good, to do something worthwhile… Huh! That's another thing you were right about, Deborah. Your brother was a fool. A fool with a heart, but isn't that too often the case? I wonder. Once he was in on your husband's little secret, what do you think he made of you? Did he see you as victim or as partner in crime? Would he have given you the benefit of the doubt, decided you couldn't possibly know about it, that you'd have left him if? Or did he finally realise he owed your contempt to your cowardice, that having married into a disease you chose to take it upon yourself to hurt him? How does that work, Mrs. De Moraes? Does inflicting pain on others really help one feel better with oneself? Is it something like "If I can't be happy neither can you"? Is that it? Tell me, did it occur to you that perhaps, just perhaps, you are responsible for your brother's death, Mrs. De Moraes? Is that why the tears? If it is, you needn't cry. It doesn't suit your looks. All things considered, I find you better looking dumb than crying. Not that you care, I know. But perhaps this is just my way of saying that if the tears are for my benefit, you're wasting your time. There's too much dirt. You're too dirty for a few tears to wash…'

He'd lost her. He'd lost her completely. She'd just freed herself from him. Her tears still flowed, running through her make-up, rolling down her cheeks to her chin and dripping onto the pearls against her chest, but she was her old defiant self again and returned his gaze in cold contempt. She was going to admit defeat but there would be no surrender…

She saw he understood, bit her lip, but against his expectation, didn't bite him. Instead, finding comfort in her regained haughty contempt, brazen-eyed again, she allowed herself to let up, turned to the handbag she'd been clasping nervously to her belly for the last few minutes, put it down on the table, wiped the tears from her cheeks with the tips of her fingers and sat back down in her chair, brooding over the contact sheet in front of her while searching her coat pockets for her cigarettes.

'Poor Leon,' she said, before lighting a Marlboro and slowly exhaling the smoke; '... How typical of him to be in the wrong place at the wrong time.'

He didn't reply, just observed her as she took another drag of her cigarette, one hand on her lap, turning the lighter between her fingers slowly round and round.

'When I called you at your hotel in Los Angeles,' she carried on, without moving her eyes from the contact sheet, 'I was going to warn you about... About Friedman. Maybe I would have if you hadn't left me waiting on the line. I hung up...'

He swallowed hard. He'd lost her all right. She wasn't even going to accept defeat. Two things. She'd said two things. Both of which absolved her from responsibility: Leonard was in the wrong place at the wrong time; and she'd have warned him if he hadn't kept her waiting on the line...

For a moment, he stopped thinking, found himself unable to, his head a dark, humming and throbbing world. And she went on gazing at the contact sheet.

'You're wrong about my being there, though,' she continued, softly, pausing once again to wipe away more tears, with the knuckle of her index finger this time; 'Carlos borrowed my car that day. His had broken down... Leon saw it, like you assumed I was there, thought he'd wait to ask for a lift. I suspect he wouldn't have in normal circumstances, would have known I was unlikely to even let him into my car, but apparently he'd spent the previous night in police custody, was tired and... Anyway, Carlos turned up from the hotel where he... Well, he turned up with the video-tape you found. He didn't know what to do. As you can imagine, he wasn't too pleased to see Leon, but with the bad conscience of those caught doing wrong, he decided to be over-friendly, drove him all the way to his place in Highgate. Leon... I don't know if the rest is tragic or stupid...' she reflected, trailing off to take another drag from her cigarette; 'A bit of both I suppose... But Leon accidentally picked up the videotape with all his photo equipment from the back seat of the car when he was dropped off. Carlos only realised it when he got home, made straight back to my brother's but got there too late. Leon had already looked at the tape. He confronted Carlos, threatened to go to the police and… And my husband panicked…'

She paused again, still staring at the print under her eyes, lips pouting, as if brooding.

'It wasn't just the tape, you see?' she eventually resumed; 'It's… He wasn't sure Leon had not seen him come out of the hotel with it, would guess it came from there, and he took the wrong decision, decided to talk to him. I don't know exactly what or how much he said, he didn't really elaborate, but he talked, too much, hoping he would frighten Leon from going to the police by telling him what was at stake, what and who were involved… From what I understand that's how Leon found out about Friedman and his business… Anyway, Carlos soon realised his mistake. Leon didn't quite react as he'd anticipated. He certainly wasn't frightened and… Well, you've more or less guessed the rest,' she concluded, looking up from the contact sheet; 'I didn't know any of this before you left for Los Angeles, Mr. Lombard,' she added, returning his scowl.

So there it was. He'd guessed right. He hadn't really needed her confession to know it, yet, now she'd confirmed his suspicions, he felt strangely foiled in his anger, and all the darker for it.

'Didn't you?' he asked, noting that she no longer was crying.

'No.'

He snarled:

'Are you really trying to tell me that you didn't guess your husband was involved with your brother the night I turned up here with *Sleeping Beauty* and the news that Leonard had bought himself a boy, Deborah? That that's not why you fired me? Because you got scared I might uncover dirt pointing straight to Adonis?'

She shook her head:

'That my brother, my husband and your Mr. Friedman were connected, that much I did guess that night. You are right. And yes, that's why I tried to fire you. But that my husband had killed my brother? No, Mr. Lombard. The possibility never even entered my mind.'

'Didn't it? So what did enter your mind?'

'I—I don't know. What—'

'What did you think might have happened to your brother once it had become clear he'd disappeared after getting involved with your husband, Mrs. De Moraes?'

'I… It's as I said, I didn't know. Could not—'

'Then why did you rehire me, Deborah? Not to mention entrust me with £20,000?'

'I—I was worried. You got me worried, remember?'

'Worried?'

'That's right.'

'Did you ever meet Friedman?'

She looked appaled.

'No. Of course not.'

He believed that.

'How did your husband kill your brother?'

'I… He…' she dithered, frowning uneasily.

'Yes?'

'It's… You guessed that right. He strangled him.'

'How? Where?'

She stayed silent.

'How? Where?'

'I don't know how… It happened in his car, that's all I know.'

'Whose car?'

'My… Leon couldn't drive. My husband's car…'

He frowned. She was right. He'd forgotten Leonard couldn't drive, but now she mentioned it, he remembered Mrs. Spitz telling him her son didn't hold a driving licence.

'Your husband's car. Is that the Ferrari in the drive outside?'

'… Yes.'

'*Nom de*—' he let out; 'Tell me, what am I looking at here, eh?' he spat.

He saw the anger in her eyes, saw her lips move, but opted not to hear what she had to say, simply switched off, so that her English words became meaningless, until her lips stopped moving again, and he turned around and made for the window overlooking the front drive, just to do something, to get her out of his sight. Or was it the Ferrari…

Carlos was in Brazil, not back until the next day, the butler had said…

'Anyway. Now this is all out of the way, what exactly did you come here for, Mr. Lombard? If it is money you want, it…' her voice drifted across the silence behind him.

Gazing at the red Ferrari sitting in the rain outside, he waited for her to complete her sentence. But she didn't, and after a few seconds he heard her exhale, guessed she'd just taken a drag from her cigarette, became aware his fingers were clasped around the pack of Gitanes inside his pocket.

He considered lighting a cigarette, but oddly, the thought held no appeal. Maybe he had no need for nicotine. No need for the hit.

'I suppose it's lucky for you he didn't borrow your car on the murder day too, eh?' he eventually remarked; 'Or wouldn't it have mattered?'

'What exactly did you come here for, Mr. Lombard?' she asked again, after a moment's silence.

Teeth clenched, he ignored her.

'Why did you send me after Friedman, Deborah? To atone for your sins?' he asked.

Again, she took a moment before speaking, did so only after a short angry sigh, and this time answered his question, or at any rate reacted to it:

'I did not know my husband and Friedman knew each other, Mr. Lombard. As I said, I guessed it after you brought me the tape, but I did not know it.'

'Don't lie, please,' he returned, grimly surveying her Aston Martin; 'I might just lose my temper.'

'For God's sake,' he heard her hiss, angry; 'What do you think I am? Do you think we spoke about it? Do you think I asked him… I've known for seven years. He's known I've known for seven years. But not once have we spoken about it. There are things one just doesn't speak about.'

He turned around, focused all the way across the room into her indignant eyes:

'Tell me, what does *one* speak about, eh, Mrs. De Moraes?'

'Think what you like. But don't presume to understand,' came the reply, sharp and icy.

'I don't.'

'Good.'

'Good? Is there anything to understand?'

'Why do I feel I needn't answer that?'

'Maybe you should. Young. Rich. Good-looking. You must at least get a kick out of what he does to his kids.'

'You bastard...'

'Seven years of it, you say. Surely. You'd have divorced him if he disgusted you.'

'You splendid bastard...'

'Are there truly no extenuating circumstances here?'

She sneered:

'I've already heard your thoughts, Mr. Lombard. At the risk of spoiling the obvious pleasure you take in listening to the sound of your own voice, we're turning in circles.'

'Yeah. And you still haven't told me why you sent me after Friedman.'

'Didn't I?'

'Did you?'

'Does it matter?'

'Why don't you try me?'

'Well. Maybe I wanted to give my husband a fright.'

'*A fright?* Seven years of cowardice culminate in your brother being murdered and you wanted to give his murderer a fright?'

'I told you. At the time I didn't know who or what had happened to my brother.'

'Of course. What was the idea then? Husband is filled with fear when he learns his child supplier is being tailed?'

'Something like that.'

'Something like that?'

'Something like that.'

'What happened? Adonis slapped you around a little and you reverted to cowardice?'

'Here we go again.'

'Where is that, Mrs. De Moraes?'

'Simplify and damn.'

'Don't you believe in simplicity?'

'Should I?'

'We all have to like what we become. Cowards included. We achieve this by complicating things a little. But it's never that complicated really,' he replied.

'Huh. You seem to know what you're talking about.'

'Well, perhaps it came to me while I was dying in a Los Angeles hospital bed because a woman set upon giving her husband a fright got slapped around a little.'

'My husband didn't need to slap me around, Mr. Lombard. I volunteered...'

'To get me killed?...'

'I didn't intend it that way. I was going to wait until your return but... It just happened.'

'What do you mean, it just happened, Mrs. De Moraes?'

'It... He heard from Lawrence that you'd been back. That we'd argued. He asked what had happened and... I could have lied, intended to, but it just happened. I told him everything. Showed him the tape. I couldn't help it. Wanted to see him scared. I had never seen him scared before, you see? I doubt you can understand it but I'd never seen him frightened before.'

'Well, I hope you found the sight enjoyable.'

'Perhaps, Mr. Lombard. Perhaps. For the short time it took for his fear to turn into panic, perhaps I did. But then panic turned into fury. That's when he slapped me around a little, told me what had happened. Told me he'd killed Leon. "You don't know what you've done," he was shouting. "We're in deep trouble." "We," he said. "We". *We'd* both be killed if Friedman ever found out you were working for us. *We* had to stop you and Friedman meeting...'

'I see,' Lombard said as she paused, all proud silence; 'Where your weak little brother showed courage you—'

'Maybe I've got more imagination than my brother had, Mr. Lombard,' she cut him off; 'Or do you think I too should have tried to blackmail him?'

'Maybe not. He might have strangled you too.'

'Huh!'

'Huh? Strange. I wouldn't have made you out to be the type scared of dying, Deborah. You remind me more of those people who are scared of living, who give up all responsibility towards themselves and, needless to say, others.'

'Aren't you frightened of dying, Mr. Lombard?'

'It depends my mood and the time of day. But looking at people like you, I find death less scary than I guess I ought to.'

'Well. Then you must consider yourself lucky not everyone is as bad as me.'

'I don't know if lucky is the right word. Or if bad characterises what you are. Let's just say I wouldn't die for you. Because of you? That nearly happened. But for you? No.'

'I told you before, Mr. Lombard. I tried calling you. I wanted to warn you of what Carlos—'

'Yes, I remember. You hung up,' he interjected.

'You... I didn't want you to die, Mr. Lombard.'

'Then what's the story, Mrs. De Moraes?'

'Fear is contagious. Is that simple enough for you, Mr. Lombard? Fear is contagious. I believed Carlos. I don't know if you can or want to understand, but the way he put it—'

'It was me or you two, right?' he cut in.

'Well... I see it is simple enough for you.'

'I'm not so sure. Perhaps you could make it even simpler. What do you think? Why don't you try me with a "What would you have done in my place?" here, eh?'

'I—Would I get an honest answer?' she returned with a sneer.

'You might. But all the same, you might not like it.'

'I see. I'm speaking to a hero, eh? Tell me. Apart from being a small-time private eye with bad manners, what exactly is your claim to fame?'

He nodded his nod. The distance between them was too great for them to read each other's thoughts, but had he been closer to her, he probably would have found her eyes impenetrable, while she might have seen...

All of a sudden, he found himself wanting to go, to step outside into the rain and...

But first, Carlos was in Brazil and...

Maybe she'd read his thoughts after all. Or maybe it was simply the right moment for her to finally say it. As she'd said herself, they'd been turning in circles for the last few minutes. He not quite sure what to do and she, well, she...

'Well,' she said; 'I still don't know what brought you here tonight, Mr. Lombard. But I guess your weren't motivated by the lure of gain. You're much too upstanding and virtuous for that, isn't that so?'

Le client est roi,' he heard himself say.

'I'm sorry?'

'Just go on, Mrs. De Moraes,' he simply answered.

'Right... Well, now you know what you wanted to know, what do you propose to do, Mr. Lombard? My brother is dead. If I understand you correctly, Friedman is gone. You have these photographs of my car, but you know as well as I do, they prove nothing. Indeed, you have no proof of anything. Unless of course you came here "wired". But somehow I doubt that. So what is it exactly you came to achieve, Mr. Lombard? If you're considering calling the police I would think again. I'm sure I needn't remind you of my parents' connections. And the bottom line really is that my poor brother is dead. However sad, there's nothing to be done about that. Nothing. Bad or good.'

It was as if the room around her had fallen into semi-darkness, or as if she was sitting at the end of a blurred and shadowy tunnel, in her mourning outfit the only clear, sharp sight in front of him.

He didn't know how long he spent gazing at her dark figure, didn't care. He wasn't looking at her anyhow, only using the time to think, and grinned when he was done, a sickened grin. His anger had all but gone.

'I'm not one for cleaning up other people's mess, Mrs. De Moraes. There's much too much of it for a little private detective like myself to make a difference. Besides, I'm not really the caring type; I learnt a long time ago the world is better left to itself. Perhaps, it needs something to read on Sundays. But you know what? I left death and ugliness behind on my way here. Uglier scenes and things than possibly even yourself. And I guess calling the police won't do me much good. But to tell you the truth, I don't think I'd mind four walls and dinner served every evening at a regular time,' he said, looking away to search for the telephone.

He came across it on a marble top not far from the photograph of Carlos, made for it.

'If you want to know, I came here hoping to have a private word with Adonis. I'd looked forward to it. But if that's the way you want it...'

'What are you doing? You can't. My parents will...' he heard her voice behind him as he picked up the receiver.

'Your parents will do what, Deborah?'

'They—'

She fell silent as he began dialling, keeping his back to her. He was calling John Fitzpatrick.

'You have no proof. You have nothing!' she cried out.

'Your brother isn't buried yet, Deborah. As I said, an autopsy will show how he died. Adonis strangled him in his Ferrari, you said. Well, unless you lied, it's the one sitting right now in your driveway. And then there's the boy you so kindly saved. I don't wish to make you regret having spared his life, but I'm sure he'll be able to identify your husband as the man who bought him and passed him on to your brother.'

'The boy doesn't know anything. He can't know anything,' she retorted.

'How do you know that?' he said, turning to face her, the receiver against his ear, listening to the ringing tone.

She stood up in front of her chair again, looking scared, too scared almost.

'He'd—he'd have told you about Carlos. You would have known about Carlos if he knew anything… Wouldn't you?'

He glared:

'So that explains your compassion. He'd have told me if he knew, eh?'

'Wouldn't he?' she asked again; 'Carlos said that anyway—'

'The boy was too doped-up to recognise his own mother if he ever saw her again, is that it?' he pre-empted her.

She didn't reply, but her uneasy eyes told him he was not too far from the truth.

'He could be right,' he went on, looking coldly back at her; 'But then again, he could be wrong. I've not asked the boy any questions yet. Partly because of not knowing what to ask, partly because I didn't know in what language to ask…'

'Hello,' a woman's voice answered in the receiver against his ear.

He recognised it as John Fitzpatrick's wife, put his hand on the mouthpiece and went on to finish what he was saying:

'The boy doesn't speak any English, you see. Is that a detail Adonis left out? Well, then let me put you in the know. The little kids people like him get their kicks with usually don't speak much English. They come straight from the third world, just to serve, and their services usually do not require them to say much… Hello,' he said, turning his attention to Mrs. Fitzpatrick; 'How are you, Mrs.—'

'He is dead. He is Dead!' Deborah De Moraes whispered urgently in front of him; 'Hang up, please. He is dead. He is dead.'

He frowned, screened the receiver's mouthpiece again.

'Who is dead?'

'My husband. Carlos. He is dead,' came the answer in yet another whisper.

'Hello?' called the voice in his ear.

'Call my parents, if you don't believe me. Call my parents. They'll tell you. Call them,' Deborah De Moraes went on, insisting, starting to cry again.

He searched her tearful eyes, quickly. They looked too distressed to be lying.

'I'm sorry, wrong number,' he said in the receiver.

Deborah De Moraes watched him hang up with such relief it was almost palpable.

'I… Thank you,' she murmured, letting herself slump into her chair, suddenly a gaunt and tired image of herself; 'Thank you,' she repeated, muttering through her sobs while mopping her tears with her coat sleeves.

'You can speak up, Deborah. I hung up,' he snapped.

'Yes,' she whispered again before coughing a few times to clear her throat; 'Yes,' she repeated, loudly, 'Thank you.'

'Your husband is dead?'

'That's right. He… Do you think we'd—' she began, pausing to correct herself; 'We just couldn't let him get away with the murder of my brother.'

' "We"?' he queried, bemused; 'You killed your husband?'

She didn't reply, just sobbed, drying her tears again.

' "We"?' he repeated; 'You and your parents killed your husband? Is that it, Deborah?'

'No. Not exactly. We…'

She sighed, felt she had better light another cigarette.

Her hands were trembling so violently she needed to hold onto her lighter tightly between both hands to keep the flame still under her cigarette tip.

The nicotine, or was it the diversion of lighting the cigarette, appeared to calm her slightly. Her sobs abated, she put her elbows on her lap and leaned forward, head down between hunched shoulders, holding her burning Marlboro in front of her eyes.

'They found his body yesterday,' she said finally; 'He drowned. In the pool of his house in Sao Paulo. He drowned. Drank too much, went for a swim and drowned.'

'Your flunkey said he was expected back tomorrow.'

'Yes. I know,' she nodded; 'The staff don't know yet. I haven't told them. I thought I'd—'

'Who killed your husband?' he cut in, impatient.

'I… The night after he hit… When I found out what he'd done to Leon, I called my parents, told them everything. I just couldn't take any—'

'Get to the point, will you?' he snapped.

'Yes. Sorry… My parents came down from Scotland. Made him tell them where Leon's body was and told him they would get him killed unless he flew back to Brazil immediately and agreed to a divorce. He flew back to Brazil and…'

She paused, peering at the cigarette burning between her fingers.

'Your parents arranged for him to drown, is that it?' he pressed her.

'Yes. They got in touch with the friends you know of…'

'Nice way to fix a family problem.'

'I—'

'And I take it they also got someone to discover your brother's body. I suppose they would have been hard pressed to explain coming across it themselves by chance in Epping Forest. Is that it?'

'Yes.'

She looked up and, meeting her eyes, for the first time he saw the girl in her who, perhaps, Leonard had been so fond of. She looked lost and scared, so much so, it was hard to imagine she was the same person he'd…

Still, she didn't look fragile. She couldn't. Gaunt, crying and humbled, she still couldn't manage it. Even though in drying her tears she'd wiped off the foundation covering the bruise over her eye and smeared her make-up, she still looked too good to look fragile. Still looked too voluptuous. Could that be her real tragedy? Her looks? She just had too much of them to ever inspire sympathy. Even bruised. Even…

'He… He took away seven years of my life,' she said, eyeing him from under her brows; 'Then my brother… What else was there to do? He was a sick man, Mr. Lombard. But perhaps it wasn't his fault… His parents bought young girls for him when he reached the age, you see? For him to gain sexual experience. When he had finished or grew tired of them, they were sold off to procurers and replaced. Apparently, it's not that uncommon a practice where he came from. Or that's what he told me, anyway. The wealthy buy children of starving parents. The Brazilian streets are packed with them. He got a taste for it…'

He nodded his nod, looked her up and down:

'So you did talk about it, huh?' he said.

Was that reproach in her eyes again? Could she already be recovering? Again? This quickly?

No. She wasn't quite there yet.

'One… Once.'

'Once?'

'Once… What are we… Sorry. What are you going to do?' she asked; 'You must call my parents. I really think you ought to call them.'

'Do you now?'

In her distress, she read the challenge as a rejection.

'What are you going to do?' she queried, worried.

'What do you think?' he returned.

'I don't know. Carlos and Leon are dead and—'

'Your parents arranged the break-in at my office?'

She nodded, put her cigarette into the ashtray and wiped the tears from her face with the palms of her hands now, finished smearing her make-up in the process.

'Yes. They have your envelope. I never read its contents.'

It figured.

'What are you going to do?' she asked again.

He peered back at her coldly, thinking. She was right, Carlos and Leon were dead. She, of course, was alive, but…

Without warning, a phrase Martin had used found its way to the forefront of his mind. *'Those who can afford our goods do their thing without upsetting anyone. Those who can't do it to kids from the street or their own family and it makes upsetting headlines,'* the red-haired man had said at some point during the evening they'd spent together.

He just wanted to get out of there. Step out into the cold rain and...

'Where are your parents?' he asked

'Now? At the moment?'

'Uh-huh.'

'Here. I mean here in London. At their town house in... Leon's funeral is—'

'Good. Tell them to be in Wales at the place where Leonard left the boy at two o'clock tomorrow afternoon. They have my envelope, so I gather they don't need the address. They better show up. And no bad things. Whatever friends they may have, I've taken precautions against bad things.'

'What are you going to do?' she queried yet again, looking both curious and relieved now.

He looked her up and down again. She was recovering. If he stayed there much longer she'd probably start hissing again, ready to bite and claw...

'Why the hell couldn't you divorce the man?' he asked.

She hesitated, nearly twisted her lips into one of her sneers, thought better of it and merely straightened up in her seat.

'You wouldn't understand...'

He didn't say anything, just went on eyeballing her, probing deep. Was that a flicker of fear that flashed behind her eyes?

It may have been. He had just let her read his thoughts, look into his mind. That was what usually happened when...

'Shame,' she said, her eyes suddenly free from tears; 'Shame... And then a good girl does not divorce... My parents wouldn't—'

She paused, as if seized by a thought, then spoke again, sounding almost surprised, which somehow emphasised her public school accent, making him realise that he'd stopped being aware of it...

'Do you know, they might pass on the family fortune to a cousin?'

Yes, he just wanted to walk out. Just… Her looks weren't the problem after all. It went deeper than that. This one could have had everything. Perhaps this one truly had no excuse…

'I said you wouldn't understand,' he heard her say.

He grinned, a mean grin, peered at her Harrods shopping bags, turned away to the photograph of Carlos on the wall, decided there was nothing worth looking at there, started towards the door.

'Don't forget to convey my message to your parents. Two o'clock tomorrow. And they better be there. Goodbye, Mrs. De Moraes.'

'I—We are burying Leon tomorrow afternoon, Mr.—'

'Leon is dead,' he cut her off, pushing the door open; 'Leon can wait.'

He stepped out into the hallway.

Her eyes followed him as he made his way through the rain along the gravel drive towards the gate. He felt them on his back, staring from the window overlooking the driveway, the same one he'd stood in earlier when gazing at her husband's Ferrari. Reaching the bottom of the front steps to walk past her Aston Martin, he'd caught sight of her dark silhouette from the corner of his eye. He hadn't looked up though. He had no wish to see her again, felt too drained for all that pride, that carnal petulance of hers. Because, there could be no doubt about it, alone with her thoughts, she'd claimed it all back. She had no choice. That was all she had to keep herself going. That and tranquillisers. He had no illusions, not that they would have given him any satisfaction, but he had no illusions; he was not walking away from a wounded animal. A frightened one perhaps, but not a wounded one. This animal couldn't be hurt. She was too cold, too wretched for that. No more damage could be done. It was too late.

He lit a Gitane soon after settling behind the wheel of his Triumph. He felt very tired again. Like before Deborah De

Moraes' arrival, when he'd sat to wait for her in the drawing room, the silence around him started buzzing. Or again, maybe it was his ears that hummed. He couldn't tell the difference, but it was not really important. His nape felt on fire again. The fire spread to his bruised neck, grazed fingers and chest. And then to his sore feet and legs. And his heart, that big and slow beating heart of his that had amazed the American doctor whose name came back to him now – *Burnswick*, no, Brunswick, he was called Brunswick – felt like a stone, heavy and pounding. It was not all bad though. At least, he could lean against the familiar contours of his Triumph's seat…

He flicked his half-burnt cigarette out the window, checked his watch, turned on the ignition; it was 22:20, time to go home. It had also just stopped raining…

He went as far as Essex Road, pulled up in front of Perkins' shop, turned off his engine but did not step out of the car. Above his flat, light shone in Jane's windows and, he guessed, she could be waiting for him, all ebullience, wanting to talk, to ask questions, rightly expecting thanks and gratitude for her help. And, as he considered waiting for her lights to go out before going in, the tall frame of Bill the pet shop owner turned up on the other side of the road, strolling in his direction with his new black and white puppy. A dark lanky figure under the street lamps' amber glow, the man seemed happy enough to be out and about with his new tail-wagging companion, and even – although this may have been due to a trick of the light – appeared to be smiling. Yet, the sight of him cast a gloom over Lombard. At first, he thought it might be due to the small bag and plastic spade in Bill's hand, many a dog owner's attribute since it had become the policy of London councils to fine people who allowed their pets to foul public areas. That a mature man should walk behind a dog equipped with a spade and bag in order to clean up its mess somehow struck him as sad, as too much devotion, or at any rate as too tangible a mark of Bill's lonely desperation. Still, it couldn't be denied the pet shop owner looked better than he had since losing his mother, most certainly walked taller, no longer hunched inside his shoulders, and, taking this in, Lombard understood the real reason for his sombre mood. It had little to do with Bill, was all about himself. He just wasn't ready to go home yet, wasn't quite prepared for settling into the comfort of his monotonous routine, which from now on would doubtless include seeing a lot of the pet shop owner and his puppy, for, assuredly, while he'd been away the two of them had become a regular feature of this stretch of Essex Road, would remain so for the foreseeable future, and soon, he and everybody else who lived along their walking route would be able to tell the time simply by catching sight of them. After the last few days' events, the change felt too violent, the routine too grim. Adjustment time was needed. The thought of being alone in his small flat with his aches and pains just didn't...

He pulled away from the kerb before Bill got too close and, reaching Upper Street, made up his mind to head for the M1. The night might as well be put to good use, for he knew that, tired out though he was, sleep would not come. Everything else aside, he'd slept for most of his flight back from America.

A moment later, without apparent reason, Patrick Walton and his hooked fingernails flashed across his mind, leaving him wondering what the tubby man was doing, how he was handling his homecoming. He barely spent any time on the subject though. There wasn't really enough there for thought.

EIGHTEEN

Under the light of the stars, the hilly Welsh landscape lay beneath a thick carpet of snow, leaving the gritted country roads looking like winding, darkly glistening furrows. For the night sky was clear, hinting that perhaps morning would bring sunshine. Still, with it had come frost, and ice on the road, making driving awkward and slow, so that Lombard took nearly three hours to cover the eighty miles between the end of the motorway and the small bridge beside the entry to the rough track that ran along the river downstream from Rhian's cottage.

Reaching the end of the track, wheels crunching on the snow, his headlights found the car-park clearing empty, which, as he'd expected, suggested Rhian was still away at her parents'. Lombard pulled up under a tree, lit a Gitane and stared across the darkness towards the surging waters of the fast flowing river, set upon waiting for dawn before heading back to the small village of Garreg a mile or so away where he would call the Welsh girl's sister to let Rhian know she could come home. It was 4:30, there was nothing else to be done, or much point in waiting for dawn anywhere else – at least in this dark clearing away from the road he was safe from the world. Only, in his suit and raincoat, it quickly proved too cold to sit, even with the engine running and the heater turned full up, which might anyway have caused his engine to overheat. So, although he'd not forgotten the perils of the riverside footpath that led through the wood to the field that rose to the cottage, despite having no torch, despite the biting wind, he reluctantly left his Triumph and headed off under the canopy of trees that covered the footpath.

He did reach the cottage, over forty minutes later, wading through the snow, numb, shivering and drenched up to his knees. In the dark, the footpath had turned out more testing than he'd anticipated, the strip of land winding between the swirling river on one side and the flooded ditch he knew to be on the other much narrower than he'd remembered. Had he not had a vague recollection of the layout of the land, he would not have made it. As it was, deafened by the all surrounding roar of water, driven on by the bitter cold, through sheer perseverance, bracing himself before every move, feeling the ground for firm land and the darkness for guiding trees, he fell on no more than three occasions – twice, steering well clear of the river, stumbling into the ditch, which, fortunately, turned out to be only knee-deep. As a result, determined not to attempt the return journey until daylight, finding the cottage dark, locked and seemingly empty, his drenched trousers and coat bottom starting to ice up, he took less care than he might otherwise have done in getting into the shelter of the stone cottage, smashing a kitchen window pane with a rock.

Stepping out of the chilling breeze provided instant comfort, and soon, having called to ensure no one was there and staggered about searching for the light switch, his fingers too numb to even flick on his lighter, he got out of his shoes, socks, trousers and coat and into a dirty and torn but warm sheepskin coat that hung by the front door, where he also found a pair of gumboots that fitted – even after drying his feet with a kitchen towel, the flagstone floor was too cold for bare feet.

Little had changed within the whitewashed stone walls. The kitchen with its rusty refrigerator and children's drawings was just as cluttered as it had been during his first visit twelve days earlier. Again, the cave-like sitting room with its low beamed ceiling and open fireplace took him slightly aback; even on a second viewing it still impressed, still looked unreal, like a sight from the past, a poor dwelling from an old picture book. Indeed, this time, the sense of unreality was somewhat heightened by a small tinselled Christmas tree that just about fitted between the stone floor and the low ceiling, together with a dozen mostly garish Christmas cards strung out along the beam above the fire-place. Be that as it may, this was somebody's home, somewhere where people kept warm, with stacks of dry mossy logs heaped against a wall.

Twenty minutes after breaking in, Lombard searched the kitchen in vain for coffee, and ten minutes after that, bare-legged and still wrapped in the sheepskin coat, he settled with a hot mug of tea in one of the old leather armchairs by the fireplace, got out of the gumboots, lit a Gitane and peered into the glowing flames of his log fire, feeling rather childishly smug for having got it going at first try, even if, pressed, he'd have to concede to having achieved the feat only by means of setting alight the pages of nearly three entire old newspapers he'd found in a pile by the kitchen stove. Still, hung around with his wet clothes, the fire was hissing, warm and getting warmer, and that was all that mattered. He might as well enjoy it, and soon, he did, was glad not to have gone home, glad to have come to Wales, no longer regretted having ventured up the river track.

At some point, a thud from the kitchen caused him to tense. But he quickly relaxed again. As it happened, it only announced the arrival of the fat tabby cat he'd met there before. Spotting someone was home, it had got in through the cat-flap in the kitchen door and, paying Lombard hardly any attention, it padded into the sitting room, jumped up onto the bed and perched itself in front of the fire, paws tucked under its chin, eyes glazed, already purring.

After frowning at it for a while, Lombard smiled, feeling somewhat fond of the animal, impressed by its detachment, its marked lack of concern at finding an intruder inside its house. He knew hardly anything about cats, had never paid them much attention, but, if they were all like this one, maybe…

He sighed. He had no garden. There was a garden at the back of the house of course, but access to it was through Perkins' shop. The butcher wouldn't like it, and anyway, now that he thought about it, Perkins had mentioned something about 'no pets' when he moved in… No. Even if Perkins could be won over, which might not be too hard a task, there were probably regulations against butchers allowing animals into their shops.

Dawn came, the cat stopped purring and seemed deep asleep and Lombard decided not to call Rhian's sister after all. There was no need for the girl to meet Leonard's parents. Not today, or not before the Spitzes had agreed to his proposition, which was at best speculative. Still, he was confident they'd turn up. He knew too much. They couldn't afford to ignore him. They'd come, if nothing else just to find out what he had in mind, and then, only then, would they decide what to do about him. But first, they'd come.

The clear night did not deliver the sun but a pale grey sky, and the day turned out dull, dry and, following the cold night, surprisingly mild for the time of year. The snow in the field around the cottage had begun to thaw when, at around midday, Lombard, back in his dry trousers, wearing the gumboots – his shoes were not yet dry and at any rate the river path would only have got them soaked again – left for Penryndeudraeth, guessing the Spitzes would come by car and follow the directions in the envelope they'd taken from his office, which entailed driving through the small town's main square. He intended to intercept them there and then lead the way back to the cottage which, instructions or not, was hard to find. Since he had not called Rhian, he thought he had better make sure Leonard's parents didn't end up asking directions of the locals, news of which would be likely to get quickly back to Rhian and her brothers and lead to trouble.

He couldn't have missed them. At 13:30, the Spitzes turned up in the town square in a gleaming chauffeur-driven dark blue Bentley. They hadn't come alone. Beside the capped chauffeur in the front of the car sat a Mediterranean-looking man who Lombard guessed was Israeli and, on meeting his eye, neither a domestic nor a worker in the shoe or leather trade. The man's presence did not surprise or worry him though for, from what he knew of the old couple, they were unlikely to entrust their safety to amateur or trigger-happy tough guys.

'I'm unarmed,' Lombard said all the same, to diffuse any potential tension, returning Mrs. Spitz's dark gaze through her open window after having flagged the Bentley down.

He'd forgotten how old Leonard's parents were, how grating the voice of the buxom Mrs. Spitz, how grey and furrowed Mr. Spitz looked behind the thick lenses of the spectacles that magnified his sad dark eyes. Still, neither looked frail, merely old, and since they travelled in comfort, there was no need to feel sorry for having made them come so far from London.

The greetings were curt. In her heavy German accent Mrs. Spitz complained briefly about having had to postpone Leonard's funeral, and then gave him a scornful look which reminded him of her daughter. He gave her a hollow apology and she started winding up her window as he was still explaining that he wanted them to follow him back to the cottage.

'Fine. Fine. Lead the way,' she said simply, in cold irritation.

Without his prompting, their Mediterranean escort remained in the Bentley with the chauffeur when they pulled into the clearing. The two old folks climbed out and, once they understood where Lombard intended to take them, changed into thick coats and identical leather climbing boots which they retrieved from the car's trunk. They were clearly used to the country, had not only come equipped but negotiated the river path with ease, exchanging a few comments between them about the wilderness in a mixture of English and Yiddish. On reaching the cottage, to Lombard's surprise, as if at home or on familiar territory, they showed no concern or disapproval at the clutter or modesty of Rhian's home, casually settled down rather stiffly next to each other at the kitchen table, with Mrs. Spitz pushing aside a pile of children's drawings to make room beside her for the small leather handbag she'd brought up with her.

He had expected they'd turn down his offer of tea, suggested it only to be polite, explaining it was all there was – after all they had just had a long car journey – but they accepted.

'*Jah*. Thank you. No milk, two sugars. Both the same,' said Mrs. Spitz, before going on to remark, while examining the room around her with a critical eye: 'So? This is where Leonard brought the boy. Huh? We own an old stone cottage a bit like this in Yorkshire. I wanted Leonard to go there after his return from America. But he would not live in the countryside because he could not drive. Terrible. Just terrible.'

'What is terrible, Mrs. Spitz?' Lombard frowned.

'Leonard. Had he learned how to drive, he might have listened to me and stayed away from London. And none of this would have happened,' she returned, dryly, as if annoyed at being made to state the obvious.

'Huh!' she let out, turning away to let out a heavy sigh.

Like the time they'd met previously, Mr. Spitz seemed content to let his wife do the talking, sat quietly beside her looking distant and sombre, at times nodding when agreeing with what was being said.

Lombard served their teas, settled across the table from them, grinned into their dark eyes, lit a Gitane and proceeded with the matter at hand. What he had to say didn't take long. They listened impassive as he explained he'd asked them there so they could see their son had found a good home for the boy. And they betrayed no more emotion when he declared that, since Carlos was dead and no good could come of letting out the truth about Leonard's death, he was ready to forget what he knew in exchange for their undertaking to regularise the boy's situation with the authorities and to provide Rhian with financial support for as long as she looked after him.

'Look at it this way,' he concluded, looking into Mrs. Spitz's steely gaze; 'Given the chance, who knows, the boy might just achieve a few of the things your son never could.'

'Huh!' Mrs. Spitz let out, once satisfied he'd finished, which didn't bode well.

The ensuing silence was brief, lasted no more than the time it took for her to exchange a glance with her husband. Whatever she silently asked the old man – Lombard saw it in his bespectacled magnified eyes – Mr. Spitz assented to it.

'Fixing the boy's legal status might be a problem,' Mrs. Spitz said, turning back to him; 'We cannot guarantee it.'

Lombard nodded his nod. They'd go for it. As he'd thought, they were reasonable people. She misleadingly fierce, he deceitfully self-effacing, but reasonable...

'Well, if you put your mind to it, I'm sure you'll find a way, Mrs. Spitz,' he said; 'You seem to have ways of getting what you want.'

She tightened her lips, once again reminding him of her daughter:

'I wish, Mr. Lombard. I wish. But. I take it the girl Rhian does not know about our ex-son-in-law?'

'She knows no more than what your son told her, that is, that he bought the boy from an Austrian called Friedman.'

'Does she know Leonard is dead?'

'She read in the papers that he committed suicide.'

She nodded, uneasy.

'And it is to remain this way?'

'I wouldn't want to give you reasons to worry about her, Mrs. Spitz,' he replied.

'Is that a yes, Mr. Lombard?'

'That's a yes, Mrs. Spitz.'

'What kind of a person is she? Apart from obviously being poor.'

'She is no threat, Mrs. Spitz. That's all I can tell you. You'll just have to trust me.'

'Trust you?' she echoed; 'You need not worry about my trusting you, Mr. Lombard,' she went on somewhat mysteriously before drinking some tea and turning away from him.

And that was it. There were no more questions. Now frowning, now sounding almost angry, she spent the next few minutes speaking in Yiddish to her husband who, bar a few words, quietly listened, nodding, staring down at the table in front of him taking small sips from the mug of tea between his broad and arthritic fingers.

At the end of it all, she turned her dark eyes back on Lombard, sighed, swallowed some more tea, grabbed hold of her handbag, stood up and simply announced they were agreed.

'Agreed to what?' he asked.

'Subject to the girl looking after the boy, she will receive a £5,000 index-linked yearly allowance and the boy £10,000 a year to provide for his needs and education. All to be terminated on the boy's eighteenth birthday. It is non-negotiable. All right?'

The offer was more generous than anything he'd expected, or in any case, more than he would have asked.

'I take it paperwork will be drawn up to that effect?' he said.

Her frown made him feel he had better elaborate:

'If something were to happen to you—'

'Ah! It will be done,' she cut in, dismissive.

His ensuing request that all decisions concerning the boy's

education should be left entirely to Rhian's discretion met only with a dark scowl, but he decided not to press on, turned to Mr. Spitz who, following her lead, was now rising to his feet.

'Well, thank you for—' he started.

'Incredible,' Mrs. Spitz cut him off; 'Incredible,' she repeated, on meeting his scowl; 'You should not have made us postpone our son's funeral just for this, Mr. Lombard. It could have waited. Or been sorted out in London. Or even on the telephone. Just incredible.'

He nodded.

'Well, I couldn't wait, Mrs. Spitz. And I felt you should see where the boy lives. But now we've agreed, to be honest with you, I had no idea you would prove so willing and understanding,' he replied.

She smiled, a wry smile:

'Huh! Willing and understanding. You are right about that. Indeed, maybe we are even more willing and understanding than you know, Mr. Lombard. Or should I call you *Inspecteur?*...'

She broke off, left him with his worries to speak to her husband, quickly, in Yiddish again.

'Laurent Delfosse,' the old man pronounced.

'Yes, of course. *Inspecteur* Laurent Delfosse,' she said, turning her attention back to Lombard; 'You see? We know who you are. So indeed we need not worry about trusting you, Mr. Lombard, if I may go on calling you this. And I hope you appreciate how unwilling or un-understanding we could have chosen to be. *Jah?*'

He couldn't hide his feelings, was too perturbed for that. She could not fail to see his dismay, and shook her head, scowling, severe, but pleased with herself, somehow reminding him of a schoolteacher who's just exposed a mischievous pupil. And just like one, sorry for him perhaps – or was it merely to stress her point so there could be no misunderstanding, so that he knew who was in charge – she decided to provide him with an explanation:

'When our daughter told us about all this we thought we better find out a little more about you, Mr. Lombard. Just for contingencies such as this. However, we found that you could not be who you claim to be. The only French citizen of about your age called *Zaveer* Lombard died in a car accident in Southern France six years ago. You should have been more imaginative in your choice of a new profession.'

He swallowed hard, tried grinning, failed, but at least managed to speak:

'Should I?'

'Should you not?' she returned; 'Too easy. It was much too easy to find you out, Mr. Lombard. For an ex-police to hide as a private detective is very foolish. I can only presume it is the only kind of work you can do. But still, it is a bad idea. I understand you murdered six people. Out in the open. Made the front pages of the French press. You are quite a celebrity. You ought to be more circumspect in your choice of work.'

He nodded his nod. There was nothing to say. And besides, if she knew this much, she probably also knew why he...

'Am I to take it that perhaps you feel secure?' she asked; 'After all, you did manage to escape from custody a mere two weeks after your arrest? Huh? I understand. But you should still change profession, Mr. Lombard.'

'What do you suggest, Mrs. Spitz?' he asked, flippantly, too flippantly perhaps; but he'd not thought about what he was saying, or how he was saying it, was merely reacting, kicking for being upset.

Strangely, unexpectedly, the old woman remained calm, reflective almost, her dark steely eyes looking right through him.

'I'm an old woman who has just lost a son partly as a result of man's vileness, Mr. Lombard,' she said; 'And I have been around and know a thing or two. And maybe I sympathise with your situation. So if I were you, whatever you think of me, I would stop behaving like my neurotic daughter; concentrate on being smart rather than sounding clever, and show due deference to experience and your elders. For what it is worth, you are too close to home, Mr. Lombard. And more importantly, with your history, in the wrong profession. Do you understand? You might do better leaving that private detective thing to others. To those immune to depravity and corruption. I understand my ex-son-in-law nearly got you murdered, *Jah?* Well, take it from me, he was no genius. You might not always be so lucky. Or meet willing and understanding people. But since, as you said, you did not expect us to be so willing and understanding, I suspect you know that.'

He looked back at her, wondering whether to feel touched or annoyed, but while he considered how to respond, a thought suddenly overwhelmed him. If she and her husband had found out so much about him in such a short time, could they also…

They'd spoken to Deborah, read the note in his envelope, confronted Carlos, who it was reasonable to presume would have known Friedman lived around the corner from him. The Austrian may not have been directly involved in their son's murder, but Martin had mentioned something about Friedman's father being a death camp commandant, and he'd told Deborah De Moraes words to that effect. Could they possibly have had him investigated while ignoring Friedman? The group they had links with was known to be responsible for the execution of over two dozen men over the years. Ex-Nazies and…

They had to.

'What did you find out about the Austrian called Friedman?' he asked; 'Or Gluck? Otto Gluck, if that is his name.'

It took a second or two for Mrs. Spitz to react, but when she did, it was with such a dark and intense scowl that he wondered if he had not just lost all of her previous goodwill.

'I would forget the Austrian if I were you,' her grating voice rang between the stone walls around them, sounding nothing short of ominous.

He hesitated. Was she warning him to lay off or could this be her way of telling him Friedman was being looked into, or even, had already been dealt with?

He wouldn't have insisted, but he met Mr. Spitz's huge distorted eyes behind his thick spectacle lenses. Unlike hers, they held no threat. Rather, the old man seemed conciliatory, appeared to want to talk, to share something.

'Just tell me,' Lombard asked him; 'I'm curious. What did you find out about the man? Somebody told me his father was a death camp commandant. Is there anything to it?'

An odd, rather sad grin formed across the old man's lips:

'Have you ever heard of a place called L—' he asked, pronouncing a German sounding name unfamiliar to Lombard.

'No.'

His answer brought a frown to Mr. Spitz's forehead. He

looked back at Lombard with a mixture of reproach and sadness, then repeated the German word he'd just mentioned.

'… Are you sure you never heard of that place?'

'I'm sure, Mr. Spitz.'

The old man took a deep breath and, almost smiling now, a perplexed smile, asked:

'How old are you? Forty?'

'Around that,' replied Lombard.

'And the name… means nothing to you?'

'I'm afraid not, Mr. Spitz,' he returned; 'But if it has anything to do with Friedman, I'd be pleased to hear about it.'

Mr. Spitz shook his head, shrugged looking disgusted, muttered something in Yiddish between clenched teeth, started towards the front door:

'Goodbye, Mr. Lombard. Come on, Ethel, let's go. We've taken enough time over this.'

Jah,' she said, without moving, her eyes still on Lombard.

'I was only—' he started.

'Just don't concern yourself with matters that do not interest you, Mr. Lombard,' she cut him off; 'And this is not a sympathetic old woman's advice, you understand? We all have a cross to bear, as you people say. To each his own. And perhaps you are right. Tell the girl, or the woman if that is what she is, that somebody will be in touch with her to discuss what we agreed. Goodbye, Mr. Lombard. And thank you for the tea,' she declared, turning away towards her husband who was waiting, holding the door open for her.

He nearly called, nearly asked if they'd got Friedman killed too, but, he knew, no reply would have come. And so, leaning back in his chair, he watched them step out of the door. First the buxom Mrs. Spitz, who disappeared behind her grey hair pinned up in a bun, and then the thin Mr. Spitz; the last he saw of the old man as he pulled the door closed behind him were his heavy brown climbing boots.

'Maybe we should never have brought children into this world,' he thought he heard the old man say through the broken pane in the kitchen window.

'Don't speak like this, Albert. Maybe we just waited too long to have ours. That is all,' he clearly caught Mrs. Spitz replying before they began to speak in Yiddish again.

He went on listening to their voices as they moved down the field, peering at his cigarette, until the roar of the river reclaimed the silence.

'As you people say,' the old lady had said after her remark about bearing crosses.

You people...

Before leaving, he rinsed the dirty tea mugs and took it upon himself to empty a tin of cat food onto a plate which he left on the kitchen floor for the tabby cat, who was nowhere to be seen. Twenty minutes later, he stopped at the phone box by the steep rock face across the road from the public house in the small village of Garreg. Rhian's sister wasn't at home, and so he left a short message on her answering machine, telling her to tell her sister she could go home, and, after a glance at the pointed mountain that commanded the snow covered valley where he'd just spent the night and the best part of the day, he drove off towards London.

He'd left a note and £20 on Rhian's kitchen table:

'Rhian, apologies for the broken window and for burning some of your firewood (hope the £20 covers the damage). Got here too late to call last night, got cold waiting outside and broke in. Would have called but decided not to for reasons not worth going into. Leonard's parents met me here this afternoon and, if it's what you want, agreed to help you financially and otherwise with the boy. Someone will get in touch with you about it. If you decide against keeping him, let them know and they'll probably help you out with that too. Couldn't find any better explanation than suicide for Leonard's death, and perhaps better leave it at that. In any case, you need not have any fear about visitors anymore. If you keep the boy, which I trust you will, hope it goes well. Look after yourself.

Xavier Lombard.

PS: Had to borrow a pair of gumboots to get down the track. Will leave them in a plastic bag in the clearing where you park. Thank you.'

He'd thought of waiting to have a word with the Welsh girl. Something still bothered him – yet another thing he'd over-looked. Both Deborah De Moraes and her mother had reminded him Leonard couldn't drive. So how had he managed to get his boy from London to Wales?

Clearly, at best, Rhian had been economical with the truth. But what good could the truth be to anyone now?

Moreau had left a message on his answer-phone, responding to the call he'd made before leaving for Los Angeles. He had managed to find information about only one person by the name of Gluck. One Oskar Gluck, an Austrian wanted for war crimes since 1946 and presumed dead. The man, according to records, had disappeared while awaiting trial in a post-war American detention camp. Amongst other things, for a period of a few months, he'd been the officer in charge of an extermination camp somewhere in Poland, called *Lublin-Maidenek,* which was the name old Mr. Spitz had mentioned. The record also showed that he had a son, named Friedrich Gluck, but nothing was known about him.

Jane was going home to Ireland on Sunday to spend Christmas with her family and, only she knew how, had got him to commit to take her to a restaurant on the Saturday. Perkins made no fuss about his not turning up at the previous Friday's football match. Doubtless, the fact that the Upper Street Traders squad had still not fully recovered from the flu epidemic that had decimated its ranks a couple of weeks earlier, resulting in yet another impressive win – seven–nil – for the Essex Road Traders, was partly to thank for the butcher's benevolence. But then again, the bald man had other preoccupations. He'd just had a word with his accountant, and the news wasn't good. The new supermarket nearby was hurting him more than he'd realised. For the very first time since opening twenty four years earlier, his butcher's shop had just about broken even, was sliding fast towards the red. Unless things could be turned around – which would take 'a miracle, a bomb or turning the shop into a delicatessen or something fancy like that', as he put it – closure would soon be inevitable, and he'd just been advised to put his shop together with the two upstairs flats on the market while property prices in the area were at an all-time high, ironically partly due to the new supermarket which contributed to making the neighbourhood desirable to the professional middle-classes. Perkins didn't want to sell, he liked being a butcher, but…

'Christ! I'm forty-six. What am I going to do with the rest of my life if I sell? It's too bloody early to retire. Too bloody late to learn a new trade. I've never been much good at learning anyway…'

'If it comes to selling, at least you'll have enough money not to worry about money anymore,' Lombard had ventured, just to say something.

'Huh. Money…' the butcher had sighed, rubbing his thumb round and round against his index finger, as he always did when he was nervous; 'Anyway, if I do put the place up for sale, I'll let you know of course. But you don't need to worry about looking for a new flat just yet. These things take time…'

On Friday morning, Nathalie turned up at the Parliament Hill café on Hampstead Heath. As usual, she was late, stoned and looking pale. He didn't let it upset him though. Not this time. He was pleased to see and smell her, that was all.

She asked no questions, and he, although he still wanted to know the meaning of the strange smile she'd graced him with before his American trip, did likewise. They just sat, silent, as they always did, smoking their cigarettes and drinking their coffees on the terrace just outside the café's windows, observing the bandstand which, just as on the Friday a fortnight earlier, was fast being turned into a colourful summery film set. For the ponytail man was back, complete with leather jacket, cell-phone, bunch of keys and two-way radio. Once again, with his crew, trucks, generators, cameras and props, he'd commandeered the bandstand, and this time, determined not to get hassled by anyone or any dog, the good general he was, he'd also brought security along, in the shape of three uniformed men who stood around looking dead-eyed at every passer-by.

'No,' said Nathalie when he asked if the ponytail man had been there the previous week; 'We've had rain. This is the first sunny day for a while. That's probably why the asshole's back.'

It was indeed sunny, the sky was blue. There was no danger of rain today, no danger of the ponytail man having to pack up in a hurry again. He would shoot his scene and then return the bandstand and its immediate surroundings to the Heath's regular visitors. Meanwhile though, anyone curious wandering too close was being spoken to or stared at by the security men.

Nathalie stayed for about an hour, at one point, without apparent reason, as was her habit, coming up with one her statements that required no reply:

'Some asshole bent my ear about the will to live yesterday. Really? As if there is such thing as the will to live. You might as well talk about the will to breathe. Huh! There's only the will to die. One day it takes you over and that's it. *Tu finis par te trouver en face d'une merde, d'un con, et... Tac!*'

'*Hein...* The movies again,' Lombard muttered soon after she had left, gazing at the ponytail man laughing with a fair young woman inside the bandstand.

Miss Johnson, the nurse with the cancer patient who she believed should have been getting better instead of dying, had come back to see him the previous afternoon, clutching the same battered brown handbag, got up in the same green duffel-coat, tatty loafers and blue pleated skirt she'd worn on her first visit. She'd thought things over, decided it would be wrong of her to do nothing, that she ought at least to find out if her suspicions about the patient's doctor were misguided, however much it cost.

'I'd be very grateful if you would let me hire you,' she'd said, like most honest people of humble means nervously asking his rates while making a point of pulling her purse from her handbag; 'I can pay you some money in advance, of course…'

Again, Lombard had not known what to make of her, had been reluctant to take her money. Only, she looked so determined, turning her down would have simply made her go elsewhere.

He'd given her his rates, told her a £100 upfront would do, made her tell her story again, asked a few questions and learnt that the dying man was a screenplay writer.

'Successful?' he'd asked.

'I—I don't know… I don't think so.'

'Why is that?'

'Well. I… I would say he is a bitter man. I doubt that would be the case if he was successful, don't you?'

He'd grinned.

'Any idea what lies behind his bitterness?'

'No. Yes… Well, maybe…'

'Maybe?'

'I don't know, but at times, when he gets low, he goes on about being betrayed by a film director. Something about a story he wrote. He's writing a book about it, he says. He wants to immortalise the man, and hopes to live long enough to complete it.'

'I see.'

'Yes. But I don't know if anyone should really read too much into it. I mean… The film director he refers to is John Segment.'

'John Segment?'

'You haven't heard of him?'

'Should I?'

'Well. He is quite well known…'

'I'm sorry. I don't go to the movies much.'

'Ah… Don't you? Well, he is quite well-known and…'

'And?'

'Well, I don't know, it's just that. Well, maybe he does know him personally…'

He sighed, noted there were no teenagers hanging around the café, then realised the nearby schools had closed for the Christmas holidays.

He stamped his Gitane out in the ashtray, frowned at Nathalie's Marlboro stubs' lipsticked ends, rose to his feet, buried his hands inside his coat pockets and walked away from the busy bandstand towards La Sainte Union Catholic school for girls in front of which, as always, he'd left his Triumph.

The teenagers were not the only ones who had failed to show up today. He had not seen the old man in the navy blue blazer and his three-legged dog either. As far as he could recall, this was the first Friday the two of them had not turned up for their walk around the bandstand. Could they too have gone on holiday or…

It looked like the ponytail man may not have needed to bring along his three security men after all.

The warmth in his nape made itself felt permanently now, had moved down to his shoulders. But this was a good sign. What you can feel, you can fight. He was beating the poison. Soon, he'd be back in control.

● ● ●